Praise for the novels of Renee Ryan

"Sumptuous fashion, thrilling espiona[ge]
The Last Fashion House in Paris has it a[ll] [th]e
resistance and the beauty of Paris fash[ion]
to life in a way that puts you right there
—Madeline Martin, [bestselling aut]hor
[of The Libr]*ary*

"Readers will love the thrill ride that is Ryan's new novel. *The Last Fashion House in Paris* is a fast-paced and compelling story complete with feisty heroines and a dash of romance set amidst the heart of the resistance. I couldn't put it down!"

—Heather Webb, *USA TODAY* bestselling author
of *Queens of London*

"*The Paris Housekeeper* is the beautifully written story of three very different women caught up in the Nazi occupation of Paris in World War II. The characters of Rachel, Camille and Vivian jump off the page. Highly recommend!"

—Karen Robards, *New York Times* bestselling author
of *The Black Swan of Paris*

"In this *Upstairs, Downstairs* look at the Ritz during World War II, three lives entwine: a wealthy American widow and two maids at the Ritz, one of whom is in deep peril by virtue of being Jewish. What will they risk? Perfect for fans of Pam Jenoff and Kristin Hannah!"

—Lauren Willig, *New York Times* bestselling author
of *Two Wars and a Wedding*, on *The Paris Housekeeper*

"*The Secret Society of Salzburg* is a heart-wrenching yet uplifting tale about the importance of art and beauty in the darkest of times. Renee Ryan weaves a masterful story of growing political tensions before World War II and the life-or-death struggle Jewish refugees faced anchored by the unbreakable friendship of two extraordinary women. A must-read."

—Julia Kelly, internationally bestselling author
of *The Last Dance of the Debutante*

"*The Secret Society of Salzburg* is a gripping, emotional story of courage and strength, filled with extraordinary characters and tender relationships. Renee Ryan reminds us that the universal languages of art, music and friendship bring light and hope amid even the most challenging of times. I loved every word."

—RaeAnne Thayne, *New York Times* bestselling author
of *The Beach Reads Bookshop*

Also by Renee Ryan

The LAST FASHION HOUSE *in* PARIS

RENEE RYAN

LOVE INSPIRED

Stories to uplift and inspire

LOVE INSPIRED®

Stories to uplift and inspire

Recycling programs
for this product may
not exist in your area.

ISBN-13: 978-1-335-09043-0

The Last Fashion House in Paris

Love Inspired
22 Adelaide St. West, 41st Floor
Toronto, Ontario M5H 4E3, Canada
www.LoveInspired.com

Printed in U.S.A.

To Harvest and Wells for letting me be your Mimi.

Chapter One

Paulette

May 1942.
Fouché-Leblanc Château. Reims, France.

Beneath the pale light of a crescent moon, Paulette Leblanc wandered aimlessly through her bedroom. She traveled from end to end, her mind working as fast as her feet. The ancient château creaked and groaned around her, like the dusty bones of an old woman refusing to go quietly to the grave. How Paulette hated this house, with its centuries of tradition and sad, painful memories. Not a home, not anymore, but a prison of her own making.

What have I done?

The clock on the nightstand read 2:00 a.m. Late by most standards. For Paulette, time had become relative. She placed her fingertips to her temples, her touch tentative at first, then harder. A useless gesture, born from restlessness and frustration.

She dropped her hands and retraced her steps, seeing nothing of the room, nothing of the decor.

What have I done?

Her mother was gone, made to disappear by the Nazis and their unquenchable hate for Jews. All because of Paulette. She'd thought her actions noble, even inspired. A heroic effort to save her mother from certain death. Good intentions mattered little in German-Occupied France.

She paused at the beveled window overlooking the acres of fertile land that had been in her family for two hundred years. Now the pilfering Germans controlled the vineyard, the champagne house, even the château itself. Not satisfied with robbing her family of the future, the enemy had also stolen their past, confiscating thousands upon thousands of irreplaceable bottles of Fouché-Leblanc champagne. Some from the previous century.

Paulette wanted to cry over the loss of a legacy she'd never appreciated until it was gone. She would have cried if she had any tears left. For two straight weeks, she'd wept for her mother. Now her soul was empty, her heart hard and brittle. Hate was all she could feel. Hate inside anger, coated in guilt.

As if catching her dark mood, the vines were awakened by a slow, wayward breeze. Their ebony limbs swayed like lost souls caught between two worlds. There were no grapes yet, only buds that had burst anew last week. The start of another growing season should bring wonder, but only reminded Paulette that her mother would not be here for the harvest.

Her lips parted, perhaps to release a sigh, or maybe a sob, but no sound came forth. She shifted her weight, and her toes hit the teakwood trunk that held her many precious possessions. Unable to stop herself, she knelt, reverently, as if in church, and reached for the shawl draped over the trunk. The garment was rather new, but had been her mother's favorite from the moment of purchase, and now was Paulette's greatest treasure. She caught the hint of roses and jasmine as she wrapped the cool silk around her shoulders.

Enveloped in her mother's scent, she unhooked the trunk's latch and lifted the lid. A shadow fell over the contents. Paulette welcomed the gloom, actually breathed it in, knowing this loneliness, this *aloneness*, was her own fault, and she hadn't even seen it coming.

Her mother had insulated her from the grief living in this house full of widows. Paulette had been so completely removed from their pain. She'd spent her days flirting with local boys, accompanying her mother on shopping trips to Paris, and, whenever the urge struck her, drawing pretty, frivolous party dresses. The sketches had brought her such joy. Sometimes they still did.

They were not the reason she was on her knees. It was the other image. Perhaps tonight she would find the courage to destroy it. Jaw set, she rummaged around in the trunk. Her fingers grazed the edge of her sketch pad. Just that small whisper of a touch and the silvery mist of memories swept through her.

Hand shaking, she captured the book, flipped to the sixth page, and stared at the face she'd so carefully, lovingly produced with her charcoals. Vicious, complicated emotion rushed through her as she studied the image of her greatest folly. Friedrich Weber. German. Soldier. SS officer. Deceptive snake of a man with poetry on his tongue and deceit in his heart.

Beneath every devoted smile, a lie. Beneath every lie, another lie.

Her hand shook harder, almost violently, with the black rage of the scorned.

She was not the first woman to fall in love with the wrong man. That's what her mother had said when the two of them sat shoulder to shoulder on the rickety cot in her jail cell. At the time, Paulette had been inconsolable in her guilt and grief. She'd begged for her mother's forgiveness between giant, gasping sobs. Hélène Leblanc, gracious even after hours of interrogation, had claimed Paulette was not to blame.

But she *was* to blame.

She'd gone to Friedrich, trusting his tender words of love, prettier than any flower in her mother's garden. She'd completely fallen for him and his smooth charm.

Now she forced herself to look at his face, really look. The rush of breath leaving her lungs was hardly new. And therein lay her shame. That he could affect her, still, after all she knew him to be. She touched the curve of his chin, snapped back her hand as if burned. Viper. Liar. Cheat. She should have seen his true nature, though she could hardly see it now.

She would keep looking. She would stare and stare until she understood his duplicity and her own recklessness. Only then would she put match to paper. The image began to waver, blur. She had the sudden sensation of falling through fog and mist.

"Paulette?"

She jolted at the sound of her name, the sketch pad fumbling in her grip. Hurriedly, she jumped up and spun around quickly, too quickly. The leather-bound pages slipped from her hand and landed on the floor with a thud. She shoved the book beneath the bed with the edge of her foot and, chin lifted, studied the woman standing in the doorway. Gabrielle. Her older sister by a full decade.

Brilliant, talented Gabrielle. Even the stingy beam of moonlight embraced her as if in a loving caress. That was her way, outshining them all with her natural beauty and impossible competency. Was it any wonder Paulette always felt somehow less in her sister's company?

That wasn't entirely fair. Like their grandmother and mother, Gabrielle had suffered the loss of her husband after only a few years of marriage. Paulette had adored Benoit, the brother of her heart. He'd never judged her, never expected more than she could give.

"Paulette," Gabrielle said again, managing to look both concerned and slightly condemning. "You cannot continue torturing yourself like this."

"I'm not."

"Except that you are. I can hear your footsteps. Day or night, you roam and you pace. You don't sleep. You hardly eat." Gabrielle shut the door with a firm click and padded across the room. "I'm worried about you."

Paulette lifted her chin a fraction higher. "I'm fine."

"Except that you aren't. Dear sister." Gabrielle momentarily took her hand, squeezed gently, the gesture reminiscent of their mother. "It's been two weeks. You cannot go on punishing yourself with thoughts of what you have lost."

"You mean *who* I have lost."

Gabrielle conceded the point with a small nod. "Isolating yourself in this room will not bring Maman back."

How easy she spoke of their mother's disappearance in that bland, unemotional tone. Where was her sorrow, her grief? It was as if Gabrielle was somehow relieved that their mother had been made to disappear by a ruthless Gestapo agent bent on destroying their family.

"Maman isn't gone. She's dead."

It hurt to say the words, hurt more to see the impassive look in her sister's eyes. "You don't know that for certain."

No other outcome was possible. Kriminalkommissar Wolfgang Mueller was the most ruthless of the Gestapo agents assigned to Reims. He'd arrested Hélène Leblanc for murdering the German tyrant who'd confiscated their home. The offense would have been equal to an act of treason had she been found guilty. She'd been cleared of the charges—no body, no crime—and that should have been the end of it. But he'd held her for more questioning, this time for falsifying her identity papers. Another treasonous offense in the eyes of men who hated anyone with Jewish blood in their veins.

If only Paulette had kept her mother's secret. If only she'd trusted her sister a little more and Friedrich a whole lot less.

"Maman would not want you to blame yourself for what happened."

A telling choice of words. "But you blame me. Don't you, Gabrielle?"

Her sister said nothing, and in her stone-cold silence, in that tight, unforgiving set of her shoulders, Paulette read her true feelings. The condemnation. The judgment. The disapproval.

"It's not a matter of blame," Gabrielle said, frowning a little too hard. "It's what you do next that will prove whether you've learned your lesson and changed your ways."

Familiar resentment clawed up her throat. Gabrielle didn't believe in her, still. She certainly didn't trust her. Their grandmother was no different. Josephine Leblanc, the matriarch of the family, had always favored her eldest granddaughter. Now, as old age waged a battle for her mind, Grandmère deferred to Gabrielle. She let her set the tone and make important decisions. Paulette would always be second-born, second-best. Second everything.

"Did you hear me, Paulette?"

She hadn't, no. And by the look of grim determination on her sister's face, she was glad she hadn't been paying attention. "Would you mind repeating that last bit?"

Gabrielle held her gaze a moment longer, the frown digging deeper, as if there were two paths set before her, and she wasn't entirely certain which she would choose. Something dark and ominous crept through Paulette, a premonition of sorts. Thunder rolled in the distance. Shadows flickered in long strips across the worn floorboards at her feet.

Finally, her sister nodded, more to herself than to Paulette, having apparently made her decision. "I wasn't sure this was the right course of action, but now I am. You must go away. You must leave this house, this city, and not come back until—"

"Wh–what?" Paulette's heart stopped beating in her chest. It actually skipped several beats. Her vision misted over, turned black at the edges. "You are banishing me?"

Her voice was low, barely a whisper, but there was a hard, urgent note to her tone, and when she looked into Gabrielle's eyes, she saw sadness. Apology. Paulette wanted neither. She wanted loyalty. Trust.

"Do not think of this as banishment. Think of it as a new beginning."

Paulette blinked in astonishment. There were no new beginnings under German occupation. France was a conquered nation. Her citizens a conquered people. A heaviness pressed down on her, and her legs shook, threatening to give way. Slowly, awkwardly, she stumbled to the bed, collapsing. She couldn't catch her breath. Why couldn't she breathe? And why… "Why are you doing this, Gabrielle?"

"It's what Maman wanted."

Paulette sat frozen in her own shock. That couldn't be true. Her mother would not want her youngest daughter thrown out of her own home. No, this was Gabrielle's doing. A fresh wave of resentment kicked in her stomach, and she dropped her gaze to her lap. Either that or let her sister see her anger, her anguish, but also her fear. "When did Maman tell you this?"

Gabrielle came to stand before her. "At the police station. Before she was sent away."

Sent away. The euphemism made Paulette shiver. Gabrielle spoke as if their mother's absence was temporary. No one came back once Detective Mueller made them disappear.

"I should have been sent away with her." She whispered the words, more to herself than to her sister. "We both should have been."

Their mother had one Jewish parent—her father—and two Jewish grandparents, which made her, by the current definition, a Jew as well. Gabrielle and Paulette were her daughters and thus technically Jewish. Though not according to Detective Mueller, who'd dragged Paulette home from the police station once her mother's secret had come to light.

Apparently, Nazi law stated that Paulette's and Gabrielle's blood was sufficiently diluted, their Jewishness cleansed by their father's noble French blood. Mueller had explained this to Friedrich. Her former beau hadn't agreed. He'd wanted Paulette transported to the death camps with her mother. She was tainted, he'd claimed. He'd called her a dirty Jew, unworthy of life, amongst other, worse things.

Bile rose in her throat at the memory, still so fresh in her mind.

"You made a mistake." Gabrielle knelt before her and took her face in her hands, then reached up and brushed a stray hair from her forehead. "A terrible, awful mistake, and now you must live with the consequences. You understand this? You understand why you must go away?"

Oh, she understood. "You think to punish me."

"I think to protect you." Gabrielle dropped her hands, and though she placed them gently on Paulette's knees, a hint of exasperation crept into her voice. "Your relationship with an SS officer will not stay a secret. Others will find out. Some surely already know. This move to a new city, a new life, where no one knows you, it could be the making of you, Paulette."

Or her ruin. "Where? Where am I to go?"

"To Paris. Maman's friend, Mademoiselle Sabine Ballard, has agreed to hire you to work in her fashion house. She has also agreed to provide you with respectable lodgings."

Paulette felt a quick kick in her heart. Sabine Ballard had been her mother's closest and dearest friend, and the only designer Hélène Leblanc would allow to dress her or her daughters. It had been Mademoiselle Sabine who'd encouraged Paulette's interest in fashion by gifting her with her first sketch pad on her thirteenth birthday. Working with her was the opportunity she'd always dreamed of, but that was before. The desire to create fashion no longer burned in her soul. "What does Grandmère have to say about all of this?"

"She is in agreement."

Of course, she would acquiesce to what Gabrielle wanted. It was inevitable, and yet Paulette felt the sting of betrayal, worse somehow, stronger, than her own self-reproach. How had she lost her way so completely that her family plotted against her?

"It's settled, Paulette. The arrangements complete. You leave for Paris in two days." Gabrielle stood, sighed. "I suggest you start packing. Wednesday will come before you know it."

Without another word, she left the room, but not before Paulette saw a shadow of familiar emotion in her sister's eyes. What did Gabrielle have to feel guilty about? Did she regret sending Paulette away, or not having done so sooner?

The reason didn't matter. Her course was set.

Nothing to be done but relent and accept. Paulette took another trip around the room. Then she did as her sister advised. She packed. The sketch pad went in last.

The day of her departure dawned rainy and gray. Gabrielle arrived at her bedroom just after sunrise and presented Paulette with her train ticket plus a small amount of money. She also handed over a single sheet of paper containing handwritten directions to Mademoiselle Ballard's atelier from Gare de l'Est in Paris. Rather pointless. Paulette knew the way by heart. "Gather your belongings. We will meet downstairs in ten minutes."

Unsure when she would return, if ever, she attempted a hasty goodbye with her grandmother. She found her sitting alone in her room, staring at nothing in particular. By the older woman's blank expression, it was clear she was having one of her bad days. No matter what Paulette said, the once strong-willed family matriarch didn't seem to recognize her. She treated her own granddaughter as a stranger. Nevertheless, Paulette grasped her thin brittle hands, kissed each papery cheek, and said, "Be well, Grandmère."

No response.

She left the room with tears running down her cheeks. Apparently, she had not fully emptied herself of grief. At the door, she looked over her shoulder and saw matching tears streaming from her grandmother's rheumy eyes. In the vain hope she'd found an ally in the other woman, she nearly rushed back and begged to be allowed to stay. Gabrielle chose that moment to call out. "Hurry, Paulette. If you are to catch your train, we must leave now."

A lump rose in her throat and she gave a wordless nod, leaving her grandmother rocking in her chair, muttering something about a missing book. The rain had stopped, mostly, but had left the roads nearly impassable by car or bike. The Leblanc sisters made the journey on foot. Paulette didn't want an escort. Gabrielle insisted on accompanying her, anyway.

They traveled in stilted silence, each pretending absorption in the scenery. They passed through the sleeping vineyard poised for the upcoming growing season. They continued past the champagne house, and eventually arrived in Reims with the Cathédrale Notre-Dame de Reims looming large and impressive. It wasn't until they were through the center archway of the train station with its bullet holes left over from the previous war that Paulette saw the signs of German occupation as she never had before. Her breath hitched at the sight of so many foul Nazi flags.

Worse yet, the soldiers were everywhere, milling about, carrying rifles slung over their shoulders, guns hitched to their belts, or holding leashes connected to vicious-looking guard dogs. Most of them were young, so very young, and so very, very German. Their arrogant expressions swollen with pride and Aryan entitlement. Victors believing they'd won the war.

The French army may have crumbled under German military

might, but ordinary citizens continued the fight. Paulette's former schoolmate Lucien was one of them. There were others, she knew. Bold men and women who conducted courageous acts of sabotage on the trains carting away confiscated champagne. Better the ground drink the wine than Nazis. Their bravery was worth celebrating, though Paulette had only recently come to understand the importance of their daring.

One of the German soldiers caught her eye and smiled with masculine interest. Paulette was familiar with the admiring look, if not the actual face. What had once brought her pleasure now made her stomach roil with nausea. She fathomed finding the will to scowl at the unrestrained appraisal. She turned away instead, and stood very still beside Gabrielle, her feet firmly planted on the platform.

The rain returned, falling from the sky in trickles.

They shared the shelter of a single umbrella. Gabrielle put a tentative hand on her arm. She seemed to want to say something, but as it had all morning, silence won the moment.

For an entire minute, they stood blinking at each other. The wind struck their faces. Steam from the train's engine coiled around their ankles. "You will let me know once you arrive at Mademoiselle's apartment?"

"I'll get word to you, yes."

There was nothing more to say, nothing more to do, but board the train. As if on cue, a porter appeared by her side. He took her suitcase, checked her ticket, and nodded. "Your seat is there, mademoiselle." He pointed to the third car from the back. "We depart in five minutes."

Through the cloud of steam, Paulette met Gabrielle's gaze one final time. Again, she saw guilt staring back at her. She simply didn't care anymore. She turned away, went to the proper car, and mounted the steps. Reims was her past.

Paris, her future.

Another German soldier sat across the aisle from her and

smiled that familiar, suggestive leer. She looked away to hide her reaction, fueled by her anger and disgust. At him, this entitled Nazi, all the others like him. Paulette's fury sparked a new resolve. She'd been given a chance to begin anew. In Paris. Her favorite city in the world. She would embrace this opportunity. She would work hard proving her worth as a budding fashion designer, and never complain. Then, maybe, just maybe, she would find redemption.

She was, after all, Paulette Leblanc. Hélène's daughter. She would find her purpose and she would fight. Somehow she would discover a way to resist the occupiers. She would do it for France. For her mother.

Maybe even for herself.

Chapter Two

Nicolle

May 1942.
La Haye-Descartes. French Demarcation Line. Zone Occupée.

Nicolle Cadieux, code name: Odette, guided her companion through the muddy, narrow streets of La Haye-Descartes. The village in central France was not her original choice for crossing the Demarcation Line. But she knew the layout well, and was nearly as familiar with the twists and turns of these streets as the ones in Moulins. Now, woefully behind schedule, Nicolle had to resist rushing her steps.

She must avoid attracting the wrong sort of notice. Only what she cultivated herself.

The network was being watched. That much she'd learned in Moulins. The additional guards at the border may not have been for her, specifically, or the man by her side, but the arrest of another couple of similar heights and builds, dressed in the same type of clothing, was warning enough for Nicolle. She'd casually slipped her companion out of line and, once clear, had immediately rerouted his escape.

Hours later, in that haunting, otherworldly moment just before dawn broke, she approached yet another checkpoint with the same man by her side. She reached out and pulled him close. It felt unnatural, treating him with such familiarity. She didn't even know his name, and he didn't know hers. Should anyone ask, he was Gaston Moreau. She, his wife, Amélie.

Their falsified papers said the same.

Nicolle added another layer of intimacy by leaning her head on his shoulder. Just a sleepy-eyed couple on their way to a family wedding in the Free Zone. If questioned, they would claim making this early start to avoid the heat of the day. The real reason was more complicated, and yet not. If Nicolle couldn't see the enemy, the enemy couldn't see her. Or, as Mademoiselle Sabine often said, "We work in the dark to serve the light."

Would Julien have approved of her secret work?

There had been no lies in him, no subterfuge, only purity of soul and a kind, generous heart. Then again, her beloved husband hadn't experienced the iron fist of German occupation. He'd died defending the Maginot Line, in a French army that had been strong only on paper. At least he'd been spared the humiliation of watching the government collapse within weeks of the first wave of battles. Nor had he been forced to live under the armistice that split their country into two zones, one controlled by Germany, the other by the collaborating Vichy government.

Worse still, Julien had missed meeting the piece of himself he'd left behind.

That Nicolle regretted, so very much.

Now her every choice, every escape and rescue she conducted, was with that precious gift in mind. She fought for him, her husband's legacy. Her efforts were small in comparison to most, but every downed airman returned to England and put back in the sky was a win for the Allies and another Nazi defeat.

"Did you hear that?"

The question came in heavily accented French, spoken in an unmistakable British accent. Nicolle had told him not to speak, but now, hearing the worry in his voice, she paused and listened, unsure what sound he meant. Then she heard it. The click-click of tiny little claws seeking purchase on the slippery concrete. "It's just the rats."

A necessary evil in their circuitous route through forgotten back alleyways.

He gave a curt nod, his face all but obscured by the wide-brimmed hat she'd insisted he wear. He was rather skittish, this Brit, and although Nicolle didn't know his name, his age, or his rank, she felt a strong kinship. They'd suffered a close call together. Moreover, they shared a common enemy. She would see him safely over the Demarcation Line, no matter the cost.

The hardest part was knowing who to trust. The enemy boldly walked among them now. Some were easy to spot. Like the men at the previous checkpoint, they wore German military uniforms. Wehrmacht, Luftwaffe, SS, Gestapo. Others hid their evil behind the crisp suits of the bureaucrats and the blue tunics of the French police. Not all were bad, but many—too many—were. Recognizing the difference was a matter of life and death for a *passeur* on the Ballard-Rochon Escape Line. Nicolle had learned this lesson while working for the Resistance network. Out of the dozens of British airmen she'd escorted from Paris to Périgueux, she hadn't lost one.

She tightened her hold. This Brit would not be her first.

From lowered lashes, she glanced up, and up farther still. He was a tall one. She still couldn't make out his features, but he'd grown tenser, more on edge. He flinched at every faraway sound—the hoot of an owl, the croak of a frog, the sloshing of river water against the stone pylons of Le Pont Henri IV.

"We're almost there," she whispered, understanding his fear, sharing it, as any wise *passeur* would. The Germans searched for men like him, accompanied by women like her. Their lackeys waited at the bridge, one of the twelve checkpoints along the Demarcation Line. Their sole job was to examine identity cards and free movement passes, checking, always, for flaws. A show of confidence was imperative when presenting fake documents, especially now that the Germans had replaced the conventional customs agents with Wehrmacht soldiers.

Using simple words, Nicolle had explained all this to her companion, especially the need to appear normal and ordinary. Yet his steps had slowed considerably, becoming a sort of dragging shuffle. She attributed the sluggish gait to fatigue and residual fear and hoped—no, prayed—there wasn't a more ominous reason.

The previous *passeur* hadn't mentioned an injury. Nor had the Brit himself. He spoke little French, and she even less English. The language barrier wouldn't have been a concern had they crossed the border in Moulins and consequently made it to the rendezvous point where Nicolle's English-speaking partner waited.

Nearly to the bridge now.

She could hear the soldiers conversing in German, a language she did know well. Their complaints about the long, boring night meant they were tired and cranky. This could be a good thing, or very, very bad. They would either be careless in their inspection—good—or unpleasantly thorough—not so good.

"Try," Nicolle whispered, "to look as if we are a happily married couple."

The Brit gave the barest suggestion of a nod. The first light of dawn chose that moment to lace through the low-hanging clouds. Nicolle slowly raised her gaze, traveling up and up to meet the man's eyes and...no. No! A face should not skew that gray.

"What's wrong?" she asked, in a voice so low the words nearly vanished in the wind. "Are you injured?"

"I…" He drew in a sharp breath that registered pain. *"Oui."*

"How bad?"

"Just…a…a nick."

Nick. She was not acquainted with this word. But she understood him nonetheless. "Where?"

"Torso," he ground out, his French almost unintelligible now. "Right side. Threads aren't…" he gritted his teeth "…holding up."

Threads? Another unfamiliar word, spoken again in his native language. Nicolle searched her limited knowledge of English vocabulary. "Do you mean sutures?"

"Oui. Sutures."

More bad news. Or maybe not. The injury probably wasn't life-threatening. What else had Antoinette failed to tell her? Perhaps the other *passeur* hadn't known. Perhaps the Brit had hid the wound from them both. Whatever the case, Nicolle had a choice to make. She knew only rudimentary first aid. Enough to assess the damage. But not here on the street.

No, not here.

Taking his arm, she guided the Brit back the way they had come. A block, then half another. Satisfied they were cloaked in shadow, she positioned herself in front of him, cupped his face in her hands, and adopted an expression as tender as that of a lover. "Look at me," she ordered past her adoring smile.

He tried. But his eyes had gone feral, and his gaze roamed everywhere, landing nowhere. Holding on to her smile, just barely, Nicolle gave his torso a fast, cursory inspection, her hands moving furiously over his long, lean frame. Not a lot of muscle, she noted, but not a lot of fat, either. More boy than man, like so many of his predecessors. Her fingers grazed a sticky, wet spot, and a queasy feeling came over her. Blood. A lot of it. Too much. She dared a peek. A mistake. Her stomach roiled again.

Taking a deep breath, she plucked at the frayed edges of her composure and slowly, carefully, slipped her fingers beneath his shirt and probed around the perimeter of the wound. The responding hitch of his breath told its own tale. As she wiped her hand free of his blood, she considered her next steps. He wouldn't make the rest of the journey without solid medical care. There were too many miles ahead, hundreds of them. And that didn't include the rigorous trek over the Pyrenees. *Staunch the blood*, she told herself. *Then seek help.*

"Place your open palm here." She guided his hand to the spot she meant. "Good, yes. There. That's it. Now press down hard. No. Harder." She demonstrated with her own hand over his. "*Oui. Très bien.* Now, keep your eyes on my face."

This time, he did as she commanded.

Holding his gaze, she unwound the scarf at her neck and went to work wrapping the material around his waist. At the sight of the wound, she lifted his hand, fit the material in position, then pressed his palm back in place. Almost immediately, blood spooled in a patchwork between his splayed fingers. Nicolle pulled in her own shuddering breath. "We need to get you patched up properly."

Another delay they could ill afford. It couldn't be helped.

Nicolle could sew—rather well, actually, fast and efficient—but that was fashion. She'd never stitched flesh together. She needed assistance, someone with skill and…*think, Nicolle.* Who in the network could she turn to at this hour?

There was no one. Except…maybe…

Yes. He would help her.

She'd come to this village because of Julien. Her husband had spent his childhood here. She'd walked these very streets with him as he'd reminisced. He'd also introduced her to his closest friend. André Dubois was not a doctor. But surely a veterinary surgeon was better suited to the task of closing a man's wound than a woman who worked as a seamstress in a fashion designer's atelier. "Can you walk?"

The Brit gave a quirky, lopsided grin. "I think I remember the basics."

His attempt at a joke gave her spirits a much-needed boost. Tucking herself under his free arm, she directed him away from the river and the looming checkpoint. They stumbled along, probably appearing inebriated. She could make that work. Thankfully, it was a short walk to their destination. When they rounded the last corner, Nicolle was all but dragging her companion. His eyes fluttered shut and his head lolled. She shook him, hard, sending his hat to the ground.

"Oh, no you don't." She shook him again. "Stay with me now."

He rallied, though his head remained bent and his gaze stayed fixed on the ground.

"Only a few more steps."

On the back stoop, she propped him up against the accompanying wall, took a deep breath, and knocked. She waited for what felt like an eternity but couldn't have been more than a few seconds. Finally, the door cracked open, revealing a small slit of light and the silhouette of the man who'd stood witness at her wedding when Julien's own brothers would not.

André Dubois was taller than Nicolle remembered, taller even than the airman swaying beside her, and clearly an early riser. Already dressed for the day, he wore a plain white shirt rolled up at the sleeves and pants as black as his hair. His intense, arresting eyes—somehow both blue and green all at once— swept across her face, passed over the airman, then back to her.

"We need your help."

There was a moment of absolute stillness in him before he wiped his features free of all expression and, inclining his head, stepped back to open the door wider. She'd barely maneuvered the Brit past the threshold when André shut the door and took over. He moved much faster than Nicolle had and with obvious purpose.

"Where are you taking him?"

"The clinic." His voice had the same gruff timbre she remembered, low and growly, as if he'd swallowed gravel for breakfast. "Second room on your left."

She hurried ahead and opened the door.

The light was better here, brighter, and Nicolle quickly scanned the small, tidy space. Sterile, almost cold, with a long metal table situated in the middle of the tiled floor. A single wall of shelves contained various medical instruments, lidded jars, and what she assumed were the tools needed to treat an assortment of household pets and local livestock.

"Help me get him on the table."

"Oh, of course. And…thank you."

He nodded. They worked in silence after that, each anticipating the other's next move.

Once they had the airman lying on his back, André was back to measuring and assessing the situation. He retrieved a pair of scissors, a bottle of antiseptic, added a roll of gauze, then set them on the table beside the Brit. Hands free, eyes narrowed, he cocked his head and studied Nicolle's bloody handiwork. The sharp planes of his face tensed. "Tell me what I'm dealing with."

"I'm not completely sure." She gave him a quick rundown of what she'd discovered, and how she'd not known about the injury until ten minutes ago. "I was only partially successful in curtailing the blood."

His gaze met hers. "You did well."

Snared in that powerful stare, she opened her mouth to respond, but he was already back to studying the airman's torso. He nodded, slipped on a pair of rubber gloves, then made a quick, decisive cut. The scarf fell away to reveal a deep, bloody gash. As Nicolle had done earlier, but with more care, his big hands gentle, André probed the wound.

The Brit bucked on the table, crying out. He would have continued thrashing had André not steadied him with a hand on his shoulder. "Easy now. I don't have the proper sedative for a man. I need you to be brave. Can you do that for me?"

Nicolle stared. André spoke fluent English, with no discernible accent. Nevertheless, the Brit was either incapable of responding or didn't seem to understand the question. André made another comment in English, then spared a quick look in Nicolle's direction. "Speak to him."

She knew what that meant. Distract him.

Jolted into action, she leaned over the airman. "He's just a boy."

"They send them up young." André hadn't acknowledged the actual situation until that moment. Yet he still asked no questions, demanded no answers.

It was better that way. A man could not reveal details he didn't know.

Nicolle looked down at the boy on the table again. She felt old, suddenly, so very old. Though she was not yet thirty, she was already two years a widow, both of them spent in war. Loss aged a woman. Grief made her ancient. She recalled those dark, endless days immediately following Julien's death. Her whole world had turned black, empty.

Then everything had changed. A single discovery, and she'd had a reason to live. A reason to fight for a Free France. Mademoiselle had stood with her every step of the way. Giving her an increase in wages first, making the necessary arrangements next, and then, when Nicolle had insisted, bringing her into the network.

The airman cried out in pain, snapping her back to the moment. She shifted her stance so that she could look directly into his face. His eyes were fringed with hot, wet tears, but he didn't let them fall. Brave boy. She touched his cheek gently, as she would a child. "Where did you grow up, *mon garçon*? What part of England?"

"Su—Surrey," he gritted out.

"Tell me about Surrey."

While he gasped through the description of the Surrey Hills and something about a chalk escarpment, André patched up the wound, quickly, efficiently. Nicolle blinked. "You've done this before?"

He said nothing, just continued sewing, tying off, cutting. What else, she wondered, did she not know about Julien's friend? Once he was finished, the Brit blew out a long sigh of relief, closed his eyes, and passed out. Nicolle followed André out of the room. Her eyelashes felt sticky, her throat gritty, but, oh, her heart was full of gratitude. "Thank you."

"I'm glad you came to me."

His voice held no softness, but Nicolle felt comforted in ways she couldn't explain. She'd always been a little intimidated by the big, quiet man Julien had considered his closest friend. There'd been great loyalty between the two men, and now Nicolle felt it, too, the trustworthiness rolling off him, the integrity. He'd always seemed so sure of himself and his place in the world. Julien had shared that trait. "When can I wake him?"

"Not yet."

She knew that much. "When, André?"

Irritation twitched at his lips. "He needs a full day's rest. Two would be better."

He might as well have said a year. "I can't afford that much time."

"How much, then?"

She did some calculating, reworked the route in her mind. "An hour, possibly two."

Her words hung in the air between them, the moment growing tense.

"Take two, and—" he touched her sleeve "—you could use some sleep yourself."

She ignored the suggestion. "Two hours, André, and then we'll be gone."

The tightness in his jaw told her he had strong reservations, and a dozen questions he wanted to ask, none of which he voiced. "He'll need a fresh set of clothing. Let me see what I can pull together."

Precisely two hours later, Nicolle was standing in front of the airman, now wearing what she assumed were some of André's clothes. The Brit was close to the same height, but not nearly as muscular. The shirt bagged on him, especially at the torso. Unfashionable, but helpful in hiding his bandages. Stepping back, she took in his appearance, then added a beret, positioning it at the proper angle. "There. You are ready." He wasn't. "You look like a proper Frenchman."

He didn't.

Nothing like her Julien, or even André, both men different in looks and temperament, yet so completely, thoroughly French, one blond, the other raven-haired. Good, loyal men, each unaware of Nicolle's precious secret, and they would remain so for eternity. Julien, because he couldn't learn the truth. André, because he shouldn't.

Bells tolled in the distance, eight reverberating strikes, reminding Nicolle they were dreadfully behind schedule with much ground yet to cover. André opened the back door himself. Golden sunlight streamed over him. Suddenly her husband's friend was reaching up, touching her cheek, as he had on her wedding day with that generous mix of understanding and acceptance. He'd been the only person in Julien's life who'd approved of their match. And now she was sad, thinking of her husband, wanting desperately to escape this terrible war and flee to somewhere safe, somewhere free of Nazis and gut-wrenching grief and gaping wounds that required sutures.

André dropped his hand. "Be safe." He stepped back, turned to the Brit. "Listen to her. She is very smart and resourceful."

"I know."

Her throat was thick with emotion as Nicolle thanked André a third time. She hooked her arm through the airman's and, noting the color still absent from his face, felt the smallest twinge of guilt. Was she pushing the boy too hard? Did she have a choice?

"Here we go," she said in English, repeating the words in French for her own benefit as well as his. *"C'est parti."*

Nicolle didn't look back. Not after she took the first few steps. Not as she rounded the first corner. Not even when André whispered, *"Faire attention—"* be careful *"—mon amie."* My friend. No, she didn't look back. Not once.

Arm in arm, she and the Brit joined the collection of men and women and a few children approaching the checkpoint. The other travelers wore some level of anxiety on their faces, in their countenance. No wonder, Nicolle thought, as she eyed the guards and their dogs, then read the sign warning ordinary citizens of the consequences for harboring the enemy.

VERY IMPORTANT WARNING
TO THE POPULATION

The Field Commander reminds the French population for the last time that the sheltering, hiding, aiding, or assisting in any manner the passing of aviators or parachutists, English or American, is done under the penalty of death.

On the other hand, the Field Commander will compensate for information leading to the arrest of these fugitives by releasing prisoners of war taken from this region.

Important warning, indeed. The Nazis played on the people's fear and greed. They'd won many battles that way and had stolen the lives of good men and women in the process, some Nicolle had known, one she had loved deeply. With every death, every new law and decree passed, they threatened her husband's legacy, and her own, and she grew more resolved, more willing to take great risks.

The Nazis would not win this war. No, Nicolle silently vowed, they would not win. And this young British airman by her side, this boy given the job of a man, would be back in the sky—God willing—by the end of the month.

Chapter Three

Paulette

Maison de Ballard. Paris, France.

Somewhere between Reims and Paris, Paulette suffered a moment of regret. She should have turned back to her sister, maybe tossed a brief wave, offered a smile—something. But she'd been so terribly upset, and the opportunity for a proper farewell was gone. Then again, she could write a letter, add a bit of sentiment, and yes, she would write Gabrielle. Make things right, or at least less wrong.

Though not now.

Now she must endure the rest of the journey with a German soldier on her left and a weary Frenchwoman on the seat to her right. One stared at her with clear masculine intent. The other shared a series of sighs and soft groans, and sported a sad little hat with a drooping feather as gray as the weather. She also smelled of moldy bread. The compartment was crowded with other German uniforms and other exhausted, tattered civilians, none of whom Paulette wished to engage in conversation. *Alone. Just leave me alone.*

Lest there be any doubt, she flipped open the book she'd brought along. Twenty minutes later, her head was still bent over the worn pages. She'd comprehended none of the words, knew nothing of the story itself. Reading was not the point, only the illusion of it.

She turned a page.

The German watched her closely and quite inappropriately. She felt his eyes brushing over her in that rude assessment common to men of a certain age who wore the enemy's uniform.

She turned another page.

Outside, the rain fell harder, heavier, and though it was barely midmorning, the sky had grown dark as night. Bursts of lightning spread thick, gnarled fingers against the black backdrop. Claps of thunder sounded on the air. One especially loud boom startled her elderly seatmate.

Paulette turned another page.

The strike of a match sounded in the stale air of the compartment. A pungent, phosphorous odor followed, and then a tiny flame was placed to the tip of a cigarette. The orange glow illuminated the German's face in hard, ruthless angles, the narrow cheekbones, the steely gaze, and suddenly Paulette felt a kind of anger wash over her. She did not, however, look up for long. She'd caught the necessary information in that first glimpse after she'd boarded the train.

He was at least twice her age and had the appearance of someone used to getting his way. He also wore a wedding ring. The bubbling anger turned into a fluttering sickness, and she clutched the book tighter, while he smoked his cigarette without a care in the world. Paulette understood what was behind that brash attitude. Only the harshest of men joined the Schutzstaffel, the SS.

She'd met many of his kind in Reims. Paris, she suspected, would be filled with more.

Paulette shivered at the thought. She was heading to an occupied city alone and vulnerable, cast utterly adrift from everything and everyone familiar. She would have Mademoiselle, that was true, but her mother had been closely connected to the fashion designer, not Paulette. Sabine Ballard had always seemed larger-than-life. Someone to be admired, not a friend. Certainly not a confidant.

"*Sie sind sehr schön*, Fräulein."

The German had broken his silence—*you are very beautiful*—and now Paulette could not continue ignoring him. Fear closed like a hawk's talon around her throat. She must be smart. Slowly, she looked over at him, blinked several times, pretending not to understand him.

He repeated the compliment.

Her stomach roiled in rebellion. Friedrich had spoken those same words upon their first meeting. He'd whispered them again and again, especially during their most intimate moments. She'd learned to decipher their meaning on her own, and then he'd taught her other words. Other things a girl of nineteen should never know. Paulette wished she could forget his lessons. And the Nazi still waited for her to respond.

When she did not, he gave the compliment again, the third time in French. "*Tu es très belle*, mademoiselle."

She blinked, startled by his perfect accent and the shocking intimacy of his phrasing, as if they were well acquainted. Just like a German to ignore the rules of the French language, using *tu* instead of *vous*. And he was smiling now, like someone who enjoyed scaring young women with nothing more than his words. Well, Paulette was scared. Terrified. The old woman by her side placed a hand over hers and squeezed gently.

That silent show of solidarity gave her the courage to say, "*Merci beaucoup*."

She meant the words for her seatmate.

The Nazi took them for himself. "You travel to Paris alone?" he asked in that sly, wickedly smooth French accent. "Without the benefit of friend or family?"

She felt the blood drain from her face, taking all her heat with it. "I…" Paulette tried to say more, but her voice didn't seem to be working.

"She is with me, monsieur."

His eyebrows lifted. "She cannot speak for herself?"

"My granddaughter is very shy, you understand. She wishes only to speak to me."

His eyebrows traveled higher. "Yet you haven't exchanged a single word since we left the station."

Oh, yes, Paulette thought, shaking now. This man saw too much.

The old woman was not so intimidated. "You know how it is with a young girl. We argued over her new beau. He wears a uniform like yours, with those lightning bolts at the neck." She pointed at the SS runes on his collar for emphasis. "I say he is too old. She disagrees."

"I see."

The old woman gave him a cagey smile. "I believe that you do."

"*Bonne journée*, mesdames. I will leave you now." He removed himself to another seat.

Paulette hardly noticed his departure. She was too busy fumbling her book closed and gawking at her seatmate. How did she know what to say? Had she seen Paulette with Friedrich, or heard about their affair? They'd been careful, meeting under the cover of night, in the vineyard or wine cellar. Even their ugly parting had been inside a police station with only two witnesses, her mother and a Gestapo agent. No, this woman hadn't seen them. Her eyes held no judgment, no condemnation. Still.

Paulette's pulse picked up speed, loud and insistent in her ears. The sound was drowned out by the brakes of the train.

They'd arrived in Paris.

Paulette welcomed the ensuing confusion as her fellow passengers stood, gathered their belongings, and fought for position in the aisle. The German joined the fray, Paulette and her "grandmother" all but forgotten now that he thought her a special friend of one of his evil brethren.

The lie had been a spark of genius.

Paulette released a sigh, not quite of relief but something close. "Thank you, madame. I…" What else was there to say? "Thank you."

"Think nothing of it." She winked. "We French girls must stick together."

The woman's weathered face was a road map of wrinkles, but her eyes shone with kindness, and her smile was contagious. Paulette found herself returning the gesture.

"Do you have somewhere to go?" the woman asked. "People are waiting for you?"

Paulette nodded.

"Then you will be all right on your own."

Again, Paulette nodded. All she had to do was make her way to Mademoiselle's apartment. The rest would fall into place. It must. The alternative was too terrible to contemplate. She shut her eyes, opened them again when the woman moved around her to claim her place in the aisle. "*Au revoir*, mademoiselle."

"*Au revoir*, madame." Still smiling, Paulette reached for her own belongings and felt the stiffness in her limbs, the exhaustion from too much pacing over too many sleepless nights. Her mind wanted to dwell on the past. But no. No more looking back. If she looked back, they won. Friedrich, the Nazis, Detective Mueller. Paulette would not let them win. She would not give up. She would embrace this new life.

Exiting the train, she stepped onto the platform in Gare de

l'Est and tightened her hands like manacles on the handle of her suitcase. She'd barely arrived, and already this was a Paris she no longer recognized. The noise, the smells, the sounds, none of it was the same.

Maybe that was a good thing. Maybe this new Paris was the perfect place for a woman who'd lost her way to begin anew. Sufficiently emboldened, she followed the signs pointing her to the main terminal, then out onto the streets beyond. Choosing to save her money, she began the forty-five-minute walk from the tenth arrondissement to the eighth. Like in Reims, German occupation was everywhere, only on a larger scale. Nazi flags. Military uniforms. Guard dogs that looked like wolves. Weapons and guns and German entitlement.

At least the rain had stopped. The sun shone bright and harsh, hurting Paulette's eyes.

She passed long queues outside shops. Lots of them, too many to count. Some went on for blocks. Through a window, she watched a shopkeeper weigh a piece of meat, wrap it in brown paper, and hand it to a woman. Paulette had never purchased food for herself or her family. That task had fallen on their housekeeper, Marta, who'd continued doing so after their home had been seized. Herr Hauptmann von Schmidt had required Michelin-star dining at every meal, despite the hardships of others and the rationing put in place.

He'd not been a real soldier, but a wine merchant in uniform who courted power. The other men at his table were always of higher rank or greater importance, Friedrich being one of them. Detective Mueller had been there, too, eyeing them all with suspicion, even von Schmidt.

Paulette passed an outdoor café. French women drank and ate and laughed with German soldiers, as if there was no war or scarcity in place. She saw her former self in those female faces, Friedrich in every soldier, and felt unspeakable shame.

Her throat clogged.

Paulette shook herself free and moved on, passing more queues. Dozens of them, with mostly women holding baskets hooked over their arms. They had the look of a conquered people in their stooped shoulders and clutched coupon books.

At the back of every line were more women, holding the hands of their small children, all of them dressed shabbier than the others, their expressions bleaker. Parisian Jews. Alive, persecuted unfairly, and suffering. Paulette thought of her own mother. Hélène Leblanc's torment was over, Paulette's only just beginning.

Do not think of this as banishment. Think of it as a new beginning.

Gabrielle's haughty speech echoed in her ears, half taunt, half promise, and at last Paulette stood outside Maison de Ballard, marveling at the scope of the operation. What had begun as a small workroom on the ground floor now inhabited the entire building, five stories in total, with dormer windows on the roof level and large plate glass windows displaying current designs on the ground floor. Mademoiselle had created an entire industry on her own, featuring both prêt-à-porter—ready-to-wear—and haute couture. She also made menswear, hats, gloves, jewelry, and even produced signature fragrances sold in bottles made from rare Rochon crystal.

Paulette was suddenly a bundle of nerves. As she studied the mannequins in the windows that flanked the salon's entrance, her confidence faded completely. Her dress was woefully out of fashion, and it hung on her too-thin frame in an unflattering silhouette.

Nothing to be done for it now.

She pushed through the main door and stepped into a world of colorful fabric and fragrance, money and prestige. House models wearing Mademoiselle's latest creations meandered across the carpeted floor in random patterns. They paused momentarily in front of patrons who sat in chairs holding champagne coupes. The clothing was simpler than in previous seasons. Paulette recognized the designer's signature embellishments on the waistband and sleeves, in the feminine draping that worked so well with a woman's figure.

Everything was so familiar yet different. Paulette no longer belonged. She felt it in the heads turning in her direction, the critical eyes watching her, judging her. The suitcase, she realized. It made her conspicuous, as did the dress she wore from three seasons ago.

Mademoiselle's customers had high standards and uncompromising taste. She wanted to run. But that would make her a coward. And so she held her ground as Mademoiselle's assistant spotted her and came over. Impossibly thin, with pointed features and hair the color of spun silver, Geneviève Durand was neither old nor young, but somewhere in her midforties, possibly. There was no real beauty in her features and no recognition in her gaze.

Had she changed so much?

"Geneviève? Do you not know me? I stood right there—" she pointed to the raised platform facing a three-way mirror "—while you supervised the fitting of this very dress."

Paulette spread out the skirt to reveal Mademoiselle's signature embellishment.

"I recognize the dress. You, I do not." She took Paulette's arm and directed her back the way she had come. "You will go now and not come back."

"But…" A blinding panic wrapped around Paulette's throat. Her chest. "Mademoiselle is expecting me. I am to meet her here, in the salon, this very morning."

The uninterested eyes swept over her—head to toe—and back again. "She told me nothing of this meeting."

Paulette thought of her mother's shawl tucked in her suitcase, of the sketch pad Mademoiselle had gifted her, and tapped into the confident woman she used to be, who she still was, beneath the guilt and grief and need for solitude. "I am Paulette Leblanc.

Hélène's daughter. Mademoiselle has dressed me since I was a child, my mother even longer than that."

Geneviève's eyes disappeared under the weight of her skepticism, but then came a sort of reluctant recognition. Paulette pounced on her hesitation. "My sister has been in correspondence with Mademoiselle for several weeks. Ask her. She will tell you I speak the truth."

"We shall see what Mademoiselle says." She turned to go. Paulette started to follow her, but Geneviève held up a hand. "You will wait here."

Alone, feeling awkward, but trying not to show it, Paulette bore the whispers with her head high, her eyes fixed straight ahead. When a minute turned into five, she went to the window and looked out, hardly noticing the activity on the street. What would she do if Mademoiselle sent her away? Where would she go? Home wasn't an option. Gabrielle had made that clear.

Where then?

Geneviève returned, her lips pulled into a tight pucker. "You will go to the other door at the back of the building and present yourself at the atelier."

The atelier? Mademoiselle must be working on her final designs for the fall season. Excited, Paulette quickly exited the salon and went to the back of the building. There was no sign designating the atelier's entrance, only a door that was made of solid wood.

She reached for the handle, found it locked. She rapped and waited. Eventually, the door swung open, revealing a young woman with pleasing features wearing a simple black dress.

Paulette gave her name.

"We've been expecting you. Please, enter."

She did as the woman requested. Once inside, she set down her suitcase, straightened, and looked around. The noise hit her first. The sound of machines mingled with high-pitched voices talking over one another. Eyes wide, heart full, she took it all in. The chaos. The vibrancy. The heat. Yet it all was somehow perfectly suited to a busy, successful fashion designer's workroom. Only women, no men, were everywhere. They were clothed in identical black dresses beneath white lab coats and wore their hair slicked back in severe-looking chignons.

Some operated sewing machines, others hemmed dresses with needle and thread, while still others sat on low stools hand-sewing beads onto colorful fabric. At the center of it all was Mademoiselle herself. She moved from dress forms to machines, orchestrating the pandemonium as if she were directing a symphony orchestra. At least five women buzzed around her. Worker bees paying homage to their queen.

Paulette smiled for the second time that day.

Sabine Ballard might not be in the prime of her life, somewhere in her early sixties, but she radiated the energy and stamina of a woman half her age. Paulette never understood why she insisted on being called *Mademoiselle* like her rival, Coco Chanel. Coco had never married or produced a child. Mademoiselle Sabine had done one of the two. She'd birthed a daughter.

Paulette felt eyes on her again, a bit more welcoming than in the salon. But not by much. The young woman who'd opened the door approached Mademoiselle and said something low. The designer nodded, then turned and caught sight of Paulette. "Ah, *ma chère fille*, you have arrived at last." She approached with her hands outstretched, kissed the air near both of Paulette's cheeks, then stepped back. "You have the look of your mother. It makes me a little sad, but also happy. I miss her desperately, you know."

There were tears in her voice, matching the ones in her eyes. And Paulette felt it herself, the loss, the grief, the unfairness of this war. "I miss her, too."

"We will remember her together, and you will work very hard to make her proud, *oui*?"

"I will work very hard."

"You will start at the machines, I think, making your own uniform as your first task, and then, when the dress is complete, you will receive your own lab coat as a sign of your new status."

Paulette blinked. "The...the machines?" she repeated, her stomach clenching and bucking, as if she were in a boat bobbing over rough waters.

"It is a good place to learn the basics of our craft. You will see. Now, wait here."

She turned her back on Paulette and, sighing heavily, approached a young woman at one of the sewing machines. She set her hand on the thin shoulders and spoke softly, her words lost in the workroom noise. At one point, the young worker hung her head and placed her hands in her lap. Then she looked over her shoulder, straight at Paulette, and she was immediately struck by the startlingly green eyes beneath thick black eyebrows. The clear skin had gone pale.

Paulette's heart skipped a beat. Something bad was happening to that woman, and she was the cause. She hadn't wanted a job in Mademoiselle's atelier, certainly not like this.

"I understand," the girl said loud enough for Paulette to hear now that they were facing one another. Her voice was tinged with a soft, lilting accent that hinted at an origin somewhere outside of France.

"I'm sorry, Basia." *Basia.* Not a French name. Eastern European. Polish, perhaps? "You will find another position."

"Who will hire a Jew?"

"Leave that to me," Mademoiselle said. "I will not abandon you. I promise."

"Yes, all right." She stood, agile as she reached for a leather tote bag. On her way to the door, eyes brimming with tears, she looked at Paulette again. She felt the girl's devastation, her embarrassment, and something else. Not blame, precisely, but a sort of acceptance, as though she'd always known this moment would come.

The terrible, awful truth hit hard. Paulette had taken the Jewish girl's job, when no one hired people like her. She'd stolen someone's livelihood, because Gabrielle had made it clear she couldn't go home. Paulette had no choice but to remain. She wished she could make it up to Basia, but that would require power and connections. She had neither. There was nothing she could do but trust Mademoiselle to make good on her promise to the girl.

"Paulette," Mademoiselle Ballard called out. "This is your machine now."

Her guilt was replaced with horror, and she felt the impostor. "I don't know how to use one of those."

"You will learn. And once you've done so, we will teach you how to make proper stitches. But not yet. Marie Claire." The designer snapped her fingers, and another young woman two machines over surged to her feet. "You will teach Paulette how to sew on the machines."

"But…" Marie Claire blinked. "Is Basia not coming back?"

Mademoiselle dismissed the question with a flick of her wrist, her attention already back on one of the dress forms. *"Non!"* She clapped her hands twice, going on the move once again. "Not like that. The other direction, Joelle. We drape the silk left to right."

Alone with the seamstress, Paulette felt the woman's anger, saw it in the narrowed eyes. Marie Claire clearly blamed Paulette for her friend's dismissal. Others in the workroom agreed. They, too, gave her accusing stares. She opened her mouth to apologize, to explain she hadn't known, but the door swung open again, and a man entered.

A hush fell over the room, and all heads turned in his direction.

He had the quintessential look of a Frenchman. Dark eyes,

dark hair, the face of a poet, and the lean build of an athlete. He surveyed the room, brushing over Paulette without a single moment of hesitation—that was new and surprisingly welcome. More looking on his part, evaluating, and then his gaze landed on the chair Basia had just vacated.

He shook his head, uttered, "Sabine, what have you done?" then lifted his voice over the din and added, "A word, *s'il vous plaît*, right now."

"Philippe, *mon ami*. You are very, very late, and I am very, very upset with you." Her words were full of censure, but she was smiling as she walked to him, extending her hands in greeting as she'd done with Paulette. "I was anticipating your arrival two days ago."

"I am here now." There it was again, the faint accent in his speech that Paulette couldn't quite place. "We have much to discuss."

"Then we will go to my office, where you will shout at me, and I will yell at you, and all will be as before."

"If only it were that simple."

"We will make it that simple, *non*?" They maneuvered toward a darkened corridor, muttering at one another. The man's limp was hardly noticeable, but yes. Paulette caught the slight dragging of his left foot. A war injury, perhaps. An unexpected twinge of compassion ran through her as she watched the slightly uneven strides. Suddenly feeling eyes on her, she glanced at the still angry Marie Claire. The other woman stood with her hands on her hips, the hard glare bleaker than before.

Paulette had made her first enemy in Paris.

Well, she wasn't here to make friends. She was here to learn. And honor her mother. With that in mind, she sat in front of the sewing machine and studied the complicated knobs and levers. A piece of shiny red fabric had been caught under a small metal foot, the material snagged in several places, and that, she decided, did not bode well for her first lesson.

None of this boded well, not the way she'd secured this job, or even the job itself, and so Paulette spoke aloud what raged in her heart. "How do I make this work?"

Chapter Four

Sabine

Sabine Ballard navigated her way through the main artery of the fashion house she'd built from hard work and hush money. She moved at a steady pace. Looked neither left nor right. Caught the eye of no one. And yet her heart filled with an overwhelming sense of responsibility. The sensation was so immediate and so complete she nearly lost her footing.

She didn't, of course. Not a single misstep. She knew her role.

Show no weakness, especially after dismissing a valuable member of the team.

In times of crisis, these women relied on her to be strong. Confident. And so she would be both. They were her girls, after all, her family. She'd handpicked each of them herself, from the finest artisans in Paris. She knew every woman by name. Understood their pain, shared in their hopes and dreams. And watched, often helplessly, as German occupation stole pieces of their souls. Motivation enough to resist the Nazis. Though not her only reason. Or even her main one.

A faint rustle of movement near her sleeve reminded Sabine she wasn't alone in the fight. Philippe. Her partner in their Resistance network. Her friend. So young, but not so innocent. Or so patient. Urgency vibrated off him, a living, breathing thing. He'd come with bad news. She'd seen the truth of it on his face the moment their eyes touched across the workroom.

He also had thoughts about her dismissal of Basia, no doubt.

There it was again. That all-consuming need to protect her own. So many souls relied on her to be Mother, Friend, Warrior, Confidant. And, for some, even Savior. Sabine would do right by Basia. She had a plan that only required a bit of fine-tuning and execution.

In the meantime, which woman did Paulette Leblanc need her to be?

Sabine paused in the shadowy hallway outside her office and glanced over her shoulder. Sorrow gripped her throat as she watched the girl attempt to operate the sewing machine with a surprising amount of grit, if not a single ounce of finesse. Apparently, she'd inherited her mother's iron will. That was something of a surprise, considering how Hélène had pampered the girl in her youth.

Philippe turned to see what had caught Sabine's attention. His eyebrows slammed together. "Sabine." He said her name as a reprimand. "I thought we agreed, no more new hires."

Of course, he would notice Paulette. She stood out from the others. *Bien sur,* Hélène's daughter was nothing like Sabine's other *midinettes,* her seamstresses. Despite the broken look in her eyes, the girl had an air that revealed her privileged upbringing. It was in the elegant way she held her shoulders, the slight lift of her chin. The perfectly manicured fingernails.

The shoes made of real leather.

So many small signs, adding up to an impressive whole. "How do you know she's a new hire?"

"The dress she wears and, no, not only because of the color."

Ah, yes. The dress. That, too, had been a surprise, an unpleasant one, leaving more questions than answers. Sabine sniffed in something bordering outrage. "It is shabby and out-of-date."

"The passage of time cannot disguise an original Mademoiselle Ballard design."

A valid, if irrelevant, point. "Flatterer."

"Truth, not flattery. Look at her, Sabine. That girl is not a trained *midinette*."

He was right. Paulette knew nothing about sewing, as evidenced by her clumsiness in the simple task of feeding thread through the machine. She'd started at the wrong place, twice, and had missed the take-up lever both times. No matter. She would find her way, eventually. If not here in the atelier, somewhere else in the fashion house. "Paulette won't be a problem."

"She already is." Philippe's voice was low and grave, and Sabine heard it now. The faintest hint of a British accent he usually controlled so well. Like fresh polish over fine wood, the faint guttural tone pointed to his formative years spent at a boarding school in Kent. Made stronger from his recent visits.

"Do not look for trouble where there is none," she warned, telling herself as much as him.

"Then perhaps you will stop giving me cause. Sabine." He set his hand on her shoulder. "I passed the Jewish girl on the street outside the atelier. She was crying. Sobbing, actually. I can only assume you released her in favor of—" he cocked his head in Paulette's direction "—that beautiful disaster."

Beautiful disaster. How well he'd described Hélène's daughter. Paulette was beautiful. And, already, a complete disaster. She'd come to Paris with no sewing skills and did not belong in the atelier. But it wasn't Philippe's place to tell her how to run her business. "You overstep."

"Do I?"

"Far too often." She shrugged out from under his loose grip and gave him a fierce scowl.

He gave her a patronizing look in return. "You rarely act on a whim, and never when it comes to your design house, which leads me to believe you have a plan for the Jewish girl and will need me to facilitate—"

The jarring ring of a telephone cut off the rest of his words. Now Philippe's urgency had become her own. Only a small number of people knew about the telephone Sabine kept in her office. Even fewer used it to contact her directly. "I should get that."

"You should."

She pushed into her office, moving with both speed and purpose. Philippe followed hard on her heels, then closed the door behind him. Only after he threw the lock in place did Sabine pick up the receiver and press it to her ear. *"Bonjour?"*

"Mademoiselle Sabine."

Relief almost brought her to her knees. *At last!* "Odette." She tried to keep the uneasiness out of her voice. "How goes the delivery?"

"The dress was presented to the client intact." Translation: The British airman was safely across the Demarcation Line with no life-threatening injuries.

"Excellent." Sabine moved the receiver to her other ear. "I trust the fit was correct?"

"Oui, Mademoiselle. Other than a few minor alterations, no additional changes were required. I left the client well pleased." Translation: The handoff to the next *passeur* went smoothly.

A heaviness lifted from Sabine's heart. Odette had prevailed despite complications. The next leg of the Brit's journey would be conducted by another escort within a different network. Sabine would never know if he made it out of France. Her concern now was for her *passeur.* "When can I expect your return?"

A soft sigh preceded Odette's response. "I missed the train to Orléans and won't be able to catch another until morning." Translation: The young woman had made her usual stop in Limoges and would be spending the night.

This wasn't the first time she'd lingered, nor would it be the last, and although Sabine had questions concerning the delays, she understood Odette's desire to spend time in Limoges. "I will see you tomorrow, then."

"Tomorrow."

Sabine set the receiver back in its cradle, reconciled she would have no real information until Odette returned to Paris and became Nicolle Cadieux once again. Assuming there were no more delays. Or setbacks. Or complications.

"What's wrong, Sabine? What's happened?"

Everything is wrong, she wanted to shout. *Too much has happened.*

The war. Heartache and loss. Death and disappearances. All of it precipitated by the Nazis spreading their policy of hate and gaining new devotees by the day. Their venom was seeping into the hearts of men and women once loyal to France, now caring only for themselves.

"Sabine. I asked you a question."

"Actually, you asked me two."

The boyish grin came lightning fast. There, then gone in a flash. "Now you deflect."

He wasn't wrong. Sighing, she shifted and noticed the change in him. His lips were set in a grim line, a sure sign of his agitation, but it was his eyes that gave her pause. They were watchful, worried, reminding her he cared as much as she about the network they'd built together, out of the dream conjured by another. As she'd done on the telephone, she spoke carefully and in code.

"Odette had several delays delivering the garment, but persevered. The client is happy. She will return to Paris in the morning."

"A day late."

She shrugged. "Alterations were required."

"Is that so?" He opened his mouth to say more, but she lifted a finger to forestall him. Parisian walls had ears, even the ones in the sanctity of a Frenchwoman's private office.

The muscles in Philippe's jaw bunched, but he held silent while she put the necessary precautions in place. First, she switched on lamps, three to be exact, enough to illuminate facial expressions clearly. Then she moved to the desk and powered up the wireless radio. It took several moments of fiddling with dials until the offensive crackling noises morphed into the even more offensive sound of a Wagner opera.

Sabine hated German music, most especially arias written by Hitler's favorite composer.

The music hit an ear-splitting crescendo, and a rush of heartbeats battered her ribs, each one sparked by French outrage. Dissatisfied with merely controlling the French capital, the Nazis had seized the airwaves. Now only German music and German propaganda touched Parisian ears. So very many reasons to resist.

Sighing again, she returned her attention to Philippe and, in the bold lamplight, noted the changes in him. The sweet, artistic boy she'd met nearly ten years ago was absent in the thirty-two-year-old man who stood before her now. War had erased his youthful exuberance, his joie de vivre, as it were. The tender soul no longer existed inside the harsh, albeit handsome, exterior.

No, this Philippe Rochon was not the son of her heart, though she loved him dearly. Nor was he the artisan of crystal and glass with an exceptional eye for beauty. This man was a black-marketeer, willing and able to buy and sell any number of goods and services. For a price. He was hard and ruthless, comfortable in the company of French gangsters, collaborating politicians, and Nazi vipers. Sabine worried he would lose his morality completely.

Perhaps that made her a hypocrite, for she, too, had made a questionable alliance with a very bad man to keep her fashion house afloat. "Tell me the news from Toulouse."

"It's not good. The Abwehr raided one of our safe houses this morning."

Her breath collapsed in her lungs. It couldn't be. German military intelligence couldn't possibly have attacked a house in the Free Zone. "Impossible."

"The soldiers came at dawn and arrested the entire household, including their sixteen-year-old daughter. The girl was a *passeur* for us."

"*Mon Dieu.*" The words echoed in Sabine's mind over and over. A brave girl. Her courageous parents. Arrested and taken from their home. They would suffer brutal interrogation and endure great pain. Possibly death.

Something hot and aching pooled in Sabine's belly. She knew the sensation as grief. It dug deep, past her defenses, pulling a waterfall of tears from her eyes. She swiped at them with an angry hand. "And you had no inkling of this raid, no hint at all?"

"None." He spat the word. And now she understood the look in his eyes was not anger, but guilt. Regret. In an effort to avoid this very thing, Philippe had made his own questionable alliances within the Abwehr, at the cost of his reputation. The loss of his friends. Even his family doubted his loyalties.

"There's more," he ground out.

Time seemed to slow as they stood in the silent moment, staring at each other. She, praying he said nothing else to break her heart. He, pulling his thoughts together to do exactly that. "The home was a popular gathering place for members of the local Resistance. There will be more arrests in the coming days."

No! This wasn't supposed to happen. From the beginning of their partnership, Sabine and Philippe had been careful. To the point of obsession. They knew the stakes, and the devastation one small mistake could bring. They'd put safeguards in place, insisted members of their network use false names and spoke only in coded messages. They plotted. They planned.

"How could this have happened?" As soon as the words left her mouth, the horrible, awful truth hit her. "We were betrayed by one of our own."

"It's more diabolical than that."

She couldn't think how. A mole in the network could erase their entire operation, either in a slow, methodical ripping apart at the seams or a quick, ruthless takedown.

"Two men, both barely old enough to shave, showed up at the pub where the girl worked every Saturday. They arrived late at night, looking lost and scared, and ultimately persuaded her that they were British airmen recently shot down by German planes. They insisted they needed help getting back to England. Believing their tale, she took them to her home."

"The safe house."

He nodded, ran an agitated hand through his hair. "There was no cause to doubt their tale. They spoke with British accents and wore British military boots."

The shoes. Always the shoes. But in this instance, she feared, a cruel, horrible trick.

Philippe confirmed her suspicions with his next words. "The two men were German soldiers posing as British airmen."

For several seconds, Sabine lost her ability to breathe. Suddenly, she was tired, so very tired. Her eyes felt grainy, her mind dizzy, and in the half second it took her to gulp down a small puff of air, Philippe was on the move. He paced and muttered and paced some more.

The music swelled with each step he took.

He hardly noticed. He was too busy vowing to be smarter,

listen closer, make better contacts with more powerful men. "And, Sabine." He stopped before her, breathing hard, eyes dark and full of intent. "No more new hires. I mean it. We cannot afford bringing in unknowns."

"Paulette is not an unknown." Although, actually, in many ways, she was. But for one important distinction. "She is a girl in need of my help."

"You say that every time."

Every time it was true. "According to Nazi law, her mother was Jewish. I helped her hide her identity and promised I would take care of her daughter should she be found out."

His eyes widened. "Her mother was arrested?"

Sabine nodded.

"And she is now without family?"

She thought about her conversation with Paulette's older sister. Gabrielle had been vague on details but clear on one salient point. *Paulette can stay no longer in Reims. It's not safe for her here.* "Paulette is on her own." True, but for Sabine. "She has nowhere else to go."

Also true.

"I…see."

She doubted that he did. No man could truly know what it was to be a woman in this world. Sabine and Hélène had known. They'd prepared for the worst, though neither suspected matters would deteriorate so quickly. Hélène's arrest had come as a shock, as had her quick disappearance. It didn't make sense. None of it. Sabine was still reeling. The false identity papers had been flawless, Sabine had seen to that herself. She'd turned to a trusted source, a client, with connections to the best forger in Paris.

"My friend is gone, and I will follow through on my promise. I will protect her daughter." *As I wasn't able to protect my own.*

Philippe reached up, touched her cheek. The sadness in his

eyes reflected her own sorrow. "You're thinking about Giselle. You're taking in this girl, the daughter of your friend, for her."

Of course she was thinking about Giselle. She was always thinking about Giselle. "Everything I do is for her."

He dropped his hand. "It won't bring her back."

That wasn't the point. "She was my daughter, Philippe."

"And she was my wife." The first crack in his demeanor showed in how he staggered away from her and collapsed in a chair, as if his legs could no longer hold his weight. She recognized the guilt in him, the grief, and loved him as the son of her heart he'd been long before the day he'd married Giselle. He'd been there on the escape that had taken her life. Injured and unable to get to her, he'd watched helplessly as his wife was gunned down by a Nazi soldier on patrol. Philippe had barely made it out alive.

He walked with the suffering of his loss every day, his limp a constant reminder.

Still injured, angry, and grieving, Philippe had accepted an invitation from the British military and traveled to England to train with MI9, a division dedicated to rescuing their downed airmen and POWs. When he'd returned to France, he'd come to Sabine, and they'd forged a partnership. Two years later, their network was vast and far-reaching. They saved lives for the sake of the one they'd both lost. Neither had moved on from their grief. They hadn't even tried. "Philippe, please. Giselle would not want us to—"

"I don't want to talk about her. Not now."

"That's the problem. You never want to talk about Giselle." While Sabine never wanted to stop talking about her daughter.

"I should get back to work," he said, though he remained sitting.

"I should do the same." Though she remained unmoving as well. Again, she felt the weight of her burdens. She had a midseason collection to design and a fashion show looming. Short two pieces, she needed to get back to the art of creating.

Slowly gaining his feet, Philippe came to stand before her. Mouth twisting, he tugged her close, kissed each of her cheeks, then rested his chin atop her head. "I miss her, Sabine. Never doubt it. I miss her with every beat of my heart."

"It's the same for me."

"I know." He gave a very long sigh. "She connects us, you and me. I do not regret that."

"Nor do I."

He pulled back, kissed her forehead. "You're a good woman and a better friend to me than I have been to you. If you need help with the Jewish girl—"

"I will contact you."

"Good enough." He released her and, with only a passing glance over his shoulder, left her office.

Feeling raw, Sabine's mind wanted to dwell on the woman they'd both lost. Giving into temptation, she went to the photograph of Giselle on stage in the title role of the ballet bearing her name. She'd been born to dance and would have become one of the greatest prima ballerinas of her generation had she lived. Grief spilled into her heart, sending blood rushing through her veins, pounding in her ears.

Sabine would never regret giving birth to her daughter out of wedlock, nor would she apologize for her affair with the wealthy Italian count. The aristocrat had known her so little, and had understood her even less. She would have kept silent about their romance without his "gift" to keep her quiet. It had made him feel important to pay her off with such a large sum. So, she'd taken the money and raised her daughter and sent her to ballet classes to teach her poise.

Giselle had become a gifted ballerina and had met Philippe at a charity event Sabine had sponsored. They'd fallen madly, instantly in love and married young. But then, war. She'd barely lost her daughter when the threat of losing her company had loomed. Hitler had wanted to move the entire fashion industry to Berlin. He'd nearly prevailed and had only relented after being presented with the impossibility of moving not just the couturiers, but the tens of thousands of workers. Seamstresses, embroiderers, lace makers, milliners, perfumers. The list went on and on. Even today, two years later, Sabine only managed to stay afloat because of compromises and a dubious alliance.

A loud knock on the doorjamb startled Sabine, and she nearly dropped the photograph of Giselle. Hand shaking, she replaced the frame on her desk and called out, "Enter."

Marie Claire poked her head in the room. "Mademoiselle Sabine, we have a situation."

Her first thought was of Paulette. Despite what she'd said to Philippe, the girl could very well prove to be a problem. She wasn't suited for hard work. Yet. "What sort of situation?"

"Basia's fiancé is at the door. He won't leave until he speaks with you, personally."

This was an interesting twist of events. Though Sabine was acquainted with the boy's father and mother, and had even met him at their home, he'd never pushed the boundaries of her relationship with his parents. He'd never shown up at his fiancée's place of work. "Does he know I let her go?"

Marie Claire shook her head. "I left it for you to tell him."

As was appropriate. She was, after all, the one who'd dismissed the girl. Swallowing back the dry lump in her throat, she forced a smile. "Send him to me here."

"Very good."

While she waited, Sabine considered what she would say to Jacob. She would, as promised, ensure Basia's future was secure. But she had yet to formulate a concrete plan, just a few ideas. In the end, she kept her explanation brief, saying only, "Basia has gone home. You will want to follow her there."

He hesitated in the doorway, hat in hand, digesting this new piece of information. Something odd came and went in his eyes, something that Sabine couldn't quite name. Resignation. Acceptance. She was still trying to piece the mystery together when he nodded and quickly left.

Moving to the spot where he'd previously stood, she watched the young man go, thinking surely it was just a series of unhappy coincidences that he'd shown up at the atelier less than an hour after she'd let his fiancée go, on the same day her network had been compromised and a safe house raided, after a routine escape had required several additional *alterations*.

Unfortunately, Sabine didn't believe in coincidences, and she couldn't help the dark, foreboding sensation pressing down on her chest, a prelude of bad things to come. Storm clouds were gathering on the horizon, warning of more death. More loss.

The Wagner opera chose that moment to hit another crescendo. Sabine marched to the wireless, twisted the knob. Blessed silence. The perfect accompaniment to the cold spreading into her heart.

Chapter Five

Paulette

The endless morning crept into an endless afternoon, and as the day finally drew to a close, Paulette wanted to burst into tears. She had little to show for her time spent at the maddening machine. There was just too much to learn. Too many terms to memorize, skills to master. It had taken her three tries to weave a simple piece of thread up and over, down and around the various levers. In, of course, the proper order.

She'd accomplished the task, eventually, with persistence and resolve, always under the watchful eye of her critical tutor. It was as if Marie Claire enjoyed correcting Paulette when she took a misstep. Which was, sadly, often. The woman was not a patient teacher. But Paulette was no quitter. She'd completed every challenge presented. Some quicker than others. None overly fast. None excruciatingly slow, either.

She was rather proud of herself.

Now, as she set the pressure foot down and then fed the two

pieces of black material she'd secured together by a row of pins, she vowed to herself, *I will not be defeated by a machine.* Or a hovering Marie Claire all but waiting for her to fail.

Head down, focused on her task, Paulette continued carefully pushing the material across the throat plate. She noticed her back ached. Her throat throbbed, and her eyes stung. From sweat. From the unshed tears. She blinked away the escaping moisture webbing her eyelashes and set about proving she was worthy of a position she'd all but stolen from a Jewish girl who surely needed the job. *You need it, too.*

New beginning. Banishment. No matter what words she applied to her current situation, Paulette was here, facing an uncertain future, on her own. She would not fail. She cast a quick glance at her suitcase parked beside the door, wishing she could retrieve her mother's shawl and wrap it around her shoulders. She wanted to feel Maman's presence. Her silent support. Not this aching aloneness. *Your own doing.*

Pulling her bottom lip between her teeth, she continued guiding the material forward, slowly, carefully, pulling pins as she went, releasing them just before the bobbing needle made contact, exactly as Marie Claire had demonstrated. This seemed a backward way to learn how to sew, as if she were starting at the end rather than the beginning. But here she was.

Nearly there now. A handful of pins left. A few more inches.

One more pin… Another…

And…

There! She'd connected two separate pieces of cloth into one, joined by a perfectly straight seam. The stitches were evenly spaced. There was no bunching. Paulette's back suddenly didn't hurt so much. Her head didn't throb so hard. "I did it."

"I'll be the judge of that." Marie Claire unceremoniously snatched the cloth out of Paulette's hands. "Hmm."

The woman turned the material over, pulled her eyebrows

together in a tight frown. She took her time, examining each stitch.

Paulette's heartbeat picked up speed. The pain in her back returned, searing and hot, and she had a flash of memory, the face of a handsome boy from school. Lucien had stared at her expectantly, in much the same way she herself stared up at Marie Claire, as if both hopeful and resigned. Had he felt this trepidation as he waited for Paulette to accept his proclamation of love? Did he fear she would turn him away in favor of another?

Which, of course, she had.

She'd been so callous with his affections. Not just his. She'd treated countless young men as if they were replaceable. One the same as another. It was not a pretty insight into her character. No wonder Gabrielle had warned her to change her ways long before Friedrich had arrived at the château for that fateful dinner party. Each time her sister had confronted her, Paulette had dismissed her with a sniff and a careless wave of her hand.

"Well, well," Marie Claire said. Her dark eyes shifted and settled on Paulette's face. It wasn't warmth staring back at her, but it wasn't the expected censure, either. "You have a rather steady hand, don't you?"

"I—" Paulette swallowed, not sure what to do with the unexpected compliment. She became aware of her defensive posture, her slouched shoulders, her folded arms around her middle, and sat up straighter, letting her hands drop to her lap. "I'm a fast learner."

The older woman sighed heavily. "Not really."

Paulette was instantly deflated. No, she silently admitted, not really. But if she said it often enough, perhaps it would become true.

"That's all for today." Marie Claire handed the cloth back to Paulette. "Tomorrow we will focus on building a dress out of a standard pattern."

"A standard pattern?"

The woman rolled her eyes. "As Mademoiselle explained, you will wear the same uniform as the rest of us. To accomplish this, you will follow a specific pattern, cut in a standard shape. It is a process that can be accomplished quickly and what we call prêt-à-porter."

Paulette knew what ready-to-wear was, in theory, though she'd never considered the process.

"Well. Don't just sit there staring at me." Marie Claire clapped her hands in a gesture reminiscent of their employer. "Clean up your workspace."

Paulette did as she was told.

Halfway through the task, a spark of defiance lit. Prior to a few weeks ago, she'd never been meek or compliant. Yet already, in a matter of hours, she'd been forced to be both, all under the condemning eye of this woman who'd been put in charge of her education within the fashion house. Another decisive clap from Marie Claire and the other girls began tidying their spaces as well. Material was folded. Machines were covered. Crystal beads were put away in cases. Soon the room began emptying out.

Few looked in her direction, and none said farewell as they filed out of the workroom. Most left via the door Paulette had entered from the alley. One or two disappeared into a darkened hallway on the other side of the room. It wasn't until she stood looking around the empty atelier that Paulette realized she didn't have the first clue what to do next. Gabrielle had mentioned something about Mademoiselle providing her with respectable lodgings.

Why hadn't she paid better attention? Why hadn't she asked her sister more questions?

She was suddenly homesick. And anxious. She was in a city with no friends, no extended family. It seemed an eternity since she'd stood in her grandmother's bedroom, attempting to say goodbye. Longer still since she'd boarded the train, her heart full of anger and outrage and very little else.

Her stomach rumbled, reminding her she hadn't eaten since this morning. Even then, she'd only taken a few bites of stale bread. Again, she thought, what now? She took a slow spin, moving in a tight circle. Her eyes caught on her suitcase resting in the spot where she'd left it this morning. Untouched, ignored. Her secrets safely tucked inside. Right next to her mother's shawl. She went to retrieve her belongings, stopped when she heard her name.

"Paulette, *ma chère fille.*" Mademoiselle's voice held genuine confusion. "Why are you still in the atelier?"

"I… I don't know where to go," she admitted, trying to hide the tears in her voice.

"No one told you?"

She shook her head.

Mademoiselle's brows knit together, adding lines to the others permanently marring her forehead. She was not a young woman, or even a pretty one, but she had kindness in her eyes. Concern, too. Here, at last, was someone on Paulette's side.

"Yes, well. I suppose it is up to me to show you the way. Do hurry now. And don't forget to grab that." She gave a dry little smile and waved her hand toward Paulette's suitcase.

The designer didn't wait to see if Paulette obeyed. She simply spun on her heel and headed toward the back of the atelier. Paulette picked up her suitcase and rushed to Mademoiselle's side. The woman moved at an absurd pace. She had to trot to keep up.

"Most of my girls live with their families," she said from over her shoulder. "A few have nowhere to go, and so they reside here, with me, in a small dormitory at the top of the building where the attic once was."

"Oh." She could think of nothing else to say. It had never occurred to her that she would be living in the fashion house itself, with some of Mademoiselle's other employees. Though now that she let the idea settle, it made sense. And would certainly prove convenient.

There was no elevator or easy way to reach the top of the building. They traveled the five flights of stairs on foot. Step by step. Up, up, up. By the third landing, Paulette was out of breath. Her suitcase swayed and bumped against her leg. She wanted to stop, breathe a bit, but Mademoiselle continued climbing.

Halfway up the next flight of stairs, she glanced back at Paulette and frowned. "You're out of breath."

"I'm fine."

"I don't think you are. You look rather pale, dear." She angled her head, measured and gauged. "When was the last time you ate a proper meal?"

Paulette thought a moment. "I don't remember." The days blended together in her mind. "Maybe yesterday, or possibly the day before. But really. I'm fine."

"You're not. But you will be. After you've eaten. You'll want to change your dress first." At the mention of her clothing, with the merest hint of insult in her tone, Paulette knew she'd made a mistake wearing the dress. She felt the designer's disappointment. Or was that pity?

She would never know. The older woman was back to climbing.

Paulette hurried after her.

Finally, they reached the top landing, where there were no more stairs, just a long, narrow hallway. "*Les toilettes* are just up ahead, on the right." She pointed to a closed door. "The dormitory is a bit farther back. Come, let me show you."

They passed the lavatory without stopping. At the end of the corridor, Mademoiselle threw open a door and revealed another set of stairs, far narrower than the others. Paulette wanted to cry. Then she heard the sound of female voices. There was also a draft blowing into the hallway, forceful enough to push a few wayward tendrils of hair off her forehead.

Someone must have opened a window. The breeze was rather nice. She shut her eyes and felt the cool air on her cheeks. It took her a moment to realize Mademoiselle had gone quiet. She opened her eyes and saw fondness staring back at her, love and acceptance, a look that could only be described as maternal. Something inside Paulette shifted. A sort of longing, but also a sense of homecoming. She wasn't on her own, after all. She had this woman. Not her mother, but a precious surrogate.

"Go on, Paulette. Go and take a look at your new home."

It was the soft smile that gave her the courage to climb the last flight of stairs ahead of the older woman. She'd barely entered the room when her feet stopped moving. Her mouth dropped open. Her mind reeled. Her suitcase slid from her hands and landed on the floor with a loud thud.

This was no dormitory. This was a room shared by friends. No, not friends. Sisters. The thought gave Paulette a strange feeling in her stomach, as though she'd missed out on something she'd always wanted but had never been able to define adequately in her mind. She'd not had a lot of friends, not good ones, and she'd never been close to her sister.

Here, before her, was the chance for both, in this large space decorated by a woman, for women. Women with nowhere else to go. It was as if she'd been deposited in a posh boarding school, a safe space, where war couldn't touch the inhabitants. A sanctuary of sorts.

A home.

There was no carpet on the floors, only a series of large wool rugs woven in intricate designs that should have made her dizzy but only added to the feeling of warmth and welcome. The beds, all five of them, had golden headboards, thick mattresses, and pretty damask coverings. The long wall on her left had a row of dormer windows with cozy blue seat cushions.

The opposite wall held bookshelves stacked with books. So many books. It would take a lifetime to read them all. There were no closets, which was expected, but there were racks upon racks of dresses in all shapes, materials, and styles. At the far end hung several black uniforms like the ones the women wore in the atelier. Paulette wanted to play her hands over each of the garments, even the ordinary ones. She wanted to feel the silks and wools and satins on her fingertips, wanted to sit at the dressing tables, all five of them, and open the jars of face creams, smell the perfumes.

Lost in the desire, she hardly noticed the room had gone silent. She did so now and took in the three girls staring at her. They stood shoulder to shoulder. Solidarity against the new girl.

She didn't know their names, but she recognized each of them. Two worked in the atelier, the shorter girl at a sewing machine, the other at the dress forms. The third was one of the house models from the salon. She was tall and slender and had hair the color of autumn wheat.

Three girls, four counting Paulette, but five beds.

Where was the fifth girl?

"Right, then." Mademoiselle touched her sleeve. "I'll leave you to unpack and get settled in before dinner. Pick any of the dresses to wear tonight. Any but the one you wear now."

Paulette's cheeks heated. Her gaze went to the rack of dresses, homing in on the collection of blue silks the same color as her eyes. Eagerness vibrated through her.

"We eat at eight o'clock, sharp. And Paulette, *ma chère fille,* welcome to Maison de Ballard."

For the smallest of moments, it was as if she had her mother back. Warmth spread through her limbs, bringing her first smile in days, possibly weeks. "Thank you, I... Thank you, Mademoiselle Sabine."

Her words earned a small nod. Then, "Girls." All three of them turned to face her. "Remember how you came to be in my employ. Like you, Paulette has nowhere else to go. She is a part of our family now. I expect you to be kind. Treat her well."

All three chimed in at once, "*Oui*, Mademoiselle."

"Charlotte, I'll leave the introductions to you."

One of the three nodded, the girl from the showroom. She looked mildly uncomfortable, and that told Paulette all she needed to know. These girls didn't want to make friends with her. She was an outsider—an interloper—a stealer of jobs—and as the door closed behind Mademoiselle, Paulette understood she would get no kindness from her new roommates. Not yet. Perhaps never.

She flexed her fingers, reached for her suitcase, and, by-passing the introductions, asked the more pertinent question. "Which bed is mine?"

Chapter Six

Nicolle

Paris greeted Nicolle with a warm, gusty wind that carried the tang of blooming flowers, the scent of pungent motor oil, and the feel of French despair. Her feet trudged across ancient cobblestone streets and wide, airy boulevards, past buildings with foul Nazi flags hanging like banners from their rooftops. The sight made her ashamed of her country and the politicians who'd thought to appease Adolf Hitler.

When their strategy proved unsuccessful, and the German dictator used military might to reveal his intentions, the French government had declared Paris a free city and then ran off to the resort town of Vichy to pretend they still held some semblance of power. Those same cowardly leaders openly collaborated with the Nazis. They passed their own antiracial laws against the Jews and organized their own mass roundups.

It was as if Nicolle's countrymen had caught a deadly virus. The fever grew with every edict they passed, the need for innocent blood an obsession that robbed them of sense. They'd already arrested most of the Jewish male immigrants living in France. Nicolle feared they would target French-born Jews next.

She'd done the right thing, she told herself. She'd erased her Jewish heritage and had reinvented herself. Fearing it wasn't enough, she'd left her future in Limoges. There was no traceable connection to her, or to Julien, not on paper. Not in pictures. Her visits, always brief, always under the guise of a special delivery from Mademoiselle, lasted but a few hours. Real names were never used. She brought gifts and smiles and died a little every time she boarded the train to Paris.

It didn't matter. He was safe. Her son. Her heart. Her very reason for living. She fought for a Free France in his name. Her little Jules, so like his father, his name chosen with her husband in mind. He would grow up only knowing love. Only mercy and justice.

Nicolle rarely cried but, as she entered Maison de Ballard and climbed the back stairs to the attic, she felt her throat close up. A few rogue drops skittered down her cheeks. She couldn't keep doing this. She couldn't keep stopping at the house in Moulins and filling her heart with joy, only to walk away with the sound of sobbing in her ears, sometimes his. Usually her own.

A flicker of longing burned in her belly. How she wished she could conduct one final escape, for herself and her sweet boy. But no. Nicolle Cadieux had a debt to pay, and a world to make better for her son.

Today, the burden felt like a millstone around her neck. If only there had been no need to turn to Mademoiselle for help. But she had, at a time when all was lost. Nicolle would continue ferrying downed pilots to safety until the war was over and the Nazis vanquished.

Eyes blurring, she groped her way up the final flight of stairs, holding on to the banister tight, her fingers white with the pressure. Mademoiselle would forgive her tardiness. The trains were unreliable at best. She would not forgive Nicolle's disheveled state. All *her girls* must be perfectly attired, in the same uniform, their hair slicked back in the same tight chignon, their faces free of any cosmetic enhancement.

Once in the dorm, there was little time for anything more than vague impressions. The area was tidy, but there was something different. The sign of a new resident. She hardly had time to investigate beyond a quick glance. The clock on her vanity table read 3:00 p.m., and Nicolle knew better than to linger. Mademoiselle would want a report. If Nicolle was right, they had a mole in the network. Or maybe it was just the Germans cracking down. There were rumors of infiltration of escape lines, raids of safe houses. Nothing conclusive.

She was wasting time.

Hurrying now, she discarded her travel clothes, retrieved her uniform from the rack, and pulled the dress over her head. Her fingers secured the buttons quickly, then moved up to her hair, tugging and smoothing, until the black curls were tamed into a slick chignon.

One last glimpse in the mirror and Nicolle nodded at the woman staring back at her. Ordinary, unremarkable, anonymous. She saw nothing of the adoring daughter born to a Jewish immigrant and his French Catholic wife. Nothing of the girl who'd lost her beloved father to an unexpected illness and her mother to her grief. She was no longer the penniless orphan raised in a convent boarding school.

No, that sad, scared little girl no longer existed in the confident woman staring back at her in the mirror. The disguise would hold. It always did. People saw what they wanted to see. When they looked at Nicolle, they saw a woman of indeterminate age gifted with needle and thread. She placed one final pin in her hair and left the attic. In the atelier, she paused, her eyes taking in the scene with a single swoop. Again, she thought, something was different.

She took another, longer study.

There was Mademoiselle, circling a dress form. There was Danielle, flitting after her. She saw Marie Claire buzzing from workstation to workstation, issuing orders like a military general. So, what was different?

The air.

There was a stifling, edgy quality to it, a sort of tension that hadn't been there when Nicolle left two days ago. Something was missing. Someone.

Basia.

Where was Basia?

A fluttering panic rose up inside Nicolle. She made her mind slow down—think rationally. Her eyes landed on a stranger. She wore the required uniform, but it didn't quite fit properly, as if it were hastily made, probably with her own inexperienced hands, and she kept tugging at the collar. Had Mademoiselle dismissed Basia, her best finisher, for this girl?

It didn't make sense.

She was too…something. Graceful, maybe. Elegant. Not unremarkable. Not plain. Not Jewish. No, she was very, very French. And very, very pretty.

Forcing herself to breathe slowly, Nicolle wiped her sweaty palms on her thighs and approached the intruder. The more distance she covered, the more confused she became. This girl didn't belong. Not just in looks, but in action. She concentrated too hard, as if the process of running a sewing machine was foreign to her.

By the time Nicolle closed the space between them, her breath was coming quicker. As if sensing her presence, the girl paused, turned her head. Her eyebrows lifted, then her chin. She looked about to say something.

Nicolle gave her no chance. "Who are you?"

The eyebrows lifted higher. The chin firmed. "I am Paulette

Leblanc." She said her name as if it was supposed to mean something to Nicolle. "Who are you?"

She started to answer, but Mademoiselle materialized beside her. "Nicolle. You are very late, and we have much to discuss."

Arm wrapped securely in the other woman's grip, she stumbled along, nodding to several of her coworkers, smiling at a very few, silently biding her time until she was in Mademoiselle's office, door shut behind them, the wireless switched on to a news report that amounted to nothing more than German propaganda. Her gaze took in the clutter that came from a lifetime of creating fashion. Piles of sketch pads littered the enormous desk. Bolts of fabric were propped against the wall. A shelf of reference books and fashion magazines looked about to collapse under the weight. "What happened at the checkpoint in Moulins? Why the change in route?"

Nicolle answered with a question of her own. "Where is Basia?"

"Ah, yes. Basia." She sighed. "I dismissed her."

A prickle of fear ran through Nicolle, and suddenly she was shaking. "But…" She trailed off, struggling to finish her thought. "Basia. She was your best finisher."

She was also Jewish. Like Nicolle. Two remained out of dozens, the others having left Paris before the invasion. Only Mademoiselle knew the shared heritage. Even Basia hadn't known. That didn't make Nicolle safe. She was shaking again. Nicolle was not usually prone to worry. Today, she was plagued with it.

Mademoiselle took her hands. "You think I will dismiss you next. You think, for all the words I have said, for all the acts of treason against the Third Reich that I have committed, that I am that cold. That callous. That I would put you out on the street, as I have done to Basia."

There it was. Her fears spoken aloud. She could not respond. She knew this woman. Knew the risks she took, the lives she saved. Yet she'd dismissed Basia, a Jew, and still had not given a reason. "Yes," she admitted. "I fear I will be next."

"Nicolle." Mademoiselle squeezed her hands gently, the gesture of a mother to a frightened child. "You are safe with me."

She dropped her gaze, wanting to believe the vow. Even if she did trust this woman, even if she believed in her, it was a risk, staying in Paris. Living her lies. The laws were getting tighter, harsher. The French government was openly in league with the Germans. They worked in tandem, vowing to rid the country of Jews. Nicolle's identity papers were good, but others had been equally so, and the bearers of those documents were still taken in for questioning, then made to disappear without a trace.

"You let Basia go," she whispered, her voice weak.

"I let her go, yes."

"She won't find another job."

"No, she won't."

It was outrageous. The deed, the calm demeanor. The air grew oppressive in Nicolle's lungs. She thought she might suffocate from the shock. "The girl has lost her father and brother to the roundups. Her mother and younger sister rely on the money she earns here for their very survival."

Mademoiselle knew all this. Yet she didn't defend herself. She gave no explanation. She simply stood there, holding Nicolle's gaze with an unwavering stare. There was meaning in that look, but Nicolle couldn't decipher the message. She made a sound deep in her throat. A sound of accusation, of fury, maybe even of betrayal. The sensation gnawed at her insides like a ravenous animal clawing at her remaining composure. "Have you nothing to say?"

The older woman sighed deeply, and with a large dose of resignation, as if she, too, were struggling with her own sense of shock. Or perhaps it was insult. "Basia has a wealthy fiancé.

He is from an old, established French family with strong connections throughout Europe."

He was also Jewish. "It won't be enough."

"No, it won't. And so—" she continued holding Nicolle's gaze as firmly as she'd held on to her hands "—we will do what we must."

Nicolle blinked. But of course. *Of course.*

Her outrage turned to relief. The shift was so sudden a gasp flew from her lips. Again she felt the prick of tears, of relief, and of shame, for having doubted this woman. Her mentor. Her protector.

She hastily wiped at her eyes and, feeling bolder, stronger, bypassed the need for further explanation and said simply, "Let me be the *passeur.*"

"This is what you want?"

She answered without hesitation. "Yes."

"Be certain, Nicolle. You have only escorted Allied airmen and escaped prisoners of war, one at a time. This rescue will be different. It could be as many as six people in your group, not counting you. Basia and her family. Her fiancé and his. It will require extensive planning, much money, and many documents."

She hadn't realized the scope, but she should have. Basia was not alone in this world. Surely she would not leave France without her loved ones. *Would you leave without your son?* A ridiculous question. No, she would not. This was a very large, complicated problem needing a large, complicated solution. Mademoiselle was very good at finding answers to impossible questions. Her plan, once it was fully formed, would be the right one for Basia.

"Nicolle, are you sure you want to do this?"

"I was Basia's mentor." They'd shared a workspace, had become friends, or at least friendly. "I want to do this."

A moment of silence passed, and then Mademoiselle nodded. "*Très bien.* I will let you know the details once I have them finalized. Now, tell me what happened at the checkpoint in Moulins that made you veer so thoroughly off course."

Right. The debriefing. She gave her report, leaving nothing out, including the moment when her instincts had taken over after the arrest of the couple who'd borne a strong resemblance to the airman and herself.

Mademoiselle stopped her there. "You think they were looking for you?"

"I don't know. If they were, it would mean—"

"We have a mole in the network."

The very suggestion turned the blood in Nicolle's veins to ice.

"*Non*, let's not get ahead of ourselves. For now, stick to the details. Let me worry about the rest."

Too late. She was worried, dreadfully so. But she was back in Paris, the airman safely on the rest of his journey. There was nothing to do but pick up where she'd left off. "I chose the checkpoint in La Haye-Descartes as an alternative because I know the village well. It wasn't until we were nearly at the bridge that I discovered the airman had a rather serious injury, one he failed to reveal to me or the previous *passeur*."

"How bad was this injury?"

"Life-threatening. I couldn't staunch the blood on my own." She stopped, took a deep breath, then told Mademoiselle about André. "He didn't ask a single question, not one. The rest of the rescue went according to plan. We were several hours late, true, but as you know, this isn't unusual. The *passeur* was waiting at the rendezvous point."

Mademoiselle's gray eyes went thoughtful. "You trust this man, this animal doctor?"

Did she? "Completely."

"You have never mentioned him before."

There had been no real need to do so, until now. Now her heart pulsed for a few beats. A memory played in her mind.

The day of her wedding. She and Julien had been waiting for his family to arrive for the ceremony before saying their vows. André had shown up instead, the bearer of bad news. *They aren't coming.*

"That's all he'd said." There had been no need to say more. "He stayed, not a single hesitation in his manner, and stood witness at our wedding. When my husband's family refused to acknowledge our match, André proved steadfast and loyal. We went back to his home for a small reception, the three of us toasting the future."

"This man, he was as you remembered?"

"More than." The man at her wedding had been intent and serious, but also resolute. The André she'd met had been the same. But she'd felt something in his presence, something strong and new. A sensation that made her feel very female, very safe, and oddly free. "Julien was always a good judge of character."

Another instant of silence. A slow nod. Then, a question. "Would you recommend we use his home as a safe house, should others wish to cross into the Free Zone at that particular checkpoint?"

Nicolle's lungs tightened as she tried to come up with a reason to discourage the idea. She didn't want further contact with André. She didn't want to see him again. Except…for one dizzying second, she wanted just that. She wanted to be near his calming presence. But that would mean deception. Could she lie to a man who gave her nothing but truth in return?

Yes, she could. Because none of this was about Nicolle's feelings. Or her desires. "I believe the idea is worth exploring."

"Then you will approach him."

"Me?" Nicolle felt the blood drain from her face. There were so many reasons it not be her. The list was long and personal. "Is that wise?"

"He knows you. He trusts you. And now there is a connection that unites you in the battle against the enemy."

Mademoiselle wasn't wrong. Nicolle and André had saved a man's life, together, and by doing so had performed an act of treason against their occupiers. A crime punishable by death. Reason enough to be the one to approach him. "I'll do it. Just tell me when."

"Not yet. Soon." Suddenly, Mademoiselle's gaze softened, and her hands came to hold Nicolle's again. "And the other reason for your delay? All is well there?"

Nicolle thought of the sweetness of her reunion, and the agony of her departure. She wondered, for the thousandth time, how long could she keep up this double life? A half day with the love of her life was not enough. A lifetime would not be enough. "It's hard," Nicolle admitted.

"Do not despair, Nicolle. This war will be over someday, and you will be together again. You will—" A knock at the door cut off the rest of the bolstering speech. Frowning, Mademoiselle called out, *"Entrez vous."*

Marie Claire appeared in the doorway. "Your four o'clock fitting has arrived. She has changed into the dress and awaits you in the salon."

"Thank you, Marie Claire. Please tell Madame Miller I will be there shortly."

"Would you like me to—"

"Nicolle will assist me with the alterations today."

It was an unintended slight, and disappointment showed on the other woman's face. She was too trained to show more than a flicker of mild irritation, but Nicolle could feel the silent accusation, as though she was attempting to seize her coveted position in the atelier. It was the last thing Nicolle wanted. She would have conveyed this to Marie Claire had she not spun around and left the room.

Mademoiselle shut off the wireless, swept a hand over her hair, and then, like a ship at full sail, set course for the salon.

She stopped only long enough to pause beside the new girl. Leaning down, she said something low and indistinguishable.

A quick look in Nicolle's direction, a hitch of her chin, and Paulette was on her feet.

"Your job today is to observe," Mademoiselle told the girl. "Watch Nicolle closely. She trained your predecessor, and now she will train you. Keep your eyes on her and say nothing to the client. *Comprends?*"

"*Oui*, Mademoiselle." She fell in step beside Nicolle. Her demeanor was not one of obedience, exactly, but there was no sign of defiance in her, either. She looked serious, eager.

Good, Nicolle thought. That was a good start to their relationship. She could train a serious, eager girl. It was the arrogant ones that proved difficult.

In the salon, Mademoiselle consulted with her assistant in hushed tones. Geneviève spoke just as low, just as quickly, her gaze shifting to Paulette, then back again. On the return journey, her smile had transformed into a frown.

Either unaware of the change in the other woman, or uncaring, Mademoiselle threw her head back and entered the largest fitting room in the salon. She greeted the client with a series of air kisses and compliments. "Ah, Vivian, my dear, dear friend. You are the loveliest of all creatures."

She said this to every woman who stepped foot in her atelier.

In this instance, it was true. Vivian Miller was spectacular and remarkable. She was so beautiful it hurt to look at her. Although older, possibly well into her fifties, her skin was as flawless as a woman half her age. She was trim and fit, elegant, and had the manner of royalty. Her hair was a spectacular red. Her smile was dazzling. She was also American, an expatriate who lived in the Hôtel Ritz year-round.

"You flatter me, Mademoiselle. I am only as lovely as the clothes I wear. Your designs make me the talk of Paris."

Vivian Miller was, indeed, the talk of Paris, though not because of her clothes. She had obscene amounts of wealth, or so it was said, with shady connections throughout Europe. She'd made herself notorious by recently engaging in a public affair with a powerful Nazi.

A horizontal collaborator, the French called women like her. Madame Miller represented everything vile and hateful in a woman living in Occupied Paris. But…

Much like Mademoiselle, the American was more than she appeared to be. She had reasons for cavorting with an SS officer, just as Mademoiselle had reasons for aligning herself with a gangster and black-marketeer.

More empty compliments were exchanged. "Yes, well." Mademoiselle took a step back and eyed the American with the eyes of a master seamstress. "Now that we have expressed our mutual admiration for one another, let us make you perfect for the party tomorrow night."

A party. Where deals would be made. Alliances created, then broken. The passing of messages would occur. In short, the perfect place to gather and disseminate information for the Resistance.

Oh, yes, Vivian Miller was more than she seemed.

Smiling warmly, Mademoiselle guided the American to a large platform facing a three-way mirror. They traded a silent look in their shared reflection. "You've done it again, my friend," Madame Miller said. "The draping is divine. The color exquisite."

Nicolle agreed. The deep green silk was everything she said, and more. A perfect complement to Madame Miller's red hair, and the warm undertones made her skin glow.

"But not quite perfect," the designer declared. "Not yet." She circled the American, examining, gauging. She reached for the invisible waistband, pinched both sides, then glanced over at Nicolle and said, "Half an inch, either side."

There was no measuring tape involved. Mademoiselle didn't need one. Nicolle nodded, then cast her gaze toward Paulette. Was the girl paying attention? Did she understand Mademoiselle wished to alter the dress by a half inch on either side?

Clearly not. The girl had lowered her eyes. Perhaps that was just as well. She looked humble and almost subservient. Almost, but not quite.

Who was she, anyway?

Mademoiselle lowered to her knees and considered the hem, setting it first at an inch, then at two. "I prefer the shorter length."

"As do I," the American agreed. "How long to make the adjustments?"

"An hour."

An hour? It would take Nicolle half that time. Still, she filled out the pertinent information on the alterations ticket—Mademoiselle required meticulous records—and, after tucking the card in her sewing kit, waited to be given the signal to exit the fitting room with the dress.

"Wonderful. I'll wait." She angled her head and studied Mademoiselle in the mirror with an intent stare. "While I do, I'd like to discuss the possibility of several more garments."

Mademoiselle rarely balked, but balk she did. "How many more?"

"Three. And Sabine..." The American continued holding Mademoiselle's gaze in their shared reflection. "I would like them completed in a week."

"So soon?"

"Time is of the essence. I am, as always, prepared to pay whatever the cost to make this happen."

Mademoiselle appeared unusually reluctant. Sabine Ballard never turned away business, especially from one of her best clients. Clearly, the two were talking about something other than dresses. An escape, perhaps. Perhaps something else entirely.

While the American gave more specifics to her request, the puzzle shaped and morphed into a dozen possibilities until Nicolle's mind landed on a rather alarming truth. Mademoiselle's network was larger than she'd realized, in both size and scope. The risk for betrayal was enormous. A mole could be anywhere. Anyone. Even this wealthy American who drank, ate, and slept with the enemy. And what of this new girl? This Paulette? Nicolle's mind went to the incident at the checkpoint in Moulins. Capture had been one mistake away. Had the guards known she was coming?

Had someone tipped them off?

"You may begin work on the alterations, Nicolle. Paulette, take the dress from Madame Miller. No, not like that. Gently. Have a care, girl. Treat the garment as if it were your own."

To Nicolle's amazement, Paulette proved wildly proficient with the folding and draping of the dress. She clearly knew her way around haute couture. So she'd come from wealth. Perhaps she'd been a customer once, but something had happened, something unfortunate that had put her in Mademoiselle's care, which explained the air of fragility.

Or was that all a ruse?

Nicolle was immediately on her guard, even as a frigid sense of dread laced its way through her veins. The timing of Paulette's arrival, it was too perfect. Or rather, too wretched. The girl had shown up on Mademoiselle's doorstep on the exact day Nicolle had attempted to cross the Demarcation Line in Moulins. And nearly been arrested. Not a close call, after all. The guards had been watching for her. Because someone had tipped them off.

Paulette?

Logic told her no. Escapes took days, sometimes weeks, to plan. The mole had to be someone already heavily involved in Mademoiselle's network. If not the mole, then who was this girl? Something about her didn't read true. Reason enough to keep a close eye on her.

Convenient that Mademoiselle had assigned her as the girl's mentor.

Oh, yes, Nicolle planned to watch this one very closely.

Chapter Seven

Paulette

Aware Nicolle's eyes were on her, Paulette draped the green silk dress over her arm with great care and much confusion. A lot had happened since Mademoiselle had leaned over her and proclaimed she would no longer be working at the sewing machines. Paulette had been beyond pleased with the news. She didn't especially like working on the electronic beast. But then she'd stood, and Mademoiselle revealed that the woman beside her—Nicolle—had not only trained Basia, she was to teach Paulette as well.

No wonder the woman watched her so closely. Like Marie Claire, she was probably waiting for Paulette to make a mistake so she could reprimand her. She said nothing, though, nor did she make rude sounds in the throat, and that was something of a relief.

Paulette sneaked a glance at the other woman. She was considerably younger than Marie Claire, but older than Paulette, by at least seven years. Somewhere near her sister Gabrielle's age. Even with the severe hairstyle, she was pretty, in a quiet sort of way, with dark hair and dark eyes filled with what could only be described as suspicion. Much like Gabrielle looked at Paulette, only without the years of history behind the stare or the knowledge of her greatest mistake.

It was hard to hold the doubt against her, considering how Paulette had taken her apprentice's position in the atelier. Another thought occurred, a more humiliating one. Had Nicolle been at one of Paulette's fittings when she'd been a customer? Had she been the one to assist Mademoiselle?

Paulette was ashamed to admit she didn't know. She'd never made eye contact with any of the seamstresses assisting Mademoiselle. She'd barely offered a smile to the designer's assistant. Perhaps that explained why Geneviève gave her scowls now. These were more reminders of how insulated her life had been, how privileged and protected. *Oh, Maman, why did you not prepare me better? Why did you not hold me more accountable?*

A light touch to her arm brought her back to the present, and she realized that Nicolle was motioning Paulette to follow her. She hurried after the other woman, noting the lack of looks in her direction this time, the absence of whispers. The black dress and severe hairstyle had made her invisible to Mademoiselle's customers. It was as if she didn't exist. This was to be her new beginning, then, a life of obscurity and a maze of dim hallways.

After the third bend, she could hold her tongue no longer. "Where are we going?"

The other woman sighed. There was something in the sound Paulette recognized. She'd heard it often enough from her sister. Not impatience, not frustration. Weariness. And that felt somehow worse, as if Paulette was already proving to be a trial. "We are heading back to the atelier."

Well, she knew that. "This is not the way we came."

Another sigh. "There are several routes."

"How many?"

"Three." With barely a hitch in her step, she reached out, opened a door, and there before them was the atelier.

The noise hit Paulette, and immediately, surprisingly, she felt an odd sort of comfort in the chaos that met first her ears, then her eyes. The frenzied activity had purpose. It was a remarkable contrast to her previous days of idleness, where her mind had been occupied with flirtations and parties, shopping trips and, then, Friedrich.

Now she could think of nothing else but him. He'd made promises to her, and had kept none of them. While here, marooned on the edge of this moment, in this loud, vital world of dressmaking, Paulette could achieve something of her own.

Nicolle stepped in the room ahead of her, then shifted to face Paulette. Their eyes met. Something passed between them and Paulette felt it, at last. The potential for something new, something wholly her own.

"Ready to get to work, Paulette?"

"I am." So very ready.

With efficient, quick movements, Nicolle organized her area. Her table was larger than the others, except for Marie Claire's, with a sewing machine built into the right side and a wide space large enough to spread out the dress Mademoiselle had created for the American woman. "Have you broken down a seam and then rebuilt it to fit the client?"

She might as well have asked the question in an ancient language. "No." Paulette had only stood like the American, perfectly still and unmoving, while Mademoiselle pinched and measured and made humming noises. "Not yet."

"We start by turning the dress inside out." She demonstrated. "Then, we locate the top of the side seams where they meet the armhole, here." Her finger landed on the spot where the straight row of stitches merged with a more circular grouping.

"Next, we place the measuring tape a half inch from the seam and insert a series of pins."

Again, she demonstrated, with a level of patience Paulette hadn't experienced often. From her mother, yes. Marie Claire, never. Her sister, rarely. Why was Gabrielle so much on her mind today? What about Nicolle kept Paulette thinking about her older sister? They didn't look or act alike.

"Now, you try on the other side."

Shoving aside thoughts of home and disappointed sisters, Paulette mimicked Nicolle's work.

"Well, huh."

"Did I do it right?"

"Exactly right." The surprise was identical to Marie Claire's reaction when Paulette had made her first line of stitches with the machine. "Well done."

"I…thank you."

They shared a smile. Their first. "Now, we mark the new seam with chalk. Then, we sew. On the machine. Remember," she said, sitting down. "Remove the pins as you go so that they—"

"Don't break the needle." Paulette had learned that lesson yesterday, at the cost of a rather harsh scolding from Marie Claire.

They turned their attention to the hem next. "Per Mademoiselle's instructions, we will take it up by two inches."

"All right." Paulette waited for more instructions from Nicolle. She got none, just a comment that this part was done by hand, and then she was told to watch.

She watched.

And immediately realized why Mademoiselle had put Nicolle in charge of her education. The woman was a marvel, quick, efficient, meticulous. As she sewed with the precision of a surgeon, she explained the technique to Paulette.

She committed each word to memory.

"What stitches have you learned?" Nicolle asked her.

"None of them."

"None?" This seemed to surprise the other woman, as evidenced by the slight hitch in her breath. "Well, no matter. I will teach you. Wait here."

Paulette waited.

And immediately realized she was looking forward to the next lesson. Nicolle disappeared through yet another unmarked door, dress draped carefully over her arm. She returned five minutes later with a handful of scraps and no dress. "I will show you the stitches now, and you will practice them the rest of the day."

The lesson went on for nearly an hour. Nicolle was a patient tutor, far more than Marie Claire. She showed Paulette how to baste, then how to perform a running stitch, a backstitch, a half backstitch, and finally a whipstitch. By the end of the lesson, Paulette discovered the great value of a thimble and, after several punctures, the cost of forgoing one.

Eventually, Nicolle left her to practice on her own. She was clumsy at first, but the more she sewed, the more vital she felt, and again realized how vapid and shallow she'd been. How utterly uninterested in learning anything of substance, certainly nothing to do with the making of champagne. Her grandmother had told her the process was both art and science. Only in this moment, as she considered what went into the making of a dress, did she fully understand what Grandmère meant.

A spark of resentment ignited into a tiny flame, hot and painful, and she felt shame for yet another betrayal toward her mother. Maman had given her so much, except the love of making champagne. To be angry at her for this—for anything— was wrong.

Being here, in Paris, alone and without her, was also wrong.

Paulette could not bring Hélène Leblanc back. Nor could she make amends hand-sewing stitches onto a scrap of discarded material. She should be at home, helping Gabrielle meet the outrageous demands put on her by the Germans. They wanted champagne of the finest quality, despite the lack of resources and workers. Paulette could be of use. She could be a vital asset to the family. But her sister didn't want her help. She didn't think Paulette cared or knew enough to contribute, and she certainly didn't have the patience to tutor her.

Whose fault is that?

Her own, of course, but also Gabrielle's. And their grand-mother's, too, for teaching only her older sister the techniques required to make the finest champagnes in the world. Again, she thought, *Whose fault is that?*

Paulette had had years to show a modicum of interest.

Now it was too late. But not too late to learn other new skills, other ways to contribute to a world gone upside down. It was small, yet something. She bent her head and poked the needle through the material, pulled it back through at the proper angle. She repeated the process, again and again. At the end of the day, her vision had blurred, her hands were cramped, and she was so very exhausted. She had to fight to keep her eyes open. A bell rang—from where, she couldn't say, but work abruptly stopped in the atelier. The lack of sound was jarring, and lasted only a moment before the chatter began again as the women closed their sewing kits, moved away from their machines, and released a collective sigh.

Paulette finished another stitch, studied her work, then sat back, smiling. As if on cue, Nicolle approached, took hold of the piece of material, and motioned Paulette to stand.

She quickly gained her feet.

Eyes narrowed, Nicolle blinked. Then her expression grew thoughtful as she rotated the material to study the underside, where the true test lay. "Well done, Paulette."

"Thank you. I…" She paused, looked around, saw that the atelier was empty but for the two of them, and knew it was time.

Time to say what was in her heart, to a woman who held her future in her hands.

With much trepidation, she broached the subject that sat between them. "I never intended..." She breathed in, out, in again. "That is, had I known my coming to Paris meant another girl would lose her position, I would not have..."

She couldn't finish what she'd meant to say. To do so would be to speak a lie. She had not asked for this job. She had not wished to take another girl's place. But she'd done both, and a part of her wasn't sorry for it, because she wanted to be here. Now, if not at first. She wanted to learn how to sew and create beauty in a world gone dark.

"Tell me, Paulette." Nicolle considered her through eyes that were not unkind, only curious. "What would you have done had you known? Would you not have come to Paris? Would you not have taken Basia's position?"

There it was. The words that had stuck in her throat plainly spoken aloud.

"No." She looked down at her hands, saw them shaking, clasped them together. "I would not have stayed in Reims. I could not. I had no choice but to come here. I'm sorry, Nicolle, truly sorry that another girl had to suffer because I have nowhere else to go."

The hushed silence that followed her statement sent a ripple of regret churning in her stomach. She'd said too much. But then Nicolle touched her hand. "I believe that you are sorry."

She tried to respond, but Nicolle wasn't through. "It's clear you have suffered a dramatic change in circumstance and Mademoiselle has offered you sanctuary. That doesn't make you and me the same. One tragedy is not like another. Nor does it make us friends. But I am willing to give you a chance, Paulette. I am willing to begin anew, with the assumption that you are as much a victim of this war as the rest of us."

It was more than she deserved, this offer, given from a

woman who knew nothing of the events that had brought Paulette to Paris. A deep sense of wrongness settled in the pit of her stomach. If Nicolle knew what she'd done, would she be making this offering?

Oh, but Paulette wanted this opportunity to put the past behind her. "I would like very much to begin anew."

"Then that is what we will do."

They entered the attic together, separating at the door. Nicolle to the left, Paulette to the right. She sat on the bed assigned to her while the other girls dressed for dinner, Nicolle included. Off came the uniform, down went their hair, and as she watched them transform themselves into individuals again, a rare moment of peace settled over her. One she hadn't felt since her mother's arrest. She let the sensation come, let it spread light into her limbs, and then into her troubled soul.

Three of the four began filing out of the room, each casting a glance in her direction, but gave her no words. Nicolle was the only one to pause at the end of her bed and actually speak to her. "Are you coming to dinner?"

She shrugged. "I'm not hungry."

"Wrong answer." Nicolle eyed her, gave a short nod, then retraced her steps toward the racks of clothing. She picked a dress made of yellow silk with white trim at the cuffs and collar. "This will do nicely with your coloring."

"Nicolle, I—I'm too tired to eat, and I—"

"Again, wrong answer. You will be of no use to Mademoiselle or to me if you get sick. We need you healthy, Paulette. Put this on." She tossed the dress atop the bed. "Then join the rest of us for dinner. This is not a request. It is a requirement of your position—a position, I will remind you, that once belonged to another."

It was that last bit that had Paulette rising to her feet and donning the yellow dress. She ate in silence and noticed that Nicolle did the same. The music of cutlery was a familiar tune, as was the sound of female voices. The absence of males at the table had been common in their home, until the Germans had invaded France and one of them claimed her family's château for himself.

The thought was enough to sour her stomach. It felt like the prelude to something more. She was going to be sick. Swallowing several times, she set down her fork and knife.

"Paulette, are you unwell?"

The question came from the head of the table. Mademoiselle was watching her with concern in her eyes. Others joined her, until silence fell over the room. All those gazes focused on her sent a tingling across the nape of her neck. "I... I don't feel well. The food. It's... I'm not used to eating like this."

It was the simple truth. Rationing was a harsh reality in most French homes, including hers. Not here, though, and Paulette could only wonder at the reason for all this abundance.

"You were fine last night," one of the other girls accused.

Last night, she'd been too tired to eat. She'd pushed her food around on the plate with very little of it finding its way into her mouth. Tonight, she'd consumed nearly all that had been set in front of her. "I guess everything has caught up to me." She glanced at Mademoiselle, ignoring all the others. "May I be excused?"

"Of course."

Grateful the woman didn't require further explanation, Paulette quickly left the dining room, then exited the apartment and made her way up to the attic. By the time she reached the top floor, she was wobbly on her feet.

She retrieved her mother's shawl from beneath her pillow and wrapped the silk over her shoulders. She wanted to go home. But she had no home. She'd been banished, and oh, how she wanted to blame Gabrielle.

But that wasn't being fair.

Gabrielle had her own share of problems.

It was time to forgive her sister.

She could call the château but wasn't sure the words would come once she heard Gabrielle's voice. A letter. She would write a letter. She went to her vanity, searched for a pen and one slip of paper. What she had to say would not take up much space.

Mouth set, she picked up the pen and poised it at the ready. Her hand shook. She steadied it by sheer force of will. She must find the words to release the anger in her heart. The Germans had taken her country. They had taken her home. They had even taken her dignity.

They could not have her soul.

Dear Gabrielle, I have arrived in Paris.

She paused, thought a moment. What else could she say? *I miss you.* Strangely, she did. *I'm sorry.* She was, for so many things. Sighing, she tugged her mother's shawl tighter around her shoulders and stared out the window, seeing nothing of the storm in the distance, but feeling it in her bones. Her sore fingers. She'd done well yesterday. Better today. A sense of pride moved into her heart. Paulette wasn't completely useless.

She was smart. A quick learner, with a steady hand. *Mademoiselle Sabine has welcomed me with kindness and put me straight to work. I have learned how to use a sewing machine and to sew with needle and thread.*

Drivel. The written equivalent of small talk, and nothing of what she meant to say. She should be telling her sister she was sorry for not saying goodbye, for walking away without a word. For killing their mother. A sob slipped past her lips. Tears threatened.

She shut her eyes and saw him there, waiting for her. That face. That oily smile. Paulette had been so naive, believing he was Romeo to her Juliet. "We'll be married," he'd whispered in her ear. "I'll make you my wife, and you will give me many beautiful babies. We will be happy."

She'd believed him, every false word. She'd given him everything of herself, only to receive more false promises spun by his silver tongue.

She'd lived three lifetimes since his betrayal, each far different than the one she'd created in her mind. None of them with the promised happy ending. Humiliation flooded through her, white-hot and real. All her life, she'd longed for a perfect suitor. Nearly every boy at school had vied for her attention, and she'd let them, had even encouraged them to compete.

It wasn't until Friedrich that she'd been the one in pursuit.

Another sob leaked out of her. This was getting her nowhere. Opening her eyes, she went back to her letter. *Dinner was a feast on a level that would have satisfied even the finicky Captain von Schmidt. Duck and asparagus drenched in real butter.*

The champagne had been a blend Paulette knew well, as she'd watched her own grandmother design the label herself. She'd not mentioned the connection. No one had asked, or had even thought to ask, though they knew her last name—they'd learned it before the first course had been served the evening before. Surely some of them suspected.

Perhaps they simply didn't care where she came from, only that she'd taken their friend's place. Hands shaking, Paulette reread the words she'd penned to Gabrielle. She added a few more details about her day—more drivel and small talk—and ended with, *Take care, sister. I will write again soon.*

She folded the paper and put it away, promising herself she would ask Mademoiselle how she could send the letter home. Shawl still around her shoulders, she stood, turned, and came face-to-face with Nicolle. "That shawl, I know it well. That's my design. My stitching. But how?" She reached out, touched the fringe. "How did it come to be in your possession?"

"I didn't steal it, if that's what you mean."

"It's not. I'm just confused. Mademoiselle commissioned the shawl herself. It was for a dear friend. That's what she called the woman." She angled her head as an indecipherable look passed over her face. "You?"

"My mother."

"But that would mean…" The look of accusation turned to pity. Then slowly, as if pieces were clicking into place, she reached out again. Not to the shawl, but to Paulette. She placed her hand on her arm, a light and airy touch that spoke of understanding that came from mutual loss. "Where is she now, Paulette? Where is your mother?"

Paulette closed her eyes. The rush of all she'd lost consumed her. She felt lightheaded and far from herself. "She's dead, Nicolle." Guilt smoldered and flared like a lightning strike to a tree. "My mother is dead, and I'm to blame. I killed her."

Chapter Eight

Nicolle

Minutes might have passed, or longer. Nicolle's sense of time had vanished with Paulette's declaration. *I killed her.* The words went round and round in her head. She knew the pain that came with the loss of a loved one. She also knew the devastating sorrow of being left to live on her own, when that one person she loved most was gone. This, she thought, this terrible sense of grief and guilt, that was what she heard in Paulette's voice. But the words themselves, they were not so easy to understand. "I'm sure you exaggerate."

Surely, the girl had not killed her mother.

"It's true." Misery coated the words. "My mother is dead because of me."

Different wording, different meaning. The candor was troubling, however, as were the tears filling Paulette's eyes. Tears of grief, but also guilt. Nicolle studied the girl more closely. The purple shadows beneath her red-rimmed eyes spoke of long nights with very little sleep. The girl was exhausted. Perhaps she *was* to blame for her mother's death, but there was more to the story.

There always was more.

The girl started shaking, and Nicolle realized she was still holding on to her arm. Letting go wasn't an option. Paulette would collapse at her feet. Her grief was that great, nearly palpable now, rolling off her in waves. She was also weeping. Soft, silent, hopeless tears. Nicolle remembered crying like that, after she'd received the news of Julien's death mere days after discovering she carried his child. Joy extinguished with a single statement. *Your husband is dead.*

She felt a sudden, inexplicable wave of compassion for Paulette. Nicolle had nearly forgotten the sensation. How hard she'd become, how utterly involved in her own pain and sorrow, caring only for a son she saw in snatches. The others, the boys she rescued, perhaps there was a level of caring there. But only in that she wanted them to live so they could continue the fight. This was not a pretty insight into her soul.

Longing for a future free of evil must start with people acting for a higher good. Somewhere along the way, Nicolle had missed that. This war had stolen more than her husband. It had robbed her of the woman she'd been. It wasn't too late, she reminded herself. She reached back in her memory and resurrected the remaining shreds of her humanity. And then, there was a memory to join all the others in her head, from a time when she'd been newly orphaned. She'd craved a sibling to share in her loss. Someone to comfort, as the nuns had comforted her.

"Tell me what happened to your mother." She spoke softly, gently, as if she were talking to her precious Jules. "And then we will decide, together, if it was truly your fault."

Paulette turned devastated eyes to the heavens. "I can't tell you. You will think worse of me. Worse, perhaps, than I think of myself."

How bad could it be? She was still so young, with so little life behind her and so much to live. She'd made a mistake, that was evident, but Mademoiselle wouldn't let this girl in her home if she were a murderer.

"I promise I won't judge you." How could she, when she herself had done so many terrible things since the war began? She'd told lies, had committed countless acts of treason. And then she'd abandoned her son.

For his safety.

But also, if she were honest, her own. It was something she rarely acknowledged. There was such freedom in living on her own, in Paris, with no husband, no son, no one relying on her. No one needing her.

More tears fell from Paulette's eyes, streaming down her cheeks. Was it fair that she looked even more beautiful in her sorrow? "I thought I was through crying," she rasped out, the sound equal parts shock and embarrassment. "Why can I not stop crying?"

Nicolle knew the answer. "You need to unburden yourself. It's safe to speak your truth with me." She would listen without judgment, and maybe that would be good for them both. "But we cannot speak here."

The others could return at any moment.

Still holding Paulette's arm, she made for the dormer window at the far end of the room. The girl stumbled along, as if the fight had gone out of her. Only once Nicolle was unlatching the lock and climbing atop the cushions did she draw back. "Where are you taking me?"

"The rooftop. We can have complete privacy up there."

They didn't speak again, until they were through the dormer window, up the slight slope, and sitting side by side with their knees drawn up to their chins. A hesitant moon was peeking through the clouds, the lights of Paris fading ever deeper into muted silver and dismal grays. The night air was cool on her cheek, and for a moment she let the feel of the soft breeze wash over her. Paulette had stopped crying. Her breathing, however, had not eased a bit. It came in quick, hiccuping gulps.

Aftereffects from her earlier breakdown.

"Now." Nicolle turned only her head. "Tell me what happened to your mother."

An aching murmur rippled from the girl's lips. "It started when they took her away."

"They?"

"The Gestapo."

Gestapo. A word that put terror into good, decent people. Suddenly, Nicolle's stomach was churning, and she thought she might be sick. "Your mother was arrested by the Gestapo, the German police?"

A sob broke through the girl's tenuous hold on her composure. "They came in the middle of the night." She brushed aside a collection of tears welling under her left eye. "They just barged in and began throwing open doors, tossing over furniture, breaking vases and precious valuables. There was no rhyme or reason to the destruction, no underlying logic to their search. None that I could see, anyway. It all appeared so random, as if they were putting on a show."

Nicolle could only imagine the fear and chaos the girl had witnessed. She'd heard tales, but had never experienced anything like the raid she described. Hugging her knees tighter against her chest, she kept her own voice neutral and asked, "Do you know why they were there?"

"The German who'd seized our home had gone missing. They believed my mother had something to do with his disappearance." She looked at Nicolle. There was more than fear in her eyes now. Agony. Guilt. "She went willingly, proof she was innocent of the crime."

Nicolle swallowed hard, thinking frantically before she posed the question hanging between them on the cool night air. "*Was* she innocent?"

"My grandmother was certain it was all a misunderstanding. Maman could not do such a thing. She would be released once the facts were revealed. I knew better. I knew she was guilty."

Nicolle sucked in a breath. "She killed the German? You saw her?"

"*Non. Non!* She was not guilty of murder, but she had committed a crime against the Third Reich. And if I knew what she'd done, then others must have known as well."

"What crime did she commit?"

Paulette stared at her with wide, wounded eyes, her face pale and gray in the dull moonlight. "She falsified her identity papers."

The words settled over Nicolle like an albatross, heavy and weighted with a sort of indictment. She struggled to swallow, knowing what was to come next, yet asking anyway. "What lie did she have to conceal on a fake identity card?"

"Her father is Jewish." Swiping at her eyes, she released a long, sad sigh. "By law, that makes her Jewish. Her papers said otherwise. She lived as a Leblanc. She went to church with the rest of us, never registered as a Jew."

"And you, Paulette? Does that not make you also Jewish?"

"Not according to the Nuremburg laws." She made a sound of disgust in her throat. "I have but one Jewish grandparent, not two. My maternal grandmother was French. My father, also French. His parents—"

"French."

"Yes, and that means my blood is sufficiently diluted." The girl's bitterness blistered the air, and now it was not only pity Nicolle felt, but also fear. The definition of what made a man or woman Jewish could change at any moment. All it would take was a strike of pen to paper, and what made a Jew a Jew would include a broader range of French citizens. People with, say, only one Jewish grandparent rather than two. People like Paulette.

Nicolle's eyes went to the shawl, made by her own hands, commissioned by Mademoiselle herself for Paulette's mother. Had the designer also provided the woman with the false identity papers that wiped out her Jewish heritage? The same as she'd done for Nicolle?

"You said the authorities found out your mother was Jewish, but you didn't say how. Was it her papers?" She glanced up to Paulette's face, seeking confirmation in the stricken expression. "Did they discover them to be fake?"

Her hands came up to cover her face. "That is not how they found out."

"How, then?"

Paulette dropped her hands. A darkness came over her features. The rest of her story tumbled out of her mouth. She told of her devastation after her mother's arrest, the need to do something. She'd turned to a friend, who'd been nothing of the sort.

"I thought he loved me. I thought he could save Maman." Her voice turned hard, angry. "He said all the right words. He promised all would be well. We went to the police station and then, he turned on me. He demanded I be arrested. He called me terrible, horrible names. Slurs that likened me to an animal and worse. So much ugliness out of someone who'd given me such assurances."

For a terrifying moment, Nicolle could not respond. Her stomach was sinking. Every nerve was screaming to stop the girl, before it was too late and she revealed something Nicolle could not forgive. She stretched out her legs and tried to gain her feet. Impossible. Her body felt boneless, and she could feel the sting of fury at the back of her throat.

Fury at this young, foolish girl who wasn't so young and foolish after all, at least not anymore, that much was clear. No, she was not so innocent, not so pure. She'd gone to a friend, a man with power in Occupied France, who'd whispered words of love in her ear.

"This friend," she said carefully, remembering her promise to withhold judgment, knowing she could very well fail with how Paulette responded to her next question. "The one who betrayed you. He was a boy from school?"

"No." Paulette looked at Nicolle with genuine pain in her gaze, a sort of tragic solemnity that said far more than words. The man had not been French. "He was older than me."

"How much older?"

"A dozen years, maybe more." Clutching her mother's shawl, she aimed a look of complete devastation at the sky. "I was so impossibly flattered by his attention. I had barely turned nine-teen, and he chose me, Nicolle. Me, over other, more sophisticated women."

Again, Nicolle forced herself to speak calmly. Something dark moved through her on Paulette's behalf. The girl had been targeted by an older man. Not surprising, since she was really quite beautiful and so utterly naive. Only someone with great power could save a woman already taken into Gestapo custody. Nicolle could think of very few who fit that description, none outside Nazi inner circles.

"You thought he could help your mother," she prompted. "You were certain of this?"

The girl nodded, then blurted out the rest of her story. How she'd met the man—an SS officer—in her own home. How he'd seduced her with gifts and fancy words. Nicolle wanted to hate the girl. She'd engaged in an affair with a Nazi.

"He claimed he wore the uniform because it was expected of all good Germans, but he didn't really believe in the Nazi ideals. He lied, of course. He did believe it, all of it, and I… oh, Nicolle, I didn't see his true nature. I let myself see in him only what I wanted to see."

"You would not be the first woman fooled by such a man." That, Nicolle told herself, was key. Paulette had been young and naive, and the Nazi had preyed on her. She was a victim.

"Maman said something similar. When I begged for her forgiveness, she said none of it was my fault." The girl gave an angry shake of her head. "She said I was only guilty of trusting the wrong man. But I should have known what kind of man he was. How did I not know?"

"Because men like that are very good at hiding the truth." Julien's brother was one of those men. But she didn't want to think about him.

She didn't want to think about herself at all.

"Because of me, my mother's lies were revealed. Had I waited for my sister to handle the situation, as she'd insisted, the Gestapo would not have found out about her father. They would not have sent her away. She is surely dead, or will be soon. It's no secret what happens to Jews in those camps."

Yes, Nicolle thought. Terrible things occurred in Nazi concentration camps. Being sent to one was the equivalent of a death sentence. "Does Mademoiselle know what happened to your mother?"

"Some of it, probably all of it, or she wouldn't have agreed to take me in."

"What do you mean, she agreed to take you in?"

"My sister does not want me in Reims. She says I am a danger to the family, but what she really means is she no longer trusts me. So here I am, banished from my home, with nowhere else to go." Again, she buried her face in her hands. "Because of my selfishness, I cannot go home. I must carry on alone…" She dissolved into soft, quiet sobs.

The girl was clearly sorry for what she'd done, but there was something she was leaving out. *I cannot go home.* The implication was that she had a home, with people who didn't support her but blamed her for her mother's disappearance, as surely as she blamed herself.

Nicolle had a decision to make. She could join Paulette's family and pass judgment over the girl. Or she could offer grace.

Condemnation or acceptance, those were her choices. This was her moment to decide who she was, at the core, a moral test.

Did she respond as Julien's family had and shun the girl? Or did she stand by her, as André had stood by his friend? And, consequently, Nicolle. The question was not so difficult to answer. If Nicolle was to survive this war with her humanity intact, she must view what she'd heard in full. The whole rather than the parts.

Sighing, she tucked the girl in her embrace. "Your mother was right, Paulette. You are only guilty of trusting the wrong man."

"You don't blame me?"

"No, and neither should you." Still holding the girl close, Nicolle's gaze caught a movement on the street below. Her eyes tracked the white Bentley making the sharp turn into the alleyway. *This is not good.* Nazis, she knew, were not the only monsters walking the streets of Paris. There were others just as vile. Men who colluded with the enemy for their own gain, while wearing perfectly tailored suits bearing the Maison de Ballard label.

Mademoiselle played a dangerous game with very bad men. She called them a necessary evil. Nicolle simply called them evil. The thought had barely materialized when the woman herself exited the building, garment bag draped over her arm, determination in every step.

No, Nicolle thought, this was not good. Not good at all.

Chapter Nine

Sabine

Sabine climbed into the back seat of the white Bentley and carefully arranged the garment bag across her lap. The driver did not open the door for her. He did not introduce himself. He did not meet her eye. No need to sigh. The blatant disrespect was nothing new. It shouldn't matter that a nameless thug thought her unworthy of a simple nod of acknowledgment, and it didn't.

What mattered was that Guy Marcel had summoned her, at a time she should be working on her collection. He wanted something from her. He always wanted something, and not just the suit in her lap. Best to avoid speculating any further. Best to clear her mind and take in the view.

Now she did sigh. Curfew had come and gone hours ago. The white Bentley was ridiculously conspicuous on the empty Parisian streets. Yet no one stopped their progress. No one dared risk the owner's wrath. Marcel was a notorious French gangster, feared by many. He'd risen from a dealer of stolen goods to the head of organized crime in Occupied France. He didn't care who bought his products, or who benefited from his black-market dealings. He didn't care who suffered, or starved, or even died. He cared only that he himself prospered.

As such, he shamelessly courted alliances on both sides of the war, pitting one branch of German intelligence against the other while wooing officials inside the French Vichy government. His ways were cruel and violent and always without conscience. Even the most despicable of Nazis treaded carefully around him.

As for Sabine, she, too, feared the man. She was too wise not to, but she also needed him. He owned the trade routes in and out of Paris. She relied on him for everything from thread and buttons to bolts of fabric. He even supplied the food she fed her girls. When Marcel beckoned, she, like all the others under his thumb, obeyed.

That didn't mean she did so happily.

Impatience boiled just below the surface. Sabine tapped out a rapid staccato with her fingertips. She didn't have time for Marcel. She had a fashion show looming and was no closer to finishing her collection than she'd been a week ago. Her mind was too full of all that had happened in a few short days to create one-of-a-kind couture dresses.

But create she must, or risk extinction.

Too many fashion houses had failed since the war began. Maison de Ballard could not be one of them. Her girls needed her for their very survival, and she needed the plausible cover for her Resistance work. Work Marcel must never know about. He must see her as just another aging designer trying desperately to hold on to her dynasty by any means possible.

She'd made many compromises. Philippe would say too many.

Sabine would not disagree.

The Bentley traveled out of the eighth arrondissement and

entered the sixteenth at a pace more fitting for a funeral procession. More tapping on Sabine's part. The driver remained silent, and she welcomed it. He was an ugly, flat-faced, burly fellow with the shoulders of a bear and the manners of a gorilla.

At last, the Bentley rolled to a stop outside the four-story building on Rue Lauriston. Placing the garment bag over her arm, Sabine helped herself to the sidewalk without the driver's assistance. She would not allow such a vile creature to touch her, not even a hand to her sleeve, not that he attempted to show her even that small courtesy. She'd barely shut the door when he gunned the engine and roared away.

Shaking her head, she considered the four-story building in front of her. Once the home of a Jewish banker who'd disappeared three days before Marcel moved in, the house was an architectural wonder, both inside and out. The top two floors were reserved for parties and decadence that made even a woman of Sabine's experience blush. The bottom two were for Marcel's criminal operations. The basement housed his side gig—the torturing of Resistance workers for the Gestapo.

Sabine shuddered.

No, she thought, Marcel must never know about her clandestine work. Lifting her clenched fist, she knocked once, twice, then waited.

Marcel's butler answered. Another flat-faced, muscular brute wearing black formal attire bearing the Maison de Ballard label. "Mademoiselle Sabine." He took the suit from her. "Monsieur Marcel will meet you in the blue parlor on the third floor."

Better than his lair in the basement, she supposed. "Thank you. I know the way."

Head high, she mounted the first step and began the climb up the winding staircase. Anger moved through her as she went. Marcel had stolen this home from a man who'd worked hard for his success. How and why he'd come into possession of the building was not his only offense. He cared nothing for the French people. While ordinary Parisians starved, his kitchens served Michelin-star dinners to Nazis and the high-society women on their arms.

Sabine's deepest regret was that she'd introduced Philippe to this world. At her son-in-law's insistence, but still. He grew harder by the day and was proving to be very good at telling lies and living with deception.

She hoped to live long enough to see him free of this awful war.

Sighing—she did too much of that lately—she entered the blue parlor and found a chair. Twenty minutes later, the room remained empty but for Sabine.

Jaw set, she rose and made a slow circuit, taking in the artwork and other treasures. Paintings by da Vinci and Monet hung on the walls. Degas and Picasso as well. A Ming vase perched precariously on top of a Louis XIV end table. A tea set made from the finest silver glittered under the thousand fairy lights blazing from a massive chandelier overhead.

None of it, not any of these exquisite treasures, belonged to Marcel.

The man was a crook.

"Ah, Mademoiselle Sabine." The high-pitched, almost feminine voice never failed to surprise her. "You are right on time, as always."

Yet he'd made her wait for more than twenty minutes.

Such a petty man. Well, she, too, could be petty. Turning in a circle, ever so slowly, she confronted the man she'd chosen to align herself with in this war. *Better than a Nazi.*

Was he, though?

He employed more than thirty career criminals in his illegal operations, men he'd handpicked from local prisons. He colluded with the enemy and did little for his fellow French. Many assumed Sabine was his mistress. She dressed him, moved in his circles, but no. She was not his lover. He preferred them young and beautiful. Sabine was neither. She was, however, Marcel's go-to designer. She dressed him, the women he seduced, his goons and lackeys, all so she could keep her fashion house operating. The compromises kept stacking up.

Smiling like the snake he was, he came to her, reached for her shoulders, and kissed her cheeks, right and then left. She resisted the urge to cringe. Under the guise of taking in his appearance, as she would any paying client, she stepped back and pointedly studied his clothing. He wore the suit she'd delivered, and now she understood why he'd made her wait.

The man was quite meticulous with his appearance. Some would say to a fault. Neither young nor old, he wore his shock of black hair pomaded to his head in the current fashion. He had pleasing features, if a bit harsh, and was attractive enough to be appealing, but not sophisticated enough to be charming.

He also required a heavy dose of drama.

Sabine gave him what he wanted. She took her time strolling around him, periodically checking the fit of the suit, knowing it was perfect. This one she'd made with her own hands. It had taken her considerable time and attention, a week of sleepless nights, all so Marcel could prove he was a man worthy of a Maison de Ballard design.

Drama, she reminded herself, *give him drama*. She made indistinct noises in her throat, tugged at a sleeve. Straightened a nonexistent wrinkle. Pulled at an invisible thread.

"Well?" Humor coated his voice. His eyes, however, remained hard and watchful. "Do I pass muster?"

"I am happy with the fit."

"As am I." He shot the cuffs, as if he was the lord of some ancient manor, and Sabine noted his hands. A man not so clean and tidy, after all. The knuckles bulged beneath the toughened skin, and the cracked fingernails had dark soot beneath their tips. "You've outdone yourself, Mademoiselle Sabine. I'm quite pleased."

Accepting the compliment with a brief nod, she breathed in a quick breath and got her first full scent of him. The pungent odor was not from the suit but from the man himself, and it was nothing she'd come across before. No rotting flower or bark of a tree or spoiled motor oil could smell that foul. Death. It was the scent of death wafting off him.

The sudden panic made her throat close, even as she became aware he was talking again. "You and me." He brushed at the suit's lapels, adding his own bit of drama to the farce. "We are alike."

Not even a little. "How so?"

"We understand the value of the finer things in life."

What else was there to say, but... "We do."

Moving to the closest mirror, he smiled at his own image, as if having a personal joke with the man staring back at him. "War is good business, *non*?"

He turned his smile on Sabine. She responded in kind, though her heart was breaking. Guy Marcel was everything she hated in a Frenchman living comfortably in Paris. He didn't resist the enemy. He used them and thrived. Worse yet, he thought Sabine was the same as he.

She'd played her role too well and would continue the ruse for the sake of the higher good. For Giselle's memory. "War is very good for business, indeed."

Mon Dieu. What had she become?

This life, the ugly choices she'd made. This man, her partner, for want of a better term. One day, she would have to answer for it all.

"You will stay for the party this evening, I insist. I have someone I wish for you to meet."

I insist. Not a request. A command. "I cannot. I have work waiting me at home. The fashion show—"

"—is weeks away."

And she was nowhere near ready to present her collection

to the critics. She said as much, earning her a vague sweep of his hand and a snort of derision. Then, "We have known each other a long time, have we not?"

"Two years is not so long."

The look of a viper was strong in his eyes tonight, his expanding smile. Sabine half expected a forked tongue to slip past the crooked, yellowing teeth. "In war, two years is a lifetime."

"You have a point." Sabine was suddenly so very exhausted. She was too old for these verbal games, always having to stay one step ahead.

"Then you know I do not make my requests lightly."

Living two lives was not so easy, she thought. "My apologies. But I must, again, decline your generous offer."

"You will stay an hour." His voice had gone an entire octave higher.

Never a good sign. She would not get her way in this. "*Oui*, an hour, then."

There was a time when she would have stayed all night, not for the party, definitely not for the guests, but to listen and learn what she could of the enemy's plans. She still needed this information, but perhaps another could take her place. Someone who understood what was expected of people at a party filled with their own kind.

The obvious answer was Philippe, but her son-in-law had responsibilities within the network that required his absence from Paris for extended stretches. It would have to be another. Someone available in the evenings, who also hated the enemy. Sabine had a person in mind.

The unknown, as Philippe had called her.

He wasn't far off. Paulette was young and untested. But she would know how to work a room. Her mother would have taught her this skill. There was resolve in her. Anger and guilt, too. Unsurprising. When she'd contacted her sister this morning, Gabrielle had been perfectly candid as to why Paulette had to leave Reims. The girl was largely to blame for her mother's arrest. Unintentional, perhaps, and the mother in Sabine battled with the longtime friend who'd lost her favorite person in the world.

Paulette was guilty, but also remorseful. Atonement was a powerful motivator. Sabine could use that. And Marcel was still talking about the man he wished for her to meet, using his typical ambiguous descriptions.

Mouth running, saying nothing, he filled a crystal goblet with ruby-red wine, no doubt purchased from a French vintner at a heavily discounted price. He didn't offer Sabine a glass. "I understand you released the Jewish girl two days ago."

The sudden switch of topics put Sabine immediately on alert. She didn't question how Marcel had come by this piece of information. He had his sources. This, she supposed, was his true reason for summoning her here tonight. To discover her motivation for releasing Basia.

"I should have let the little Jew go sooner. Although she was cheap labor, and her work was acceptable, I grew tired of employing one of her kind." She nearly choked on the words. "I wish for all of them to be gone, not just out of my employ, but out of Paris altogether."

"Perhaps this is your lucky day." Marcel drained his glass and poured himself another. There was a pleased look in his reptilian gaze, and she thought he could not have looked less attractive than in that moment. "More roundups are coming, Sabine. More arrests."

She wanted to be surprised, both by the use of her given name and the words themselves. But she understood the climate in which they lived. Recently, the Nazi Occupiers had passed an ordinance requiring Jews to wear a yellow star. It was a way to make them visible and easy targets. Parisians looked the other way, and too many of them wished for their disappearance. "I assume they will arrest the remaining immigrants living in our city."

He nodded. "*Oui*, then women and children. They will all be purged from our city in a single day, possibly two, if necessary."

Targeted. Purged. Ugly, miserable words. Women and children. A strangled sound caught in her throat, and her lungs filled. She was cold, then hot, then cold again. Never had the roundups included women and children or the elderly. "When is this to happen?"

He studied the rim of his glass, an unreadable look in his small, beady eyes. "Soon."

Careful, Sabine. Stay calm. Speak slowly. "When, Marcel? Tomorrow? Next week?"

"Soon," he repeated, his eyes narrowing, no doubt curious why she was so concerned.

She gave him a blank expression for his efforts, while her brain worked frantically. She would have to move up her timeline to get Basia out of the country. She owed it to the girl, the last of her Jewish employees.

Except, of course, for Nicolle. She was safe. Hiding in plain sight under an assumed name, her real one a secret from all but the two of them. Basia was a different matter. The girl was foreign-born, and her time had run out.

You can't save them all, Sabine.

She could try.

"When?" she asked again, forcing herself to sound a little calculating, wily.

A menacing smile appeared on his lips. "What is this information worth to you?"

There it was. The view of his ugly underbelly. Always the gangster. Sabine knew this man, this game, its rules, and so she gave a very brief, very French shrug. "I have a collection to show, and as I have made perfectly clear already, I am woefully behind schedule."

"I wonder." He closed the distance between them, stopping only once they were inches apart, so close she could smell the horrid scent clinging to his hair and skin. "Is that the only reason? Or does some other motivation drive you?"

Be smart, Sabine. Think as Marcel would. "Dresses do not sew themselves, and while I would prefer only Frenchwomen touching my garments, perhaps I was a bit hasty firing the Jewish girl." *Forgive me, Basia.* "If I can hire her back and perhaps acquire others like her, at a third of the usual rate, why would I not do so? At least in the short term."

"You think like a mercenary. I like it."

The man was a monster. But she had him convinced. She saw it in his beady eyes and pressed a little bit more. "If Jewish women are to be rounded up before my collection is complete, well, that would be unfortunate." She let the implication hang in the air between them.

Any minute, Marcel would agree with her. Unfortunately, any minute turned into two.

She sighed.

The man was nothing if not thickheaded. "You see my predicament, don't you? If I replace some of my current staff with Jews, and they are arrested before my collection is complete, I will be in a worse position than I am now."

"Ah, yes. I understand. But, darling, I don't know the date. Sometime in July, perhaps."

It took great effort to swallow back her outrage. Surely, the authorities wouldn't coordinate a roundup on the same day France celebrated the storming of the Bastille, when they honored the ideals of liberty, equality, and fraternity. "The Germans are nothing if not obvious."

"There you are wrong. This will be a solo effort by the French police."

Shock washed over her, stark and hot as a lightning strike. "You jest."

"I speak truth."

Her country had descended into unconscionable evil. There was no other explanation. Sabine continued speaking about the arrests, digging for information, while her mind calculated the number of days she had left to organize Basia's escape. Not enough. She had to acquire documents, create the route, decide if it would require more than one wave of departures.

The clearing of a masculine throat heralded the entrance of Marcel's partner, and Sabine's thoughts scattered. Gabriel Bergeron had added a mustache to his otherwise unremarkable face. Not quite the same as Hitler's square patch, yet it put her in mind of the German leader. Sabine hated this man, for very different reasons than Marcel. Marcel had never pretended to be anything but a crook, a liar, and a cheat. Bergeron had once been a member of the French police. His corruption was somehow more foul, more unforgivable.

May you both rot in prison, she thought, while planting a small smile on her lips as the odious traitor took her hands. "Mademoiselle Sabine, *enchanté*." He bent and placed an air kiss near her knuckles. "You are here for the party?"

"Only for a little while. I have much work awaiting me at the atelier."

"Perhaps I will change your mind."

Not possible. She knew better than to spend time in his company. Unlike his partner, Bergeron preferred older women and had made it clear he would happily entertain the notion of an affair with Sabine. Nothing would ever happen between them. She preferred men with souls.

"Pity you won't be here long. We have a very special guest arriving tonight from Reims. He brings us gifts of the sparkling variety."

Everything in Sabine stood at attention. Reims. The city Paulette had recently left. The coincidences, there were too many of them. "Is he someone I know?"

"You have never met him." He seemed certain. "He is a captain in the German wine corps. He brings champagne, at a discounted rate."

Another thief, no different than the two standing before her, stealing champagne and serving it up to these men, at a *discounted rate*.

Fury made her vision turn black at the edges. She swallowed, hard. This war would not end well for either of these men. Or, by association, Sabine.

She wasn't worried about herself. She was not so naive as to think she would survive much past the next year. She'd designed her network accordingly. Much as a spider spun her web, Sabine had forged intricate connections held together by thin, almost invisible bonds. Whenever those tenuous links broke, as they so often did, she replaced them. She rebuilt.

One safe house gone, another would go up in its place.

Now, as she made small talk and let Bergeron take her hand so he could escort her to the fourth floor, Sabine understood she was the weak link in this den of thieves. A younger, prettier version must take her place.

Her decision was made.

She would not send in the girl unprotected, at least not at first, and not yet. She would give her a small, preliminary test, the passing of a simple message. Important, but not especially dangerous. Then Sabine would know. In her heart, she already knew this was the right move. It wouldn't take Paulette long to prove her mettle. The girl was too much like her mother. Did it make her callous, pulling her friend's daughter into the network?

Probably. She would do it anyway. Because the war raged on. The roundups continued. Innocent lives were lost daily, and resistance was her only countermeasure.

Chapter Ten

Paulette

Paulette thrashed and kicked and thrashed some more. The sheets tangled around her legs like a snake wrapping his prey in a deadly embrace. Tighter, tighter. She kicked again. Then, suddenly, her eyes were open and she was blinking into the shadows. She'd been here before. In this haunting moment between wakefulness and sleep with a sick feeling in her stomach.

Something had startled her awake. A noise? A movement, perhaps?

The dream. It had to be the dream. The troubling images were there, in her mind. She rubbed her eyes, but the image remained. Friedrich, rumpled and alluring, his collar unbuttoned, standing on the edge of a misty vineyard. His face was ghostly pale, his skin the color of death as he reached out, beckoning her to join him. His striking blue eyes were full of promises, as heady as the vintage champagne her family made.

A lie. All of it a lie.

She'd shouted at him. "Go away. I don't want you anymore."

His smile had widened. His voice came to her muffled, as though moving through a thick wall of water. "You can't get rid of me, Paulette. I'm your terrible secret no one knows about but the two of us."

Another lie.

People did know about him. Her mother. The Gestapo. Gabrielle. And now, Nicolle. Paulette had confessed to her on the rooftop, and the other woman hadn't turned away from her.

She'd offered Paulette grace.

The one thing she craved from her older sister. Gabrielle had given her lectures. Nicolle had treated Paulette with words of comfort. So very different, the two women. There'd been no ridicule or judgment in Nicolle. Just an arm around Paulette's shoulders. That small gesture, accompanied by warmth and kindness, had brought a glimpse of forgiveness. Even as they'd retreated back into the attic, the eyes of her dorm mates not so warm and kind, Paulette had been able to breathe again. She'd gone to sleep with hope and a conscience slightly less troubled.

Until Friedrich had shown himself in her dreams.

Paulette wanted to howl in frustration. Would she ever be free of him?

Sitting up, she stared into the dark broken only by a sliver of moonlight. She felt the aloneness again. The despair. Telling Nicolle had been but one step toward atonement. There was much work left to do. Paulette knew that now, accepted it. There would be more dreams with Friedrich's image haunting her, but she prayed they'd not be as frequent.

She drew a deep breath. Her head was groggy with guilt, but Nicolle had gifted her with a glimmer of hope. Warm and intoxicating. Glancing at the bed beside hers, Paulette drew a deep breath. Nicolle was gone.

Heart beating against her rib cage, Paulette looked around the room and to the window. The moon still hung in the evening sky. Morning was hours away yet. Where was Nicolle? She wasn't at her dressing table. Another quick sweep, and her heart stuttered. There, in the doorway, a silent figure in a white nightgown, slipping away. The faint sound of footsteps followed.

Torn between curiosity and concern, Paulette slid noiselessly out of bed. With fast, measured steps, she padded through the room, pausing only long enough to stuff her feet into a pair of slippers and drape her mother's shawl around her shoulders. The other three slept undisturbed. Paulette moved to the doorway without breaking stride. At the threshold, she hesitated. What if Nicolle didn't want her company?

What if she did?

Only one way to find out.

The moonlight had not reached the skinny stairwell. Paulette blindly fumbled for the banister. Finding it, she clung tightly to the worn wood and descended the steps as quickly as she dared. In the corridor, she spied further movement. A shadowy shape of a woman, bypassing the lavatory, then disappearing into the wider stairwell that led down to the atelier.

Paulette hastened her own steps. She didn't know why she sensed something had pulled Nicolle from her bed. She just… knew. It was like hearing a mosquito buzzing in her ear right before it took a bite out of her flesh. Maybe this was a mistake.

Maybe Nicolle didn't want her company.

She considered turning around, but in the next instant discarded the idea. Nicolle had been good to her tonight. It was Paulette's turn to reciprocate. If the other woman told her to go back to bed, she would. Halfway between the attic and the atelier, she paused and listened to the gong of some distant clock tower toll three times. A strange hour for prowling around in the dark. Paulette had done it before, too many times, always at Friedrich's insistence.

How had she not seen the wrongness of those clandestine meetings?

She pulled the shawl tighter around her and continued searching for her friend. Friend. It felt good to think of Nicolle that way.

Inside the atelier, a single lamp burned, illuminating Nicolle sitting at her workstation. Paulette watched her pull out a small item from a basket and set it before her with unspeakable tenderness. Her face transformed into something she couldn't describe. An aspect of sadness in her brow, but also love. Raw and naked and deeply felt. Somehow the sight of that much emotion on a woman who'd always seemed so composed loosened something in Paulette's chest.

She forgot about Friedrich, her anger. Even her shame, and felt only distress for another.

"Stop skulking in the shadows, Paulette. I know you're there."

She flushed. "I didn't mean to disturb you."

Nicolle met her eyes with a thoughtful expression, void of emotion now. "Didn't you?"

"I suppose I did. I couldn't sleep. Nor, it would seem, could you." As she spoke, she inched out of the shadows, her eyes on the other woman. Nicolle was beautiful in the semi-darkened room. Her black hair curled long past her shoulders. "What are you working on?"

Her unflinching gaze met Paulette's and held. "Nothing important. Just a little token for one of Mademoiselle's clients."

She looked down again, her gaze fixed on the object beneath her hand. She stroked what appeared to be a lump of faux fur. Paulette peered closer to see a tiny stuffed bear. Her confusion spiked. "That seems an odd project for a client of Maison de Ballard."

Nicolle shrugged, her hand still atop the lump of faux fur, and Paulette was struck by the distant vagueness in her expression, as if she were watching a sad memory being played out before her. Paulette had seen a similar expression whenever her mother stared at the watch that had once belonged to her father. The sorrow, the misery, was the same. "You've lost someone in this war, someone you cared about deeply."

Her shoulders caved. "I have lost several someones, Paulette. We all have."

"Well, yes. But that's not what I meant." She sat beside Nicolle, touched the gold locket around her neck. It was too dark to make out the etchings, but there was no denying its value. "You keep his picture in there. He is your sorrow, but also your comfort."

Nicolle's eyes widened, and some time passed before she spoke. "Or perhaps it's simply a pretty bauble a customer gave me."

For a deflection, the response fell flat. Paulette dropped her hand, smiled softly. "My mother wore a similar locket. She kept a picture of my father on one side and me as a baby on the other."

But no photograph of Gabrielle. A peculiar regret tripped along her spine, one she couldn't quantify. She told herself the revelation didn't signify, but perhaps it did. Paulette had always resented her older sister, because their grandmother had favored Gabrielle. Now, she realized, their mother had favored her. That must have stung. The tension between them made more sense, and for the first time ever, she found no comfort in her mother's shawl.

"Who do you keep in there, Nicolle?" she asked. "Who means so much that you place them close to your heart?"

Her head dropped, and a tear dropped onto her hand still clutching the tiny bear. She said nothing. Then she sighed and her hands lifted, moving behind her neck. Off came the necklace. "See for yourself."

Paulette snapped open the locket. There was only one picture. Why had she thought there would be two? She studied the image of a young man. He was quite attractive. Tousled, tawny hair, an open face, humor on his lips, love in his eyes. "Who is he?"

"My husband." Her tone was nothing short of wretched, and the tears came quicker, a steady stream of watery sorrow.

At the sight of all that pain, a peculiar pressure pushed between Paulette's shoulder blades. Her tongue was heavy with a thousand questions, but she thought it best to lead with a sort of vague prompt. "Is he…" She touched Nicolle's arm, held on as gently as Nicolle had done with her earlier in the evening. "Is he…?"

"Dead? Yes, Paulette, he died in the war, almost two years ago now." She wiped at her eyes with a trembling hand. "It was during one of the first battles, right after the Germans bypassed the Maginot Line and entered France near the Ardennes."

Paulette had heard her sister and grandmother arguing about the Maginot Line. The matriarch of the family believed the miles of concrete fortifications were impervious to attack. She'd claimed the structure would hold back the Germans. Gabrielle had vehemently disagreed.

She'd been right.

The Germans had simply breached the weakest point near the Ardennes. Their tanks had advanced through the forest, crossed the River Meuse, and encircled the French army. Many men had died, including Nicolle's husband. "I'm so sorry." The words felt insufficient. "Will you tell me about him?"

"Julien was the best of men. He was so very good." She pressed a fist to her heart. "At the core. Not a deceitful bone in his body."

Paulette had heard of men like that, but had known few of them. Gabrielle's husband had been one. How little she'd understood her older sister and the pain she'd endured at Benoit's passing. He'd been Gabrielle's childhood friend first, then her husband. A double loss, and Paulette had been oblivious. "He sounds wonderful."

"He was my very own fairy-tale prince come to life." She picked up the little bear, smiled softly, sadly. "We had so little time together. A few months as husband and wife, so sweet and lovely, before he was conscripted into the French army."

Paulette pressed a steadying palm on Nicolle's shoulder. "So now, when dreams of him chase you from your bed, you come here, to this child's toy, and…" She lifted her hand as something quite shocking occurred to her. "Wait… Is there a child?"

The face that turned toward her had drained of color, as white as the nightgown she wore. And her eyes had gone empty, round and glassy. "Have you seen a child in this building? Have you?"

Something cold scurried over her skin. "No. Never."

"Then *that* is your answer."

Paulette had obviously crossed a line. Regret coalesced in her throat, joining the lump that wanted to steal her breath. "Nicolle, I'm sorry. I didn't mean to upset you. I only meant to listen, as you listened to me earlier."

"I know."

Chest tight, pulse spiking, Paulette covered the hand still holding the bear and squeezed. "We will forget this conversation entirely. It will be as if it never happened. I will go back to bed, and we will never speak again of tiny bears or brave husbands gone too soon."

Staring at their joined hands, Nicolle was quiet for a while. Then she turned her head. There, in her eyes, was the look of a friend. "Nor," she began, "will we speak of disastrous love affairs or courageous mothers gone too soon."

"Our secrets," Paulette said. "It will be as if they do not exist outside this moment."

"What secrets?"

As if in silent agreement, they released each other's hands. Paulette stood. "You will be all right on your own?"

Another nod. "I want to finish this bear."

For a child, Paulette suspected, that had never been born to a couple that had so little time together. Grief came in many forms and made people do strange things. Nicolle made a tiny stuffed animal. Paulette kept drawings. They were so very different and yet very much the same.

Smiling softly, she touched her friend's cheek. "Good night, Nicolle."

"Good night, Paulette. Try to get some sleep."

Back in the attic, Paulette liberated her suitcase from beneath her bed, quietly released the latch, and pulled out her sketch pad. It was time to purge herself of the albatross she kept within the pages. She hadn't opened the book since her arrival in Paris.

Had it been only a few days since she looked at Friedrich's face?

He didn't belong in her new life. Yet his presence was with her, always there, right there, on the plane between shadow and light. Where evil lived. The man had been evil. She could accept that now. A predator. And she, his prey. Her fault had been in her own actions, in the lies she'd told her family. Evil for evil. Lie for lie. That was her past.

What she did now, in the present, would determine her future.

Hand shaking, she sat on her bed and placed the sketch pad on her lap. By the light of the moon, she studied the drawings of dresses born from her youthful innocence. Now that she'd seen Mademoiselle's work, Paulette recognized the frivolity in her attempts at fashion, the silliness, the lack of understanding of how a woman's body was formed. No wonder Mademoiselle put her to work in the atelier. Paulette wasn't ready to design.

Maybe she never would be.

Her cheeks hot, she turned the pages quickly. Faster and faster, past drawings she was glad no one had seen—the party dresses with their ridiculous flounces and unremarkable bodices. Even the rendering of Friedrich received only a glimpse. Flip. Flip. Flip.

Finally, a blank page where she could begin anew.

Tonight, she would draw. She would create. It had been too long. She went to her suitcase again and took out a piece of charcoal, and a towel to wipe her fingers. Then she drew.

The first mark brought a familiar joy. Her soul filled with the elixir of discovery. The act of drawing had never felt so calming, so right. The turmoil in her head quieted. An image quickly took shape on the page, and details appeared. A dress like none she'd formed before, like none she'd seen in the atelier or salon. Sharp lines merged with soft folds. Hard with soft. Dark with light. Her mother's shawl slipped from her shoulders. She let it fall to the floor.

This was who she was, today, in the quiet hours of the morning. One foot in the past, one in the present. A future not yet realized. Would her time in Paris bring healing? Would she grow into someone else entirely? Someone who was…more. Someone better.

Someone good.

To become that person, she would have to face the past. Face *him*.

Outside, a dog howled. That mournful sound could have come straight from her own tortured soul. Suddenly her hand was moving of its own accord. Back she went, flipping through the pages, until his image stared out at her.

Suppressing a shiver, she held his gaze. Nicolle had known love. Paulette had known passion, obsession, but not love. Her stomach clenched. Her breath knocked from her lungs. The fury inside her was strong, evoking a gasp from her lips. She wanted to slam her fist into the face staring up at her.

Shocked at the intensity of her feelings, she closed her eyes and forced herself to breathe. Softly, slowly. After a moment, the anger slid away, like a snake slithering back in its hole.

Scratch.

Scratch. Scratch. Scratch.

Paulette snapped open her eyes and immediately came back to herself. More scratching. She searched for the source of the sound. The wind, nothing but the wind whisking through tree branches, bending them into the glass. Suppressing a shiver, she slammed the sketch pad shut on Friedrich's face. She would not destroy the drawing today.

Soon, she vowed. She would soon forget the past.

It would not be easy—perhaps impossible—but Paulette would try.

Chapter Eleven

Sabine

The morning after an endless evening in Guy Marcel's company, Sabine left her apartment on the fourth floor. She'd slept little, her mind too focused on the horrible knowledge that Jewish women and children were soon to be arrested. Already set apart with yellow stars and discriminations. Pushed to the back of lines, fired from their jobs. Soon to be rounded up by the French police and sent away.

The very idea was unconscionable. What sort of evil was imprinted on the hearts of her own countrymen that they could systematically plan the destruction of innocent human beings?

The world had turned upside down. There was no other explanation. Nothing felt right anymore, and all Sabine could do was save as many as possible. It wouldn't be enough. It was never enough. With leaden feet, she made her way down the back stairwell to her atelier. At the bottom of the steps, a familiar rise of voices brought a blessed moment of comfort. She let the sensation become part of her like a thin invisible shroud.

Already, her girls were hard at work.

Her mood lightened all the more at the sight of all that efficiency on display. Her eyes took in the scene, moving until she found Nicolle Cadieux. The young woman sat at her station, Paulette faithfully there beside her, her head bent over a shimmering piece of silk.

Nicolle spoke softly, firmly, while Paulette sewed.

Pride filled Sabine's chest.

She'd been right to put the two together. One had needed someone to nurture and look after, and the other had needed guidance. That they would become friends had not been a requirement, but if that was the direction their relationship took, then all the better. Sabine watched them for several seconds. As if sensing her, Nicolle looked up.

Sabine presented a brief nod, produced a quick jerk of her chin, then turned on her heel and continued to her office. She didn't wait to see if the other woman followed. Nicolle always understood her silent messages.

Leaving the door ajar, she touched the picture of Giselle, a soft, breezy brush of fingertips, then perched on the edge of her desk and waited. One second turned to two. By the third, Nicolle stepped into the room and shut the door. Her eyes darted about, always assessing. There was something sorrowful about her this morning, as though her loss haunted her more than usual. Clearly, she'd had a bad night. The evidence showed in her unusually pale complexion.

Worry stirred deep inside Sabine. "My dear girl, you look absolutely wretched."

To her credit, Nicolle didn't deny the charge. "I didn't sleep well."

Nor had Sabine, and now her mind was on all that was not yet done. She was no closer to finishing her collection than she'd been yesterday. Two weeks, that was all she had, and yet this was not a time for creating pretty clothing. If Marcel was right, and he almost always was, Basia and others like her were in grave danger.

"I have another delivery for Madame Dumas." She didn't bother turning on the wireless before saying this. No need. She and Nicolle always spoke in code. "The order is nearly complete but for a few minor embellishments on several of the garments. You will make the delivery in two days, assuming all goes well on my end."

Translation: New identity cards had yet to be obtained.

Not a single blink or look of surprise. Just acceptance. Resolve. And as always, absolute trust in Sabine to pull off the impossible. "I'll be ready, Mademoiselle. Whenever you say it's time to go, I'll go."

Sabine nodded. "I don't yet know how many garments you will be delivering. At least two, possibly four, but as many as six. And Nicolle, this would be the perfect time to reach out to your friend in La Haye-Descartes and determine if he wishes to become a client."

Translation: We need his home for a safe house.

A peculiar sort of resignation fell over her face. Replaced just as quickly by a look of renewed determination. "I believe," she began, "it is always wise to expand your business."

"Indeed."

"If that is all…"

"Not quite. I have one final question." Nicolle rocked back on her heels, her head slightly tilted, but she didn't interrupt. She merely waited. Sabine pressed on, seeking confirmation for what she already knew. "What is your estimation of the new girl?"

As though needing a moment to consider her response, Nicolle moved to the shelf with the array of photographs chronicling Sabine's life as a fashion designer. She ran her finger along the shelf, her attention lingering on the picture of Giselle on-stage. The two women had never met, but they were very much alike. Loyal, hardworking. Brave. Perhaps that explained her affinity for the young woman.

"Paulette is a fast learner," Nicolle said, turning slowly. "She has quick hands, a good brain, and, I suspect, hidden depths to her character. She is more than she seems."

A telling comment. "How do you mean?"

Nicolle looked Sabine straight in the eye. "The girl watches everything, everyone, and thus she sees much. She listens in the same way. Nothing gets past her. No nuance, no contradiction. She understands people, women especially, and isn't afraid to be wrong. Though, surprisingly, she rarely is."

"Helpful skills for someone beginning a new life in an un-known city."

"Agreed. Overall, Paulette is an asset. She would do well taking on more duties."

This was the recommendation Sabine had been seeking. It did much to settle her doubts. She kept her face blank. Inside, she let out a long sigh of relief. Nicolle had just confirmed what she herself had sensed in the girl. It was settled, then. She would approach Paulette with her first task for the network, something small, a test of sorts, the mere passing of a message. "Thank you, Nicolle. That is very helpful. You may return to work now."

As she watched the young woman leave her office, Sabine had the first of her own tasks to complete. She must deter-mine the final number of escapees. Convincing a family to forsake the life they'd always known would not be easy. Let-ting go of the wealth acquired from generations of hard work and sacrifice even trickier. The son would be swayed with little effort—he would go wherever Basia went. The parents would be a much harder sell.

Naomi and Abraham Lindon had populated their home with

all manner of treasures. Abandoning such luxury would not come natural to either of them, Abraham in particular. Like so many men who'd been successful before the war, he still believed his wealth and status protected him from the antiracial laws applied to other Jews.

It was an illusion made of cardboard and paste.

Sabine traveled to the Lindon home on foot, a brisk forty-five-minute walk that helped clear her head and organize her thoughts. As she had the evening before, she carried a garment bag over her arm to disguise her true purpose. She knew she was being watched, not by the Nazis, but by Guy Marcel. He considered her a partner, but not one he could trust. He trusted no one.

Surely, probably, he had someone following her this morning.

Glancing in a shop window, Sabine met her own reflection. A tired old woman looked back at her, unexceptional in every way. Ignoring that disturbing image, she studied the street behind her and counted any number of potential enemies. The girl on the rickety bicycle, looking in Sabine's direction without actually looking. The man in the dark suit, hat pulled low over his brow. Did they work for Marcel?

What about the shopkeeper sweeping his front stoop? The café owner wiping down the outdoor tables in anticipation of the lunch crowd?

Any one of them could be in the gangster's employ. Reminding herself of the stakes, Sabine switched the garment bag to her other arm and continued her trek at a pace that could be construed as a woman in a hurry to make her delivery. The Nazi flags seemed obnoxiously large today, the bloodred background in stark contrast with the pale limestone of the beautiful Parisian buildings.

Once outside the four-story mansion that had been in the Lindon family for generations, Sabine couldn't help but notice the similarities to Marcel's home, the one he'd seized from a Jewish family much like the one naively living within these walls. Naomi and Abraham must be made to understand the danger they were in. Their French citizenship, their diplomatic connections, even their wealth—especially their wealth—could not save them. In the eyes of the Nazis, and the collaborating Vichy government, they were undeserving of their hard-won success. To them, a Jew was a Jew was a Jew.

Urgency had Sabine lifting the lion's head knocker and releasing it with a loud bang. The door opened a moment later, and she came face-to-face with yet another stiff-backed, stone-faced gatekeeper.

This one was dressed as well as the butler serving Marcel, though clearly more comfortable in his role. Of indeterminate age, he was cadaver-thin, with coal-black eyes, and had the uncompromising stare of a man charged with preventing undesirables access to the house. That look probably intimidated many, but would hold no authority over a Walther PP, the favored pistol of the SS.

Sabine gave him her calling card.

He stared at a spot just over her left shoulder, a none-too-subtle dismissal that only managed to irritate her. No, she thought, this man would not keep the SS, Gestapo, or even the French police from storming this home.

He had yet to acknowledge her directly. Enough. She stated her business in a cold voice that matched his hard expression. "I'm here for a fitting with Madame Lindon." She lifted the garment bag to illustrate the statement.

"You do not have the look of a *midinette*."

It was something, she supposed, to be seen as more than an ordinary seamstress. Except there was nothing ordinary about her girls. Each one was exceptional. And while she would like to point this out, this was not the battle she'd come to fight.

"My staff is otherwise occupied. Please inform Madame Lindon that Mademoiselle Sabine has arrived for her morning fitting."

"I was not informed of a fitting."

This nonsense had to end. "Yes, well, my time is valuable. You will announce me to your employer, or I will find her myself."

He must have sensed she meant what she said, because he stepped aside to let her cross the threshold. "You will wait here."

"Of course." Sabine took a moment to look around the ornate foyer. The air left her lungs at the sight of so much luxury untouched by Nazi greed. Abraham's "connections" must be with very important men quite high up the food chain. And yet...it would not be long before this home was seized. There was too much wealth here. Too much to pillage. The custom rugs and marble flooring. The Lalique and Rochon crystal. No doubt several fur coats stowed away in closets. Naomi's jewels. Abraham's Cartier watches. Fair game, all of it.

The butler reappeared. "Madame Lindon will see you now."

Sabine followed the man, trying not to sigh. His spine was so straight, she thought timber might be more pliant. They passed one treasure after another.

Warn them, Sabine. This is why you are here.

The butler stepped into a small parlor dominated by blue-and-gold furnishings. He announced Sabine in a nasally tone, then slithered away.

Naomi greeted her with a frown. "I don't understand. I did not order a dress."

"I'm well aware." She set the garment bag on a chair and studied her friend with a grave expression of her own. Other than a few new wrinkles around her mouth, and the streaks of gray in her dark hair, Naomi Lindon was still a beautiful woman. She had a trim build that harmonized with her small, delicate features. "I came to explain my intent concerning Basia."

Sniffing inelegantly, Naomi gave a hard flick of her wrist.

"The girl is fine. Or she will be, once she and Jacob marry at the end of the week. She will be a Lindon then, and all will be well."

Sabine's impatience spiked. Naomi spoke as if a new name would change everything. Paulette's mother, Hélène, had been Paris-born, like Naomi. She'd been a French citizen, too, and none of it had been enough. Not the marriage to a Frenchman. Not the official name change. Nor the fake documents that had erased her Jewish heritage. "The Lindon name won't be enough to save Basia. She is a Polish-born immigrant."

"The authorities don't know that."

Not true. "The girl registered at her local police station along with her family." Sabine had let her off from work that day to obey the edict. "You know this, Naomi. You also know that based on that census, her father and brother were arrested in the *rafle du billet vert*."

It had been a horrible day for France in general, and for Basia and others like her specifically. Nearly seven thousand foreign-born Jewish men who'd followed French law and registered as Jews had received a green postcard instructing them to report to their local police station for a status check. The summons had been a ruse. They were immediately arrested and deported to a detainment center.

Where they were now was unknown.

What *was* known was that those same monsters who'd sent the postcards planned to arrest women and children next. In quick, decisive words, Sabine told Naomi what she knew. "Now you understand why it's not safe for the girl to remain in Paris."

The other woman didn't give a single indication she'd heard Sabine. She simply tossed her a sidelong glance and said, "Basia won't be arrested with the others. She will be safe in this home, as a protected member of our family."

Sabine blinked in astonishment. It was suddenly hard to breathe. She forced out a breath that sounded like a hiss. "You delude yourself, Naomi. The Lindon name will keep none of you safe." Lowering her voice, she leaned in close. "I can get her and Jacob out of France. I can get all of you out."

"Why would we leave our home?"

"It's not safe to remain."

Naomi gave a snort of dismissal.

Now Sabine was angry. "Do not be naive, Naomi. No Jew is safe in Paris. Foreign-born, French-born, it will not matter. Eventually, you will all be targeted."

How did this woman not see this?

"You speak nonsense." Naomi moved away to run her fingertips over a brocade settee, skim across the rim of a Rochon vase. "My husband has connections deep within the Vichy government. They will protect us."

Sabine no longer bothered with soft words. "The worst of the anti-Semitic laws have come out of Vichy."

"We are safe." Her finger continued its swirling motion, faster now, firmer. Her voice, however, was surprisingly calm. "Basia will be, too, once she marries Jacob."

The woman truly believed her own lies. It was there in the dismissive tone, the complete and utter lack of worry in her manner.

"Safe for how long?" Sabine went to her friend, touched her arm. "Let me help you escape France, before it is too late."

"Run away? *Non.*" Naomi pulled away from Sabine's touch. "We are not cowards."

Her words were low and crisp. A slap. The other woman understood the danger. Deep down, she understood, and yet still clung to a false narrative. Held fast to a lie. As Naomi said nothing more, as she just stood in cold, unrelenting silence, the tenuous strands of their friendship strained.

It was hopeless.

Sabine was no quitter. She could not—would not—leave this house without making her case. She began again, battering the other woman with what she knew to be true. She led with facts and logic, listing every ordinance, pointing directly to the roundups that had taken Jewish men and their sons in the harsh light of day. "All you have to do is look to Basia's family to know what the future holds for yours. They arrested her father and brother without warning. There will be no warning for you, either. Except for this, Naomi. *This* is your warning. Let my word be your guide to what is to come. Let the Bermans' example be your prediction."

"The Bermans." She sneered. "Their obedience was their downfall. They never should have registered."

"What else were they to do? Their neighbors knew them. Their Jewishness was not something they could hide. It's not something you can hide, either."

Naomi's jaw ticked, and Sabine sensed she'd made a dent in her stubbornness, a tiny fissure that showed in the quick flutter of eyelashes. The quick glint of fear.

She pushed harder. "At least think of your son and his future wife. Do they not deserve a chance at a happy future, in a place where being Jewish is not a death sentence?"

Away went the touch of fear, and in its place—anger. "You speak in hyperbole. It is childish and beneath us both."

A wave of defeat washed over Sabine. Such venom coming from a friend. "I speak the truth, Naomi. You know this. You *know* what I say is not an exaggeration."

There in the flattening of Naomi's lips was Sabine's victory. She'd inched through the woman's confidence, just a quick, nearly imperceptible slide through that tiny crack of doubt. "I can get you out of France." It would require a good cover story, or perhaps a more clandestine escape through woods and shadow. "I can make it happen this week."

"Abraham has worked hard to provide for our family. He will not abandon the fruits of his labor, and I will not abandon my husband. *Non*, we stay." The words held unwavering resolve. "But…perhaps…Jacob and Basia can go on an extended honeymoon after the ceremony. To, say, the south of France."

She'd finally gotten through to the woman. It was a hollow victory. "I can make that happen."

"They must not know it was you," Naomi said. "We will tell them Abraham has arranged everything. He will do this, thinking he has helped his son and future daughter-in-law enjoy a few days of respite. But we will know differently. You and I. We will know that they will be taking a one-way trip to the Free Zone. You can make this happen, Sabine?"

"I can and I will." It was only half of what she'd come to do. She'd gained two escapees. She'd lost two. Naomi could not be moved. Arguing further would be futile. Then she remembered the others. "What about Basia's mother and her sister? What do you know of them?"

"They won't leave France without the father and brother."

Sabine hadn't considered that possibility, but she should have. "Will Basia be persuaded?"

"We won't tell her. A honeymoon, that is what she will think of this trip."

A lie for all the right reasons. A young Jewish couple would have a chance to live in freedom. They would have children and expand their family and never see the inside of a concentration camp. "I will arrange the details myself. When I have made the arrangements, I will send word through a messenger. You understand, Naomi? Tell me you understand."

"I understand. And, Sabine?" She came to stand before her, all signs of haughtiness gone. "Thank you."

Trembling all over, Sabine left the Lindon home feeling like a failure. Her friend stubbornly clung to her comfort and her husband, even knowing their house was built on quicksand.

It was so unbelievably tragic. Sabine's eyes were hot as she commandeered the sidewalk, but tears were stubbornly absent. She reminded herself she had the chance to save two lives.

There was much work to do. She must set aside her sorrow and acquire the necessary documents. Determine the best route. Prepare a dedicated *passeur*.

Two lives.

It had to be enough.

Chapter Twelve

Paulette

The wealthy American widow Vivian Miller returned for her next fitting three days ahead of schedule. No one but Paulette seemed to notice the discrepancy in dates. Even Mademoiselle's salon assistant, Geneviève, gave no indication her sudden arrival was anything out of the ordinary. An excellent client deserved excellent treatment, no matter how unusual or unexpected the request. As before, Nicolle was tasked with assisting Mademoiselle. Paulette was brought along to watch and observe from the shadows.

There was an odd feeling in the air this morning, a sense that they were each playing a role. Except Paulette didn't have any lines, and she certainly added nothing to the scene.

She was window dressing, irrelevant, a mere prop worthy of indifference.

How far she'd fallen from her days as a paying customer, when she and her mother would come for a fitting much like this one, then take tea at a fashionable café. How important she'd felt at the time. How unimportant she'd become. It was all so completely humbling and yet, oddly, remarkably, freeing. This sudden change in circumstance wasn't especially pretty—it was actually cold and scary—but it was real. And Paulette wanted real in her life. Everything with Friedrich had been false— smoke and mist wrapped inside lies and deception.

Now, as she stood against the wall, she performed the three tasks assigned to her by Mademoiselle. She watched. She listened. She learned.

Vivian Miller posed in front of the three-way mirror, her eyes a study in privileged indifference. She pivoted to the left, swiveled to the right, repeated the process twice over. "Hmm."

Indeed. The half-finished evening gown all but hung on her trim figure. The dress was actually rather ugly, completely drab and unappealing, and yet weirdly garish. Certainly not at all up to Mademoiselle's usual standards. Paulette certainly didn't remember the American ordering formal wear during her previous visit. She'd requested three garments and had been both specific and somewhat vague with her preferences. Something feminine. Something on the masculine side and, finally, a whimsical piece that showcased a schoolgirl feel.

No evening gown.

How very odd.

Odder still was Mademoiselle's solicitous behavior. She buzzed around Madame Miller, barking out instructions to Nicolle while throwing out random measurements that couldn't possibly correspond to the garment itself. Paulette had learned enough to know that much.

Mademoiselle made a gesture toward the American's feet. "Are these the shoes you will be wearing?"

"They are the same height."

Not exactly an answer, but Mademoiselle made a sound of

approval, adding, somewhat offhandedly, *"Très bien,"* before lowering to her knees.

As she adjusted the hem to reveal the smallest peek of the woman's shoes, Paulette eyed the confection of silk and gauzy tulle. Again, she thought, the dress was no Mademoiselle Ballard creation. The construction felt rushed. The embellishment was barely tacked on with only a few strategically placed stitches. From a design standpoint, the diagonal row of fabric flowers was too much, the outlandish creation nothing close to the American's preference for subtlety. Yet Mademoiselle marked the hem with great care. She pinned it, then sat back on her heels and studied her handiwork. "That will do."

She gained her feet. Nicolle moved in to help the client remove the dress, her eyes cast downward. Paulette had no such qualms, which was why she caught the exchange of a quick, meaningful look between Mademoiselle and the American.

Much was said in that brief eye contact. Questions were asked, answers given. She knew the signs of subterfuge. Secrets coated in deception. Paulette had become proficient in that particular language. Friedrich had taught her well. Something clandestine was happening between the two women. And… none of it was her concern.

She followed Nicolle toward the exit. Compelled by some unknown urge, she shot a final glance over her shoulder. This time, she caught the two women exchanging envelopes. It was done quickly, without comment, giving Paulette the impression there was some hidden purpose to the transaction. What was in those envelopes? Again, none of her concern.

Brow furrowed, she exited the salon and entered the winding corridor that led to the workroom. She'd lost sight of Nicolle and felt the aloneness that had become a part of her new life in Paris. The air was heavier, the light dimmer. Secrets congregated here, in the transition from elegant salon to busy workroom.

A cloud of anticipation cloaked her in its heady embrace,

the sensation stoking some hidden excitement deep within her. She'd felt this sort of fearful thrill before. Whenever she'd slipped out of the château to meet Friedrich under the moon and stars. There had been something mesmerizing in the way her heart had beat in time with her quickened steps. The heady sense that she had a secret life found only in the dark, separate and unique from the one she lived out in the open, had been exhilarating.

Paulette could admit that now, as she hurried through the shadowy maze of twists and turns. She'd enjoyed the rush of blood in her veins. She'd relished the sense of danger and the risk of discovery, nearly as much as she'd enjoyed attending parties and being the center of attention. Neither had brought her happiness, only heartache and loss.

So why did she still crave both worlds, one for its danger, the other for its validation?

Not liking this insight, she picked up the pace, all but stumbling over her own two feet. Secrets were everywhere in this hallway, calling to her. Her lungs filled with the musty air, her breath clogging in her throat until there, up ahead, stood the door to the atelier, left ajar for her by Nicolle.

She all but ran through the opening. The familiar sights and sounds had her heart easing back down her throat. Nicolle was already laying out the dress at their workstation. She took a step in that direction, but stopped at the mention of her name.

The voice seemed to come from everywhere and nowhere. When she looked behind her, Mademoiselle was striding toward her. "I'd like a word with you. In my office."

The older woman disappeared back into the corridor. A chill settled over Paulette. She blinked, suddenly unsure of herself. She'd done nothing wrong. Except witness an exchange that she was not supposed to have seen. An encouraging nod from Nicolle was all it took to set aside her nerves enough to follow after her employer.

Inside the cluttered office, Mademoiselle sat at her desk, attention on a stack of papers. She'd placed the envelope off to the side, visible but not quite forgotten. Paulette took a tentative step, heart pounding. Other than the faint patter of rain on the window, the room was silent as a tomb and nearly as dark. Why had Mademoiselle not turned on the lamp?

"You may sit down, Paulette. You are not in trouble."

The blunt sentiment sent her elevated heart rate into a sporadic jumble of thumps and thuds. She breathed in a steadying breath and did as she was told.

Looking up, Mademoiselle folded her hands on the desk and leaned slightly forward. "Tell me, *ma chérie*. Why are you here?"

The question was so unexpected, her arms closed around her body of their own volition. "I—I…" she stammered. "That is, I wish to begin anew."

A sound of disappointment prefaced Mademoiselle's slap of palms to the desk. "I ask for candor. You give me rhetoric. I will repeat my question. Why are you here, Paulette? And this time, I want the truth."

She tucked her chin, shamefully, and tightened her arms around her waist. "I have made mistakes, or rather, one mistake. I committed a terrible, awful deed that can never be undone." Now that she'd begun, the words tumbled out of her mouth, one on top of the other. "That is why I am here, in Paris. I am here to atone for my behavior. I wish to make amends for the pain I have caused my family."

"Ah, my dear, dear girl. Wishing does not make a thing so." The soft voice was that of a mother, and it was Paulette who leaned forward now. "The past cannot be changed. To begin anew, as you suggest, you must look to the future. You must take one small step forward, then another and another."

One step forward. She made it sound so simple. "I don't know how to do that. I don't know where to begin."

"But you have begun. You have come to me, and now I will

guide you. It will take courage and many, many selfless acts, until you have become a different woman. A kinder, braver woman who has changed lives for the better."

How lovely it sounded. How utterly impossible. "If you knew what I have done, you would not say these things to me."

"There, now you speak with candor. So now, I will do the same. I know what you did, Paulette. I know about the SS officer and the events that led to your mother's disappearance."

Her earlier shame shifted into a hot, hard feeling she couldn't name. Something dark and ugly, something that lived deep inside her heart. "I betrayed my own mother."

"Hélène does not think this of you."

"You can't know that."

"I know her mind as well as I know my own. She does not judge you, *ma petite chérie*, nor do I."

"You should."

"To do so would make me a hypocrite. You see, I, too, have made mistakes. My past, it is not so pristine." She looked at the photograph of her daughter and smiled softly, sadly.

That look proved the rumors true. Mademoiselle had given birth out of wedlock. It explained why she hired women with nowhere else to go. Why she gave some of them lodgings and food. Paulette thought of Mademoiselle's fondness for Nicolle. A bond that seemed stronger than employer and employee. She thought of the stuffed bear.

Could it be...?

Was Nicolle a mother? Did she have a...?

Non, it was impossible. There was no child in this building. No signs of one anywhere, but for that small toy.

It took her a moment to realize Mademoiselle was speaking again. "We have each suffered a great loss because of this war." She stood and went to the wireless. A quick twist of a knob and classical music filled the stilted air. "I wonder," she said, her attention on Paulette's face as she perched on the edge of the desk. "What would you do to begin anew? What small, brave act would you commit to finally put the past behind you?"

Thoughts buzzed in Paulette's head. Thoughts of the people back home. Of Lucien and the pamphlets he'd distributed for the Free French. Of her mother's daring choice to cozy up to a Nazi to protect her family. Of the acts of sabotage back home in Reims. The sneaking into the rail yard by Resistance workers to wreak havoc on shipments in and out of the city. The emptying of wine barrels overflowing with confiscated champagne on its way to Berlin. It was like hearing a mosquito in the dark, knowing it was there, waiting for the bite that was sure to come. "Anything. I would do anything."

"No matter the risk to your safety?"

"No matter."

"What of your reputation?"

The tips of her ears burned as she remembered Gabrielle's parting words of warning. Her sister had intimated people in Reims knew of her affair with Friedrich. If that were true, her reputation was already stained. Even if that weren't the case…

"My answer remains the same."

"Good. This is good." Mademoiselle replied calmly, but there was a steely look in her gaze, and Paulette knew she was in the presence of the woman who'd built a fashion empire despite the scandal surrounding her daughter's birth.

Mademoiselle returned to the other side of the desk and sat. "I have a task for you."

Sensing the importance of this moment, Paulette scooted to the very edge of her seat.

"You will go to this address." She rattled off a number and street name, then gave rudimentary directions. "Once there, you will knock on the door and ask to speak to Madame Lindon. You will recite to her this exact message."

Paulette listened, then repeated the random collection of words and sentences. She waited for more, then realized Mademoiselle had gone silent. The moment felt unfinished. "Would you like me to repeat the message again?"

"Have you committed it to memory?"

"I have."

"Then that is your answer."

It was, Paulette realized, all the instruction she was to receive. Mademoiselle confirmed this by lowering her attention to the stack of papers on her desk and saying, "You may go now. And Paulette." She looked up, briefly. "I urge you to hurry. Time is not our friend."

"Je comprends." She left the room without another word.

In the darkened hallway, she shook off a shiver, then set off for the address Mademoiselle had given her. She paused only long enough to tell Nicolle she was being sent on an errand for their employer. The other woman was not surprised, nor did she ask questions.

Outside in the alleyway behind the building, Paulette noticed the rain had stopped, but the clouds remained. Under the grainy canopy, she told herself she was up to this task. A simple one, really. She was to go to a specific address and knock on the door. She would then ask to see Madame Lindon. Repeat Mademoiselle's confusing message. And, lastly, leave the house.

Knock. Ask. Repeat. Leave.

She would not let Mademoiselle down. She would not let herself down. The address she'd been sent to turned out to be a four-story elegant structure made from Paris limestone in the wealthiest part of Paris.

Knock.

She lifted the large metal ring caught in the mouth of a golden lion's head, let it drop with a bang. A dour-looking man answered the door.

Ask.

"I wish to speak with Madame Lindon."

After a brief inspection, he directed her into the entryway, then left her waiting under an enormous chandelier. A moment later, he returned. "You will follow me."

He escorted her into a small, intimate parlor, then disappeared without a single word to Paulette or the other occupant in the room. An elegant older woman stood alone near a floor-to-ceiling window. The stream of sunlight did not show her to advantage. She looked haggard, anxious even, her hands clutched at her waist.

"You are Madame Lindon?"

"I am."

"I have a message for you, from Mademoiselle Sabine."

The woman's eyes immediately sharpened. Her lips flattened. All signs of her previous anxiety gone but for a small muscle twitch along the right side of her neck. "I'm listening."

Repeat.

"The arrangements are complete. Report to Gare de Lyon tomorrow at dawn. You will know your travel companion by the blue scarf at her neck. She is prepared for two, but will accept as many as four. Please reconsider."

The last piece of the message still confused Paulette, but Madame Lindon seemed to understand. "Anything else?"

"That is all."

Paulette had delivered the message. Only one task remained.

Leave.

She shifted her stance, prepared to go, but suddenly, an alarm went off in her brain. The air in the room had changed. She and Madame Lindon were no longer alone.

A young couple had entered from a side door, all smiles and happiness. The man was handsome, the girl beautiful and quite familiar. Basia, the seamstress from the atelier. But where was her sadness? Her fear? This was not the dejected woman who'd left the atelier in tears.

There was no weariness in her, no quiet acceptance. Just joy. And happiness. So much happiness. The man at her side, also happy. The way they held hands, their soft glances, the sweet, delighted smiles. This, Paulette realized, was the definition of love and the antithesis of what she'd shared with Friedrich.

"I know you." Basia let go of the man's hand and approached Paulette. "You are the girl from the atelier. The one with the suitcase." *The one who took my job.* She didn't say the words, but they were hanging in the air between them.

Leave.

Paulette should—must—leave this house. Her feet refused to obey. A strange energy had rolled over her, holding her firmly in place. "Yes," she managed to say, "I… I took your job. And I… I'm sorry. So very sorry."

"You mustn't blame yourself." The young woman took Paulette's hands. "My dismissal was inevitable. The laws are changing every day. We are forced to wear yellow stars so that we are known for our ethnicity. Already, we struggle to find work in Paris, and only the most menial of jobs. It is the way of my kind."

My kind. She meant Jews. Basia had just confirmed what Paulette had known all along. A spark of anger flashed in her heart, but the other woman didn't seem to notice. She was still smiling, even after delivering the harsh truth of what it meant to be Jewish in Paris.

Paulette's hands started to shake.

Leave.

Basia's grip tightened. Her smile softened.

Leave.

"I'm sorry, Basia. I'm sorry Mademoiselle let you go."

"I'm not." She squeezed Paulette's hands again, then let go and returned to her young man. "Jacob has asked me to marry him. He will make me his wife this very afternoon. We leave for our honeymoon in the south of France tomorrow morning. So you see, all is well."

Paulette knew the young woman was telling the truth. Or at least, her truth. She also understood she wasn't supposed to know anything about a marriage or a trip to the south of France. She was supposed to have delivered the message and be gone by now.

The message. It ran through her mind, piece by piece. The train station. The traveling companion. Mademoiselle had arranged for the newlyweds to go on a honeymoon in the south of France. In the Free Zone, despite the impossibility of Jews crossing the Demarcation Line. How?

The envelopes. Falsified documents? That was a lot of subterfuge for a brief holiday. Perhaps not a holiday, then. An escape. The rest of the message fell into place. *She is prepared for two, but will accept as many as four. Please reconsider.* The last part had been for Madame Lindon, and possibly her husband. Like so many French-born Jews, they'd decided to stay in Paris.

It was a death sentence. As Basia had said, the laws were changing daily. No Jew was safe. Urgency had her rushing to stand before the woman of the house. She had so much she wanted to say. She could tell her what was happening outside of Paris. She could tell her about her own mother. About the Gestapo agent Detective Mueller and his penchant for making people disappear. "Please, Madame Lindon. Please reconsider."

The woman's response was a cold, hard glare. "You have delivered your message, mademoiselle. You will leave my home now."

All the blood rushed out of Paulette's face, and now she knew just how far she'd fallen. Madame Lindon would not listen to a girl dressed in the uniform of a lowly seamstress. Paulette had no power. She went over to Basia and pulled her into a tight embrace. "May you live a long, healthy life and be blessed with many children."

"I wish the same for you."

Saying nothing more, Paulette left the room, her failure sharp as a blade in her throat, her feet heavy as stone. She stepped outside into a perfect spring day. The clouds had lifted away, leaving blue sky. And still she shivered. Her stomach churned with the sickening mixture of heartbreak and remorse. She'd taken one step, just one, but was no closer to atonement. In many ways, she was farther than ever before.

This was not the end.

There would be other messages for her to deliver. She would make sure of it. More steps to take. And as she lay in bed later that night, her mother's shawl thrown over her, Paulette vowed to help Mademoiselle put together other *honeymoons* for other Jewish couples. She drifted in and out of sleep, always with the same resolve in her heart. A full hour before dawn, she was awake again, staring up at the ceiling, which was why she heard Nicolle stir.

The other woman slipped from her bed as quiet as a wraith. She was fully dressed, and when she tied a blue scarf around her neck, then reached for a garment bag, Paulette understood Nicolle to be Basia's travel companion. Afraid for her friend in ways she couldn't explain, Paulette reached for her hand and whispered, "Be careful, Nicolle. Please. Come home safe."

Her responding smile was soft and full of silent gratitude. "I will, as I always do."

Chapter Thirteen

Nicolle

The weather turned nasty an hour outside La Haye-Descartes. Another escape with unexpected challenges along the way. First, the storm. Now, the thick, misty rain had become a heavy, milky-white shroud, all but strangling any hope of visibility. Testing the depth of the fog, Nicolle thrust out her hand and immediately lost sight of everything below her elbow. She would have to proceed on memory. That was no problem. She knew the trajectory of each street in the center of town and, more specifically, the three that fanned out toward André's home.

Nicolle was ready to proceed.

Were the escapees?

She rearranged the scarf around her neck, moved closer to the couple, and tried not to sigh. Basia leaned heavily on her new husband, her eyes wide, her face twisted with trepidation. She was clearly terrified. She should be. They were about to enter the most precarious leg of their journey, the actual crossing of the border into the Free Zone. But that wouldn't be until later. First, the couple needed rest and food. Nicolle counted on André providing both.

At least so far, the journey had gone well enough. The train ride from Paris to La Haye-Descartes had presented nothing out of the ordinary. Their false identity papers had held up at each checkpoint, as had the couple. Basia's fear had only presented itself when Nicolle explained she wasn't going on an extended honeymoon but was, instead, escaping France permanently. "But why would we not return?" Her eyes had filled with tears and confusion. "Our family is here."

Nicolle had looked to Jacob, who'd been equally confused, equally upset. Clearly, the two had not been included in the planning of their own escape. At that point, with time not on their side, she'd been blunt. "You know why. You are Jews. Arrest is only a matter of time."

"But—"

She held up a hand. "As to your families..." Nicolle didn't know. These two were her only priority. "You will know more once you arrive in America." Or so she assumed.

This had only elicited more questions, most of them about the people they'd left behind. "My mother," they'd said in tandem. "My sister," Basia had sobbed. "They will worry. We cannot abandon them like this."

"Jacob, your parents have decided to stay in Paris." Mademoiselle had been clear on this. "Your mother, Basia. Your sister." Mademoiselle had said nothing about them, and so Nicolle improvised. "I will personally see to their safety."

The two had fallen silent after that, each digesting the news. Eventually, Jacob had stepped into the role of soothing his new wife, leaving Nicolle to focus on their route. She needed to proceed with patience and a cool head. One small mistake on her part, a lack of cold, clear thinking, and someone would die.

Perhaps all of them. "From this point on," she told the pair, "no more talking. We proceed in silence."

The couple blinked at her.

"Do you understand?"

Two silent nods were her only response. Excellent. She gave them a signal to follow her.

Cloaked in the impenetrable fog, she took slow, careful steps, approaching the house from the southeast corner. The last time she'd come to André, she'd been in desperate need of his help. He'd proven faithful. This visit would be trickier. Different. Because she would solicit more than a few hours of his time.

She would ask him to join Mademoiselle's network of Resistance workers ferrying refugees to safety. His home was perfectly placed to be a safe house.

Rounding the final corner, she guided the escapees to the back of the house. She held up a hand, signaling they stop. There was no light coming from inside, no shift in the fog, but something felt wrong. She had a vague sense that eyes were on her, watching. Time slowed down to an almost dormant trickle of seconds. Taking a calculated risk, she whispered, "Wait here."

Uneasy and restless, she investigated the perimeter of the yard, discovered nothing suspicious. She expanded her search to the neighboring houses, then the entire block. All quiet. She emerged from the cocoon of fog and found the escapees where she'd left them. Mounting the back stoop, she knocked softly. As before, the door opened within seconds.

He wore the same garments she remembered. Black pants, white shirt, sleeves rolled up past his forearms. The only difference was that his dark hair was in full disarray, as if he'd been running his fingers through its thick depths. A sign of worry.

Consumed with deciphering his mood, she didn't see him reach out. She jumped at his touch but recovered quickly. "We need your help."

Seeming to turn to stone, he didn't move. His silent gaze

stayed locked with hers. Then he swept his attention behind her, over to the left, surprise evident in the slight widening of those remarkable eyes. "Two of them."

"*Oui*, two."

He stepped aside without further delay. A thousand little thoughts filled her mind as she directed Basia and Jacob to proceed ahead of her. Once they were tucked safely inside the kitchen, with only the gloomy outdoor light filling the tiny space, André wasted no time with pleasantries. He took the garment bag from Nicolle's possession, then gave their entire sad little group a single swooping glance. "Which of you is hurt?"

The calmness that surrounded him brought such relief, Nicolle found herself moving closer. Closer. Until she could see the striations of both green and blue in his irises. "None of us is hurt."

His jaw softened, even as his eyes filled with confusion.

"I'll explain later," she said before he could ask. "First, they are in need of—"

"Food and rest."

"Precisely. We will leave in a few hours, just before dusk." Right before the guards changed shifts, when they were at their most tired and, hopefully, least attentive.

As if reading her thoughts, and understanding her logic, André smiled. His eyes crinkled at the edges, and Nicolle instantly knew why she'd agreed to approach him. It wasn't because she trusted him, or maybe not only because she trusted him. It was the promise of seeing him again. She tried to convince herself his presence made her feel more connected to Julien.

Was that true?

As he went to work settling the newlyweds at a small breakfast table, she took the opportunity to study him. Her eyes landed on a small strip of skin at the edge of his shirt collar, and something pleasant moved through her.

She quickly looked away just as he came to stand beside her.

"You should also sit and eat," he said. She started to argue, but he added, "Please."

His kindness was so genuine, her need to rest so great, that there was nothing to do but sit and eat. "Thank you."

The food went down quickly, and now, with her belly full, it took great effort to keep her eyes open. The newlyweds seemed to be having the same difficulty. Nicolle wasn't the only one to notice. André took charge, and oh, how nice it was to let him. If just this one time. "You will rest now," he told Basia and Jacob. "Come, I have a room set up for this very purpose."

He led them toward the basement. Basia balked at the top of the stairs, her eyes wary, her feet seemingly frozen. "Must we go down there?"

"I wish I could offer a better solution," André said, his voice full of apology. "Unfortunately, I have patients scheduled all morning. They cannot know you are here."

His words did nothing to release the tension from her shoulders. Her eyes remained on the gaping hole in front of her. "But it is so very dark down there."

Understanding, sympathizing even, Nicolle attempted to calm the girl's fears, but her husband was faster. "Basia, my love. This man knows nothing of our story or why we are running from Paris, yet he has been kind enough to offer us refuge at great risk to himself. We will thank him by obeying his wishes."

It was a sound argument and seemed to get through to the frightened girl. Her head bent in silent acknowledgment. "Will you hold my hand?"

"You know I will." He kissed her cheek, then whispered something solely for her ears.

She laughed a little, a very little, but looked to André, who said, "I will lead the way."

He made a polite noise deep in his throat as he moved in front of the frightened girl. Nicolle watched him descend, one step, two. By the third, she could no longer see him. His footsteps continued sounding loud and with grave purpose, and she felt relief with each strike of heel to wood. Jacob went next, then Basia. Nicolle took up the rear. She was halfway down when André, now at the bottom, reached to a single light bulb hanging from a fine, frail wire.

He pulled the string, and Nicolle blinked at his tall silhouette, more shadow than man. She hardly noticed him, so busy was she looking at the contents of the basement itself. Shelves filled with rationed goods lined two entire walls. Sacks of flour, pasta, rice, sugar, coffee. There were also piles of neatly folded clothing. Pants for men, dresses for women, children. And there, on the edge of the third shelf, was what looked like a stack of ration coupons. Forged? Or stolen?

Following the direction of her gaze, he said simply, "I supply my neighbors with what they cannot acquire on their own."

How very vague. How very telling. Nicolle swallowed, knowing she would never look at him the same way again. "I see."

"I don't think you do."

She said nothing as unwanted suspicion filled her. Was André profiting off his fellow French citizens? Nicolle was aware of the *marché gris*, the gray market. She knew some Parisians bred rabbits and guinea pigs in their bathtubs to sell as meat to their neighbors. Others took the train to the country, where food was in more abundance. They bought these types of goods to sell back in the city at a small profit.

What role did André play?

Clearly unaware of the direction of her thoughts, he pulled back a thick green curtain, revealing a lone cot, a blanket and pillow, a small table with a water jug, a tin cup, and a stack of books. The place had a lived-in feel, and Nicolle tried to make sense of what this setup revealed. He'd harbored other refugees. She could practically hear the whispers of the people who'd come before. She could feel every breath of every person who had ever sat on that cot, drank from that pitcher.

As her thoughts swirled, he went about settling the newly-weds into their temporary lodgings. He gave them rather precise instructions, speaking quickly, almost sternly, but not without kindness. Who was this man? An opportunist or savior? "Do not come upstairs until one of us—" he pointed to himself, then to Nicolle "—comes for you."

Giving their agreement with identical nods, the two sat shoulder to shoulder on the cot, huddled together as if they were a single unit. A moment of nostalgia filled Nicolle. She and Julien had moved like that.

Lost in the memory, she was hardly aware of André leading her back up the stairwell until she found herself standing in the kitchen. The sun had broken through the clouds, erasing the fog and turning the small space into a kaleidoscope of pastel colors, smoothing out the hard edges of the table, the counter, André himself. She eyed him closely, looking for some flaw in his character under the soft glow of light. When she found none, she began gathering the empty dishes, moving to the sink, aware—so wholly aware—he watched her every move.

"You have questions."

Her tongue was heavy with them. "I have many, many questions."

"I let you see my contraband for a reason."

She turned then, hands empty, eyes searching. It would be so easy to let down her guard. But to do so would be to put two innocent people in danger. "How much?"

Puzzlement met her gaze. "I don't understand the question."

"How much?" she said again. "How much money do you charge your neighbors for the supplies they cannot get on their own?"

"I do not accept payment." Now his eyes filled with disappointment.

At her. She'd made a mistake, asking him this, failing to trust him, when he'd given her no cause to doubt. Nicolle was suddenly hot. Dizzy with regret. André was one of the good guys, and she'd insulted him with her suspicions.

"I work with three others," he explained. "We are a small band of Resistance workers, offering means of survival for our neighbors. We also shelter refugees passing through our small town. Our efforts are small in comparison to other operations, such as—" he held her gaze for a beat "—the secret networks that help escapees out of France."

All the air left her lungs. She struggled to take a breath, nearly dropping to her knees as relief settled over her. Then came the shame. "Oh, André. I thought—"

"I know what you thought." He shook his head, the epitome of a man let down by a friend. "You assumed I traded on the black market for my own gain."

"Yes, but also no. Not necessarily for your own gain." Except yes. She had thought that very thing. For at least a second or two. "All right, that's not true," she admitted. "I thought the worst of you, and I'm sorry. So very, very sorry."

He walked toward her, and she saw the purple shadows under his eyes, the hollowed cheekbones that seemed sharper than the first time they'd met. She'd missed the signs, hadn't bothered noticing that he had the look of a man who slept little and ate less than someone his size required. He denied himself so that others could eat the food he had stored in the basement, or wear the clothes, or use the ration coupons. He supplied anything they needed to survive the worst of German occupation. "I'm sorry," she said again. A sliver of guilt had her adding, "I should have known better."

Now he smiled, and she was certain she saw the sun in his eyes—all light and warmth.

"How could you have known?" He briefly put a hand on her shoulder, weightless, unintrusive, then gone. "You and I, we have met but a few times. We know little of one another except that we both lost a good man, your husband, my friend."

It was true, all of it.

"Not to mention," he continued, "in your line of work, you have met some of the lowest of men and women, as have I. It is hard to trust."

Again, he was right. Still, she should not have painted him with the same brushstroke as the people she trusted the least. For one relevant reason. "Julien would not have made you his closest friend if you were not a man of integrity."

At the mention of her husband, André's eyes went glassy. He rubbed the back of his neck, sighed. "War changes people, some for the worse."

"Others for the better."

A smile passed between them. "Yes, others for the better."

Which was she? She didn't know. After all, she stood here, again, with a very large lie between them. They fell silent, neither moving, neither speaking, both knowing this moment mattered. What they said next, what they *did* next, would determine each of their futures.

André's expression softened. "What you are doing, Chloe. For men like that Brit and the young couple downstairs, Julien would be proud of you. I know I am."

The words brought great inner peace, but also fear. "You mustn't call me that anymore. Chloe no longer exists. She cannot exist." He knew why, knew of her Jewish heritage, the reason Julien had been shunned by his family. "I am…" She paused, considered whether to give him the name on her official identity papers or her code name. There had to be some truth between them. "You will call me Nicolle."

"Nicolle." He repeated the name as if testing the sound of it on his tongue. He knew she had lied. It was there in his eyes, in the heavy sigh he heaved, the frown that twisted his lips.

"It's what they call me in Paris," she blurted out, hating that this conversation had become so stilted, painful even, with both of them going through the motions, but not completely giving of themselves.

"It is a strong name for a strong woman. A good woman."

"I'm not good." Even now, she stood before him covered in lies. He knew nothing of her life in Paris, her work there. Her son.

"You are good, Chlo—I mean, Nicolle. Julien would not have made you his wife otherwise." A sad smile crossed André's face. "He would want us to be friends, I think."

He looked so serious and sincere, no different from Paulette a few days ago when she'd said something similar. Two offers of friendship given, and now a lump was rising in Nicolle's throat. "He would, and so we will try."

"I have appointments scheduled for the next two hours. You should get some rest yourself."

How lovely that sounded. How impossible. She had preparations to make, routes to consider. A question to ask on Mademoiselle's behalf. "André—"

"Let me show you where you can lie down."

Lie down. She couldn't fathom setting her head on a pillow. If she closed her eyes, even for a few seconds, she would never open them again for hours, possibly days. That was the level of her exhaustion. Better to focus on the work, the question she'd come to ask. "André, would you be open to providing refuge to others?"

He said nothing, merely cocked his head.

"We—that is, the network—would like to use your home as a safe house."

The spark of amusement in his eyes was not what she'd expected. "I assumed this issue was settled the moment I opened the door to you last week and again this morning."

"How easy you are. I ask, you agree. It's really that simple?"

"It's really that simple." He reached to her, let his hand drop before making contact.

Oh, but the tenderness in his gaze. It was too much. Something inside her cracked open and spilled into her throat, burning up, up into her eyes. "I need a desk. A pencil. And access to a telephone."

"You need rest."

The man was like a dog with a bone. "I must let my employer know I have arrived and that you are willing to become a client." She explained the cover story Mademoiselle had crafted for her ongoing stops at his house. "Hence the garment bag."

Proving he was a born strategist and an extremely quick thinker, he asked, "How do you explain the additional people with you?"

"My assistant, or family, depending on my companion. A man, he is a tailor. A woman, a finisher." She went on to explain the difference. "A tailor specializes in creating, altering, and repairing garments, particularly men's clothing. A finisher is relatively self-explanatory. She is responsible for the garment's final look, focusing primarily on buttons, zippers, cutting threads."

The lines around his eyes smoothed out, and there was an almost imperceptible shift of light in them. "That was quite a thorough explanation."

"Do you have questions?"

He gave a shake of his head. "None."

"Good. The telephone," she reminded him. "Once my employer knows I am safe and the issue of your continued patronage of her fashion house is confirmed, then I will rest."

"I do not like seeing you this way. Exhausted, sad. Full of grief." He reached to her face, brushed away a stray tear with his thumb.

When had she given in to her emotions? "I miss him so much," he admitted.

"As do I."

The air grew heavy with their shared grief. She didn't resist when he pulled her into his arms. She let her head fall against his chest, his heartbeat strong against her ear.

He eventually stepped back. Something was there in his eyes—grief, of course, but also something new that didn't involve Julien. Yet she felt him with them, in this small, cramped kitchen. Smiling down on them. The sensation was so peaceful and good and right that it didn't make sense in this ugly, fallen world, with war raging outside and so, so many secrets held in her heart. She wanted—needed—to end this moment and blurted out the first thing that came to mind. "The telephone."

"Right. Of course. Come with me." He escorted her to another part of the house, along winding wood-paneled corridors. André's home was larger than she'd thought, his strides twice the length of hers. He moved with fast, fluid movements. At the end of the hallway, he directed her to enter the room on her right. She stepped inside and saw him everywhere.

The rich, dark wood and earth tones reflected his personality. Bookshelves lined three walls. The fourth had the same wood as the hallway, but no windows. Newspapers lined the surface of a large mahogany desk. The sought-after telephone rested on the far edge.

André rounded the corner, studied the contents strewed across the top of the desk. An imperceptible nod and then he was pushing aside the stack of papers. Nicolle moved to sit before the space he'd just cleared. He unlocked a drawer and there, inside, was a surprise.

"This is the latest map of France under German occupation." He unfolded the paper, spread it before her. "I urge you to study it closely, commit it to memory."

"What are these red marks?" She pointed to one on the other side of the Demarcation Line, another near the Spanish border, just north of the Pyrenees.

He swiveled his head, his expression grim. "The sites of recent ambushes by the German army."

Ambushes. *Ambushes.* She fell into an immediate silence. Her heart beat fast and erratically, and it became hard to breathe. An ambush was the worst scenario for a *passeur*. Her fear wanted to make itself known in a soft gasp. She pushed the sound down, opened her mouth, but her pulse continued pounding in her ears, and she couldn't sort her thoughts into words.

"I'll leave you alone to make your call." At the door, he paused, looked back. "I know I don't need to tell you to stay silent and out of sight until I come for you."

"And yet you just did."

He smiled, a flash of teeth and humor, and her heart gave two quick thuds in response. For a brief moment, the darkness that lurked in her soul disappeared.

"Try to get some rest. For me." A moment later, he was gone and the sense of doom was back, reminding her two lives were in her hands.

She considered the map, her fingertip running along known escape routes, pausing at each red mark. Grimacing at the one in Toulouse, she reached for the phone. When Mademoiselle answered, she gave her employer a quick update on the escape. She used their agreed-upon code, finishing her report with news pertaining to the other task she'd been assigned. "As of this afternoon, I have secured another menswear client for Maison de Ballard. I will bring back his first order after I complete my current deliveries."

Chapter Fourteen

Sabine

Sabine set the telephone receiver back in its cradle, her head in a whirl. So far, only good news, barring the delays, which was a matter of course in matters such as these. The pertinent piece was that they had another safe house in the system and a new, twice-tested escape route.

Despite the late start, there'd been no trouble at the checkpoints. No sign of a mole leaking information to the German or French authorities. Of course, that could be because Nicolle had diverted the escapees along a route no one knew about except her and Sabine. The brief pause in La Haye-Descartes was also a secret only the two of them shared.

Still, Sabine worried, and would continue to do so until her most trusted *passeur* was safely back in Paris. She'd told Nicolle to take an extra day if she wanted. The atelier would survive. And a few days with her son would restore her spirit.

As for Sabine, nothing could restore her spirit. Exhaustion

made her consider all that could go wrong. Giving in to the bone-rattling fatigue, if only for a moment, she collapsed into a nearby chair and closed her eyes. She'd worked through the night, well into the morning, and then past noon. She was still dressed in the previous day's garments. Her back ached worse than usual. Her fingers had cramped into something resembling claws, the nails stained black from the charcoals. But she'd done it. She'd completed her collection.

The final two designs were the best of her career.

She felt nearly restored, almost renewed, because inspiration had not come from within, but from without. From the two women she'd lost, symbolized in the two women she'd gained. Now, on this rainy afternoon, Sabine had the final two pieces that had eluded her. The war had stalled her creativity for only a while. Somewhere in the middle of the night, she'd made the decision to show her designs on a smaller scale, in her own salon, for a curated group of clients and reporters. That choice, along with her focus on herself instead of the masses, had opened the floodgates of her imagination. She'd beaten self-doubt. She'd won.

Smiling in satisfaction, she opened her eyes and climbed to her feet. A series of creaks sounded from her bones and caused her to limp across the room to her worktable. She fanned out the final two dresses and found tears welling. Her daughter and closest friend were both gone, but here in these sketches, they lived on. She traced the lines of the first design, past the cinched waistline, along the draping. Did the same with the second, noting the similarities, the differences, seeing the women of her past as they melded with the women in her present.

Nicolle and Paulette. They were part of this, as surely as Giselle and Hélène.

A quick glance at the clock warned of the day slipping away. Her girls would be breaking for the night. Some would make their way up to the attic to dress for dinner. The others would head home to their families. They would wonder when or even if the designs would be ready for their hands. Sabine would leave them waiting. Once Nicolle returned home, she would deliver the sketches. The showstoppers. War might be all around, but here was beauty. Here was the future of Maison de Ballard.

A knock on the door startled her. Another glance at the clock pulled her eyebrows so high they skimmed her hairline. She'd specifically requested not to be disturbed. Who would dare interrupt her creative time? Her girls, they knew better. There were no sounds of war, no bullets or warplanes. Then who?

A single glance through the peephole answered her question.

Sabine threw open the door to a very calm, unusually stoic Vivian Miller. Even in the pale light of the approaching dusk, caught in an unceasing drizzle, her hair was a thing of beauty, not a strand out of place. She was dressed in one of Sabine's designs, a true work of art, if she did say so herself, created solely for the American. The elegant draping, the minimal embellishment. She wore black gloves to complete the ensemble, while a smart hat with clean, crisp lines covered her head.

The only sign of her agitation showed in the lines around her eyes, thin as a spider's web, a visible warning of her dark mood. "Vivian?" They rarely met in Sabine's private domain. Rarely, as in never. "What is it? What has happened?"

"My hem has slipped." Even had Sabine not recognized the urgency in the other woman's tone, her words would have been enough to alert her to a serious concern. *My hem has slipped* was code for *We have a problem, assistance needed.*

"Come in."

"Thank you." The other woman pushed past her. Without breaking stride, she walked over to the wireless and switched it on with a fast flick of her wrist. "Let us catch up on the news out of Berlin."

Sabine tried to ignore the heavy German accent mutilating the French language and did as the other woman suggested. She listened to the broadcast and heard nothing but the usual propaganda, followed by another reminder that frequenting Jewish-owned establishments was cause for arrest. Another warning that handing out pamphlets for the Free French would not be tolerated. On and on and on. Clearly, there was nothing in the report she was meant to hear.

Something else, then. "What brings you out in the rain?"

She laughed, a joyless sound. "Is it raining? I hardly noticed."

"You have much on your mind and many obligations."

Another laugh. A heavy sigh. Then her eyes went blank, and she moved to look out the window. The hand that clutched the pane was bloodless, the knuckles bleached of color. "He expects me to be at his disposal, day or night."

He. She meant the Nazi. The SS officer who operated out of Drancy. She'd become the mistress to a powerful man in the Third Reich, also a cruel one, as evidenced by the loss of light in her once beautiful eyes. There were advantages to this unholy liaison. Information was gathered and then passed on to the Resistance. Countless lives were saved, but at a heavy cost to Vivian's soul. She hated the man—it would be hard not to—yet she let him court her. "You have chosen a difficult lie to live."

She gave a bitter laugh. "A lie that is not a lie." She turned to face Sabine, a look of self-disgust curling her lips into a morose pout. "He won that particular battle months ago, when he made me his mistress in deed as well as name."

"That does not make it any less difficult."

The rain outside filled the silence for the length of a heartbeat. "I fight with the weapons I am given. My looks. My skill as a hostess. These are valuable assets in a world where men of power see women like me as nothing more than a lapdog to be spoiled and petted." She spoke boldly, sullenly, with the eyes of a troubled soul.

Sabine had strong thoughts toward what many termed *horizontal collaborators*, women who indulged in affairs with Nazis to make their lives easier. Vivian Miller was one of them, and yet not at all. She'd entered a dangerous alliance to save innocent lives. Sabine understood the reasoning, the cost, the toll. She shared her own ugly entanglement with a monster, though she was only metaphorically in bed with him. Vivian could not say the same.

Lines of fatigue fanned around the American's mouth. The gaunt frame that had grown thinner in the past months presented Sabine's clothes to their best advantage but also meant her friend had lost even more weight. Too much for a woman in her fifties. "You're suffering."

She gave a very French shrug. "I have made my choices."

As had Sabine.

Moving to the worktable, Vivian picked up the top design. "This is good." A rare smile bloomed on her lips. "Very good. You have outdone yourself, my friend. You—"

A disembodied voice from the wireless cut her off. "It is no secret the Jews are liars and thieves. We know they are behind Bolshevism. Many have changed their names, dyed their hair, wishing to pass as Aryans. They are conniving, manipulative, and you must not be taken in by their evil ways."

"Idiots." Vivian shot a furious glare at the wireless, as if her outrage could slide through the airwaves and annihilate the speaker. "Hideous, awful men, every one of them. They think they will win this war."

"They are wrong."

"Yes." Their eyes met over the designs, Vivian's sharper than before. Harder. Determined. "They are wrong."

Resolve and purpose filled Sabine, followed by a sliver of anticipation. She took a breath and said, "Tell me why you are here."

Setting down the sketch, Vivian pushed away from the worktable and took to pacing the perimeter of the room. She completed a full circuit before coming to a stop in front of Sabine.

The woman frowned like there was a battle waging inside her. When she spoke, her voice was hardly above a sigh. "If I needed to coordinate a…trip for a friend or…" she paused "…two. I wonder. Where would I begin?"

Sabine reached out and rested her fingertips on the other woman's shoulder. "You would tell me something of the situation. And—" she glanced at the wireless, which now broadcasted flute music "—you would speak in the vaguest of terms."

There was a long stretch of silence as Sabine dropped her hand. She tried to read the other woman's expression, but she'd turned her head, giving only a profile for her to consider. "A woman of foreign birth and her French-born daughter wish to leave France. Traditional travel is not an option. I need to find an alternative quickly."

For the smallest of moments, Sabine's muscles went taut. Vivian was asking her to coordinate an escape for two women, at least one of them an immigrant, both of them Jews. Women, her mind repeated. A mother and daughter, ages unknown, but soon to be targeted for arrest by the French police.

"Is such a thing possible?" Her voice became cautious. "Can this be done?"

"It can," Sabine said. "To be more accurate, you have already begun the process. I would need to know a bit more. For instance, the date of this trip."

"As soon as possible."

The words came out with a weight Sabine wasn't expecting. She could appease, or she could give truth. "Matters such as these take time."

"How much time?"

"Hard to know. There are many moving parts that must be coordinated." She rattled them off in her mind. A route needed to be determined, a *passeur* chosen, documents acquired. "Perhaps two weeks." Train tickets had to be purchased, safe houses lined up. "It could be as long as a month. Are they currently safe?"

"I have been assured of this, yes. But, Sabine, I do not exaggerate when I say this must be done as soon as possible."

Sabine went to the window. Rain obstructed the view beyond the watery image of an old woman too tired to continue, too resolved to stop. "Their documents." Pivoting, she placed her own disturbing image at her back. "They are up to date?"

Vivian's expression became one of absolute resolve. "They will be soon."

"One other question." Sabine held the other woman's stare. "Will they be able to make a trip over rough terrain?"

Vivian hesitated, then gave a stubborn lift of her chin. "They will make it."

Her resolve was personal. "This one is important to you, more than the others."

"I have a duty to uphold, a debt to pay, so, *oui*, this is very important to me."

"I'll let you know when the plans are in place. You will need to get them to the rendezvous point, perhaps at a moment's notice. Will that be a problem?"

This time, the hesitation was longer, the silence thicker. *"Non."*

A beam of weak sunlight slid into the room, sun in the midst of rain, unusual and eerie. A bad omen. "I'll make the arrangements. Now you must go. No, not that way. Come with me."

She directed Vivian into the hall, then to the back stairwell. "Take these to the bottom level. There will be a door that will lead you into a dark passageway. Travel ten paces, then take a right out into an even darker corridor. Follow it to another door, into the alley. From there you will use the building as your guide, and—"

"Ah, my friend." Vivian patted Sabine's arm in a rare show of affection. "You need not go on. I am well acquainted with back alleys."

Sabine did not respond directly. She simply pulled the American into a brief hug, another rare occurrence between them. When she stepped back, they shared a look full of a hundred unspoken words. In that moment, Sabine feared she would never see her friend again. "Be careful, Vivian."

"What would be the fun in that?"

The joke fell flat. Sabine laughed anyway. *"Au revoir*, Vivian." *Goodbye until we meet again.*

"Au revoir, mon amie."

Sabine watched the door close behind the American, her lips clamped together in silent contemplation. Another rescue to plan with not enough time and limited resources. Not impossible. The network had a new safe house and a new escape route that had been tested twice in a matter of weeks. She smiled, pleased with herself, but it faded when she realized how quickly matters could change. A whisper in an ear, the leaking of a small piece of information, and the network would be compromised—again. Her stomach turned and twisted at the thought.

Then again, it went both ways.

A whisper in an ear, the leaking of a small piece of information could also give Sabine the advantage. Oh, yes, it was long past time to be proactive and hunt down a mole. She knew where to begin, at one of Marcel's parties. She knew when. Tonight. She even knew who to send. Paulette. She'd been faithful in her first test. The second would prove harder, but would ultimately reveal her true worth to the network.

Sabine would not send her in alone. That would be cruel and unnecessary. He would be there to receive the message, easiest that way, but he would know nothing of its contents until Paulette relayed the information. With only hours to prepare the girl, Sabine went to her closet and studied its contents. She would put Paulette in a beloved design made with motherly love.

Touching the smooth silk, she prayed he understood this was a test for the girl, not him. His reaction, Sabine could predict. It would not be pretty. Paulette's response was the unpredictable piece. Should she be the quick learner Nicolle claimed, with the courage and fortitude of her brave mother, there would be more duties to come, more responsibilities.

But first, the party.

Chapter Fifteen

Paulette

"Are you certain you want to do this, *chère*?" The words came from a surprisingly nervous Mademoiselle and were so completely out of character, Paulette took a moment to respond. Her employer's sudden reticence must have to do with some promise she'd made her mother and was completely unnecessary.

This was Paulette's chance to join the fight against tyranny. As she stared at her image in the full-length mirror in Mademoiselle's private apartment, she looked as ready as she felt. The timid seamstress was all but erased. There were no signs of the frivolous girl she'd once been, no hint of doubt. Only resolve in her eyes, commitment in her heart. "I want to do this."

"There will be very bad men at this party. Some of the women, also bad."

This was not the first time Mademoiselle had warned Paulette of the dangers she would find lurking inside Guy Marcel's home. Again, she wondered why her employer seemed uncertain about sending her to the party, when this was her idea. The guest list would include high-ranking Nazis and notorious French gangsters, true. There would also be dishonest policemen and dirty politicians and collaborators. And not one of them caused Paulette a moment of worry.

The last two years of her life had prepared her for tonight's party. "I have attended many of these types of parties. All of them held in my own home."

And always, always, at the insistence of the Nazi billeting there. Herr Hauptmann von Schmidt had been a true sycophant, wishing to impress his peers and men of higher rank with lavish parties and private dinners, many of which Friedrich had attended.

"Then this is the last we will speak of backing out."

"Agreed." Paulette studied her reflection, dressed in a sleek evening gown made of shimmering green silk plucked from her employer's own closet. The fit was astonishingly perfect. Paulette wondered over this, knowing she and the fashion designer were neither the same height nor build. She was taller, thinner, Mademoiselle shorter and fuller-figured.

A sigh sounded from behind her. "You look wonderful."

"It's the dress." It was remarkable, something otherworldly. "I feel invincible."

The other woman merely smiled. "These parties start early. Cocktails at five, hors d'oeuvres at six. Most of the guests will be far past sober before dinner at nine."

"Which is why I'm to arrive at five, before matters get too wild."

A fuller smile curved along Mademoiselle's lips. "Now, let me have a proper look at you."

Paulette stepped away from the mirror, turned, opened her arms, then did a slow, graceful twirl. "Will I do?"

"I think…" Mademoiselle covered her mouth with her hands. "I think you look like your mother."

She could not have paid Paulette a higher compliment. "I still miss her," she whispered. "So very much."

"Your mother is not gone. She is with you, always. I see her every day, living in your image and, more, in your heart."

"Why can I not feel her?"

Taking her shoulders, Mademoiselle spun Paulette back around to face the mirror. She moved in behind her, until their faces were cheek to cheek in their shared reflection. "She is here, if you pay attention. Close your eyes, *chère*, and you will hear her in the night air, in the sound of the rain hitting the Parisian streets. Open your eyes, and you will see her in the tilt of your chin. In the shape of your face, your smile. Look, Paulette. Look at yourself and see her."

Perhaps she was a version of her mother on the outside. On the inside, she was not as good. Not as strong. "I want to make her proud."

"Then remember her sacrifice. She knew what awaited her, but instead of crumbling, she prepared for your future. You are with me, here in Paris, because your mother planned it to be so. It was her idea, executed by your sister."

It's what Maman wanted. Despite Gabrielle's words, Paulette had thought her sister had been the one to orchestrate her banishment. But it had been their mother all along. Hélène had sent her to Paris to live with and learn from her most trusted friend. A dozen questions arose in Paulette's mind, but Mademoiselle had moved to another topic, adding instructions for her to follow.

She listened carefully, then recited the message she was to give to a person who would find her at a party full of Nazis, French gangsters and collaborators.

"The car will be here soon." What sort of car, she didn't say.

Paulette could not hold back from asking, "Who will be driving me to the party?"

The question received a careless wave. "He is nobody. A goon. Do not speak to him. Do not make eye contact."

At this, Paulette felt the first stirrings of fear. "Should I be afraid of this man?"

This earned her a faster, vague flick of Mademoiselle's wrist. "*Non*, he won't hurt you. He is not that clever, nor that stupid. This is not something to be concerned over. Now, sit." She guided Paulette to a dressing table littered with pots and jars and several crystal atomizers. "Rouge your cheeks. Kohl your eyes. While I pull your hair into an elegant chignon."

As she opened pots and sniffed at jars, she tried one more time to discover the name of her contact. "Who did you say is to be the recipient of the message?"

"I didn't say. He will find you."

He. A man. Why could it not have been a woman?

At the door, Mademoiselle had one final request. "I seek a specific date, sometime in this month or possibly the next, certainly soon."

"Will there be an event attached to this date?"

"You ask the right question." Mademoiselle dropped her voice to a whisper. "Listen for any discussion about another roundup, one not yet executed."

Paulette's heart slammed against her ribs. Another roundup was coming, more mass arrests, countless lives lost. She was still digesting her shock when Mademoiselle, clearly finished with her, yanked open the door and nudged her out into the hallway. "Now go."

"You have no other instructions for me?"

"I do not, except this. *Bonne chance*, Paulette."

Her mouth opened to respond, but already Mademoiselle had shut the door, leaving her alone in the darkened corridor. There was nothing to be done but put on her gloves and descend to the bottom of the building.

A thousand thoughts collided in her mind. Paulette had been

charged with watching rather than being watched. Observing rather than being observed. Except now she was supposed to seek out a specific piece of information that could save lives. She could not do that from the shadows. She would have to mingle and possibly even speak to the other guests.

Did she still have the skills to charm a room full of strangers? Paulette wasn't sure. She hadn't done so well with her fellow seamstresses. Other than Nicolle, most still treated her with suspicion, some with contempt. Tonight's party would be another important step to beginning anew. From this point forward, she would become two people. A humble seamstress working to earn her way at a famous fashion house. And a stronger, braver version of her former self, no longer a girl, but a woman who knew how to harness her female attributes to full advantage.

You can do this, Paulette. The words were whispered in her head, in a voice that sounded very much like her mother's.

As Mademoiselle promised, a car waited for her outside the atelier. A large white Bentley she'd seen before, the night she and Nicolle had sat on the roof. Tapping into the confident ingenue of the past, she settled in the back seat, her dress spread out to prevent creasing.

The driver didn't speak to her. He didn't even glance at her as he put the car in gear and pulled away. The journey was blessedly short. In case she should need to make her own way home, Paulette paid close attention to the street names, the outdoor cafés and other businesses, even the buildings themselves. Not long after turning onto Rue Lauriston, the car drew to a stop. Paulette helped herself out onto the sidewalk with no assistance from the man behind the wheel.

The party was in full swing. She could hear the music and laughter from the street. The door was opened before she could knock. A man stood before her, legs spread, feet planted as if he were a gatekeeper of a medieval castle. Barrel-chested and built like a military tank, there was a hint of cruelty lurking under the thin veil of servitude. He was half-covered in shadow, as if he were sculpted from the darkness itself.

Alarm bells went off in her head, and she had to hold back a shiver of revulsion. There was not a hint of approval in his black gaze, but no leer, either. Then why, she wondered, did she feel so…exposed? He didn't question her being here. He simply said, "The party is on the top floor," then added as he stepped aside to let her pass, "Take the stairs to your right."

She'd barely mounted the first step when something that sounded like a scream punctuated the air. Or was that some sort of twisted laughter? No, there had been fear in the sound. And it had come from below, not above. Another shiver worked its way up her spine. What sort of home was this, where laughter and screams mingled?

Trying to steady herself, she placed her hand on the black lacquered banister and continued her climb. One flight, two, a final third. She hurried across each landing, noting how the music grew louder. American jazz, a tune she didn't recognize or particularly like. There was no melody, just a lot of disjointed notes strung together.

Pausing at the entryway of what appeared to be a grand ball-room, she took in the assembled crowd. She recognized none of the men and women, and yet she knew them. This was her world, or rather her former world. They were in constant motion, moving in and out of groups like stylish waves rolling on the seashore. Women in their long shimmering dresses, men in their pristine white dinner jackets and black bow ties. Their smiles seemed strained, their laughter a little too loud, and Paulette sighed at the thin coating of cheerfulness.

Mingle, she told herself. *Make friends.*

Not likely, but she moved deeper into the room. Almost immediately, a woman caught her attention. Yes, over there, by a potted plant, she stood conversing with a rather ordinary man. He had a glint in his eyes she'd seen in others, more leer than masculine interest, and she was instantly reminded of von Schmidt. The Nazi on the train to Paris.

Friedrich.

She thought she might be sick.

Mingle.

It would help if Nicolle was with her, but her friend had her own responsibilities, and this was Paulette's job. In a world she knew well. She paused only long enough to pluck a glass of champagne off a silver tray. She never once lost sight of the woman. She stood in profile, a cigarette in one hand, a glass of champagne in the other. Something in her countenance wasn't right, as if she were playing at sophistication rather than it coming from within. Paulette had seen her share of women like that, false and ordinary, thinking they were more.

The woman turned. Paulette went hot, then cold, then hot again. Cheeks aflame, she automatically slipped into the shadows, then wondered if she was overreacting. The woman could be her contact. But no. Mademoiselle had said *he*. Besides, she could have told her assistant the message in one of their morning meetings.

No, Geneviève Durand was not Paulette's contact.

She continued scanning the room, cataloging the guests. The sheen of elegance was all wrong, a veneer covering something dark and ugly. Mademoiselle had been right. These were not good people, and Paulette was far, far out of her league. She also had a reason for being here.

Mingle.

Stepping out of the shadows, she moved into the crowd, knowing she should avoid gaining Geneviève's notice.

At once, she felt as if she'd stepped into a farce. The forced laughter, the pseudo gaiety, the nod to decadence in the clothing, the conversations. Did these people not know there was a war on? Had they not lost loved ones? Had they not heard of the roundups and the death camps?

Did they not suffer rationing? She took a sip of champagne and knew it at once. The 1919 from her family's own cellars.

A movement caught her attention. Paulette snapped her head in that direction, and her breath clogged in her throat. Her heart slammed against her ribs as she watched the man weave in and out of groups, smooth as smoke despite the limp. She recognized him at once. Though she'd barely had a glimpse of him at the atelier, she remembered the dark eyes, dark hair, and that face. The face of a poet, with sculpted cheekbones and a strong chin, a perfect complement to the lean, athletic build. He surveyed the room with an intensity Paulette remembered, his gaze brushing over men and women without much interest.

He looked good in evening attire. Too good. And Paulette did not like the way her pulse picked up speed or how her mouth went dry. He was the quintessential handsome stranger, directly connected to Mademoiselle, and…he was her contact.

She hoped she was wrong. Oh, please, let her be wrong. Disaster had struck her in the form of a handsome stranger once before. *Mingle*, she told herself a third time, again wishing Nicolle was here. The other woman was strong and capable, but so was Paulette.

Watch and listen.

She could do neither if she continued gaping at the man. Legs shaking, she went back into motion, deliberately, carefully, not looking behind, only ahead, eyes on the opposite side of the room. Oh, but the urge was strong to cast a glance in his direction.

He was exactly as she remembered. The strong features. Those wide, muscular shoulders. The intense brown eyes. The hair, that was different. A shade nearly as black as a raven's feather, it was trimmed and combed, both neat and expertly tousled at the same time. A professional job.

No ordinary Frenchman could afford the cost of a barber's expertise nowadays. Reason enough to find the man suspect.

Who, exactly, was he, and what, exactly, was his relationship to Mademoiselle?

Others took note of his arrival. "That's Philippe Rochon."

Rochon. Paulette knew the name, though she couldn't remember how. She searched her memory. Rochon. Rochon. Of course. The glassmakers, specializing in crystal perfume bottles. Her mother had at least a dozen in her boudoir.

More whispers floated on the air. She approached a pack of women huddled closely together. They spoke in rapid, hushed voices, in a language Paulette had grown to hate. German. The women were German, probably office workers or wives of diplomats, and they were gossiping about Rochon. Occasional pauses accompanied their swift glances in his direction.

He paid them no attention. He'd seen Paulette and now held her gaze in a wholly impolite manner. She welcomed his interest like a cold rush of biting air on her bare skin. Moving slower now, seeking a column, a shadow, anything to hide behind, she passed another group of women. These were younger, clearly French, their manner more sophisticated than the Germans. But that wasn't saying much. "I hear he dabbles in the black market."

So the man was a gangster.

Paulette was not surprised.

"I hear he does more than dabble." More glances were tossed in Rochon's direction, including Paulette's.

"He does have the look of a pirate about him." More glances, a few heartfelt sighs. Then one of them said, "I'd willingly be his captive."

The others enthusiastically agreed, their manner turning bawdy and mildly vulgar.

Paulette shook her head, dismissing them as easily as Rochon had dismissed her at their first meeting. She knew men like him. Reserved. Brooding. Which was really only code for callous and unfeeling. The complete opposite of Friedrich, who'd been engaging, romantic, full of smiles and soft words and compliments. This was a point in Rochon's favor.

And still, she trusted him even less than a Nazi.

"He was married once, to a ballet dancer. I hear she died in some sort of tragic accident."

Paulette had barely had time to register this new bit of information when the man went on the move. In her direction. She nearly bobbled the champagne as he made his way to her casually, a stern sort of look on his face. She didn't move, couldn't move. Men had always been drawn to her, their attraction intense and obvious, which had given her all the power. But she had no power in this situation. Rochon was not the same as the others. He was not attracted to her. He was angry and unimpressed, as if she were a chore that must be endured.

Pausing beside her, he wasted no effort on pleasantries. "Where did you get that dress?"

His anger was thick and real. An unmistakable tension coated the air. She'd offended him, in ways she couldn't understand. "I... I... Mademoiselle Sabine." She was babbling. "She chose my attire."

Recognition came and went in his eyes. "You are the new girl."

The impatient tone was hard to miss, as was his condescension. It was as if he could see past her facade, to the smoldering guilt of her soul, the truest, ugliest part of her. Suddenly, Paulette had had enough of being judged and misunderstood by her fellow seamstresses. Mademoiselle's clients. This man. "I am Paulette." She worked to keep her voice level. "Paulette Leblanc."

He did not appear impressed. He opened his mouth, but then his expression softened ever so slightly, as if understanding dawned. "I knew your mother. She was a special woman."

Paulette hadn't expected that admission, and her response came as quickly as her accelerated heartbeat. "She was."

A quiet understanding passed between them. There, then gone. Replaced with an odd look in his eyes. He took her measure again, his jaw set, and she could see his mind calculating, his gaze full of thoughts as intricate and tangled as a spider's web. "How old are you?"

"Twenty." Her birthday had come and gone two weeks ago, and she hadn't thought to mark the date. No one had.

"Mademoiselle gave you this dress to wear tonight?" Something in his tone warned her to tread carefully.

"It is from her personal closet." Which still confused her, as much as it seemed to confuse Rochon. Only in his case, the bafflement had a layer of shock. Or possibly outrage. Certainly anger. "I've offended you."

"Not you. Mademoiselle." His voice was flat, his gaze mild, and both were at odds with his mood, because now there was a strong hint of sadness threaded inside the anger. "The dress belonged to my wife."

Chapter Sixteen

Nicolle

Nicolle opened her eyes and let out a deep, weary sigh. She'd fallen asleep in André's office chair, her head resting on his desk. It was a dangerous luxury she could ill afford. Any number of bad things could have happened while she slept.

The sound of a lock giving way jolted her upright. A creak of hinges, and in strode André. He shut the door behind him with a soft click, then spun the lock back in place. An added precaution, she knew, as it had been when he'd left. Yet it felt odd to be in this room, filled with his scent and his personal possessions. She watched his approach, eyes hooked with hers. There it was again, that sense that he saw her as she was, deep inside her marrow, where even Julien hadn't looked.

The sensation was not altogether unpleasant, and that somehow felt wrong, like a betrayal. She took a deep breath, held it in her lungs for several beats, then let it go in a rush of air. There was no reason to feel uncomfortable. This was André, her friend. Nevertheless, when he flashed a fleeting smile as fast and as brilliant as a lightning strike, she scrambled to her feet.

"Did you get some rest?"

"I did."

"Good to hear." The smile came again. "You'll be wanting to depart soon. The shift change at the checkpoint is in less than an hour."

"Thank you. And André…" Still holding his gaze, she moved around the desk, aware of her tattered attire. Mademoiselle's idea. Clothing could just as easily make a woman disappear as stand out. "What you're doing for your neighbors, it's important."

"As is what you do." He reached for her. As his strong fingers closed over hers, she felt a moment of peace so strong she feared her knees would give way. "Please know you can come to me anytime, day or night. No matter the weather or the circumstance. My home is your home. I will never ask questions."

"That was quite a speech."

He inclined his head, a glimmer of amusement in his eyes. "I have been known to make them. Julien always said I was too verbose for my own good."

The mention of her husband made heat spread across her cheeks. "Your offer is for him, for Julien."

"For you." He squeezed her hands. "My offer is for you."

His arresting eyes settled on her face with such intensity she wanted to look away. She couldn't. She was too compelled, too mesmerized. A hot burning began in the backs of her eyes, making her sniff lightly. She blinked, cleared her throat. "*Merci*, André."

He took a breath. She did the same. Looking down at their joined hands, at her fingers where calluses had grown from the needlework, she saw how well they fit together. "Do you carry a weapon, Chloe?"

The way he said her name. It was too intimate, too personal, as if the world had stopped revolving around the sun and it was only the two of them on earth. "Nicolle. I am Nicolle now."

"All right, *Nicolle*. Answer my question."

She adopted the same uncompromising tone. "No, *André*. I don't carry a weapon. Well, actually, I do. Right here." She wiggled her fingers. "Ten of them, to be precise."

He didn't smile. "I meant something other than your hands."

"Ah. Well, then, no. And don't glare at me like that. It's insulting. I am not without skills. I know how to defend myself." In theory. She'd never had to test her skills, learned in a brief tutorial from Mademoiselle's son-in-law before her first rescue mission.

André shoved his hands in his pockets and gave her a thorough once-over, as if assessing her size and weight as he would one of his unruly patients. "We are at war, Chloe, Nicolle, whatever you call yourself. The enemy does not think twice about harming civilians who threaten their efforts to stamp out our freedom, and that includes women."

He wasn't wrong.

"I cannot allow you to leave my home unarmed."

"You did before."

He heaved a sigh. "My mistake, one I won't be repeating. Come with me."

"André, I don't think—" She was talking to his back.

At the door, he glanced over his shoulder. He said nothing, only frowned, then motioned for her to follow him into the hallway.

She trotted after him and soon found herself in the animal clinic where he'd stitched up the wounded airman. There was a distinct antiseptic odor, as if he'd taken the time to clean away any unpleasant scent left by the various animals he'd examined that morning. The last time they'd been in this room, she hadn't asked about his practice. She did so now. "Do you only treat household pets?"

"I travel to local farms as well."

Hence the fresh produce, milk, and home-baked bread he'd provided earlier.

Mouth set, he opened a drawer, moved around the contents. She dropped her gaze to his neck, to that patch of skin just above his shirt collar. Warmth stole up her cheeks, and she had to avert her gaze to gather her bearings. When she looked back, he was holding a thin metal instrument with a short blade at one end. "What…what's that?"

"A scalpel. In a hospital or clinic like this, its purpose is to make incisions, most often during surgery. In war, it's an elegant, deadly weapon due to the small, extremely sharp blade."

She took a step forward. "It's quite thin."

"Lightweight, too, which makes it easy to conceal. Here, see for yourself." With a flick of his wrist, he presented the instrument, handle first. "Go on. Take it."

Careful to avoid the blade, she did as he requested, testing the weight in her hand. Sturdy and almost weightless. Perfect for a woman like herself, one with small hands and unused to wielding a tool meant specifically to slice open another human's flesh. She tried to give the instrument back.

André shook his head. "I want you to keep it."

Impossible. Too dangerous. "I wouldn't know how to use it."

"I'll teach you." She started to argue, but he held up a hand. "Julien would want you armed."

And so began her first lesson in close combat with a weapon.

"You will want to come from behind." He bent his knees, lowering until he was eye level with her. "The position and angle matter. Do you understand?"

Her gaze skipped around the room, her insides churning. "I understand."

"Patience is your greatest ally. Wait for the opportune time to strike. Resist showing him your weapon."

Him. She tried not to shiver at the image that popped in

her mind. A Nazi soldier, in a back alley or over rough terrain, murderous intent in his eyes.

"Your goal is to move quickly and strike fast." Nicolle watched as he took the scalpel from her, set it down, and picked up a pencil, turning the blunt end toward her. "Pretend this is the blade."

"All right."

"Watch carefully." He spun her around to face the lone mirror in the room and moved to stand behind her, his eyes dark and intense in the low light. There was at least eight inches difference in their height. He literally towered over her, and she could hear her heartbeat in her ears.

"Do not hesitate. Commit fully, and remember." His left arm came up and snaked around her neck. "Move fast, strike hard. Your goal is the heart. You get there by sliding the blade through the tender flesh between the fourth and fifth ribs, here." He pressed the pencil into her side. "Make sure to go deep. The blade will do the rest."

Her eyes went wide. "That's it? That's all I have to do?"

"That's all."

She hadn't known killing another human being could be so quick and easy. She began to shake with the knowledge, and she thought, hoped, prayed the lesson was over.

It was not.

André's arm wrapped tighter around her throat. "Do not release your opponent until you've made the cut and pushed the blade in deep. Keep him close until you know you hit the mark."

"How long before he's dead?"

"Not immediately. The punctured heart will eventually drown itself." He removed the pencil from her torso and finally—finally—let her go. "Your turn."

She didn't want to stand behind him, didn't want to embrace his neck or feel his heart beat against hers. "André," she whispered, her mind racing for a way out of this exercise. "I can't imagine a scenario where I would need to use a deadly weapon."

It was a lie. She could picture a thousand.

"You think I would give you a weapon without you knowing precisely how to use it?" He spun her around to face him, his eyes hot, his breathing sporadic. "Do you think it doesn't scare me, knowing you are out there somewhere, taking risks, moving through woods and checkpoints, without sufficient protection?"

He was clearly angry. Well, so was she.

"How many times must I tell you? I *know* how to protect myself."

He proved her wrong with a single move. She'd been standing one moment. She was on the ground the next. He hadn't hurt her, cushioning her fall with his own hands. But now he was hovering over her, eyes fathomless, and she thought she might expire from mortification. Her pulse picked up speed. Her vision blurred. What was happening to her? The answer was there, then gone, leaked from her mind like water through her splayed fingers. She blinked, just once, and was back on her feet as quickly as she'd found herself on her back.

"How...how do you know these things?"

He ignored the question. The muted light of the gray afternoon gave his face an ashen hue. He, too, was breathing hard, his gaze darting around erratically. But when he spoke, his voice was steady. "Now, show me how to use a scalpel to kill a man."

They went through the process several times, then found a quiet moment to say goodbye before retrieving Basia and Jacob from the basement. There weren't many words exchanged, just a very long look full of meaning and a promise on both ends to stay safe, "until we meet again."

Thirty minutes later, Nicolle was standing in line at the checkpoint with a remarkably calm Basia and a rather stoic

Jacob. The time in the basement had brought them some level of peace with their situation.

The three of them joined the queue at the checkpoint behind a girl on a bicycle and a family of four. Two guards stood with guns slung over their shoulders. They were, as she'd predicted, visibly tired, as was the dog sitting on his haunches and panting miserably in the heat. A third guard checked identity cards and free movement passes, the latter harder to get than the former.

When he asked for their names in a bored tone, Nicolle stepped up and handed over her papers first. "I am Callie Napier."

He consulted her identity card, then glanced at her face, then turned his attention to the free movement pass. "What is your business in the Free Zone, Mademoiselle Napier?"

"My sister's wedding. I am to be her bridesmaid. This is my dress." She gave him an ironic smile and lifted the garment bag she'd brought from the atelier. If he looked inside, he would find several dresses, including an ugly, frothy concoction no self-respecting woman would choose for herself.

He didn't look. He simply handed back her papers and told her she was free to go. Basia and Jacob had a similarly easy time posing as her cousins. They, too, were free to go.

They traveled by train to Périgueux, where Nicolle would hand them off to the next *passeur*. The café was full. German soldiers dominated the space with a few exceptions. Elderly French men stared into their half-empty coffee cups. A few shady-looking characters sat in the shadows surveying the area with beady, intense eyes. But it was the young women that held Nicolle's attention. They sat at tables with the enemy, their expressions desperate, as if willing to do anything to feed their families. Some of them, too many, appeared to enjoy their companions, despite the enemy uniform, perhaps even because of it.

Nicolle could not bear the sight of any of it. She purchased three cups of watered-down coffee and escorted the newlyweds to a table outside. Despite the thickness in the humid air, others sat outside as well. She noted each one. A businessman reading the newspaper. A group of four well-dressed ladies chattering not-so-kindly about their friend who was not present. A mother and her child.

Satisfied none were a threat, she guided the newlyweds to a table beneath a striped awning that appeared new. It was hard not to think about where the money came from to fund a fixture so blatantly unnecessary. Money that could have been spent on a starving child's dinner or a pair of shoes for an elderly woman. Defeat fluttered in her stomach, souring with each glance at that green-and-white eyesore.

Averting her gaze, Nicolle tracked the activity on the street. The first few minutes were the most crucial, when the odds of detection were at their highest. Newcomers were always conspicuous. She slipped her hand into the pocket of her coat, deep, all the way to the seam, where the scalpel rested, deadly tip facing down, a small metal cap covering the blade. André's lessons were still fresh in her mind as she touched the handle. The cold steel brought an odd sort of comfort and hardened her resolve to finish this mission strong.

Unlike her usual refugees, Basia and Jacob would not return to the skies to fight the enemy. They would escape the country altogether and live to see another day. A lifetime of days. And wasn't that vanquishing the enemy as surely as a fighter put back into the sky? Wasn't a Jewish couple making Jewish babies the most gratifying of all strikes against the Germans?

She checked the time on her wristwatch. The *passeur* was late. Only by a few minutes, but with each delay came another chance of discovery.

Glancing at the couple, she saw her nerves reflected in their wandering eyes. "Try to look happy," she told them under her breath. "Bend your heads together and whisper softly."

"What should we say?"

"Anything, anything at all."

They moved in close, their foreheads touching. Two becoming one. The image reminded Nicolle of the moment André leaned in to her to whisper final instructions. He'd also produced a name, a woman in Périgueux should things go wrong. Margarete. And now Nicolle couldn't shake the image of a beautiful Frenchwoman receiving an intimate lesson in scalpel combat. André leaning down to whisper in her ear. Nicolle forced her thoughts clear. She didn't want these feelings running through her.

Julien. She whispered his name in her head. *Julien. Julien.*

Any second she would pull his image from her memory. His beautiful face would form, and Nicolle would know a sense of calm. If she could see him one more time, even in her mind, she would find her balance and ignore the confusion creeping into her heart.

Basia's tentative voice broke through her thoughts. "I have a favor to ask. Will you check on my sister and mother? They still live in our family's apartment." She rattled off an address near the Paris suburb of Montmartre. "Tell them I am happy and safe. I don't wish for them to worry."

"I'll check on them myself as soon as I arrive in Paris. It will be my first stop."

"*Merci.* You are a good friend."

She started to respond, but a movement to her right caught her eye. A woman strolled to their table and sat. She barely spared a glance at the newlyweds, her attention reserved solely for Nicolle. She wore a smart beret, a coat that had seen better days, and, most importantly, a blue scarf around her neck identifying herself as a *passeur*. Once their eyes met, she quickly removed the scrap of silk and stuffed it in the pocket of her shabby coat.

The girl was impossibly young. Fourteen, possibly fifteen, with the look of an old woman in her pale, slightly feral green eyes, a cat who'd run through several of her nine lives, but not all of them. This was not the girl's first time on an escape.

Without ceremony, she gave the coded greeting. "It's a lovely day for a walk."

Not at all. The heat was unbearable, but these were the words Mademoiselle had decided upon, as well as Nicolle's response. "Quite lovely."

For the next few minutes, they spoke a series of nonsensical pleasantries. The weather was the main topic. Rationing next. The conversation seemed endless, until finally it was time to separate. Nicolle wanted to feel relieved, but she knew Basia personally. They'd worked side by side for nearly two years.

Maybe if she stood and simply left the café, their parting would be easier.

Maybe if she thought about her brief stop in Limoges, her stomach would settle. But then she thought of her last escape, and the near miss in Moulins, and her instincts reared. Her blood hummed. Nicolle must have shown her suspicion, because the girl touched her hand. "I am the same as you."

A thousand unspoken words passed between them. Something like relief settled inside her and, as planned, she stood first. The other three followed her lead. They left the café together. Two blocks later, they separated. No farewells, no promises to see one another again. Just a subtle change in direction and four became three, with one now alone.

Nicolle retraced her steps, moving quickly toward the train station. A car coughed and wheezed to life. A dog barked in the distance. A baby wailed from the building on her left. She let the sounds of a typical day in a lovely French village wash over her. She didn't look back. Not once. The future lay ahead, not behind.

Next stop, Moulins.

Chapter Seventeen

Paulette

Paulette had no idea how long she stared at Rochon or he at her. There was a hollow quality in his eyes. *Haunted* was the word that came to mind. *The dress belonged to my wife.* How could she have known? No wonder he'd been offended. She was offended on his behalf. "Your wife was…"

"Mademoiselle's daughter."

Paulette wanted to respond. The words were there, forming in her mind, rising up in her throat, but they seemed to flee from her head when she looked into Rochon's eyes and saw the fury. No, not fury. Something deeper. A sort of angry grief.

Why would Mademoiselle toy with his emotions like this? There seemed to be no good explanation, and now Paulette was left with a choice that wasn't really a choice. She could keep staring or walk away. Both seemed cruel. "I saw her dance once. In *Swan Lake*." Giselle's Odile, the black swan, had been bold and dangerous. But also beautiful. Paulette had been inspired, charged with a bursting energy to do something great with her life. Something bigger than herself. "She was magnificent."

"She was, in every ballet she performed." His face contorted with raw pain, and a spreading realization filled Paulette. This was a man who'd loved and lost in a way she could never understand. Her own heartache over Friedrich seemed shallow and childish. A schoolgirl's silly infatuation.

"I'm sorry for your loss." The words were simple and true, and seemed to upset him more.

Rochon's eyes clouded over. He was the very essence of her own misery and grief.

Shyly, Paulette touched his hand. A mere brush of fingertips across knuckles. "I can't understand why Mademoiselle would wish to torment you in this manner. I've never known her to be cruel."

His flinty eyes betrayed little emotion now, only quiet resignation. "She warned me. She said I would know you by your dress. I had not thought she would be so heavy-handed."

Paulette replayed her recent conversation with Mademoiselle in her mind. When she'd asked about her contact, the designer had been vague, only saying: *He will find you.* Clearly, she'd been equally cryptic with her son-in-law. But why not tell him the message herself? Why this complicated meeting? "I'm sorry."

"I believe you are." He looked about to say something more, something profound, but another man approached them, and everything in him went hard. Maybe even a bit mean.

Not an ounce of softness left. More warrior than man.

She sensed layers in Philippe Rochon. He'd once loved deeply. That required a heart. But parts of him contained darkness. He was a black-marketeer, after all. And he was here, in this house, mingling with women who gossiped behind their hands. Socializing with Nazis and French gangsters, like the one who stopped before them and leered at her.

A wave of revulsion washed through her. That smile, those

eyes, they reminded her of a snake. He addressed Philippe first, in a shockingly high-pitched voice that was completely at odds with the inflexible features on an extraordinarily plain face. "Rochon."

"Marcel."

So. This was the infamous Guy Marcel, the host of the party. He was also the same man she'd seen speaking with Geneviève earlier. Paulette took him in, recognizing the cut and fit of his perfectly tailored suit. Mademoiselle's fingerprints were all over that garment. And now Marcel was staring at her again. Paulette knew that look. She also knew the malice lurking beneath.

Eyes still on hers, he clapped Rochon on the back. "My good man, you've been holding out on me. Who is this lovely creature you keep to yourself?"

Rochon's eyes flicked over the whole of the other man. "A friend."

"Does this friend have a name?" Marcel asked the question of Paulette, his eyes moving slowly down her body, all the way to her toes and back up again.

There'd been a time when she would have ignored the brazen perusal. That time had passed. No longer would she allow a man to make her feel dirty or ashamed. Rochon must have had a similar thought, because he attempted to step in front of her, as if to shield her.

Paulette wanted nothing of a man's protection. That time had also passed. "I am Paulette Fouché-Leblanc. My family is in the business of making the champagne you have chosen to serve your guests tonight." She held up her glass in a silent toast, all smiles and thinly veiled disdain. "The 1919 was an inspired choice."

She felt the rage growing inside her, bubbling to the surface like the golden liquid in her glass. Marcel dared to serve one of the rarest vintages from her family's cellars that was not for sale to the general public. Oh, yes, Paulette knew what she held in her hand. She'd paid attention to the conversations between her sister and grandmother. The knowledge had been inside her for years, baked into her soul.

"Well, well, well. What do you know, Rochon, we have an aristocrat among us."

He was laughing at her, and Rochon was no happier than Paulette. She could feel his ire as he took the champagne glass from her hand, set it aside, and, again, attempted to move in front of her. Paulette was faster, shifting in the opposite direction and, unfortunately, closer to the man with the voice of a woman and the eyes of a viper. She started to speak.

In this, Rochon was quicker. "Excuse us, Marcel. Paulette and I have another pressing engagement at my private residence." His voice was all insinuation, as if they were off to indulge in a naughty tryst. "We don't want to be late, now do we, *chérie*?"

She was too shocked at the unexpected tenderness in the endearment to respond.

As Rochon had clearly wanted, Marcel seemed to apply a carnal meaning to their departure. "Ah, yes, I see. I see. You landed a sweet little morsel for yourself. Well done, my good man." Another clap on the back. "Well done."

Rochon could have responded in a number of ways, many of them violent, but he proved a man of remarkable restraint. He nodded, then began guiding Paulette through the room quickly. Despite the slight limp, he moved smoothly across the floor. It was really something to behold and…no, no. She would not be impressed. In many ways, most ways, he was as bad as Marcel. Maybe worse.

He was a thief. A black-marketeer. And the man could move when he put his mind to it. Well, so could Paulette. She kept pace with his long strides. They took the stairs in a coordinated rhythm. It wasn't until they reached the first landing that she realized what he was doing. "Wait just a minute. Stop, Rochon. I mean it. Slow down."

When he kept moving, she pulled them both to a halt, heart palpating in her throat. "I can't leave the party yet."

His eyes narrowed. "Can't or won't?"

A wafer-thin distinction that had only one truthful answer. "Both."

He sighed. "You came to give me a message, is that correct?"

"Well, yes."

"Then we go outside where there are no eyes or ears waiting to intercept."

The man was being difficult. He had to know she would be speaking in code. She'd opened her mouth to make this rather obvious point when two large, burly men dressed in head-to-toe black shoved past her, sending her tumbling into Rochon. He steadied her and, with his arms still around her waist, they glanced after the two men. Who were actually three. She'd missed the third one.

Shoving away from Rochon, Paulette hurried to the banister to get a better look. The trio continued descending. This was why she was here, after all, to watch and gather information.

Her unwitting assailants did indeed flank a third man. The shabby suit he wore had seen better days a decade ago. As if he sensed her eyes on him, he looked directly at her. His gaze was unfocused and wild with fear. "Are they throwing him out?"

"No."

Rochon seemed certain, which helped her not at all. She continued leaning forward and lost sight of the trio completely. She bent a little more at the waist, craned her neck, and was rewarded for her efforts when she saw the three men on the bottom floor. They went in the opposite direction of the front door and—

Rochon yanked her away from the banister, saving her from a nasty tumble. "Where are they taking him?"

Silence.

"Do you know?"

More silence.

"Rochon—"

"No questions, Paulette. You didn't see anything in this house, absolutely nothing."

His voice was low and menacing, and that was one angry man gripping her arm. "You're scaring me."

"Good. I meant to. Now…" He slid his hands down her arms, released one of her wrists but kept hold of the other. "We're leaving."

He didn't loosen his grip until they arrived on the first floor. Taking advantage, she tugged free and glared at him. "I can't leave. I must discover—"

"Stop. Talking."

"But—"

"Not another word." He looked pointedly at the butler, who was not really a butler. He was watching them too intently. Apparently, Paulette was not the only person gathering information from the party guests. "It's a lovely evening for a walk," Rochon said, rather loudly. "Don't you agree, *chérie*?"

Of course, it was a lovely evening for a walk. This was Paris in the summertime. The heat of the day had vanished, the sky was clear, and she'd made a grave error. Rochon was taking command again, marching her through the foyer.

Over the threshold.

Out into the night air.

"You," she sputtered. "I…" The door shut behind them with a bang, and she nearly jumped out of her skin. How had she let herself be finessed so completely? She felt her shoulders slump. "Mademoiselle will be so disappointed in me."

"Maybe not. Maybe you heard what you needed to hear."

Except that she hadn't. The gossip had included not a single mention of a date and certainly nothing about another mass arrest of Jews. "I must go back in there." Although the prospect of interacting with Guy Marcel brought nothing but revulsion. "I have a job to do."

"Admirable, but foolish."

"Did you just call me a fool?"

"I would add prickly, too."

The man was full of insults, and not exactly wrong. She'd been called both before, usually by her sister. As if she were speaking to Gabrielle, Paulette snapped out her response. "I prefer to think of myself as tough and resilient."

A smile appeared, not condescending but actually genuine, and his face was instantly transformed into something handsome and rather roguish. "You are those things as well. You handled Marcel quite masterfully."

"I…oh." Had he just complimented her? "Thank you, I think."

Moving quickly, Rochon pulled her into the shadows just as two white Bentleys roared past, each carrying a well-dressed man and a giggling young woman. The same car that had brought her to the party, times two. Another followed at a slower pace, with Marcel and a lone woman in the back seat. One Bentley per couple seemed wildly unnecessary. "How many of those does he own?"

"At least a dozen."

"That's obscene."

Rochon didn't disagree.

She continued watching the large white Bentleys as they squealed around the corner. "Where are they going in such a hurry?"

"A nightclub."

That surprised her. "It's rather early."

"Not for Marcel. He enjoys a decadent lifestyle."

That did *not* surprise Paulette.

A lazy breeze was making itself known, and Rochon reached

for her hand. His hold was light, his touch soft. Anyone look-ing at them would see a couple fascinated with each other. It was a ruse, and yet she felt her heart do a fast little skip. "All right, Paulette." He said her name with quiet affection. "Tell me the message from Mademoiselle."

Right, the message. The reason he held her hand and looked into her eyes like a long-lost lover. She wet her lips with the tip of her tongue, then rattled off the strange assortment of words and phrases. "Two croissants, one éclair. Track OTP. No delays." She took a breath. "Odette to Brontë, alterations complete. New customer secured. One final stop for porcelain."

A long beat of silence stretched between them.

"Well?" she asked. "Did you hear me?"

"I heard you." He shifted a little, his gaze dropping over her face. Even though the sky was dark, she caught the slight tick at his jaw. "I only wonder why she couldn't tell me this herself. Unless…hmm. Yes, I think I understand."

"At least one of us does," she muttered.

The door opened again, and several men and women stum-bled out onto the sidewalk. The sight of the drunken group reminded Paulette she still had a second task to complete. It wasn't too late. The night was young. The hors d'oeuvres hadn't been circulated yet. She could still go back inside.

Her body turned and surprise, surprise, Rochon stopped her with a single word. *"Non."*

The ominous tone in his voice sent a shiver up her spine, like nails on a chalkboard. "Why not?"

"This is not a place for someone like you."

"Someone like me?"

"An innocent."

She nearly laughed at that. "I have attended parties before. Many similar to this one."

"I find that hard to believe."

"Mademoiselle would not have sent me here, on my own, if she thought I could not handle myself."

"You aren't alone, Paulette. You were never alone. I've been with you since the moment you stepped into the ballroom."

That couldn't be true. He'd been visibly upset. At her. No, not her. The dress. Rochon had been taken aback by what she wore. And that meant Mademoiselle had indeed sent him to watch over her.

Insulted, again, she stared up at him. She stared and stared. And he stared right back, his shoulders straight and incredibly wide, made wider by the tapered waist and lean hips.

"Do you know about the second task Mademoiselle gave me?"

He frowned. "Mademoiselle told me nothing about a second task."

"I go back inside. And before you start issuing threats and gloomy warnings, I can go in there alone, or you may join me. Your choice."

His eyes took on a hooded expression, and she thought she saw a sort of grudging respect in their depths. By offering him a choice, even a superfluous one, Paulette had taken back a portion of control. "With me," he said, surprising neither of them. "You go in with me."

"I thought you might say that." Smiling, she patted his arm in a way that earned her a cold, hard glare, which only managed to make her feel more confident and very much like her old self. She actually fluttered her eyelashes at him.

And received a very masculine sigh.

"Let us be off." This time, she took his hand.

The butler lifted his eyebrows at their return. They both ignored him and climbed to the fourth floor, hand in hand. At the ballroom's entrance, she released her hold and glanced his way. "We should probably separate."

"Not a chance." He offered his arm and escorted her into the social equivalent of shark-infested waters.

It took nearly an hour for Rochon to relax enough for Paulette to make her break, with the excuse of needing to visit *les toilettes*. Once there, she sat in front of the mirror and took a much-needed breather. The man was relentless in his refusal to leave her side. She would think it sweet, and maybe it was, but she couldn't focus with him so close. He was so very big and impossibly male and mysterious and…no. She was not going down this road again. She was not falling victim to a man with a handsome face and a mouth full of lies. To be fair, Philippe Rochon was no Friedrich. But he was not a good man, either. He worked in the dark and made friends with Nazis and French gangsters.

The door burst open, and two giggling women spilled into the room. Paulette quickly opened her purse, took out a compact, and pretended to powder her nose. A wasted effort. The intruders paid her no attention but for a fleeting glance. She swallowed her anxieties and studied them in the mirror of her compact.

They wore evening gowns that looked a bit cheap, one in bright blue silk, the other in strips of gold satin that almost passed for a dress. Both women were pretty, if a bit hard, and each spoke German, a language Paulette knew not nearly well enough. She could count to twenty and, thanks to Friedrich, recite a handful of endearments.

She swept the powder puff over her nose and nearly gave up, but then she heard the mention of an important prison in French history—the Bastille—followed by the German word for Jew, *Jude*. Disgusted glares came next, accompanied by what Paulette sensed were very unflattering words, including *Schwein*.

When Blue Silk said *Polizei*, the hair on the back of Paulette's neck rose to attention.

France celebrated the storming of the Bastille in July. The day of celebration was officially called Le 14 Juillet. The connection could not be random. But the women were still talking, arguing it would seem. Blue Silk was adamant, continually repeating the German word for fourteen. *Vierzehn*. Gold Satin offered up several *nein, nein, neins*, then a stream of unintelligible words, something about French outrage—at least, that's what she assumed it meant—followed by *fünfzehn*. Fifteen.

They could be discussing a tourist trip to the famous prison. But what if it was something to do with the roundups?

She must get this information to Mademoiselle. With slow, deliberate steps, she left *les toilettes*. Rochon was waiting for her in the hallway. Eyes locked with his, she asked, "Do you have access to a motorcar?"

"I do."

Good. This was good. She forced herself to speak calmly. "I need you to take me to Mademoiselle at once."

Chapter Eighteen

Sabine

Sabine opened her apartment door in response to the rapid, impatient knocking that could only belong to a man. A very exasperated man, she concluded, as she took in the sight of her scowling son-in-law standing beside an exceptionally tense Paulette. Sabine hadn't expected the two to arrive together, though she probably should have. Philippe might have become hard and cynical over the past few years, but he was still decent at his core. He would never leave a young woman in Marcel's company, or allow her to travel the Paris streets alone at night.

She'd been wise to throw the two together, and not just to protect her friend's daughter. Her initial decision to send the girl to the party had been a good one. That anxious look on her face. The slight shaking. She'd watched and listened. "You have a date for me."

"I do. I…" She glanced at Philippe, then back at Sabine. Giving one quick shake of her head, she said nothing more. Evidently, the girl didn't want to speak in front of a man whose loyalties she had yet to determine for herself.

More proof Sabine had been right to send Paulette into Marcel's lair.

"What were you thinking, Sabine?" This from Philippe as he strode into the apartment ahead of Paulette, who entered at a more sedate pace, her eyes assessing her surroundings with sweeping glances. She had the look of her mother tonight, not only in her physical appearance, but in her regal posture and the graceful way she moved. How she watched Philippe, with female wariness, was all hers. A young woman coming into her own who was not so gullible anymore.

"Well, Sabine? Have you no answer for me?"

She switched on the wireless, then pretended utter confusion. "I'm sure I don't know what you mean."

Although, in truth, she knew exactly what he meant. Philippe rarely showed his anger, and only when it came to matters of Giselle.

"Don't play coy. You put her in my wife's dress." He made a vague gesture in Paulette's direction. "Badly done, and completely unnecessary. I would have known the girl had you put her in any of your signature designs."

Fair point. "I may have overstepped."

"May have?" He roared the question as his feet propelled him into the small sitting room off the foyer. He roamed the cramped space like a hungry lion seeking prey. The limp was more pronounced at this hour, but did nothing to stall his progress. That was one frustrated, unhappy man.

"All right, yes," she admitted. "I overstepped." And she was only half-sorry for it. She'd gotten his attention, hadn't she? As no phone call or coded message had been able to do for weeks. Now he was in her apartment, and they could finally have that overdue discussion about the changes she wished to make in the network.

A few that involved Paulette.

Sabine noted the embarrassment in the girl's wide, steady gaze. Another unexpected consequence of her underhanded tactic to make a point. She'd used Paulette like an expendable pawn. Philippe was right. Badly done. "I'm sorry for putting you in the middle of this, Paulette. That was not my intention."

"Wasn't it?" And now Sabine had two unhappy, frustrated individuals in her home. Paulette, the bigger surprise.

If Hélène were here, she'd be terribly proud of her daughter. This was no spoiled child. The show of strength was an added point in the girl's favor. "Not in the way you think."

And that was the end of Sabine defending her actions. Time was running out for Parisian Jews. Everything else was a distraction. She twisted the knob on the wireless, increasing its volume. "Tell what you've learned."

Paulette looked taken aback. Her eyes slid to Philippe, brushed over his face, then returned to Sabine. "You are certain you want me to do so here?" Another glance at Philippe. "Now?"

"You may speak freely in front of my son-in-law. He is heavily involved in the network."

He'd stopped pacing and was eyeing Paulette with interest. Silence had fallen over the girl. Seconds might have passed, or longer, but eventually she took a deep breath, exhaled through her nose, and presented what she'd discovered at Marcel's. "I heard two German women speaking in *les toilettes*. I don't have a strong command of the language, but I'm quite certain they mentioned the Bastille and two specific days in July."

"Two?" Sabine had not expected that extensive an operation.

"There seemed to be a bit of confusion over which was the more important day, the fourteenth or the fifteenth. But then, the woman with the stronger personality insisted on the fifteenth. She mentioned something about French outrage."

So. Marcel had been telling the truth. The mass arrests

would occur on or near the day France celebrated the unity of her people. There would be no open celebrations on the fourteenth—the Germans had stopped those—but there would be recognition that day. All while the French police systematically planned a mass arrest of Jewish women and children.

"Sabine, I'm talking to you."

She startled at Philippe's voice. "Give me a moment. I need to think." What could she do with this information? What could any of them do except try to save as many souls as possible? They didn't have much time, and she was wasting too much of it in her head. In quick, concise terms, she explained the situation to her son-in-law. Her voice was clear and precise, carefully under control. Throughout her explanation, his expression never changed. Not once.

"You knew about this," she accused, unsure why he hadn't shared the information.

"I've heard rumblings, mostly among the Germans, not the French, and nothing concrete. It seems your protégé has been more successful in gathering information from a pair of gossiping Fräuleins than I have been from my contacts in German military intelligence." He sounded a bit perplexed, but the smile he gave Paulette held a large dose of respect.

That was interesting. Philippe respected very few, and trusted even fewer.

"It seems I have underestimated you," he told Paulette, his smile still in place. "Something tells me I am not the first."

"No, you are not."

"Do not lose that quality. It will serve the network well."

Paulette nodded, and now she was the one smiling. As she should. Philippe had given the girl his official stamp of approval. Sabine was proud of them both. Each had conquered something inside them tonight. Something that had kept them from fully embracing life without the ones they'd lost. But this wasn't about them and even less about Sabine.

"We have to do something, Philippe."

He went back on the move. "What can we do? If your information is correct, this roundup will be a large, coordinated effort. Thousands of arrests will occur in a single day, or perhaps two. We don't have the resources to stop it."

Nevertheless. "We have to do something," she repeated. "We cannot sit on this information and do nothing."

He went to Paulette and paused before her. A silent moment passed between them, a quiet understanding. The connection was unexpected and distracted Sabine momentarily. Somehow, it didn't hurt to witness their bond. Tentative and new, but there all the same, an invisible tether. Deep down, Sabine had known they would relate on a personal level and no, it did not hurt as much as it should.

"How certain are you about what you heard, Paulette?" The way her son-in-law said the girl's name held the kind of patience he'd abandoned years ago. "Think hard before you answer."

Her hesitation was the length of a single heartbeat. "I am confident I heard three very distinct words." She ticked them off on her fingers. "Bastille, fourteen, and fifteen. As to their connection to a specific event, I cannot give you a clear answer."

"I appreciate your candor." He considered her a moment longer, and then, as if coming to a decision, turned his attention back to Sabine. "Even if you are right about this roundup, we are not set up to rescue civilians. We ferry physically fit young men who are trained for warfare and have the skills to travel over rough terrain."

A knot of helplessness twisted in her stomach. "Yet we made an exception for Basia and her husband, for reasons you know well."

"They aren't safely out of France yet."

"We have to try, Philippe. We cannot sit on this information. Too many innocent lives are at stake."

"Let's not get ahead of ourselves. We aren't even sure there will be another roundup. And besides." He took out a cigarette as if he would light it, then pocketed it again. "How would we choose which lives to save? What makes one soul more worthy than another?"

It was a moral question with no good answer. Sabine thought of Vivian's unexpected visit that afternoon. "Perhaps it is not a choice of worth but of opportunity."

"You have someone in mind."

"A mother and daughter. Their travel papers are already secured." Assuming Vivian had been telling the truth. "We would only have to determine the route, coordinate transportation, and choose the *passeurs*."

"None of which are simple matters, especially in the time frame we've been given."

Sabine thought of all the Jews she'd known in her lifetime. The rich ones, like Naomi and Abraham Lindon, the poor ones, the hardworking ones. The exceptional, the ordinary. "We have to do this, Philippe."

"Je sais." He rubbed at his chin, stippled with the beginnings of a day-old beard. He looked resigned, and not wholly in agreement with her. So when he said, "Let me look into it," Sabine had but one response.

"Thank you."

"Do not thank me yet. This is out of our purview, Sabine. I can give you no guarantees." He headed for the door, yanked it open. "I'll be in touch in a day or two."

He left with only a cursory goodbye to her and a nod to Paulette.

He'd barely disappeared when the girl was offering her assistance. "Tell me what I can do, Mademoiselle."

"You've done much already. You uncovered the date."

"I don't think I did. I…no." She shook her head. "I didn't." Her gaze darkened with purpose. "I will go back to the party and determine if the arrests will begin on the fourteenth or fifteenth. I can do this, Mademoiselle. Please, let me try."

Sabine smiled at her friend's daughter. Paulette was proving a rare young woman. Capable, determined, motivated. But returning to the party was not a good idea. Nor was it necessary. "I have the information I need. You may go to bed knowing your actions tonight have saved lives."

Sabine would make it so.

"You are certain there is nothing more I can do?"

"Go to bed, Paulette. I need you rested and ready to work in the morning." She took the girl in her arms, kissed each of her cheeks, and smiled softly. "Garments, as you know, do not sew themselves."

She smiled a little at that. "You are certain I've done all I can?"

"For tonight, very."

"Très bien." She turned to leave. At the door, she paused, looked down at herself, spun back around. "I forgot to tell you I saw your assistant at the party."

A string of thoughts rushed through her brain, none of them good. "Geneviève was at the party? You are sure?"

"It was definitely her."

Geneviève. Her trusted ally, at least here at the fashion house, or rather, in the salon. Sabine tried to reach the place where she could feel surprise, but she'd passed that point years ago. All she could feel was relief that she'd kept her assistant ignorant of her Resistance work.

"She was speaking with Guy Marcel. Their heads were bent close together, as if they were sharing secrets. I thought at first she was my contact. But you told me it would be a man."

Geneviève and Marcel, when had they met? Had she been the one to introduce them? Sabine tried to remember. But all she could hear was a low, rhythmic knocking in her head. A warning, telling her Paulette had uncovered important information. The knocking grew louder, and Paulette wasn't through hitting her with difficult words to swallow.

"The dress. It belonged to your daughter. You will want it back, surely."

A day ago, yes. Sabine would have demanded Paulette return Giselle's dress before leaving the apartment. Her heart was not in the same place, not when it pertained to her daughter. It was as if a switch had been turned on and her burden was lighter, her soul not so empty, and this young woman had much to do with the transformation. "The dress is yours, *ma chère fille*. It is my gift to you for a job well done. There will be no arguing over this."

Paulette nodded solemnly. "Thank you, Mademoiselle. Every time I step into this dress, it will be in honor of the magnificent Giselle."

An apt description of Sabine's brave daughter. Her heart swelled. All this emotion, it was too much. "Yes, yes, do go and get some rest."

"*Bonne nuit*, Mademoiselle."

"Good night, Paulette."

Sabine worked through the night, not on her art, but on the ramifications of a liaison between Geneviève and Marcel. She would like to think it meant nothing, but that would be irresponsible. At 3:00 a.m., she came to the decision to keep a very close eye on her assistant. In the meantime, there were lives that needed saving, specifically a mother and a daughter.

Setting aside thoughts of Geneviève, Sabine worked on a training program that would prepare Paulette should she be needed as a *passeur*. Nicolle was the better choice, but Sabine preferred having more than one option whenever possible.

At sunrise, she dressed for another day. Too tired to eat, she swallowed down a piece of dry toast and weak tea anyway, then made her way downstairs. She'd barely entered the workroom when Marie Claire intercepted her progress. "There is a man waiting for you in your office."

Philippe had worked fast. Perhaps too fast. He'd hit a snag. She did not want to hear his bad news. "Tell my son-in-law I will be there shortly."

"It's not Monsieur Rochon." Marie Claire lowered her voice. "It's that ugly man who insists you sew his suits with your own hands."

Marcel. Guy Marcel had come to her this morning. After a party where he'd been seen in secretive conversation with one of Sabine's trusted employees. This could not be a coincidence. "Do you know what he wants?"

"He didn't say."

"Thank you. I'll see him now." She hurried to her office. The door had been left ajar. The sound of drawers opening and shutting again told her Marcel was rummaging through her belongings. Her suspicions were confirmed when she crossed the threshold and saw him studying a stack of invoices. She said his name. He looked up, grinning, as if he cared little that she'd come upon him snooping. "Marcel," she said again. "I don't believe we had an appointment."

Setting the papers down, he rounded the desk. "Ah, Sabine. Business partners such as ourselves need not make appointments."

He was not her business partner. He was a necessary evil and a cruel man. Helping a cruel man succeed was not noble or good or even right. She would have much to answer for when this war was over. "I do not have time for games. What do you want?"

His eyes glinted with something malicious. "It has come to my attention that your newest collection is still incomplete."

A flare of irritation sparked. This man, whom she detested, should not have this information, wrong as it was. The real question was: How? How did he know anything about her collection beyond what she'd told him herself? He couldn't know.

Unless...the mole was inside her own atelier. A woman came immediately to mind. "Your information is out-of-date. My collection is complete."

His grin had a cruel edge to it now. "So brave. So bold. It will be your undoing, this pride of yours."

Said the cat to the mouse. She held his gaze, saying nothing. A charged silence filled the space between them. She saw his mind working frantically, wondering if he'd made a mistake, if his information was wrong. It had happened before. This man was not infallible.

His gaze suddenly cleared, as if a veil had been lifted, and then he clapped his hands together, slowly, with two entire seconds between each loud clasp and release. "You lie so well. A heroic effort, truly, but for one fatal error on your part. You have not delivered the final designs to your team."

"You know this, how?"

He gave a careless flick of his wrist. "I have my sources."

Sources. He meant Geneviève. Or maybe not. Sabine opened her mouth, clamped it shut, and her mind worked fast, arranging names with faces. Geneviève, others, any of them a traitor. Or was this Marcel being a thug as usual? He was not creative or especially clever. He was probably bluffing. But then, why would he care if her collection was complete? "What do you want?"

To his credit, he didn't pretend confusion, confirming her suspicions. "I want you to include my friend's designs in your fashion show."

Well. That was unexpected. Apparently, she was still capable of being surprised. Marcel had never pushed himself into her business for the sake of one of his paramours. She tried to hide her reaction, then decided, why bother? It would not change her answer. "No. I will not do this."

"You will, Sabine." With startling speed, he closed the distance between them. Up close, he was a great mass of middle-aged flab and sweat.

His fingers locked on her arm, so deep she felt them skim bone. "Let me go."

He did, surprising her yet again. "You will include several of her designs in your show."

"Or what?"

His expression transformed into something base. "Or you will witness, firsthand, what goes on in the basement of my home."

His threat transported her soul into the darkest of places. The fiend was threatening her with a trip to the bowels of his building, where he and his fellow thugs applied torture for the SS, the Gestapo, and their own ugly purposes.

No one came out whole from a trip to that chamber of horrors.

Sabine shivered and had to look away to find her balance. She was not a young woman. She would not survive Marcel's brand of torture. "One dress. I will include one dress designed by your...*friend*."

"Two."

"One." She held firm, knowing a show of strength was her only recourse in the face of such evil. "And I will choose the garment myself from her portfolio. That is my offer, Guy. My only offer." She lifted her chin and held his ugly, evil gaze. "It's a fair deal, one I suggest you take."

"Always the savvy businesswoman, eh, Mademoiselle."

She stood as straight and calm as she could, her heart hammering. "To the bitter end."

A flicker of something unpleasant passed over his face. He wanted to continue negotiating—the blackmailing, lying, cheating swine—but he must have seen her resolve. "You drive a hard bargain. She will present her portfolio this afternoon."

"Not in the atelier," Sabine said quickly, not wanting anyone to know about this wicked deal. "In my apartment. Twelve o'clock, sharp."

The knock came at exactly noon. Sabine walked into the foyer of her apartment, as Marie Antoinette had walked to the guillotine, her head high, shoulders back, her spirit not yet beaten. Her bravado wanted to disappear at the door. She would not give in to such weakness. A twist of her wrist, a squeak of hinges, and her world crushed at her feet.

The woman at her door was not young. She was not innocent. And none of the rules Sabine had set for this meeting applied. "Come in, Geneviève."

She nearly choked on the words. This woman, who Sabine had elevated to the second most important position in her fashion house, had gone to a known gangster and let him push his weight around on her behalf. It was the wrong move—she should have come to Sabine herself—and revealed a certain lack of character.

Geneviève had betrayed all Sabine had given her. But was she the mole?

Chapter Nineteen

Nicolle

The extra time Mademoiselle offered Nicolle made visiting her son a fait accompli. Spending an entire afternoon with Jules was a wonderful prospect—for her. But would it be good for him? He seemed to love playing with her on the floor with his blocks, or listening to her read fairy tales, or dancing with her while she sang a silly tune. Even sitting on her lap brought him pleasure, as did the little stuffed bears she gave him. But the moment he realized she was leaving always brought suffering.

His cries and whimpers broke her heart.

Was it worth it, putting them both through that agony so she could kiss his baby cheek one more time, or place his little hands in hers, or smell his powdery scent?

She wished she knew the answer.

Somewhere in the distance, church bells rang. She pictured herself missing the train to Limoges and hurried her steps. Not too fast. Not too slow. The trick to avoiding notice was somewhere in the middle, applying just the right amount of French indifference. The Germans had no use for a bored, sullen, over-worked Frenchwoman.

That's what Nicolle told herself when she arrived at La Gare de Périgueux unnoticed. The train station wasn't much to look at, just a two-story building fashioned in a style much like Nicolle herself, neither small nor large, not especially bold or pretentious. Just a sturdy, necessary structure made up of solid angles, a few rounded curves, and no frills.

The train to Limoges was waiting at the platform. Nicolle purchased her ticket, climbed aboard, and took her seat. The compartment was only half full, which suited her just fine. Fewer people meant fewer attempts at conversation. The lack of German soldiers was an added bonus.

As hoped, the journey proved uneventful, until the train stopped a mile outside of Limoges and the passengers were in-structed to exit for a random examination of credentials. The makeshift checkpoint was nothing more than a flimsy table manned by three German officials. Two were soldiers. The other wore a dark suit.

Nicolle took her place in the middle of the line, not under-standing why she was suddenly nervous. She'd been through this drill a hundred times. It was nearly her turn. She would present her actual identity card with confidence, knowing the lies read as truth.

She *was* Nicolle Cadieux. She *did* live in Paris and worked for a well-known fashion designer. She'd come to the Free Zone to deliver garments to several of Mademoiselle's special clients.

Nothing to hide, she reminded herself, yet she approached the table with her pulse roaring in her ears. The sound over-whelmed the hisses and groans from the train. The soldier thrust out his hand. "Papers."

So cold, so demanding, so German. The uniform wasn't even SS. He was just a regular soldier in the Wehrmacht. Impossibly young, yet already drunk on power. What would the world look like if the enemy won this war and rude, arrogant boys walked among them?

"Papers," he repeated, his eyes narrowing over her face, as if he enjoyed intimidating hardworking, ordinary Frenchwomen. Best, she decided, to play her role.

She presented her identity card with the blank stare of the vanquished. The soldier took his time studying her information. When he looked up, his expression was full of German suspicion. "Where do you live?"

Keep it simple. "Paris."

"Where in Paris?"

She took a quick inhale and said, "Maison de Ballard," then recited the atelier's address.

More questions followed. More answers given. Then, at last, she was back in possession of her identity card and allowed to reclaim her seat on the train. Once all passengers had been processed, a whistle blew, metal scraped against metal, and the train jerked into motion. The entire nerve-racking experience had taken less than fifteen minutes.

It was midafternoon when the train drew up to a stop at the main railway station in Limoges, France. Gare de Limoges-Bénédictins was much grander than the one in Périgueux with more German soldiers in residence. The distinction between the Occupied and Free Zones was becoming more blurred by the day.

Her senses heightened, Nicolle gathered her belongings, including the gift she'd brought for Jules. The weather had taken a blustery turn, but at least the rain had moved to the east.

Clutching the tiny bear in one hand, the garment bag in another, she leaned into the wind and traveled along a circuitous route that followed the river Vienne. Limoges was a lovely city, but would not have been her first choice to hide her child. It was too far from Paris. But Mademoiselle had found a young Catholic couple willing to harbor a Jewish child. Louis Lavigne worked as an accountant at the famous porcelain factory. His wife spent her days running their tidy household and raising Jules as her own son.

It grated every time Nicolle heard her son call the other woman *Maman*. A small price to pay for his safety. She turned the final corner just as a burst of golden light bathed the house down the lane. The two-hundred-year-old structure was charming in every way. The lawn was perfectly manicured, the rosebushes neatly trimmed. There was a willow tree, a sturdy oak, and even a tidy vegetable garden that Monique Lavigne tended with her own hands.

This was Jules's home, where he lived the life Nicolle could not provide for him herself. Squaring her shoulders, she knocked on the front door. Monique greeted her with a smile on her young, pretty face. "Nicolle, how lovely to see you."

The warm greeting should have comforted her. A wave of resentment came instead. This woman, with her kind smile and sweet nature, was raising Nicolle's son. In a world free of death and pain, she reminded herself. That mattered. A lot. "I have brought the dress you ordered from Mademoiselle."

"How wonderful." Still smiling, Monique escorted Nicolle to a sunny parlor that overlooked the expansive backyard.

They went through the motions of a normal dress delivery, the garment payment for her kindness. When the fitting was over and the dress was back on its hanger, Nicolle asked, "Can I see him now?"

"I'm so sorry." Regret filled her expression. "I just put him down for his afternoon nap before you arrived. Would you like me to wake him?"

Nicolle felt a fresh surge of resentment. Monique put her son down for naps. She fed him, bathed him, and Nicolle wanted those moments for herself. "No. I…no." She shook her head. "No. Don't wake him. Let him sleep a little longer."

In a show of solidarity, Monique touched her hand. "I know how hard this is for you."

She couldn't possibly.

"Come with me." Moments later, Nicolle stood shoulder to shoulder with the other woman, just inside the threshold of her son's bedroom. Her heart filled with love so powerful she feared it might burst in her chest.

Her beautiful baby boy lay on his side, eyes closed, his arm roped around the bear she'd brought on her last visit. Her stomach gave a hard flip, and suddenly her chest hurt even more. Everything hurt. Her son had her coloring and Julien's sandy-blond hair. He was the sum of their parts. It wasn't fair that she couldn't raise him herself. She tore her gaze away and glanced around the room, taking note of the other bears.

A blind panic filled her throat. Those toys were all her son had of her.

Monique's arm came around her waist, and she pulled Nicolle in close. "He adores your visits."

The woman was being especially tender, and it did nothing to ease her pain. It was as if she stood between two worlds, one of flesh and blood, the other fashioned from dreams, the two divided by a glass wall, unbreakable, impenetrable. A sudden fatigue washed over her, and she swayed on her feet.

"You're exhausted. Come back into the parlor." Nicolle had neither the energy nor the wherewithal to resist the suggestion. "Sit. Let me get you some tea."

Tea. What a normal, reasonable activity.

"You'll feel better."

Not waiting for a response, Monique left Nicolle in the fancy room by herself. Alone, she took a cursory glance around at her immaculate surroundings. So clean. Nothing out of place. Order and stability. Comfort and security. These were the things she'd dreamed of for her son.

But this wasn't a dream. It was real.

Did she take this from him, when the weapons were finally laid down?

Children were resilient, she reminded herself. Nicolle was his biological mother. But Monique was the woman he called *Maman*. She gave him love.

Nicolle was just the lady who brought him stuffed bears. She wanted to cry. But Monique returned and went through the ritual of serving her tea, as if they were living in another time, another world. She drank the warm liquid and engaged in small talk as she waited for her son to awaken.

Half an hour passed. Then a familiar laugh had her snapping her eyes in the direction of his room, then back to Monique.

"He's awake," they said in tandem. Nicolle reached for the gift she'd brought, then paused. "May I?"

"Of course."

Hurrying now, she let the sound of toddler babbling guide her. She was rewarded with another baby giggle, and her heart leaped into her throat. Such joy in her son's little voice.

At the edge of the room, her feet ground to a halt. The sight of her child gave her a strange feeling in the pit of her stomach. Perhaps it was the way he sat in his crib, talking incoherently to his bear. His first best friend. It was such a wondrous, beautiful scene. Nicolle leafed through her emotions, love, joy, hope, then set them all aside and said, "Hello, darling."

She heard the wonder in her voice, felt it expand in her heart. Then Jules looked up and smiled directly at her. Restraint shattered. Calm vanished. Longing came fast and hard. Ignoring the stab of pain, she moved to stand next to his crib. "Who do you have there?"

With one chubby arm, he lifted the bear high over his head. *"Nounours!"*

"I've brought *ton ours* a friend."

She lifted her boy from the crib, careful to include his bear. He kicked and giggled in her hands, such a sweet baby, and smiled broadly. She knew that smile. It had once belonged to her, before death had come into her life. Setting him on the ground, she set the new bear beside the old one. *"L'ours!"*

Grinning, Jules crawled into her lap, a bear in each hand, and she thought, *This is where I belong. With my son in my arms.* She lowered her cheek to the crown of his head, breathed in his clean scent. The smell washed away all her sadness and she knew, from experience, this unspeakable joy would be replaced with melancholy once she returned to Paris.

She didn't want to go back to war and responsibility. She'd already missed every milestone in her son's life. The first time he rolled from his back to his belly. His first steps, his first words. If she survived this war, Nicolle would take him away from France and share other firsts with him. His first bicycle. His first crush on a girl.

It was not meant to be yet. Someday, she promised herself. In the meantime, he must remain in this home, living as a French Catholic.

The visit lasted another two hours. Nicolle helped feed Jules and stayed for his bath and suffered a horrible first with her son. He didn't cry when she told him she had to leave. At the door, Monique hugged her hard. "Be careful, Nicolle. We live in dangerous times."

And this woman protected her son from the worst of the threat.

Due to a delayed train and a mix-up with her ticket that had required a bit of sorting out with the conductor, Nicolle arrived in Paris past curfew. This was a first she was glad her son would never experience, in a world where being a Jew meant persecution. And now her mind was on Basia, and the promise she'd made the young woman. Nicolle could not fulfill her vow. Unless she made herself one with the dark.

Which she would have to do anyway, if she wished to get

back to the atelier tonight without notice. Keeping her word would require nothing more than a slight detour.

Decision made, she took the long way home, moving from shadow to shadow, avenue to avenue, neighborhood to neighborhood. The voices of German patrols carried over the concrete arteries, filling her ears and skating across her skin.

At last, she turned onto Rue Rochechouart and arrived at the address Basia had given her. The interior of the building was unnaturally silent, eerie even, as she made the climb up the two flights of stairs to the third floor.

The light was dim in the hallway, but so dark that Nicolle couldn't see to the other end, where one door, just one, stood wide open. The smell of rotten cabbage and a hint of brine drew her forward and into the Berman apartment. A thorough investigation of each room told her the awful truth. Basia's mother and sister were gone. Arrested? Or in hiding? She prayed for the latter and traveled back into the night.

Caution drove her deeper into the shadows, even as her mind wanted to dwell on her failure. Or maybe not a failure. She would never know. Her feet kept moving. Her mind kept whirring. She didn't remember entering the atelier, or climbing the back stairs, but she must have moved quickly because she now stood inside the attic, taking inventory. Three of her roommates slept in their beds. The fourth was missing. The slit in the dormer window sent Nicolle to the roof. She found Paulette sitting under the moon and stars, her mother's shawl around her shoulders, her knees drawn up to her chin.

Nicolle sat beside her.

Paulette turned her head. "You're sad. Something has upset you."

She attempted a swallow, but it was too late. The schism in her heart. The fracture. It could not be closed. Paulette had a similar sorrow about her. "I could say the same of you."

"I am always sad and upset. This war is ugly and unpredictable. Terrible things happen all the time. Mothers go missing. Husbands die too young. Jews get rounded up."

"Yes," Nicolle agreed. "Terrible things happen all the time. But there are some working to make things better."

She went thoughtful. "The world desperately needs better."

"It does."

"Let us find some of that better now. You are home at last, Nicolle. You are safe and unharmed, and we are both a little less alone." She linked their arms together, pulling her close with the same tenderness as Monique had displayed. "I'm so very glad you're back."

It took her mind a moment to make sense of the emotions running through her, the gratitude. "You were worried about me?"

"I was."

Nicolle blinked into the inky night. Paulette cared about her. Despite her efforts to keep herself separate and apart, she'd gained a friend. A real friend, who'd worried about her.

"I think I have it figured out." Paulette's gaze went up to the sky, as if she were trying to examine the moon and stars. "Where you go with the garment bags."

Nicolle attempted another swallow. This time, it went down without maiming her lungs, but still hurt a bit going down. "I deliver special orders on Mademoiselle's behalf to her clients in the Free Zone."

"You escort Jews out of France. No, don't deny it." Her gaze settled on Nicolle's face. "I have done my job, you see. I have watched and listened. Maybe I was not meant to know quite so much, but I was given coded messages to recite that weren't so hard to crack. One to Basia's in-laws, the other to Philippe Rochon."

Nicolle shook her head, more in confusion than denial. "I don't escort Jews out of France." She heard her voice echo oddly in the night air. "Or rather, not usually. Usually, it's downed airmen or escaped Allied POWs."

"I knew it." She looked back to the sky. "You save lives, while I dress in fancy evening gowns and attend parties."

"Parties? What parties?"

"At Guy Marcel's. He throws them nearly every night. I go to watch and listen for anything that can help the network succeed. I have attended two already, with a third scheduled for tomorrow night."

It made sense, pulling Paulette into the network this way. She would easily move among Marcel's rich and famous friends. But the career criminal also invited all sorts of German scum into his home, and Paulette was still so young. "You go to these affairs alone?"

Paulette made a face. "Mademoiselle sends Philippe Rochon to watch over me. It's rather humiliating, certainly unnecessary, but I understand. I am the daughter of her dearest friend, the only thing she has left of my mother. It is enough to make her worry."

"This is not a bad thing, Paulette. Mademoiselle is a strong ally to have on your side, as is Rochon."

"I don't disagree."

"But…?"

"But nothing. Except…" She straightened the shawl around her shoulders a little self-consciously. "Mademoiselle will probably tell you this herself."

"Tell me what?"

Paulette moved her hands to her knees. The gesture did nothing to hide their shaking. "We think there is to be another roundup, the largest yet." She turned solemn eyes in Nicolle's direction. "We don't know when, exactly. Oh, Nicolle, it's terrible. Thousands of Jews are slotted for arrest, most of them women and children."

It couldn't be true. But Paulette would not make something like this up, and Nicolle needed to think. "Have the French authorities been made known of this?"

"They are the ones in charge."

Mon Dieu.

"Mademoiselle and Rochon are attempting to rescue as many people as possible, but with the time constraints and no exact date in mind, they can only hope to get them into hiding."

"Even that will prove difficult." There were too many Jews left in Paris and too much indifference over their plight among the French. "This terrible thing can't be stopped, can it?"

"No."

Mon Dieu, she thought again. Paris was about to descend into complete darkness, and there was little they could do but watch the lights go out.

Chapter Twenty

Paulette

"My collection is complete."

Paulette blinked at the announcement, more than a little confused. She'd anticipated some sort of profound revelation, something macabre and terrible. After all, Mademoiselle looked not quite herself. Her eyes were red-rimmed and drooping with fatigue. Her skin had taken on a grayish, sickly pallor. Even her signature *clap, clap, clap* had lacked enthusiasm.

"We will show the designs in the salon, with a select group of clients and reporters. We will do this on Le 14 Juillet. We are, after all, a French fashion house, and we will honor our heritage on our most important holiday."

This earned another round of applause and cheers that stole any chance of hearing the rest of what Mademoiselle had to say, something about adding an additional design, something different from her usual. Paulette's shoulders knotted. She understood why Mademoiselle had chosen such a significant date to

show her designs. It was a silent rebellion against their occupiers. But it didn't feel right, celebrating a new collection so
close to the day thousands of women and children were to be
arrested, detained, and ultimately deported.

She could hardly watch her coworkers as they smiled and ap-
plauded and cheered. She definitely couldn't look at Mademoiselle. She wanted to yell at these silly women, getting caught
in something so frivolous when lives were at stake.

As if sensing the direction of her thoughts, Nicolle leaned in
close to her ear. "Do not judge them too harshly."

"I wasn't—"

"You were. Remember, Paulette, they don't know what they
don't know." Patting her arm, Nicolle sat back with a sort of
sisterly lift of her eyebrows, and sometimes, in moments like
these, the other woman was just a little too much like Gabrielle.

The frown she presented her friend felt all too familiar, as did
the surly tone when she spoke. "But *I* know. And you know.
And Mademoiselle knows. Yet she carries on as if this is just
another day."

"It *is* another day, and an important one at that." She spoke
in whispers now that the cheers were settling into excited chatter. "The business of creating fashion must continue."

She understood this. Of course she did. In theory. "It seems,
I don't know, excessive. An affront to what is coming."

"There you are wrong. If Maison de Ballard does not produce new designs, clients will look to another fashion house
for their wardrobes. Dresses will not be sold. No sales, no more
work here. No more work here means none—" she paused for
emphasis "—elsewhere."

Paulette flushed. She had not fully considered the connection between the two worlds she and Nicolle navigated. The
sewing, the fittings and alterations, these were the chores that
made attending parties relevant and special deliveries possible.
She'd been naive, thinking the latter existed without the former.

And so, when Mademoiselle called the team to Marie Claire's workstation, Paulette made her way across the workroom with a portion of the excitement she'd once felt for fashion. "Come closer, my lovelies," the designer crooned in a melodic voice. "Yes, yes, quickly now. We haven't much time before the show. Only a few short weeks."

The deadline sent Paulette's mind to another day, another event. She tried to steady her nerves, but could not. By the time Mademoiselle showed her designs, the roundups would be either underway or about to happen. The thought made her want to howl with frustration. She'd attended a party with the express purpose of spying on the men in charge, and had come away with only pieces of information, most of which Rochon and Mademoiselle already knew.

"This is such a happy occasion," one of the seamstresses whispered. "At last, at last."

Paulette tried to make herself small, which proved obligatory. It was a tight space for so many bodies. She could hardly breathe as more and more of her coworkers pressed in for their first glimpse of Mademoiselle's designs. The crush of people was made worse because they were forced to share the limited space with rolls of fabrics. Linens and wools and cotton twills.

The heat was oppressive. A trickle of sweat slid down her spine, yet she managed to squeeze in next to a pair of dress forms modeling simple muslin patterns, the first step in the making of a dress. She found an opening and moved in closer still to take her own glance of the sketches.

Her heart stopped, then sped up like a rabbit's caught in a snare. These were no ordinary renderings. They were art at its finest. One of the dresses had Mademoiselle's signature embellishment, an intricate row of flowers running diagonally from shoulder to waistband. A gasp escaped her. Not just any flowers. Roses, her mother's favorite. She bit her tongue and looked up, found Mademoiselle watching her. The designer mouthed two words: *For Hélène.*

Gratitude swelled in Paulette's heart. So many things to say. She needed to respond. Too many words were jumbled in her mind for any of them to break free.

Mademoiselle's eyes softened, and the older woman was no longer so pale. Paulette managed a very low, whispered, *"Merci,"* which earned her a solemn nod.

The other dress was a masterpiece of draping, and Paulette was immediately reminded of the dress she'd worn to her first Guy Marcel party. Giselle's dress was now wrapped in tissue, carefully folded and stowed away in her suitcase next to her mother's shawl. Clearly, this new one was inspired by Giselle.

Applause broke out again. Sighs of pleasure were interrupted by shouts of "Brava, brava!" Mademoiselle accepted the praise with more nods. Then, suddenly, she was turning away and announcing, "I sleep now."

And that was that. She didn't present the third design with any fanfare, or actually not at all. She just pushed the paper over to Marie Claire, said, "See what you can do with this," then exited the atelier. Marie Claire looked down, frowned, then copied Mademoiselle's *clap, clap, clap* and sent the team back to their workstations.

When Paulette was again sitting next to Nicolle, she asked, "Who will make the dresses?"

"Marie Claire will decide. In the meantime, I suggest you practice your hand sewing. Start with a simple backstitch, but this time I want you to work with one of the more difficult fabrics." Nicolle handed her a scrap of shiny blue silk. "Take your time and concentrate. Keep the area flat, free of any wrinkles, and don't pull too tight on the thread or you will ruin the material."

Paulette did as Nicolle instructed. It took her many attempts to get it right. The silk was slippery and prone to snags. While she worked, Nicolle attacked the pile of alterations awaiting her expert hands.

They were barely an hour into their individual tasks when Mademoiselle's assistant appeared just inside the atelier as she did every morning. Geneviève's face revealed nothing of her late nights drinking rivers of champagne with the rich and notorious, or riding in the back of one of Guy Marcel's white Bentleys.

Had she not seen it for herself, Paulette would never believe the woman moved in the same circles as Nazis and career criminals. As she swept an impassive glance over the room, only the edge of shadow in her eyes hinted at something dark in her character. By the time she finished her inspection, her gaze had changed, and she hid none of her disapproval, as if her role was more important to Maison de Ballard than anything else that happened in the atelier. She didn't seem to understand, or especially care, that without the women in this room, Mademoiselle's creations didn't exist.

There had been a time when Paulette might have thought something similar, unaware of what it took to build a dress out of a dream. She'd been on the other side of that curtain, poised on a platform, elevated above even Geneviève. She'd been full of her own thoughts, hardly aware that a seamstress— or three—buzzed around her, pinning and draping, rearranging folds, all while she'd stood and admired her own reflection in a three-way mirror.

Marie Claire joined Geneviève at the edge of the room. They each held a notebook and, as if performing some sort of coordinated dance, flipped open the covers at the same moment.

With her wide-rimmed glasses perched on her nose, Geneviève began ticking off her needs for the day. "We have three fittings in the morning, two this afternoon."

She rattled off names in rapid succession. Marie Claire scribbled away in her notebook.

"One of the afternoon fittings is a loyal customer with exacting requirements," she warned. "The other is a new client. An Italian contessa who has recently arrived in Paris. She wishes to embrace our culture and desires to wear only French designers during her stay. We will want to show her our very best service."

"I'll take that one myself," Marie Claire declared, her pencil flying across the page.

Geneviève looked up, nodded. *"Très bien."* She returned her attention to her book, then sped through the rest of the day's appointments, listing names, special requests, more warnings.

When she stopped talking, Marie Claire waited a beat, then asked, "Anything else?"

"That is all." With unnecessary curtness, Geneviève snapped her notebook shut and exited the atelier.

Despite the tension that hung in the assistant's wake, Paulette recognized the efficient way she and Marie Claire performed their duties. A superior blend, as her sister would say, each part coordinated perfectly to make a remarkable whole. Considering the connection between her former world and new life, Paulette went to work earning her place on Mademoiselle's team.

Nicolle had warned her it would take years to become proficient at finishing, up to seven. Paulette vowed to do it in three. Absorbed in her sewing, she didn't notice Marie Claire's approach until the other woman cleared her throat.

"Nicolle. Paulette. You will take the Beaumont fitting this afternoon. Mademoiselle Isadora is fourteen years old and can be rather difficult. She believes she has an eye for fashion. Her mother indulges her in this, to a point. Arguments often ensue. You will correct neither mother nor child, but rather accommodate both. Understood?"

"Understood."

Three hours later, Paulette was down on her knees, in a posture of supplication, confronted with a fourteen-year-old girl who didn't seem to notice she was caught in the awkward stage between adorable child and attractive young woman. Her limbs were too long, her knees a bit knobby, and her hips had not quite revealed themselves. Add in her rude manner and dismissive attitude, and Paulette decided Isadora Beaumont wasn't difficult. She was impossible. Nothing seemed to please her, except her own reflection.

The mother was worse.

She managed to insert herself into the process at the most critical moments. As a result, Paulette had more than her share of pinpricks. In a nasally voice, the woman criticized the weather, the lack of ventilation in the fitting room, the slowness of the staff, specifically Paulette and Nicolle. They moved too quickly, then not quickly enough. "Do a little spin for me, *ma chère*. I wish to see how the material flows."

Sitting back on her heels, Paulette shared an exasperated glance with Nicolle, then waited as the girl took a slow, measured turn, much like Paulette had done in Mademoiselle's apartment the night of her first Guy Marcel party. With the swish of chiffon falling elegantly into place, Isadora asked her mother, "Well?"

"Hmm. One more time, please."

Paulette could see the wheels in Isadora's head churning as she tried to decide whether to execute another spin or stomp her foot in rebellion. The storm brewed on, but then she gave in and performed the requested pirouette.

As she waited, as they *all* waited for the older woman to pass judgment, rain began to patter on the sidewalk outside the salon, first soft and indecisive, then in a steady drumming.

"Pretty," Madame Beaumont declared. "You will be the loveliest of your peers in that gown, once the alterations are properly complete, of course."

Much like the rain outside, the storm in the girl's eyes took on momentum. "It's satisfactory, I suppose." Isadora smoothed her hand down the yellow fabric. "But I think we should take up the hem by at least two inches."

It was a hideous choice, Paulette thought. The shorter length would ruin the look, but Madame Beaumont seemed to have no real opinion. She simply gave a wave of her hand and said, "Whatever you want, *chère*."

Grinning smugly, the girl returned to the raised platform. In silent agreement, Nicolle and Paulette moved into place, manipulating the hem, Paulette wondering if she'd been this difficult at Isadora's age. She'd been through many fittings in her life, but how little she'd known of the workings of Maison de Ballard. Or the people who worked here.

Her life was so completely different than what she'd imagined when she'd boarded the train in Reims. She watched her hands tuck and drape the chiffon as Nicolle had taught her. She caught a peek of herself in the mirror. The serious young woman in the black dress and severe hairstyle was not the same person who attended parties at Guy Marcel's.

Which was the real Paulette?

Isadora caught her looking at herself. She opened her mouth, but Nicolle ordered her to remain still. Taking advantage of the girl's silence, her mother, reclining back on the divan, began chattering about a litany of parties she'd attended and the who's who among her fellow attendees. Caught up in her own musings, and seemingly unaware she carried the one-sided conversation with only herself, she prattled on and on.

Suddenly her tone changed, and she was up on her feet. "The dress needs more lace at the neckline. Maybe a few more flowers at the waist. Or perhaps some ribbon." She sauntered to a table of accents and studied her choices. "Something that will draw attention to your lovely long neck and fine figure."

Two seconds. That's how long it took Nicolle to gain her feet and say, "No."

Hand reaching for a spool of lace, Madame Beaumont glanced over at Nicolle. "What's that?"

"Mademoiselle's design is complete. The dress needs no lace." Nicolle circled around Isadora, brushing away wrinkles as she went. "No additional flowers." She straightened a sleeve. "And absolutely no ribbons."

There was a long pause. The other woman's eyes narrowed ever so slightly. She opened her mouth to speak, but then another voice joined the conversation, one with honey dripping from the vowels and oozing over the consonants. "The seamstress is correct. Additional embellishment would only detract from the exquisite cut of the dress and the girl's lovely figure."

Nicolle all but forgotten, Madame Beaumont flung her wrath at the newcomer. "Who are you?"

Undaunted by the brash tone, the woman struck a pose in the doorway. "I am Contessa di Cappelletti."

Chapter Twenty-One

Nicolle

Nicolle had made a series of terrible mistakes. If she had not been so bold with the client, if the rushing in her ears had not been so loud, she would have heard the sound of approaching footsteps. She would have remembered to lower her eyes and step away from the entrance of the fitting room, away from the prying eyes of whomever strode across the threshold. Most of all, she would have remembered to melt into the woodwork. To become a part of the decor. To make herself completely unimportant.

She'd done none of those things. She'd allowed her loyalty to Mademoiselle to take over her sense of self-preservation. Now she was forced to watch a woman from her past confront a difficult client on her behalf. It would be a happy co-incidence if Francesca Cappelletti had been a friend. Or even a mere acquaintance. But the girl who'd been a year ahead of her at boarding school had never liked Nicolle, and had treated her with nothing but disdain. At first she'd thought Francesca was snobby because Nicolle had been orphaned as a child and raised by the nuns at the convent, but her Jewish blood had also been a factor.

Thankfully, she hadn't recognized Nicolle. Yet. She was too busy glaring at her current rival, who appeared to be in an equally foul mood.

As the staredown continued, Madame Beaumont's body language changed subtly. She drew her shoulders closer together, entwined her fingers, but she did not break eye contact. Nor did she wilt under Francesca's withering stare. "You say your name as if I should know you." She sniffed. "I do not."

It was an impressive show of strength, but if Nicolle knew anything about her former classmate, it was that no one challenged Francesca. True to form, she began a dressing down of the other woman. Her accented French wove through the room, filling the space with Italian arrogance reminiscent of an operatic diva.

This was Nicolle's chance for escape.

Dipping her head, she slipped back a few steps, all but bumping into Paulette. She murmured an apology, slinking farther away, nearly reaching the curtain that led to the hallway. Never once did she take her attention off Francesca.

The woman hadn't changed much in the ten years since they'd attended school together. Her arresting, exotic features had matured into something breathtaking. The mass of chestnut curls that had once hung down her back was artfully piled atop her head. Her dress was made from the finest material, crisp and utterly unblemished, the color of burnished amber, old gold, a perfect match to her eyes.

Isadora Beaumont wedged herself between Nicolle and Paulette. The girl was shaking and clearly afraid of the passionate Francesca—wise child—and, though Nicolle's desire to flee was strong, it wasn't in her to abandon a young girl, not even a difficult one. Any minute, Francesca could turn her wrath from mother to daughter. Or to Nicolle. Neither option was ideal. At a distance, perhaps, at a passing glance, when her temper was high, and with Nicolle dressed in severe black, Francesca might not recognize her.

Why was Francesca Cappelletti here at all? She'd graduated a year ahead of Nicolle, following in her French mother's footsteps, but had returned to her Italian roots and her father's home in Florence. There was no explanation, save for the obvious. Italy and Germany were allies. Francesca was Italian. She could freely move between the two countries. And that made her, for all intents and purposes, the enemy.

Nicolle took another step toward the hallway, automatically tugging Isadora with her. As if sensing the movement, Francesca turned her head and looked directly at Nicolle. Her mouth stopped spewing words. Her eyebrows slammed together. Nicolle turned her head away. Her body slowly followed, a body that had changed dramatically since her school days. War and grief had stolen her figure.

Would it be enough to disguise her from a woman with a sharp tongue and sharper eyes?

Francesca drew closer, her full lips forming into a pretty pout that had won her admiration from more than a few boys. "Do I know you?"

Lowering her gaze, Nicolle dropped her voice two octaves. "I am nobody."

Gold eyes pierced through Nicolle's composure like a shard of broken glass. "I never forget a face. Let me think. You are… oh, why can I not remember your name?"

It was a small victory, to see the haughty woman falter, even for an instant. Nicolle pressed her advantage. "I assure you, mademoiselle. We have never met."

A moment of hesitation crossed her face. And then she was too close, the air between them snuffed out like a candle, replaced with the scent of jasmines in bloom. "I know you. We were young, forced to endure that wretched school run by those mean, awful nuns."

Mean? Awful? Nicolle had thought them kind, more mothers to her than teachers. They'd given her a home and had, quite literally, saved her life.

"What fun we had, *amica*. Do you not remember all those nights we escaped to the roof?"

Nicolle had never been invited to those impromptu soirees, though there had been a time when she had desperately wanted to belong to Francesca's inner circle.

"We drank champagne straight from the bottle and watched the sun set over the hills. It was such fun, hiding from the hall monitor. What was her name?"

Emeline.

"Céline. See. I never forget a name. My mind is very, very good." She tapped her temple to punctuate her point. "I will remember yours soon. Give me a moment."

She grinned then, a small, smug smile, all teeth, feasting on her triumphant grasp of attention. No one spoke, not even Nicolle. She couldn't think. Couldn't move. Time shifted and bent in her mind, memories bombarding, a shocking assault on her senses.

Francesca in their dorm room, much like the one upstairs, ignoring Nicolle completely…

Francesca speaking only to the girls she thought worthy…

Francesca prattling on about her latest beau…

Francesca always at the front of every classroom, hand raised, smug smile in place…

Francesca offering her opinion, her criticism, her expertise on everything…

"Chloe! Yes. That's it. You are Chloe Nahum!"

That name, spoken from Francesca's lips, it struck like flint to stone. Fear clawed against Nicolle's bones. Years of secrets and careful manipulation, lies and subterfuge, false papers, all of it undone in an instant.

There was nothing in her head, nothing but a sense of defeat, no mother and daughter bickering over a swath of chiffon, no Paulette moving to stand beside her, reaching for her arm, pulling her close.

Nicolle was alone, utterly alone, but for the pounding of her own pulse in her ears and the desperate hope to find a way free of this moment. The solution was obvious. Deny. She must deny, in a voice that was not her own. "You have mistaken me for someone else." Deny. "My name is not Chloe." Deny. Deny. Deny. "It is Nicolle. Nicolle Larousse Cadieux."

The name on her false identity card.

Francesca was having none of her lies. "You have lost much weight. I suppose that would be expected in times such as these." She stepped closer, her gaze narrowed. "Your face is rather gaunt and quite thin, but yes. The eyes are the same. You are that orphan from... I don't remember. But what is this hideous dress you wear?" She turned more Italian with each critical word. "It does not belong to the stylish girl of my past."

The years fell away, bit by bit, dragging Nicolle to the narrow existence of her life in the convent without friends, save for the kind nuns. She'd made her own clothes, by hand, each stitch carefully executed. She'd copied her dresses from magazines, then attempted her own designs. Until she was the best-dressed girl in the school. "You are mistaken, mademoiselle. I never attended school with you."

Her delivery was slower, less emphatic.

"For what reason do you pretend to be someone else? Except... oh. Yes, I see." The gold eyes turned a little mean, and when she spoke again, the tenor in her voice had shifted. "Of course you lie. You are a Jew. It is in your very nature to manipulate the truth."

Nicolle felt her face drain of color. Her mind went blank. It was over. She would be sent away now. Her first coherent thought was not for herself, but for her son. *Oh, God,* she begged to the deity of her ancestors. *If I am carted away, keep him safe. I will do anything. I will…*

The prayer stalled in her mind.

Run, she told herself.

"But where is your yellow star?" Francesca demanded. "Why do you not wear it on your dress, as all Jews in Paris are required to do?"

"I do not wear a yellow star because I am not a Jew. I am French, born in—" she hesitated, looked at Paulette "—Reims."

The lie stuck on her tongue. Denying her heritage was a betrayal to the Jews who wore the yellow stars with pride. She'd seen them on the streets. Had been awed and frightened and conflicted by their courage, wishing she'd been able to join them, knowing to do so would reveal her lies and expose her son.

But Jules wouldn't be exposed, would he? Not now that he lived in the Free Zone and carried the last name of Lavigne. Monique raised him as her own and would continue to do so after Nicolle's arrest. What scraps of dignity she had left required her to admit her lies and claim her truth.

She opened her mouth, but Paulette was quicker, speaking for her. "You are mistaken, mademoiselle. This is Nicolle Cadieux. One of Mademoiselle's most gifted seamstresses and my closest friend. We grew up together in Reims. Her family grew grapes for mine."

How easily she lied, Nicolle thought.

The declaration thudded dully in Nicolle's head, even as Francesca shifted her attention to Paulette. "Who are you?"

It was the same question Madame Beaumont had asked of the haughty Italian, but with far more venom. Nicolle's heart knocked in her chest so loud she could hear it, and she was smothered with the weight of her fear, pulling her deeper within herself.

Paulette reacted quite differently. Her posture straightened. Her eyes filled with entitlement, a match to Francesca's. "I am Paulette Fouché-Leblanc."

She had Francesca's attention. "I know this name. I have tasted your family's champagne, and yet I do not understand. Why do you work in a dress shop sewing seams?"

Brushing at her skirt, Paulette gave a very French shrug. "I wish to become a fashion designer. One day, I will own my own shop. But first I must learn the basics of my craft. Sewing seams, as you put it, is an important skill."

"Hmm. Yes, that makes sense." Seemingly satisfied with the answer, Francesca turned back to Nicolle. "You look very much like someone I once knew." She sounded less sure of herself. "You are certain we have not met?"

Emboldened by Paulette's support, Nicolle gave the Italian a wry grin. "I am mistaken for others a lot. It is my face. Very ordinary."

Geneviève chose that moment to peek her head into the room. "Ah, Mademoiselle Cappelletti, there you are. We are ready for your fitting."

Now it was Geneviève on the receiving end of Francesca's displeasure. "At long last."

She swept out of the room as she'd entered, after striking a pose that ensured all eyes were on her. Nicolle watched her go in stone-cold silence and with no small amount of concern that the drama wasn't over, only paused. And yet, as upsetting as the interaction had been, the greatest shock came from Madame Beaumont. "That woman is absolutely horrid."

Taking charge, Paulette spoke with a tone full of apology. "I am sorry you had to witness her outburst."

"As am I. To interrupt Isadora's fitting, with such accusations and ridiculous theatrics. Stupid, horrible woman. Mademoiselle Sabine would never hire a Jew."

Her racism was appalling, but in this moment, it covered Nicolle in a hedge of protection. For that, she was mostly grateful.

"As for you," she said to Paulette, "I had the honor of attending a party at your family's château before the war. The champagne was exquisite. Your mother was a sparkling hostess, as effervescent as the wine itself. It was a lovely affair I will remember long into my old age."

"I am pleased to hear this. And, yes—" something sad came into Paulette's eyes "—my mother was always the consummate hostess before the war."

Misunderstanding, Madame Beaumont offered a kind smile. "Do not worry, dear. She will be again, when the fighting is over. Perhaps, if you work very hard, one day Paris will toast your first collection with Fouché-Leblanc champagne."

Paulette bowed her head in a show of silent acknowledgment. "That is my greatest wish, madame. Now, let us finish what we started."

The rest of the fitting went quickly. Isadora behaved herself, almost, and her mother stayed quiet as Nicolle and Paulette bustled around the girl. When they finished making their adjustments, they left Isadora to change back into her dress. Paulette took the gown, Nicolle grabbed the sewing kit, and, in unison, they thanked both mother and daughter before leaving the fitting room. In an odd switch of positions, Nicolle followed Paulette down the hallway.

The girl walked a little taller, her steps were surer, and Nicolle could see why Francesca had been beaten. Paulette was meant for bigger, brighter things than the sewing of seams. One day, she might even change the world.

Once they were behind the curtain and deep into the darkened hallway between the two worlds of Mademoiselle's operation, Nicolle reached out to Paulette. When she turned, eyebrows lifted, there was only one thing to say to her friend. "Thank you."

Chapter Twenty-Two

Paulette

Perhaps Paulette could have handled the Italian woman with more tact and humility. There were a hundred different ways she could have steered the insufferable woman's attention away from Nicolle. She'd known this, had begun to sort through a few, but there had been something in Francesca's behavior that had reminded her of herself, and she hadn't liked that glimpse into her former personality. Especially after witnessing Isadora's disagreeable behavior. There, too, Paulette had recognized too much of her younger self.

How had her family let her be so awful? They hadn't. She knew that now. Her sister had consistently scolded her and urged her to change her ways. Her grandmother had tried to ignite her interest in the business of making champagne.

Paulette had ignored one and been indifferent to the other. But that was the past, irrelevant now. The condescending

Italian woman had recognized Nicolle and openly accused her of being a Jew. This was not a small thing.

If Nicolle was, indeed, this Chloe, she was in grave danger. She'd committed a crime. She'd changed her name and falsified her official documents. *Like Maman.* Paulette would keep Nicolle's secret, as she'd failed to do for her mother.

Stopping abruptly, she pivoted to face her friend. It was dark in the corridor, so dark she couldn't separate her friend's features from the shadows. She took a step closer, but Nicolle shrank back, much like a cornered animal. "How much of what she said is true?"

"All of it." There was a ghostly timbre to her voice, like gossamer drawn over a dress form, and she was shaking. Actually trembling in the darkness that surrounded them.

Paulette wanted to reach out to her friend, but she feared that would only upset Nicolle further. "Does Mademoiselle know?"

She nodded.

Keeping her voice steady, calm, she asked, "Do you think she will let the matter drop?"

"Hard to know with Francesca."

Paulette's hand went to Nicolle's arm. "Then we will—"

"Not here, Paulette. We will not speak of this here. Later, on the roof."

"You're right."

She'd known fear like this once before, fear for another woman who'd hidden her identity behind a false name and fake papers. Her mother had shared her secret with Paulette, and Paulette had betrayed that trust. She would not fail Nicolle and made the vow aloud. "Your secret is safe with me."

Not waiting for a response, she resumed walking, once again in the lead. They didn't speak of the incident again until they were up on the roof under the pretext of watching the sun set over Paris. Nicolle brought up the subject herself. "You stood up for me today, when a woman spoke a name I thought I would never hear again."

She sounded surprised. "I will stand by you, Nicolle. Always. You are my friend."

"You say this now, up here, where there is no threat, no Nazi holding a gun to your head."

"I will remain true."

Hands shaking, Nicolle lit a cigarette. The flash of light wobbled, just a bit, revealing her very real fear. "You broke once before."

Paulette was dizzy with remorse and guilt, but also resolve. "I failed my mother. I will not fail you."

"I want to believe you."

Paulette understood her friend's reluctance as a long silence fell over them. She took the cigarette from Nicolle and took a deep pull as she'd seen her mother do countless times. The smoke filled her lungs before catching in her throat on the way back out. She coughed and coughed, hard, unrelenting, until tears ran down her face. Nicolle reached to her, not to comfort, but to take back the cigarette.

Watching her friend smoke, as she'd watched her mother a hundred times over, an answer revealed itself. "We have to get you out of France." She would turn to Mademoiselle. No, Rochon. Mademoiselle had too much on her mind. The fashion house, the upcoming show of her new collection. Besides, Rochon was the man with the resources, the contacts.

"Paulette, did you hear me? I can't leave France. Not yet."

"You wish to continue your work for the network."

"I…yes. That's it, exactly."

She sounded a bit too bright, the kind of tone used to cover a lie. "What holds you here?"

"We have stayed on the roof too long. You have a party to attend." She stubbed out the cigarette, flicked it over the edge, and stood. "We must get you dressed."

Paulette wanted to argue. She wasn't in the mood to spy on Nazis and French gangsters tonight, but Rochon would be there. The little kick in her stomach had nothing to do with the man and everything to do with speaking to him about an escape for Nicolle. At least, that's what she told herself as she followed her friend back into the attic.

She repeated it as she stood in the center of Marcel's foyer, wearing a pale pink dress with matching elbow-length gloves and simple gold jewelry around her neck. The laughter grated more than usual. She followed it up the stairs and into the ballroom. It was in moments like these that she missed her mother most. Hélène Leblanc erased the shadows. She filled any room with warmth and light. Paulette tried to emulate her tonight, but her heart was too broken and her mind too filled with worry for her friend. Nicolle was hiding something that kept her in France, at risk of discovery, working for Mademoiselle's network. Was she, like Paulette, seeking atonement for past sins?

Paulette would not find out the truth here. She would, however, seek Rochon's help. Mademoiselle trusted him, and so would she. Or rather, she wanted to trust him. Her instincts had been wrong once before.

He was late. She retreated to a strategic position near a potted plant, close enough to hear several conversations at once, but not so close as to be pulled into any of them.

Guests twirled past in a silken spool of color and texture, stirring the dark green leaves beside her. A young woman giggled from somewhere nearby. Paulette flinched. Only a few months ago, that girl was her.

She needed to get away from that laugh. She needed air.

The balcony beckoned.

She answered the call, moving quickly, but not too fast. A light breeze stirred a tendril of hair that had fallen loose from its pins. She passed a couple in a scandalous embrace. Their kiss brought heat to her cheeks. She knew what came next.

Friedrich had been a master at manipulating her emotions into a physical response.

Shame turned hot in her veins. She found a dark corner and leaned her head against the wall. Shrouded in the safety of the inky night, she looked up just as a group of swift-moving clouds covered the moon. She belonged here, alone in the dark, where secrets lived. But she wasn't alone. A shadow approached her, lengthening and then morphing into the form of a man. He wore black, from boots to jacket to tie. "It isn't wise to be out here, *mon pétale*."

My petal. An endearment reserved for a fragile, poetic girl. How little he knew her. She'd never been fragile. Selfish, flirtatious. Coy. But never fragile. Nor could she prevent a small shiver of anticipation from moving through her. She knew this feeling. And hated herself for it.

Had she met this man before the war, he would have been the cause of several girlish dreams. Now she stood alone with him in the black night, with a war raging across Europe, and she needed his help. With chilled, trembling fingers, she reached for the wall behind her, and found a reassuring anchor when her palm pressed to the cool stone. "I think it's time a mutual friend leaves France."

He didn't ask for a name, only, "What has led you to this conclusion?"

She moved closer, nearly touching him. In the dark, as she lowered her voice, she felt it again. The shiver that had no place in this conversation. And for a traitorous second, she wished to have met him another time, in another place. "She was recognized today in the salon, and while I convinced the client she was mistaken, there's no guarantee the woman will let the matter drop."

Rochon muttered something under his breath. "Why come to me with this? Why not Mademoiselle?"

It was a good question and something Paulette had worried over all day. "It's hard to explain."

"Try."

"It's just… I don't know. I guess it's that, in many ways, she's become something of a mother to me. I owe her so much." *Everything.* "She carries many burdens, mine included, and I don't want to add more if it isn't necessary."

"So you come to me instead."

"Oui."

The way his brow furrowed, then cleared, told her she'd been right to come to him. His next words solidified her confidence. "Mademoiselle will have to be notified."

"I'll do so myself."

He said nothing for a very long moment. When he spoke, it was the voice she'd come to know, but lower. Deeper. "I'll handle the rest. In the meantime, let us get back to the party."

"All right."

She placed her hand in his, the move as natural as breathing. As she allowed him to pull her into the laughter and light, he said, "Have faith, Paulette. All will turn out as it should."

His eyes held sincerity, the look unguarded, with not a hint of irony in his voice. Paulette wanted…she wanted…

What she did not dare name, even in her own head.

Her pulse pounded in her ears, nearly deafening her with its roar. She'd known this yearning before. And yet, this was different. Stronger. The discovery made her blood charge through her veins. Suddenly, they were back in the main room, and he was releasing her hand, and they were heading in opposite directions.

Two hours later, she'd learned very little. Certainly nothing she didn't already know. The alliances between French women and Germans were the same. The silly, unhappy actress who'd fallen in love with a much younger man was still silly and unhappy.

"You're frowning."

Paulette startled at the high-pitched voice. She'd let her guard down, and Guy Marcel was next to her, leering at a spot far below her eyes. She felt dirty, violated, none of which she showed on her face. "Was I?"

"A beautiful young woman such as yourself should be smiling, not thinking." He leaned in close, the scent of too much cloying cologne wafting off of him. "Tell me, beautiful girl, what makes you smile?"

She could feel his ugly thoughts, the feverish heat coming off him. A wave of nausea rolled heavy in her belly. *Be smart, Paulette. Discourage this man without alienating him.* The old lie from their first meeting showed itself in her mind.

"Philippe," she said dreamily, a little breathless and husky. "He makes me smile. In very inventive ways."

Marcel's lips quirked into a crooked half smile. "Tell me more."

Here we go, Paulette thought. She knew this game, understood the rules. Tapping into the terrible flirt she'd once been, she indicated the foul man should come a bit closer with a crook of her finger. "A woman never tells her most intimate secrets." She batted her eyelashes for good measure, absently wondering why the vapid feminine trick worked so well on men like Marcel.

Something twisted crossed his features, deeper than a leer, uglier. "Be careful, my dear. Rochon is a dangerous man."

As are you, she thought.

"The man is not what he seems."

Paulette could say the same of this man, of most of the people in this room, even of herself. "Are any of us?"

Laughing now, Marcel looked at something over her shoulder, grinned that hideous, wicked smile of his. "Look behind you, toward the mirrored ceiling, and see the kind of man your lover calls friends."

Although there was envy in his tone, a sort of surliness she'd not heard before, Paulette didn't look. She didn't need to look.

Rochon allowed all sorts of vipers into his inner circle. He did so for the network, for the greater good. And now she was curious.

She looked for Rochon and found him with another man. Both in profile. Both in head-to-toe black. One in a suit. The other in a uniform. Both tall. Both lean. Dread filled up her heart. Time bent and shifted in her head. Past overlaid present.

"What do you think of Rochon now?"

She couldn't think. Couldn't breathe. Her lungs actually emptied of air. There stood Rochon, engaging in idle conversation with her mother's murderer. The two looked friendly, familiar, as if this wasn't their first meeting.

Smile, Paulette told herself. *Reveal nothing of what is in your head. Play this game.* "I think…" She swallowed back the bile rising in her throat, drew a breath. "Rochon is no different from any other man in this room." More bile. More swallowing. "He lies. He cheats and makes friends with all sorts. But what is this to me?" She flicked her fingers in the air. "When we are alone, he is mine and quite capable of satisfying me."

"A prince among men." Chuckling softly, Marcel slithered away, leaving Paulette to stare at Rochon without distraction, to watch him in conversation with…him.

A Nazi. The worst of his kind. Gestapo. Kriminalkommissar Wolfgang Mueller. Her mother's murderer. Mueller. The name ricocheted in her mind. Mueller. Monster. Instrument of death. And there was Rochon, speaking to him as if they'd known each other for years.

Paulette's heart went cold. She wanted to scream, to rage, to sob. This couldn't be real. She looked away. Back again. Caught the barest incline of Mueller's head. The movement of Rochon's lips. Outside, thunder rolled in the distance.

Lightning flashed.

And then, Mueller was turning his head. His piercing, pale blue gaze met hers and held. Recognition came next. She willed herself not to give him the satisfaction of retreat, not to be the prey to his predator, but it was hard. She knew what the man was capable of. Adrenaline surged. She fell back a step. Another.

Then she fled.

Chapter Twenty-Three

Paulette

If Paulette had expected escape, she'd been living in an illusion made of smoke and mist. Her small, hurried steps were no match for Mueller's ground-eating strides. She'd let him see her. *Stupid. Reckless.*

"Mademoiselle Leblanc. I am not here to harm you. I only wish to speak with you."

She pretended not to hear her name, uttered in that rigid German accent. Or the vow of guiltless intention. She didn't look back, either. She simply kept moving, faster, faster. Her mind worked twice as quick, trying to make sense of the Gestapo agent assigned to Reims showing up in Paris. At this house. This party. This night.

"Mademoiselle." He was all but on her now, his voice so close she could feel the vibration of the sound waves. "Slow down."

She picked up the pace, fear gushing through her veins, turning her blood hot.

A hand landed on her shoulder and she was suddenly being dragged backward, into the dark, into a world of shadows and nightmares she thought she'd left in the past.

Where was Rochon? He was supposed to be Paulette's one true ally in this den of liars and thieves, but he was absent. Mueller was slowing their steps and turning her around. She could see his hard, almost beautiful face in the slice of moonlight coming in from the window at her right. The pale blue of his eyes seemed paler tonight, almost unnatural. She met that cold gaze and suddenly, as if a fog had been burned away by the sun, the tragedy that had become her life was laid bare before her. All this time, Paulette had thought Friedrich the source of her pain. That was only partially true. The bulk of her grief, the worst of it, could be laid at this man's feet. "I hate you."

He stepped forward, into the beam cast by the moonlight. Shadows settled in the hollows of his face, and the blue eyes glittered, silver on white. "I know."

He didn't defend himself. That would make him human. And there it was again, the crippling hatred Paulette felt for him, the man who'd arrested her mother and released Paulette, despite her pleas to share her mother's fate. He'd denied her even that small chance at redemption. "What do you want?"

His hand dropped away from her shoulder and came to rest in the open space between them, palm facing forward. "I wish to have a conversation."

The Gestapo didn't have conversations. They interrogated.

Paulette was scared. Not for herself. For Nicolle. Mademoiselle. The network itself. She had names in her head, pieces of the whole, some from personal experience, others she'd put together on her own. If compelled to tell what she knew, lives would be lost.

"I have nothing to say that you will want to hear."

Mueller frowned, and a groove formed on his forehead, marring his smooth features. She was reminded of the final moments she'd spent in his company. He'd dragged her out of the jail cell, then home. He'd put her in her grandmother's care while he...

What? What had he done? What had he said?

She searched her memory. He'd demanded to know Gabrielle's location. Her grandmother had been silent, possibly confused, then had told him she was in the wine cellar with another German—the wrong one—and Mueller had rushed out of the house, muttering, Mein Gott. *Pray I'm not too late.*

The words had been uttered with no discernible accent. The same voice he was using now. "You should not be in this house, Mademoiselle Leblanc. The people here, they are not good."

"Your presence is proof of that, *non*?"

His smile flashed hollow. "You should take better care with the company you keep. Your sister, I think, would be disappointed."

"You judge me? You, the man who sat at von Schmidt's table nearly every night, the man who attended his parties much like this one, the man who drank stolen champagne from my family's cellars?"

"Things aren't always as they seem." His voice dropped to a whisper. "You would do well to remember that."

He was so close she could see something different in his eyes, but she couldn't decipher its meaning. "Was it not enough you arrested my mother and sent her to her death? Now you hound me here in Paris. What next? Will you go back to Reims and target my sister? My grandmother?"

"You speak too boldly. These walls have ears, more than most."

"Is that a warning, or a threat?"

He leaned in close, with the ease of someone used to holding all the power. "A piece of advice, mademoiselle." His delivery was slow, but no less emphatic. "You would do well to think hard about the men you choose as allies."

"Philippe Rochon is not my ally."

"I was referring to Guy Marcel."

Enough of this game. "Tell me, Detective Mueller. What happened to my mother? Where did you send her?"

He was silent for several seconds. Then, when he spoke, he was very precise. "Your mother is with her people."

She drew back from his words, from him, from the images running in her head. And now Mueller was turning to go. Not fast, and not without hesitation, as if he wanted to say something more. She'd seen him look like this before. She tried to remember all the times she'd crossed paths with this man, this Nazi. He'd been silent, hard, quick and decisive, but had he been cruel?

Not overtly. He'd arrested her, at Friedrich's insistence, but he'd placed her in the same cell with her mother. Where she'd found comfort, even in her grief and guilt. There'd been other options. Cruel options. Or maybe, putting them together had been the cruelest act of all. Giving them a chance to know what they were losing.

Your mother is with her people. "Is my mother alive? Is she—"

"Paulette." Rochon appeared behind Mueller. Large, menacing. No less dangerous than the Gestapo agent himself. "Is this man bothering you?"

This man, as if he didn't know Mueller. As if only moments earlier, they hadn't been engaged in a conversation like two old chums renewing their friendship.

"I was just leaving." This from Mueller. "Before I go, a word of advice, Mademoiselle Leblanc. Be careful who you trust in this city. There are some who mean you harm, others who wish to keep you safe."

It was a typical Gestapo warning, full of double meanings. He didn't look at Rochon. Rochon didn't look at him. They were too busy staring at her. "I bid you adieu, mademoiselle."

She said nothing, just continued watching Mueller watch her as he spoke. He shifted to his left. Rochon shifted to his right.

And there. A brief look shared between the two men, a single, split-second glance that held a thousand unspoken words. The kind of look that indicated a silent agreement. And then Mueller was gone, melting into the shadows.

Rochon cleared his throat. "Let's go, Paulette. I'm taking you home."

Suddenly tired of intrigue, and walls with ears, and wanting to know just what Rochon was playing at by aligning himself with a man like Wolfgang Mueller, she let him take her hand and guide her away. They left the house in silence, fingers threaded together.

Paulette had questions and concerns. Doubts and suspicions. And she sensed Rochon had much of the same. They voiced none of what was in their minds, but sat in silence as he drove the short distance to the fashion house. Taking advantage of the silence, Paulette replayed the evening in her head. The tender moments on the balcony. Mueller's appearance. Rochon's knowledge of the other man, a possible alliance. "Who are you, Philippe?"

He glanced at her from the corner of his eye. "No one you want to know."

"Are you a good man?"

"Not anymore."

She let that sink in, knowing the loss of his wife had changed him, as the loss of her mother had changed her. She was still pondering his response when they reached Mademoiselle's building. The moment he cut the engine, she asked, "How do you know Wolfgang Mueller?"

"He gives me information, and I repay him with lies."

A chill slipped into her pores. Paulette knew Rochon made alliances for the benefit of the network, but she had not understood the danger of such partnerships until now. "Philippe—"

"Go inside, Paulette. It is safer for us both."

"Why?"

He didn't respond. He didn't need to; his silence was answer enough. He'd shut her out. There would be no more talking. She entered the atelier, realizing only after she'd made the climb to the attic that Philippe hadn't asked her how she knew Mueller. She couldn't help but wonder why.

Her roommates were asleep, including Nicolle. There her friend slept, on the bed next to Paulette's, a small smile on her face. She was dreaming, probably of the husband she'd loved and lost. A man nothing like Friedrich. Or even Rochon, with his dark alliances and friendships with Gestapo agents. Nicolle's husband had been pure of heart, good and noble. By his own admission, Rochon was none of those things. There'd certainly been nothing good or noble about Friedrich.

And yet Paulette had fallen for him. The secretive nature of their trysts had excited her.

Tonight, when she'd found herself alone on the balcony with Rochon, the two of them standing together in the shadows, her heart had pounded with old longings. She'd thought him different from Friedrich. Then she'd seen him with Mueller and knew herself to be a fool.

Even after all that had happened, all she'd learned, she was once again attracted to a man she couldn't trust.

Still in her party clothes, she retrieved her sketch pad, but not her mother's shawl. It didn't feel right, seeking comfort from Maman while she was enduring hardship *with her people*.

The moon hung low against the black fabric of the sky, revealing trees in a distant park standing in dark clumps. It wasn't quiet, Paris was never quiet, but it was peaceful. Paulette set the sketch pad on her knees, opened the cover, and leafed to the sixth page. As she stared at Friedrich's face, she thought of Rochon. Then of Mueller. Then of serpents, waiting in a garden, ready to tempt.

Mouth grim, she raised her eyes to the gauzy clouds twisting around the moon and vowed, aloud, "No man will manipulate me again."

"I'm glad to hear it."

Paulette didn't react to the sound of Nicolle's voice. In truth, she'd expected her friend to find her here. Had hoped, at any rate. She placed her hand over Friedrich's face and asked, "Trouble sleeping?"

"Always. Here. Take this." Nicolle wrapped a blanket around Paulette's shoulders then sat beside her. "I told Mademoiselle about our encounter with Francesca this afternoon."

Had it only been this afternoon? It felt like a lifetime ago. "What did she say?"

"She already knew. Geneviève told her."

Of course. Francesca would have mentioned the incident to her. They'd been naive to think she wouldn't. "Is Mademoiselle worried?"

"A little. We both are, but my papers are good, Paulette. They will hold up under scrutiny."

Her mother's papers had been good, too. *She is with her people.* She lifted her hand and stared at the drawing.

"Is that him?" Nicolle pointed to the pad. "The SS officer?"

Paulette had a moment of hesitation. Shame filled her, but this was Nicolle. She already knew the story, and Paulette didn't want secrets between them. "I drew this the first night after we were intimate. I should have burned it long ago."

"Yet you haven't. Will you tell me why?"

She stared into Friedrich's face, drawn with a hand guided by love, or what Paulette had thought was love. "I keep him close to remind me of my own foolishness. One day, when I have earned redemption, I will destroy the picture."

"You put a lot of power in a few lines and squiggles. May I?" Nicolle indicated the pad.

Paulette handed it over and, while her friend studied the

drawing of Friedrich, she let her mind take her back to the beginning.

"This is very good, but his face is unsettling. It's the eyes. They are not kind."

"How did I miss that?"

"Because you were infatuated. He saw to that. Then, when he betrayed you, you were ashamed. But I think all along you detected something ugly in him." Nicolle gave her back the sketch pad. "He does not deserve to be immortalized on paper or in your mind."

Paulette gave a bitter, brittle laugh. "It's not Friedrich I preserve. Not really. Every time I look at his face, I see my mistakes, my sins, my guilt."

"Burn the drawing, Paulette. Do it tonight. Now."

Desire warred with guilt. Hope swirled with shame. "I don't know if I can."

"We will do it together." Nicolle dug in the pocket of her robe and pulled out a box of matches, the ones she used to light her cigarettes. "Do you want to hold the flame or the paper?"

This was it. She was really going to destroy the drawing. "The flame."

"Then give me the paper."

Hands shaking, Paulette ripped the page free of the pad. Nicolle pulled out a single match. They swapped, and now it was Paulette with the matches, Nicolle with Friedrich's image.

It took three tries to light the paper. Finally, a spark, the scent of sulfur. Then the flame burst from matchstick to paper, devouring the page. It consumed Friedrich's face. Smoke and fire joined in a heated dance, pluming up and up. As if compelled, Paulette reached for the paper, held it aloft, until only a tiny piece remained in her hand, the fire approaching quickly. "Let it go," Nicolle urged.

She stared at the flame a second longer.

"Now, Paulette." Nicolle shook her arm, hard enough to

dislodge her grip just as the last bit of paper turned to ash and swirled to the sky.

It was done. Friedrich was gone.

"You're free," Nicolle whispered.

"I am." And she wanted the same for her friend. No matter what deals she had to make or alliances she had to forge, Paulette would make it happen.

She would see Nicolle safely out of France.

Chapter Twenty-Four

Sabine

Sabine stood in the center of her atelier and watched the hive of activity. Her girls worked hard, harder than usual, all to ensure Sabine's fashion show was a success. They had only three days remaining. Not a lot of time to turn her vision into beautiful confections of silk, satin, and various other fabrics. Her girls would not let her down. They never did. That's what came from curating a team with the best the city had to offer—nay, the world.

Three days, she reminded herself as she began her morning rounds, stopping at each workstation, checking progress, giving guidance when warranted, redirecting when needed. All but one of the dresses received her personal touch. One hideously derivative red evening gown that fell far short of her standards.

Proof she'd lost control to a common thief. Guy Marcel had inserted himself into her business with his foul demand, and now Sabine had a collection that was no longer cohesive. She also had an assistant who grew more and more presumptuous with her new power.

Geneviève had actually dared to call Sabine's integrity into question at the word of a new, unvetted client. The Italian anti-Semitic snob who would never be allowed in the salon again. Sabine had made that clear to her assistant. Francesca Cappelletti had been right, of course. Nicolle was not the woman she claimed to be, and that was a problem, especially with the yellow star ordinance, the upcoming roundup, and the overwhelming French indifference to the plight of Jews in the city. Safest to get the young woman out of Paris for a while.

Sabine would send her on a rescue mission immediately following the fashion show, under the guise of fulfilling a special order from the new collection. It was a risk, she knew. Someone who actually understood the process of creating haute couture might take notice of the quick turnaround between show and delivery.

By then, Nicolle and the airman currently hiding in a safe house in Montmartre would be out of the city, a full day ahead of the mass arrests. It was times such as these that Sabine was glad her son-in-law moved in dangerous circles. Philippe had been the one to uncover the exact day of the roundup, easier once Paulette had pinpointed the general timing.

A movement caught her attention, just as Geneviève appeared by her side. For the first time in their twenty years of working together, the other woman wouldn't meet her eyes. *Good*, Sabine thought, and slid just a hint of ice in her voice. "What is it, Geneviève?"

"A client wishes to speak with you in the salon."

Sabine frowned. She had insisted no appointments scheduled until after the fashion show. "What client?"

"The American widow. She says it's urgent and insisted, despite my objections, that I make you aware of her arrival."

This could not be good. "Tell her I will be with her shortly."

"You...will?" Geneviève stared at her, all the humility gone from her face, replaced with suspicion, and Sabine knew she was trying to figure out the nature of her relationship with Vivian Miller, why she would make an exception such as this. Let her wonder. Let her speculate. Not for the first time, Sabine Ballard was glad she'd never brought Geneviève into the network.

Mostly because she hadn't wanted to cross-pollinate. Keeping her two worlds as separate as possible had always been the goal. The exceptions being Nicolle and now Paulette. And though Marcel had sunk his claws into the fashion house, Sabine was still in charge. She gave no explanations, especially to this woman.

"You may go now."

"*Très bien.*" Her mouth quirked at the edges, a small, familiar smile, but this one didn't reach her eyes. Had any of the others? The smile was almost impertinent as she passed the workstation where two seamstresses worked on the dress she'd designed.

Now it was Sabine watching her assistant with suspicion, drawing up memories and images from the past, thinking back to conversations. Had Geneviève's insolence been there all along, or was it more recent? A woman who aligned herself with Guy Marcel, with the sole purpose of forwarding her own agenda, was not made of much integrity. That rendered her either an enemy or an annoyance.

Either way, Sabine would keep a close eye on the woman. She could not fire her. Marcel would not allow it. In an effort to keep Geneviève guessing, she waited a full ten minutes before making her way into the salon. Her assistant was busy with another client, which gave Sabine a chance to approach her friend without hindrance.

Vivian was looking not quite herself. Sabine greeted her, scanning the beautiful face. The small vertical groove between the thin, perfectly plucked eyebrows was never a promising sign. Her unexpected arrival could mean any number of things, none of them good.

"Can we speak somewhere in private?"

Now Sabine was truly worried. Private conversations with Vivian Miller always revealed trouble. But she immediately granted her friend's wish, and as she escorted the woman through the salon and into her office, her thoughts converged on a terrible possibility. The Nazi was on to Vivian's extracurricular activities for the Resistance. But if that were true, she would not be here, walking freely in a fashion house.

Still, Sabine had been against her friend's decision to become the man's mistress from the start, knowing the personal toll it would take on a woman who was not so hard as she appeared. And yet she'd appreciated the advantages to such an alliance. Vivian was privy to conversations that provided their network with information. Coupled with what Philippe uncovered and, to a lesser degree, Paulette, lives had been saved from such information.

Hoping she misread her friend's agitation, and trying not to fear the worst, Sabine put the usual precautions in place and asked, "Has he found out about your secret work?"

"He grows suspicious and watchful, but that is not why I have come."

Sabine could feel her friend's agitation, a sort of rising panic that had no place in the confident woman's demeanor. "Is this about the situation you came to speak with me about a few weeks ago? Have the mother and daughter been compromised?"

"Yes, but also no." Vivian moved to the wall of photographs. Touching one, then another, she said, "They are quite safe, for now. But their documents have been delayed, and—" her hand began to shake "—that is not the worst of it."

Sabine took Vivian's hand and drew her away from the wall, toward the center of the room, where the chance of being overheard was at a minimum. "What is the worst, if not a delay?"

Vivian let out a sort of howl as she cradled her head in her hands, the pose one of absolute defeat. "I have learned, quite by accident, that the housekeeper hides the mother and daughter in a bunker beneath the house in Drancy. Right there under my feet. And—" she dropped her hands "—his."

Sabine blinked. In her darkest moments, she could not have come up with this stunning piece of information. Jews, hiding in a Nazi's home, right under his nose. "Why, that's…" Her own hands began to shake. "Lunacy. It cannot continue."

"No, it cannot." Something hard and dark flickered in her friend's eyes. But there was also fear swimming in their depths. "We must move up our plan for their escape."

"This is no easy request you make." But one Sabine would make great effort to accommodate, because it was important to Vivian, and every life saved mattered. Her mind went to work on the particulars, sifting and sorting, landing on the one piece out of her control. "How long will it take to secure the documents?"

"I have met with a new forger just this morning. I will have what we need in a week, possibly two."

Too long. Sabine's eyes shut, and her chest pumped with a breath as strong as a swell of water breaking against a cliff. A mother and daughter, two Jews, living in a Nazi's home. It really was quite remarkable. Detection could occur at any minute. Arrests would be made. Deaths would surely follow. A foreboding filled her, and the sense that Vivian would not survive her liaison with the Nazi.

"Can it be done?" Vivian asked.

Sabine gave her the truth. "I don't know. Possibly."

"Thank you, Sabine."

"Don't thank me yet. We have much to do." An entire escape plan had to be reworked. "We will begin with a new rendezvous point. Somewhere near the house." She moved behind her desk, lowered to her knees, and dislodged a floorboard.

She reached inside the hole and retrieved a recent map of Paris, then smoothed it out on her desk. "Show me where you live."

"Here." Vivian pointed to a spot on a street within walking distance of the Drancy detention center. Sabine understood the enormous, dangerous task that lay ahead.

It would be the network's most daring rescue mission yet.

Chapter Twenty-Five

Nicolle

Preparations for the fashion show began before dawn. The air in the atelier was charged with excited energy. Today, there would be no mention of war. It was still there, on everyone's minds, pulsing underneath the frenzied activity and busy hands. Scheduling the event on the National Day of France was its own mini-rebellion, as was Nicolle's assigned duty. Per Mademoiselle's instructions, she traveled from garment to garment, sewing on tiny *cocardes tricolores*.

The designer had fashioned the pleated blue, white, and red circular ribbons with her own hands, but allowed Nicolle to decide where to attach the little rosettes. She chose spots that would not take away from the design's overall aesthetic, or cause unnecessary attention. They would be recognized only by discerning French eyes aware of their significance.

As time for the show drew near, the whir of activity grew more fever-pitched. Models were helped into the dresses. Hems were checked. Threads were searched for and found. Missing beads were reattached. Loose embellishments secured. Mademoiselle arrived dressed in all black so as not to take away from her designs. She buzzed between the main salon and the workroom.

The show itself would be small and intimate. Only Mademoiselle's best clients and select members of the press were invited to witness the official unveiling of Maison de Ballard's midseason collection. Later, once the models were out of the dresses and Mademoiselle was toasting her success, the doors would be open to the public. They, too, would see the designs, but on dress forms rather than live models. Geneviève and her staff would take orders. Hopefully many, many orders. But not yet. Not until after the show.

Nicolle tied off the thread, patted the rosette she'd sewn inside a brocade rose, then moved on to the next dress. She visually studied the garment, zeroed in on the ruching at the waist. She wished Paulette was helping her make these choices, but Mademoiselle had given the girl a different job. One that would put her at the center of attention.

Pride filled Nicolle's heart as she approached her friend. She wore the blue silk gown inspired by her mother. The two of them had handcrafted the showstopper from Mademoiselle's designs, knowing that Paulette would be the one to wear the dress. Her hair hung in loose waves, the sides pinned up and back from her face.

Smiling, Nicolle swept around her friend, inspecting the fit, knowing it was perfect. The fabric had been Paulette's idea, the color Nicolle's. The silky material shimmered down her body, a waterfall of movement and light. "Flawless."

"We did a rather fine job, didn't we?"

"We did, indeed." After learning the inspiration behind the design, Marie Claire had put Nicolle and Paulette in charge of making the dress. It was a kind gesture, meant as an olive branch to the girl she'd been rude to on her initial arrival. Paulette had shown her gratitude with a fierce hug that had sent the head seamstress into sputters about overzealous young ladies who needed to know their place. She'd been only half joking.

Paulette sighed. "It should be my mother wearing this dress."

"You will wear it in her stead and make Mademoiselle proud."

She nodded, but her eyes turned sad, as they always did when her mind traveled to the past. And now Nicolle was sad, too, but she also felt a burst of affection lined with hope. Against all odds, she and Paulette had become friends, as close as sisters. They stood metaphorically shoulder to shoulder, operating as a single unit against the other seamstresses who still hadn't warmed up to Paulette, though she'd been a member of the team for months now. Paulette didn't seem to mind their snubs, claiming, *What is their meaningless rejection when I have you?*

It was true. She had Nicolle, and Nicolle had Paulette. The threads of their lives were tangled now, and while the younger woman had been candid, baring her soul on more than one occasion, Nicolle had shared only a portion of hers. She would do better in the future, when she returned from her latest rescue. Or rather, she would try. Old habits were not so easy to break.

"Why are you looking at me like that? Is there something wrong with the dress? Did I get something on the skirt?" She spun around in a circle, like a dog chasing his tail, trying to catch a glimpse of the garment from every angle.

"Stop that. You'll make yourself dizzy. The dress is perfect, as are you." She meant to say more, but Marie Claire's elevated voice cut her off.

"Charlotte!" she shouted. "Charlotte Leduc. Where are you? Show yourself at once."

Silence met the order.

Marie Claire huffed out a frustrated breath. "Where is Charlotte? Has anyone seen Mademoiselle's house model?"

The question unleashed a multitude of hurried responses. *Not me, I haven't seen her… I saw her last night…*

Then, from one of the finishers, "Isn't this the dress she is meant to wear?"

Clicking her tongue, Marie Claire wove through the room and reached for the garment in question. The discovery was met with gasps and whispered *oh no*s, but not a single person said what they were all thinking. Charlotte's absence could be temporary or permanent. People disappeared in Paris all the time with no warning, no explanation. There one minute, gone the next. Sometimes they were brought in for questioning and released days later. Sometimes they were never seen or heard from again.

"What is this? What is happening?" Mademoiselle swept into the atelier with a dramatic flourish, a cloud of lilac perfume trailing in her wake. "What is the cause of this commotion?"

The pause that followed was only heightened by the sound of shuffling feet and the lowering of heads.

"Well?" she demanded. "Does no one have an answer for me?"

"Mademoiselle." Marie Claire hurried over to where the designer stood, the dress still in her hand. "It's Charlotte. She's gone missing."

"Missing?"

"I…yes. *Oui*." Marie Claire seemed to shrink in on herself, a little of the light in her eyes dimming. "We can't find her anywhere. She was selected to wear the black gossamer gown." The words were pouring out of her, fast and desperate. "We have the dress, but no model."

The room braced for an outburst of curses and accusations, but Mademoiselle was not a hotheaded neophyte. A missing model was just another problem to be solved, even if that model was slotted to wear one of the two showstoppers.

The very image of control, the designer looked around the

room, then narrowed her focus on Nicolle. Without missing a beat, she said, "You. You will model the dress."

Nicolle took a step back. What she suggested, it was impossible. Madness. She couldn't put herself in the salon, in a position where all eyes were on her. Not so soon after Francesca had recognized her. It was too dangerous. And the reason Mademoiselle was sending her on another rescue mission later that afternoon. She should be preparing for her departure, not traipsing around the salon in a cocktail dress. "I... I cannot do this. Please don't ask it of me."

Mademoiselle maintained her calm but for the narrowing of her gaze. "Come with me, Nicolle, and bring the dress with you."

She opened her mouth to argue. But Marie Claire was shoving the dress at her, and Mademoiselle was already marching away. Even Paulette conspired against her. "Go on," she said, sending her off with a little nudge.

Sighing, Nicolle rushed to catch up with the designer. The sound of a German opera carried her the final steps. At the threshold, she paused, looked down at the dress, and shook her head. "Mademoiselle, this isn't a good idea. I—"

"Come in and shut the door, Nicolle." The gravity of her tone snapped her into submission.

She quickly obeyed, then chose her words carefully. "I'm confused. I thought I was to avoid being seen. Isn't that why you're sending me on the, uh, special delivery to Périgueux?"

"That's enough, my dear. And please, give me the dress before you cause lasting damage."

Nicolle's gaze slid to the garment and saw that she was holding it all wrong. She quickly adjusted her grip. "I apologize. I'll iron out any wrinkles myself."

Seeming not to hear her, Mademoiselle shook out the garment, smoothed her hand over the complicated bodice, touched the tiny rosette Nicolle had secured inside one of the folds. "Do you know what inspired this dress?"

It was not a hard question. All she had to do was look at the picture of Giselle on stage as the Black Swan. It wasn't just the color, or the thin gossamer material reminiscent of a ballet costume. It was the vertical stitching, the feathering at the peplum-style waist. "Your daughter, she was your inspiration."

"And that is why you must model it today." She set the dress carefully on the desk and came to stand before Nicolle. "You are not Giselle, but you have become important to me. You are the daughter of my heart. It is only right that you wear the dress."

Nicolle was eaten up by emotion, absolutely gutted. The tears came fast and hard, and all she could do was let the older woman pull her into her arms and sob on her shoulder. After Julien's death, her whole world had felt like fog, empty of form, yet thick enough to drag her under. Mademoiselle had saved her from drowning in that dark abyss. She'd given her work, and a purpose beyond herself. "You are the mother I never knew." Her own had died so young. "But also, my mentor and friend."

Now Mademoiselle was crying, too, patting Nicolle on the back. Then she was pulling away, smiling, sighing, wiping at her cheeks. "Do this for me, Nicolle. Wear the dress and I will do what I must to keep you safe. Let me show you what I mean." She went to a cabinet and pawed through an assortment of hats. "This one, I think, yes. It will do."

She pulled out a hat with a satin cap and a swirl of netting that, when positioned properly, would cover the top portion of Nicolle's face. It was a brilliant solution, and now she had no reason to deny Mademoiselle's request. "I will do this, for you and our friendship. But I warn you, I have never modeled before. You may regret asking me."

"This is a problem easily solved. In this, Paulette will be the teacher, you the student. Now, let's get you dressed."

It was a perfect fit, once Mademoiselle worked her magic

with needle and thread. The hem had required a bit of restructuring to accommodate Nicolle's shorter height, and then there was the matter of Nicolle's hair. The slick chignon didn't work with the hat. The wide brim required a looser style. Mademoiselle proved as proficient in arranging hair as she was at draping fabric over a dress form.

Nicolle didn't know how long it took them to complete her transformation, but when they arrived back at the atelier, the other models were already lining up in order of appearance.

"Take your place beside Paulette." Mademoiselle gave her a light pat on her shoulder. "The two of you will finish the show together, as a pair."

That hadn't been the plan when Charlotte had been chosen to model the evening gown, but Nicolle liked the idea. Paulette in the dress inspired by Mademoiselle's dearest friend. Nicolle in the dress inspired by her beloved daughter. Symmetry of the old and new.

There was a moment of utter silence as she took her place. She wasn't surprised by the shocked speechlessness. She was, however, a bit insulted. "Stop staring," she growled at the group in general. "It's just me."

The outburst earned her a soft laugh from Mademoiselle, several shrugs from the house models, and a series of compliments from her fellow seamstresses. Once Mademoiselle was gone and the attention was no longer on Nicolle, Paulette whispered, "You are absolutely stunning in that dress."

She didn't feel stunning. She felt nervous and impatient, and her legs had gone suddenly boneless. It was an odd sensation, as was the sense of doubt coursing through her veins. She was Nicolle Cadieux, code name Odette, Mademoiselle's most trusted *passeur*. She'd crossed checkpoints with wounded airmen in her care. She was in the possession of a vicious scalpel and knew how to use it to kill a man. But wasn't that the point?

Nicolle's greatest skill was making herself invisible. There was no hiding in this dress.

As if reading her mind, Paulette squeezed her hand. "I especially like the hat. Very chic."

"Mademoiselle's idea."

"It's a nice touch, completely hides the top half of your face."

They shared a knowing smile, and Nicolle felt marginally better. She squared her shoulders, lifted her head, and nearly, almost, convinced herself she could saunter into the salon with some level of confidence. But then the music began, a soft, mesmerizing tune played by a string quartet, and they were moving into the corridor between the salon and atelier.

The music hit a crescendo, the first model hit her cue, light bulbs flashed, and the show was fully underway.

This was real. It was happening. Too fast. Nicolle gripped Paulette's arm. "I don't think I can do this."

"Not to worry. I'll be with you every step of the way. Just follow my lead."

For the past two years, her whole life had been dedicated to the shadows. She'd become comfortable in the dark. Now she was supposed to step into the light and become the center of attention. She felt a headache coming on. "What do I do? I don't know what to do." She gripped Paulette's arm. "You have to tell me what to do."

Paulette chuckled, pulled her close, and gestured with her head. "Watch Amelia."

With grim determination, Nicolle peered into the salon, saw the model moving at a leisurely pace. Not too fast. Not too slow, much like she herself approached a checkpoint.

"See how she makes a slow circuit of the room. We will do the same, only together, like two friends out for an afternoon stroll in the park. Oh. Okay, good. This is good. Look, see how Amelia has paused before that guest, her hip thrown out, head cocked, one hand in a pocket, the other thrust at an angle in the air."

Nicolle frowned. "She's just standing there, looking pouty and bored."

"Exactly. That's all you have to do."

Paulette made it sound so simple. And maybe it was. Nicolle had adopted a similar pose at the border only a week ago. The very picture of French indifference.

Three more models took their turn in the salon. Each time, applause broke out, with one glaring exception. It happened when the model wearing the red dress entered the salon. The crowd fell silent, and then murmurs of confusion filled the moment. Nicolle remembered the design had created a similar reaction in the atelier.

Marie Claire had begged Mademoiselle to rethink the gaudy lace and gauche ribbon at the hemline. Mademoiselle had been unmoved. No changes were to be made to the dress. She'd been wrong. The assembled crowd agreed. And yet, if Nicolle wasn't mistaken, the designer didn't look embarrassed. In truth, she displayed a rather smug smile, as if she secretly enjoyed the negative response. Meanwhile, Geneviève looked positively apoplectic. Something was going on there. Any number of reasons came to mind.

"Okay, Nicolle. We're up." Paulette took her hand and tugged her forward. "Shoulders back, head high. That's it. Perfect. Remember, stop, pose. Wait for the flash of light bulbs. Then we stroll, pause. Stroll, pause."

"Got it."

Out came the model wearing the hideous red dress, looking a bit shaken, and in went Nicolle and Paulette. They stopped, posed. Another extended hush fell over the crowd, a series of blinding light bulbs flashed. Then thundering applause broke out, and now they were strolling, pausing. Strolling, pausing.

Pencils scribbled on notepads. Gazes lit with pleasure. Words like *remarkable, amazing, innovative* were bandied about.

More strolling, pausing. Hands reached out to touch the fabric. Then it was over, and they were back in the corridor, Mademoiselle kissing each of their cheeks. "I will go now and take my bows."

She entered the salon to a standing ovation and a chorus of "Brava! Brava!"

While the designer accepted the praise, Paulette and Nicolle hurried back to the atelier, where they removed the dresses and handed them over to the sales staff. The process was slow. The garments were as valuable as any treasure the Nazis stole from French homes and museums. At some point, bottles of champagne appeared. Corks popped. The mood was happy, indulgent. Even Paulette received a positive reception from the other seamstresses.

It was the perfect distraction. Nicolle slipped away to prepare for her departure. She climbed the steps to the attic quickly, padded across the hardwood floor polished to a fine patina, and donned a dress made of faded cotton she'd chosen for the journey. The scent of soap lifted from the freshly laundered cloth. One glance in the mirror told her she looked the part of a humble Frenchwoman doing her best to survive occupation and rationing.

As a precaution, she placed the deadly scalpel in her pocket, then retrieved the garment bag from beneath her bed. After a short analysis of the available garments, she placed two glittering evening gowns and four stylish day dresses atop the man's suit Mademoiselle had supplied the night before. For the first time in months, she skipped packing a small stuffed bear. There'd been no opportunity to make one. She could only hope Jules wouldn't be too disappointed.

Another glance in the mirror, the choice of a hat, and she was ready. Yet something held her in place a moment longer, something she couldn't quite work out in her head. As she took a long, slow study of the room, a kick of foreboding struck fast and hard, like a swift jolt in her gut that made her a little queasy. Something dark pressed in on her mind, giving her the sense that she would not be returning to this attic. Or Paris.

This was the end of the line.

Terror welled up inside her, making her waste valuable time. She needed to get to the safe house and retrieve the airman. They must board the train out of Paris before nightfall. *Leave, Nicolle. Leave now.*

She took a step and froze again at the sound of familiar footsteps coming from the floor below. Paulette entered the attic, wearing a concerned expression and gripping a small brown item in one hand. It took Nicolle a moment to realize her friend held a tiny stuffed bear.

"I thought you might want this for your..." She paused, worried her bottom lip. "For, you know. The boy."

Nicolle's mind emptied. Then roared back to life with a dozen thoughts. "You think there is...a...a child?"

"Am I wrong?"

"I..." She couldn't bring herself to confess, even now, after silently vowing to share her secrets with this woman. She found a compromise instead, four words that admitted the truth indirectly. "How did you know?"

"The same way I learned how to hem a dress and sew a straight seam." She fiddled with the bear's ear. "I watched. I listened. It was not so hard to put the rest together."

Paulette Leblanc was proving to be a shrewd, clever young woman. And every time Nicolle thought she had an understanding of who she was, what she was capable of, her friend proved to be something more.

"Thank you, Paulette." Hand shaking, she took the bear, immediately saw the splendid craftsmanship and wondered where she'd found such a treasure when she spent her days in the atelier and her nights at Marcel's raucous parties.

"I made it myself."

At once, she was awed and sad. Paulette pulled her gently into her arms. It was hard not to cling. "Safe journeys, *mon amie.*" There was an uneasiness in her voice. "Come home in one piece."

Stepping back, she lifted her chin and gave her standard reply. "I will, as I always do."

By the time she stood in the street outside the atelier, looking up at the building she'd called home for two years, tears poured from her eyes. Tears of gratitude, of grief. Nicolle felt the kick of foreboding again and she knew, deep in her core, that this would be her final rescue.

Chapter Twenty-Six

Paulette

Paulette waited to begin her search until she was sure Nicolle wasn't coming back. Charlotte was still missing, and Mademoiselle was worried. Paulette was, too, and so when the designer had pulled her aside and asked her to snoop in the model's belongings, she'd agreed without hesitation. She hadn't expected to come across Nicolle. That had been something of a shock. She'd meant to put the bear in the garment bag and let her friend find the toy later.

But then she'd seen Nicolle, standing in the middle of the room, looking alone and a bit lost. The sight had unsettled Paulette and, to be honest, left her with a bad feeling.

A creak coming from the roof, or possibly somewhere outside, sent her moving to the other side of the room. Quickly, quietly, she sat at Charlotte's vanity and listened. When she heard no more sounds of a possible intruder, she continued, investing a full minute surveying the array of jars, bottles, and perfume atomizers. She immediately felt at home. She could be sitting at her own dressing table. The contents were that familiar.

How had she not seen the similarities between her and the house model? Because she hadn't tried. To be fair, the girl had never been friendly to her, either—quite the opposite, actually—but her sudden disappearance didn't sit well with Paulette, and she was genuinely concerned.

She began opening drawers and searching the contents. She found nothing out of the ordinary. Just more cosmetics and bits of a life lived under German occupation, ration coupons, ticket stubs to shows, matchbooks from restaurants, but no identity card—that was concerning. It wasn't until she opened the final drawer and found the false bottom that her snooping paid off. She removed the diary, and when the photograph fluttered to the ground, she thought, *Oh, Charlotte, what have you done?*

Paulette knew, of course, having traveled a similar path. Sighing, she retrieved the picture off the floor and studied the image of the impossibly attractive SS officer. He could be Friedrich's twin. The chiseled angles and smooth planes were the personification of Aryan perfection. The arrogant smirk, that, too, was pure Nazi. Bile swirled in her throat, but Paulette managed to swallow it down. A picture was just a picture. It could mean nothing. Or everything.

She was here to find out which.

Bolstered, she opened the diary and began reading. The early entries held nothing but descriptions of customers and opinions of coworkers. None of which were flattering. There was an entry from the day Paulette had arrived in Paris. Also not flattering. She quickly flipped the page. Then she found success with the last half of the entries.

His name was Franz. Charlotte had met him at Café de Flore. There'd been an instant attraction. He'd given her pretty words. Vows of devotion. Small, meaningful gifts. Promises. It was as if Paulette was reading about her own life. The only difference was that Charlotte hadn't yet discovered his true nature. She'd engaged in secret trysts, chronicling the various places they'd met. Cafés, nightclubs, picture shows, restaurants, the bar at the Hôtel Ritz.

It was clear Charlotte was devoted. Prepared to run off with her Nazi lover. And that, Paulette discovered, was exactly what she'd done. *I am to meet him at Gare de l'Est tomorrow morning just after dawn*, she'd written in an entry dated the day before. *It is the perfect moment to slip away. The fashion show will take priority. By the time they realize I am gone and not coming back, I will be his wife.*

Paulette doubted Franz had shown at the train station. A man who joined the SS was not the kind of man who would abandon his ideology or his Führer for a woman.

So where was Charlotte? Surely, the model wouldn't have gone looking for him. But that's what Paulette would have done. She would have worried for him at first, then grown desperate. Mademoiselle must be told. Or…

Perhaps it wasn't too late to save the girl. Paulette could go in search of her and bring her back. She could save Charlotte from herself, use her own story as a cautionary tale to convince her to come home. They would claim it was all a misunderstanding. She'd gone to see a family member and had forgotten to leave a note. Something, anything. Paulette would help her craft a believable story.

Who better than she?

It would mean striking out on her own. She knew Paris well enough to find the café mentioned in the diary, all the other places as well. That would put her out past curfew. Unwise.

There was another option, no less risky. She could wait until morning. She didn't know exactly when the French police would begin carrying out the mass arrests, but surely not before dawn. That was still hours away. Maybe the girl would return on her own. Paulette would give her a few hours to come to her senses. In the meantime, she would make a plan. Or rather, a list of the places Charlotte would go looking for her lover. At least a dozen showed up in the diary entries.

Paulette went to work. She committed the business names to memory. Then she placed the photograph back in the diary and slipped the lot back in the drawer. Her remaining two room-mates returned to the dorm just after nightfall. As was their habit, they completely ignored Paulette. Tonight, she was having none of it. "Do either of you know what happened to Charlotte?"

"Non," they said in unison, then burst into fits of giggles. Clearly, they'd consumed much champagne and not enough dinner.

"Does Charlotte have a beau?"

This time, she received shoulder shrugs and wandering gazes. They knew something.

"Are you not worried for your friend's safety?"

More shrugging. Oh, yes, they knew something. Paulette continued peppering them with questions. They continued giving nonanswers. Finally, she gave up. The two weren't talking. Their loyalty would have been admirable given a different scenario. She left them to their whispered giggling. All was not lost.

Nightfall came, then curfew, and still no Charlotte. The moon rose in the inky black sky, the stars came out, and still no Charlotte. Paulette spent the quiet hours between midnight and dawn alternating between worry, indecisiveness, and resentment. Maybe the girl had indeed run off with her lover. Maybe she'd found the one Nazi in Paris willing to give up his allegiance to the Reich for love.

She should tell Mademoiselle what she knew. But to do so risked exposing the girl to expulsion from the fashion house. The designer was lenient and forgiving. She gave her girls any number of privileges and freedoms. But openly cavorting with the enemy was not the same as frequenting a nightclub.

Another hour ticked away. By 4:00 a.m., Paulette's patience

came to an end. Her mind would not settle until she did her best to find Charlotte. If she couldn't find her, then she would tell Mademoiselle what she found. She hurriedly dressed in all black: trousers, sweater, cap. She placed her identity card in her back pocket.

Her plan was simple. Check every venue Charlotte had frequented with Franz the Nazi, and do it before the roundups began.

She had at least an hour before sunrise. Surely, the roundups would not begin before first light. She went to the café first, found it shut down. She hadn't expected it to be open. She eased around to the back of the building. There was movement within the dark. Activity. Someone, like herself, slinking in the shadows. She risked a single word. "Charlotte?"

No response, only silence. Stillness. But she knew he—or she—was there. Paulette could feel another presence in the black air. Was this person also searching for a lost friend? Or perhaps going into hiding before the roundups. If Rochon could uncover the date, so could others. Whatever the reason, an uneasy feeling had her backing away, slowly, one careful step at a time, hand on the wall for support. Soon, she was free of the alley. The other person hadn't attacked. Hadn't actually made a move at all.

She decided to check one of the restaurants next, a little bistro in Montmartre. Not far into her journey, the tempo on the streets changed. Movement out in the open. She stifled a scream. This was wrong. It was too early. The sun wasn't even up. Paulette ducked around another corner and froze. Her hand flew to her mouth. French police were everywhere. Dozens of them, hundreds, moving down the avenue in groups of three and four. Their footsteps pounded on pavement.

No, no! The arrests had begun.

She should not be here. She must get home. She ducked into the shadows and ran. She kept to the shadows. At this hour, it was not so hard. One block blurred into another. Paulette could hear fists pounding on doors. The air vibrated with the noise, shrill yells and raised voices. Sobs and pleas. Too many went willingly, carrying a pillow or a blanket. No suitcases. Those weren't allowed. And Paulette was out here among the chaos, looking for a wayward girl who didn't want to be found. One who'd prioritized romance over what was right. Why did she care so much? She knew, of course.

Go home. Her feet continued carrying her across the pavement, shadow to shadow, avenue to boulevard. No one seemed to notice her. Was she that good at keeping to the shadows? Or was it something more straightforward?

The arrests were brutally organized, the targets inside buildings, behind closed doors, as if the police were working their way down a preordained list of names and addresses. Of course they had a list. Lists upon lists. The whole reason behind the census became clear. The foreign Jews that had registered at their local police stations were being systematically rounded up and loaded onto buses.

Paulette thought of Nicolle. She was safely away from Paris, but would return. A new rush of heartbeats. She must convince her friend to leave France. If her identity was discovered, this would be Nicolle's fate. Buses choked and spit their way down the streets, a parade of innocent people deemed unworthy of life. *Help them.*

How? Mademoiselle. She must get to Mademoiselle.

Paulette hurried to the atelier, sticking to back alleys, avoiding Jewish neighborhoods, avenues and streets where many of the immigrants had settled. Hundreds, possibly thousands of people were forcibly taken out of their homes. Some women carried their belongings in sheets and towels. Others carried small children in their arms. Elderly women dragged behind their families, silent tears in their eyes.

All of them looked panic-stricken and haggard. They'd lost their husbands and sons to previous roundups, and now it was their turn. Surely, they knew what was coming next. It took only a single look into the hard eyes of the men in French uniforms to know. Deportation, death.

Those men, they were traitors. They weren't following orders. They were committing a crime against humanity.

More buses rumbled past. More shouting, crying. She ran faster.

Some of the police carried large rolls of tape. For what? To secure a door, she guessed, a sign to their fellow officers that this apartment had been cleared of the Jews living inside.

She entered another neighborhood and thought she'd come to the end of the world. French children were playing in the streets, as if this was just another day, while Jewish children were crammed into buses. It was terribly unfair. The buses seemed to be heading her way now. Paulette stood not far from the Eiffel Tower, on Rue Nélaton. One after another, buses joined a line that wove toward the entrance of the Vél d'Hiv, where sporting events and competitions usually took place. The police unloaded their human cargo in orderly fashion.

Where was the uprising among the French people? Where was the rebellious spirit that had defined generations? Just yesterday, they celebrated the storming of the Bastille. Today, they remained silent. She walked for what seemed an eternity, her mind full of sadness, outrage. She lost her way, twice.

Up ahead, finally, she saw Maison de Ballard. A light shone from a window on the fourth floor, like a beacon calling her home. Paulette sprinted across the street, rounded the corner, and entered the building through the atelier. She heard classical music coming from Mademoiselle's apartment. Beethoven, she thought. Or possibly Mozart.

Mademoiselle opened the door within seconds of Paulette's knock. Without preamble, she said, "The roundup has begun."

"We know."

We. Mademoiselle wasn't alone. She was also fully dressed, her hair coiffed, her eyes alert but full of sadness and rage. Behind her stood Rochon. Paulette's spine tingled at the sight of him. Like her, he wore all black, not a suit, more casual. The kind of clothes meant for moving through the shadows.

"Get inside, Paulette, before someone sees you dressed like that."

She hurried into the apartment, her gaze on Rochon. The last time they'd met, Detective Mueller had stood between them. Nothing had changed since then. The Gestapo agent was still in the middle of their tenuous relationship, a dark, menacing presence that brought doubt and ugly suspicion. Her heart squeezed with too many emotions to sort through at once. She wanted to trust Rochon, but there was too much mystery surrounding him.

Huffing out a breath, Mademoiselle stepped between them. "Where have you been, Paulette? And why are you dressed like a common thief?"

"I went to search for Charlotte." Realizing she could no longer protect the house model, she explained what she'd discovered in the girl's desk, the photograph, the diary, and what conclusions she'd drawn. "I left before dawn, thinking I would go to all the places she'd met the Nazi in the past before the roundup began. I went to the café first, swung over to Montmartre, and discovered I was wrong about the timing. The police were everywhere, swarming the streets like cockroaches crawling out of hidden nests."

"They started earlier than we thought," Rochon supplied. "Just after four a.m. And you were out there, in the middle of it?"

"Yes."

He did not look pleased. "You weren't stopped or questioned?"

"I know how to stay out of sight." She described the winding route she took, what she saw from her vantage point in the shadows, what she heard. She left nothing out. By the time she finished, Mademoiselle had tears in her eyes. Rochon seemed angry, but also full of respect.

"Paris has fallen," she said to him. "Too many look the other way. They pretend nothing is wrong. I used to be one of them. Those days are over. I want to do more for the network. I *have* to do more."

Rochon nodded. *"Très bien."*

His easy agreement left her momentarily speechless. She'd anticipated a fight. She actually welcomed one. She was still gaping at the man, but he was no longer looking at her. "Get the maps, Sabine." To Paulette he said, "Wait here."

He went to the wireless and turned up the volume. Then, taking the maps from Mademoiselle, he set them on a tabletop and began shoving aside debris left over from what looked like a breakfast of fresh-baked pastries and strong coffee. Paulette's mouth watered. She hadn't eaten since yesterday morning before the fashion show.

"We run escape lines for people needing to get out of France—downed airmen, Jewish refugees, political dissidents and the like." He smoothed out one of the maps, left his palm on top. "We locate them and then, when necessary, feed and clothe them. We also provide false identity papers and ferry them across southern France and into Spain."

"I had no idea your operation was this organized."

"We call the people who assist us along the way helpers. They number in the hundreds. Include the other escape lines and that reaches into the thousands. The most perilous job in the network is that of a *passeur*, the people who shepherd the escapees along the route."

"Like Nicolle."

"Correct. Now." He lifted his hand. "Tell me, Paulette, what do you see?"

She leaned over and studied the map. "I see several hand-drawn lines fanning out from Paris. Five to the north, four to the south, and one west toward England. All the southern routes end in Spain." She looked up. "These are the escape lines?"

He nodded. "We primarily use the southern routes by train through France and cross the Pyrenees on foot. Is this what you want to do, Paulette? Become a *passeur*?"

Before answering, she ran her finger along one of the escape lines. Paris to Orléans, then on to Limoges, Périgueux, Toulouse, and ending, finally, in Spain. She retraced the path back to Paris, knowing that here, beneath her fingertip, was her personal route to redemption. "I'm ready."

"Paulette." Mademoiselle took her arm in the soft, gentle hold of a worried mother. "We know you're ready or we wouldn't be having this conversation. What we need is for you to be certain. What we are asking is dangerous. It requires daring and nerve, and an ability to improvise when things go wrong. And things always go wrong."

Mademoiselle was trying to scare her. But Paulette wasn't to be deterred. She had the daring, the nerve, and, yes, all the other skills. She'd learned them from sneaking out of her family's château to meet Friedrich. She'd used them skulking through the Parisian streets littered with French police. Even navigating a party at Guy Marcel's had prepared her for this moment. "I'm certain. I want to be a *passeur*."

Chapter Twenty-Seven

Nicolle

Nicolle's portion of the escape went without a hitch. Every piece fell into place. The airman was waiting for her in the safe house, uninjured, dressed properly, and ready for the long journey south. He answered her questions correctly, posed to determine he was not a German spy. They sailed through the checkpoints. The trains ran on time. The weather held. Even the handoff in Périgueux went smoothly. Everything went so well, in fact, that Nicolle wondered if all the fuss about a mole was really just a series of unfortunate coincidences.

So why this sick feeling in her stomach?

Why the sense that she would never see her son again?

It was the weather, she decided. The wind had shifted, and clouds were moving in swiftly overhead, creating a gray, marbled ceiling poised for a watery attack. The air went still and Nicolle hurried her steps, taking the most direct route to the train station.

The rain let loose, and she sought shelter under an awning connected to a business that sold watches. The street was empty. No one to her left or right. But there it was again. The feeling that something was wrong. Something was off. She slipped into the shop and wandered around, always aware of her surroundings, the single entrance in and out, the display cases. The sleepy-eyed man in his fifties sitting behind the counter read a book with tattered pages and a scarred cover. He didn't acknowledge her, and she decided that was good. She pretended interest in a watch in one of the cases, then left.

The rain was coming down harder, and she decided to wait it out in the café across the street. It had outdoor seating protected by an awning larger than the one over her head. Steeling herself, she dashed out into the rain and found a table a minute later. Soaked to the bone, she placed the garment bag on the seat beside her, then ordered a coffee, paid the ridiculous price, and felt outrageously uneasy. As if she were being watched. A glance revealed nothing out of the ordinary.

She closed her eyes and conjured up her son's image. Usually, this exercise brought her peace. This afternoon, she felt nothing but anguish. Her son was safe, but only because Nicolle wasn't in his life. What had begun as a temporary solution had become something more permanent. Her Jules had a new name. He was Jules Lavigne, a happy, healthy little boy who lived in Limoges with his parents. He wasn't hers anymore. He was theirs, Monique and Louis's.

It wasn't fair, but it was right. She jumped to her feet, needing to move. She wandered aimlessly through the quaint streets of Périgueux that still showed signs of the Roman conquest. She passed the remains of an amphitheater, a villa, a temple to some ancient goddess, and found herself in a park. She'd lost her way a bit and had to backtrack along the river.

There was time, still.

A crack of a twig had her freezing midstep. She looked down, saw nothing beneath her feet. Not her fault. Another's. She moved quickly, seeking the shadows, where she was most comfortable. The rain helped, not a downpour anymore, a steady drizzle that cloaked the air in misty gray fog. She turned down a back alleyway, looking left, right. Behind. No one there. She kept moving, turned another corner. A new sound. She held her breath, listened. The noise came again. Footsteps. Too heavy for a woman. A man.

Cocking her head, she listened to the cadence of the heel strikes. One man, walking with authority. A steady, measured approach. Nicolle made another turn, then realized her mistake. A dead end. No way out, not without a fight. This was why she carried a weapon.

She stuffed the garment bag in a dark corner, flexed her fingers, then pulled out the scalpel and removed the metal cap covering the blade. It felt light in her hand. She wished it were a gun. A bullet could be discharged from a distance. This weapon required intimate contact. *Him or me*, she told herself. Only one of them would walk away. Only one would survive.

If it was him, her son would still have a mother. Monique would raise him for Nicolle. And that was the precise thinking that got a woman killed. She melted into the shadows, crouched low, cleared her mind of such thoughts.

"I know you're here, Fräulein. Show yourself." That voice. It was familiar, but the German accent confused her. "I killed your friend. Now I will kill you."

The enemy came around the corner. Nicolle stifled a scream. Blood rushed into her ears. It was the airman she'd just handed over to the next *passeur*. And he had a gun. Not a British airman. A German spy. Where was the other girl? He'd just told her. Now he'd come for Nicolle.

She cleared her mind and let André's instructions flow over her. *Come from behind*. She made herself one with the dark and watched him come closer. Closer.

Patience is your greatest ally.

He was nearly on her now. She held her breath, watched him continue past her.

Strike fast. Commit fully.

She pounced, wrapped her arm around his neck, held firm. The gun dropped to the ground. A shot fired. She felt a sting in her belly, ignored it. She found the spot on his rib cage, slid the blade in deep.

Then she took off at breakneck speed.

Horror at what she'd done rolled through her. She'd taken a man's life. A man who'd come to kill her. She hadn't known she had it in her.

She had to think. No, she had to run. The gunshot. Too loud. Others would come for him. She needed a weapon. The scalpel. It was still in her hand, dripping with a man's blood—and she was still running hard. Her lungs burned. Air caught in her throat. *Breathe.* She had to breathe. In a rush, the air ripped out of her. Then came the hard gasps peppered with sobs.

And still, she ran.

Hard, fast, her feet pounding the ground. Too much noise. She stopped abruptly, regrouped, found herself on the outskirts of the city. A hedge appeared out of nowhere. No time. She pushed and fought her way through. Her teeth chattered. Sweat poured in her eyes.

For a terrifying moment, she felt something tear below her ribs. A cramp. She pressed her hand to the pain. Her fingers came away bloody. She'd been shot. Fear clogged in her throat. She couldn't board the train with blood pouring from her side.

She needed to find a hiding place, treat the wound. Staunch the blood. Then decide her next step. She found sanctuary in an abandoned shed connected to a farmhouse. Her hands were shaking, and she must be quiet. Absolutely silent. The wound wasn't bad. A stroke of good luck. The bullet had only grazed her. Somehow, she managed to retrieve the blue scarf in her pocket, make a few rips with the scalpel, and wrap it around her waist without making a sound.

Tears flooded her eyes, all but drowning her vision into a watery blur. She didn't know how long she stayed in the shed. Minutes, hours. Finally, the rain stopped. The moon came out. Nicolle needed to get moving and find a way to contact Mademoiselle. Suddenly everything cleared. Her body became light, her mind freed itself of any pain. André. She would go to him.

First, she must survive the night.

She stepped out of the shed into a moonlit clearing. She was exposed. She looked for the dark, where she felt most comfortable. And there, up ahead, her old, constant friend waited in a clump of trees and shadows. Fifty feet to safety. Then she saw it. The truck, abandoned near a decrepit barn beside the dark house listing slightly to port. The going would be slow driving over foreign terrain. But faster than on foot.

Nicolle paused, listening for any indication the owners of the house were in residence. She heard the wind shifting the leaves, but nothing of people or farmers. She made her move, her senses alert to sounds not of nature but of man. The house lay dark, silent. Abandoned. She didn't want to think why.

She moved in a crouch. A few more steps and she was at the truck, on the wrong side. She opened the door anyway, crawled across the seat and bent down to have a look at the ignition. No key. Big problem. She searched the floorboard. Pulled down the visor and nearly lost an eye as a set of keys hit her head and then fell into her lap. She prayed there was petrol in the tank. After a grinding of metal against metal, the motor turned over, the vehicle coughed to life, and again, Nicolle was on the move.

What would she say if she was stopped?

She wouldn't be, and if she was, there would be no incriminating evidence. She tossed the scalpel out the window, drove without the headlights, and kept to a roundabout route. The moon had retreated behind the heavy cloud cover rolling in from the west, which made crossing fields and hills a challenge. She kept going forward, circling back twice, grateful she knew the terrain because Julien had loved his little drives in the country. Even in death, her husband protected her. Still, a journey that should have taken two hours lasted five. She stopped a mile from the village of La Haye-Descartes and abandoned the truck in a field.

Sleep beckoned. Her body ached. A few hours of rest would restore her strength. She could go back to the truck and stay in the dark a little longer, and leave herself vulnerable to capture. But she pushed on instead, past her physical and mental limits, until she saw the house. A spurt of energy filled her as she slunk around to the back door. The shadows embraced her almost lovingly. She'd learned to crave the dark. Not a single light shone from inside, and while she appreciated this, she also wondered if André was home or on a mission, like her.

At the door, she tried to remember the sequence of knocks they'd agreed upon. Was it two fast raps, pause, then three more? Or was it three first, then two?

Think, Nicolle.

She was so tired. Her mind was a jumble of thoughts.

Think.

Three. It was three first, two second. She fisted her hand, knocked. Waited an entire thirty seconds before daring to repeat the sequence. Another fifteen seconds passed, Nicolle counted, and then, finally, André opened the door. They exchanged no words for several seconds. She gave no explanations. He asked no questions, except one. "Are you alone?"

"Yes."

His eyes ran across her face, down to her blood-soaked shirt. "You're hurt."

"I…" Queasiness rolled over her. "I…" Her vision blurred.

She saw him reaching for her, felt herself leaning toward him. She slumped.

He swore.

And then, relief. The world went black, and her last memory was being lifted in André's arms.

Chapter Twenty-Eight

Sabine

Sabine stood at her apartment window, watching the sun set over Paris. As if in defiance of the war, the sky glowed rosy and warm, casting the world in a soft pink blush. It seemed wrong that the city could look so pretty, so full of light, when evil lurked around every street corner and inside every building. Thousands of homes that had once belonged to Jewish immigrants lay empty. Swept clean by French policemen in open collaboration with the enemy. They'd had a plan for the roundups and had executed the mass arrests with cold, swift, unprecedented efficiency.

Now women and children were trapped in the Vél d'Hiv, scheduled for deportation or worse, and there was nothing Sabine could do. A pang of absolute uselessness shot through her. She'd helped only a few, not even twenty, managing to get them into hiding throughout the city. A *sou* in the ocean. Even the two women she'd vowed to rescue, Vivian's friends, were in a precarious position, entombed in a bunker beneath the home of a Nazi.

Purpose wiped away all other emotion. Sabine would get them out. She must, for the sake of the thousands she couldn't save. It would be tricky, but it could be done, with the right *passeur*. The thought made Sabine want to howl in frustration. She settled for a low growl deep in her throat, then shoved away from the window. Her joints creaked like old hinges as she made her way across the room and stared hard at the telephone, willing it to ring.

Nicolle was late. It wasn't uncommon. She'd often been late due to her side trips to Limoges, but never this many days. And never without contacting Sabine first. Any number of problems could have arisen, some as simple as a delayed train, faulty telephone lines, a problem with the handoff. Others reasons were far worse: detection, discovery, death.

She shuddered. The SS was getting smarter, infiltrating entire networks with German soldiers posing as British airmen. Their own safe house in Toulouse had been compromised that way. She was back to dwelling on the worst outcome for her *passeur*. Death. "Ring!" she commanded the phone.

Silence met her demand.

Sighing, she went back to the window, gripped the windowsill with fingers going arthritic at the knuckles. Sabine felt old and tired. She'd spent much time avenging the deaths of the women she'd lost, and for what? A network submerged with a traitor. A *passeur* who hadn't checked in. And then there was Paulette. Sabine had lost control with that one.

She'd promised Hélène she would take care of her daughter. Instead, she was training her to take on the most dangerous job in her network. Paulette was inventive, smart, full of courage, with a strong need to do the right thing. Young still, but more than capable. And there was her answer to one of her problems. If Nicolle didn't reach out soon, Sabine would send Paulette to find her.

The sun finished its slow decline, and another long, endless day dipped into the gray margin between day and night. Sabine's eyes began to strain against the failing light. They grew heavy, but just before she let them close, the harsh sound of the telephone rent the air.

Nicolle!

She made it across the room before the third ring. Despite her breathlessness, she pushed out a single word. *"Bonjour?"*

"We go tonight." The voice did not belong to Nicolle, but Vivian.

Two days ahead of schedule. A cold, familiar wind swept over Sabine's soul. Something was wrong. Her friend's voice sounded ragged, agitated, but the message was clear. There was no need for conversation. No questions. Vivian had secured the documents or she wouldn't have made the call. They'd planned for this eventuality. Any day, the Nazi could discover the Jews living beneath his feet.

The sooner they got the mother and daughter out of France, the better. Sabine cleared her throat, and when she spoke, it was softly, with a heavy tone. *"Très bien."*

As the line went dead, her legs lost their bones, and she found herself sitting on the floor, receiver still in hand. Not Nicolle, she thought again. Vivian. In trouble. Two Jews in need of rescue. A new and willing *passeur* ready to take on the challenge.

Sabine managed to stand up, set the receiver back in its cradle, and pick it up again. Rochon answered on the second ring. She gave the same three words to him that Vivian had given her. "We go tonight."

She went in search of Paulette next. As expected, she found the young woman on her bed in the dormitory, sketch pad on her lap, her mother's shawl draped around her shoulders. She looked like a young art student honing her craft. Even the black trousers and sweater beneath the gauzy shawl added to the overall picture. The choice of clothing was in preparation for this moment, when Sabine tapped her for the extraction of Vivian's friends from the Nazi's home.

"Paulette," she said. "Come with me."

Without speaking, the young woman calmly rose, set the sketch pad on the bed, and discarded the shawl in favor of the blue scarf. "I'm ready."

Yes, she was. Sabine led the way out of the attic. Back in her apartment, she put the necessary precautions in place, then spread out the map the young woman had already committed to memory to the sound of a Mozart opera. Much better, Sabine decided, than Wagner.

She'd ensured Paulette knew the route by heart, and the alternatives should she need to improvise. Still, Sabine wasn't leaving anything to chance on this, the young woman's maiden voyage. "Philippe will drive with you as far as the edge of Drancy, where you will set out on your own for the rendezvous point. There will be two women waiting for you, a mother and a daughter."

She nodded solemnly.

"You will guide them on foot through the forest, then reconnect with Philippe here." She indicated a different spot on the map. "He will drive the three of you to Fontainebleau." She pointed to the small village sixty miles south of Paris. "Then it's on to Nevers. At that point, you and the refugees will board a train bound for Clermont via Montluçon, where you will hand the pair off to the next *passeur*. Any questions?"

She had only one. "Why him? Why Philippe?"

This was not the first time she'd asked the question, but all the others had been with her eyes only. A look of distrust, a reluctance to stand too close to him. Understandable. However, voicing her concerns aloud now, minutes before she was to take on her first rescue, changed nothing. "He's done this before. You have not."

"I don't trust him."

Considering her past, she was wise to be leery of a man, any man, Philippe included. Her son-in-law had cultivated dangerous alliances. Paulette had witnessed his interactions with these men at Marcel's parties, one in particular that had given her genuine cause for doubt. Sabine had not been able to ease her concerns. That left only one response. "Philippe won't let you down, and *maintenant*, we are out of time. You must go."

In an instant, her expression cleared. "I'm ready."

She gave the girl her identity card. Her code name: Clara. Then she kissed her cheeks and showed her the door. "Philippe will be waiting for you outside the atelier."

In the entryway, Paulette reached for the doorknob, paused. "Have you heard from Nicolle?"

"No, I haven't. But there's no cause for concern. This is not unusual." Not a lie, precisely, just a little fib to ease both their minds. "She'll be home soon. Now, go."

As soon as Paulette left, Sabine hurried to her bedroom and looked out the window to the alley below, where Philippe's car idled. A dark figure exited the building, head down, shoulders hunched. The passenger door swung open, and Paulette slipped inside. The car pulled away at a slow and steady pace. She was breathing a sigh of relief when the phone rang. *Nicolle.* It must be her.

Sabine hurried back out into the main living area, all but stumbling over a pronounced wrinkle in the rug. Moonlight cast moody shadows over the room, obscuring the map still laid out on the table. She hastily picked up the receiver and pressed it to her ear. *"Bonjour?"*

A man's voice came through the line loud and clear, a deep, rich baritone, speaking with a cultured French accent. "Mademoiselle Sabine."

Her heart stopped in her chest. Her grip tightened. "This is she."

"The suit I ordered has arrived."

Relief wanted to bring her to her knees. How desperate she was to hear those words. *At last!* News of Nicolle. But…two days late. Sabine tried to keep the anxiousness out of her voice as she asked, "I trust the fit was correct?"

"I'm afraid there was need for quite a few alterations." Translation: Nicolle was injured.

Sabine's hand started to shake. She forced herself to remain calm. That this man knew to speak to her, in this specific code, gave her hope. He would have needed to be coached in what to say. Nicolle was alive. But not well enough to call herself.

"This is not happy news." Sabine had no ability to keep the worry out of her voice. She didn't even try. "Is the garment fixable?" Translation: Will Nicolle survive her injuries?

"Yes, but the required alterations are extensive and will take time."

A heaviness weighed on Sabine's heart. She moved the receiver to her other ear. "How much time?"

"Several days."

Her stomach contracted into a hard pit. It was too much time away, added to the days she'd already been gone. Nicolle's absence had been noticed, commented upon in private. Now it would be talked about openly. Speculated over. "No sooner?"

"Non." His voice was soft, barely a whisper, but there was an urgent edge when he added, "I believe I should look for another designer for a female friend, one who can provide a Spanish flair to the garment. Do you have any recommendations?"

The man had gone off script, but she understood what he was asking. He wanted help getting Nicolle out of France. Sabine wanted the same thing for the young woman who'd become a surrogate daughter, a friend. She'd kept Nicolle long enough. It was time to let her go. Time to set her free. "I'll look into the matter myself. You'll hear from me soon."

"Merci."

For the second time that night, Sabine set the receiver back in its cradle. All her strength, all her fight dissolved from her body. She felt deflated, empty. Her knees gave out, and she collapsed into the closest chair. Her gaze tracked around the room, seeing nothing but Nicolle in her mind. The day she'd arrived on Sabine's doorstep, her belly not yet swollen with her husband's child.

Sabine lunged to her feet. The boy. She'd forgotten about Nicolle's son. He would have to stay behind, perhaps not forever, but for now. Leaving behind her child would tear Nicolle's heart in two. Maybe there was a way. Sabine wouldn't know until she investigated the various possibilities. Course set, she moved through the room, switching on lamps.

At the table, she leaned over and studied the map of France. She would construct another rescue plan. The most important yet.

Chapter Twenty-Nine

Paulette

Paulette did not speak to Rochon as she settled into the seat beside him. She simply let him drive. His hands—the hands of an artist, she realized with a jolt—guided the car expertly through the empty, silent streets. He kept the headlights off, navigating from memory. The man was so incredibly competent. Mademoiselle trusted him without reservation. Paulette tried to do the same. She could never quite get there.

For days, he'd trained her, drilling into her head the route she would take, the layouts of the various train stations, the words she would say at the border, the many lies she would tell: her name, her purpose for crossing the Demarcation Line, the names of the women with her. And always, he reminded her that one mistake on her part and lives would be in danger.

On several occasions she'd asked him, "Who are you?" and "How do you know all this?" Each time, he'd told her to stay focused on the task at hand.

The man was an enigma. He was also a good teacher. Paulette was prepared.

She was also edgy.

Mouth set, she gazed out the window, determined not to reveal her nerves. Her eyes strained against the gloom. Paris at night was full of secrets. They passed a large park. In the distance, she made out the silhouette of a man, rifle slung over his shoulder. Her heart gave a stutter as one became two, moving in lockstep. Good guys, bad guys. SS, Resistance. Hard to know. She squinted, leaned forward, and they were gone. Vanished into shadow and night.

Sighing, she sat back, resting her head on the seat cushion.

Rochon's hands continued guiding the car with cool, quiet efficiency. The confined space grew suddenly hot, intimate. He sat too close. She could smell his clean, masculine scent. Something composed of spice and wood. Tiny doubts flared in her mind, until she could think of nothing but the sight of him in conversation with Wolfgang Mueller.

Paulette hadn't asked him for an explanation since that first night, nor had he volunteered one on his own. That left them at a stalemate, not friends, not quite enemies, but something nebulous and blurry. Rochon steered the car around another corner, slow and steady, his eyes never leaving the road. Never touching on Paulette. She chanced a glance at his profile and had to stifle another sigh. His expression was one of carefully studied boredom. A mask only. She could feel the tension wafting off him.

He took another unhurried turn, winding his way toward the edge of the Parisian suburb where he'd let her out of the car to make the rest of the journey on foot. Time seemed to slow. Endless seconds turned into endless minutes until Paulette had had enough. "How long until we reach the drop-off point?"

"A quarter of an hour."

She couldn't take fifteen more minutes trapped inside her

own head. She made several attempts at conversation. And received one-word answers for her effort. Then she went for something more personal. "How did you get the injury?"

His head turned in her direction, revealing two dark eyebrows scrunched into a frown. She expected a nonanswer. Instead, he said, "During an escape."

Three whole words. Progress. "Things went wrong?"

"Disastrous." Back to one-word answers, but then he surprised her again and added, "I was the lone survivor."

He didn't expand. She hadn't expected he would. Rochon was a master at revealing just enough information to leave her wanting more. She waffled over asking more questions. But then she saw the raw, unfettered pain brimming in his eyes. A glimpse beneath the mask. She'd seen that look once before, when he'd come upon her wearing his wife's dress.

Had Giselle been on the mission with him? Paulette wanted to ask, but they'd crossed into Drancy, and he was pulling the car to a stop beneath a cluster of trees with low-hanging branches.

All business now, she shoved a hat on her head and pulled the droopy bill over half her face. Rochon shifted in his seat, drawing closer. She made an involuntary gasp. A shudder. He was all muscle and sinew, strength and bones. "You're nervous," he whispered.

"I'm not."

"You're trembling."

Was she? Her blood was so loud in her ears, rushing like a river, she wasn't aware of anything but the sound.

"You're ready, Paulette. You have the skills, the brains. Go now, and save the lives of two women in desperate need of rescue."

Her heart became a drum in her chest. Thumping, thumping. Rochon's belief in her reminded Paulette that she wasn't the flighty, vapid girl who once toyed with young men's affections.

Nor was she the secretive, slightly older girl who'd lied to her family so she could engage in a scandalous romance.

"Remember. The escapees will be frightened. Rightfully so. They are Jewish women on the run from men who want them dead. They will be skittish. One look at me and they will not want to get in the car. You will convince them."

This, she knew, was the reason Mademoiselle had insisted Paulette was to be their first contact. She had five miles of woods and brush to build a bond with the mother and daughter. "I will do my very best to ease their minds."

That got a smile. "I'll be waiting for you on the other side of Drancy." He shifted closer still, placed a torch in her hand. "Don't switch on the light until you are deep in the forest."

"Right." She reached for the door handle.

He stopped her with a hand on her arm. "Be careful, Paulette."

"Always." Outside, she adjusted her oversize jacket. Underneath, she wore men's clothing far too big for her small frame. The hat had been Mademoiselle's idea. Even in clandestine operations, she knew how to dress a woman properly.

An owl hooted from a tree branch overhead. A small woodland creature scampered in the brush below. These were familiar noises, heard in her own part of France on other late-night jaunts. She set out feeling confident, working her way systematically over terrain she'd studied and memorized from maps in Mademoiselle's apartment.

Residual heat of the day pulsed off the forest ground, turning the air into a wet, sticky stew smelling of the night and something foul, the stench of sweat and unwashed bodies. Paulette wrinkled her nose, paused, gathered her bearings. How close was she to the Drancy detention center? Too close, she decided from the scent, and her heart slipped to her toes. All those people, thousands of them, waiting for deportation, crammed in a facility meant for seven hundred.

A shout rent the air, and Paulette resumed her trek through the forest, happy for the lack of light. She couldn't see well, but that meant she couldn't be seen. Rochon had chosen this particular torch for this purpose. Its weak light was just a shimmer.

Paulette cleared the brush. Three figures appeared before her, hidden in shadow. Three? There were supposed to only be two. She studied the trio. Two huddled close together, an older woman and a younger one. The mother and daughter, then, each carrying canvas bags thrown over their shoulders. There was something especially harrowing in the way they clung to each other. Something had happened. Something bad. Their fear, it was fresh. Tangible.

And who was the third woman? Paulette scowled. *Rescues rarely go as planned.* Adjust, she told herself. Improvise. She could always abort should there be a need, should any of the three lack the proper papers. Introductions first.

She gave her name, low and quick, wishing to hurry along this process so they could be on their way. "I will be your *passeur.*" The older woman met her eyes, mumbled something in a foreign tongue. "Your escort," she clarified.

The tallest of the figures shifted into the thin beam of light. "This is Rachel," she said, tugging a young woman forward who looked close to Paulette's own age, "and her mother, Ilka."

She recognized the names. But, again, who was this third woman? "I was told to expect only two, a mother and daughter."

"*C'est vrai.* I'm not making the journey."

This seemed to surprise the youngest of the escapees.

"Why not?" She reached to the other woman, her distress vibrating on the air. "You can't go back to that house."

"I can't leave Vivian." Paulette recognized the name, and her mind raced back over the days and months since her arrival in Paris. The American widow, always insisting Mademoiselle fit her garments personally. The extra fittings that had not been scheduled, the passing of envelopes.

"Yes, you can leave her." The young woman spoke low and with urgency. "She is the woman who…" The hesitation hinted at some terrible act. "What if she didn't survive? What if *he* did? Don't go back, Camille. Please."

Paulette tried to piece together the words. There'd been a fight involving Vivian Miller and some unknown man. They were both injured, but these three were not. A battle over them or something else?

The tall French woman, Camille, shook her head. "I won't abandon her. I can't. And there is my family to consider. They need me." She held Rachel's stare, unspoken meaning in her steady gaze. "No, I can't leave France."

As the two argued, Paulette thought of Nicolle and the day they would have to part ways like this, on the edge of a clearing or in a train station, saying their final goodbyes. She didn't want that, but for her friend's safety, for a chance at a life free of persecution, she would endure the loss.

"Thank you, Camille. I won't forget what you've done for my mother and me."

"I would do it all again."

"I know."

The young women reached for each other and held on tight. "Thank you," Rachel said again.

"De rien." You're welcome.

They pulled apart, and Camille was turning away, but Rachel was calling out to her. "Camille, wait." She reached inside her tote bag and pulled out what looked like scissors—no, garden shears. "For protection."

Rachel said nothing more. But Paulette saw the loss in her eyes. The grief. She took her mother's hand, nodded to Paulette, and the three of them were moving deeper into the woods.

Once they were swallowed up by the forest, she stopped and addressed the pair with a single glance. "From this moment forward, you are no longer Rachel and Ilka. You are Eva and

Yvonne Tremblay. I am Clara, your cousin. We are traveling into the Free Zone to attend our uncle's funeral. This is a tragic event for our family. He was young, only fifty-three, and we are very, very sad over this terrible waste. We are grieving, and this explains our outward distress." Mademoiselle had made up the general story of the funeral. Paulette had added the details. "Any questions?"

They shook their heads.

"Good. We continue."

Five miles later, Paulette caught sight of Rochon's vehicle, right where it was supposed to be. Ilka, or rather, Yvonne, put up a minor fuss when she laid eyes on the big, dark-haired man. Paulette tried to ease her mind. "You can trust him."

She realized it was true. For all the mystery surrounding him, all the things he said and many he didn't, Paulette knew he was the man Mademoiselle claimed. A man of integrity who lied, cheated, and made unholy alliances with men like Wolfgang Mueller for a higher purpose.

In the end, Rachel was the persuasive force, convincing her mother they had no other choice but to trust the *passeur*. Not, Paulette noted, the big man behind the steering wheel, but her. She prayed she would prove worthy of such confidence.

They spent the sixty-mile drive to Fontainebleau in relative silence. The mother and daughter in the back seat, Paulette in the front with Rochon. The Jewish women were close, their bond apparent in the way they linked arms and bent their heads together. She heard words like *yarn, knitting needles, books, shawls*. It was a scene straight out of Paulette's childhood. She and her mother had been that close, sharing small conversations about shared interests. *Oh, Maman, I miss you so.*

If her mother knew what she was doing here tonight, she would be proud of Paulette. That helped ease her sorrow to a low rumble beneath the surface. Rochon looked at her, must have seen something in her face, because he covered her hand with his and pressed their palms together. His touch, easy and light, said far more than words. In that moment, with his heat joining hers, she felt a peace that had eluded her for months. His soft expression told her he felt the same. When he pulled away, his warmth remained on her skin, in her heart.

They reached Fontainebleau just before dawn. Rochon pulled to a stop outside the train station and reached to the floorboard for a small bag. When she lifted her eyebrows, he explained, "Your free movement passes and some money."

She tucked both into her own satchel and exited the motorcar without another word. The two women followed her lead. As she watched Rochon drive away, Paulette realized she was on her own. The refugees were solely in her care.

The first train took them to Nevers, where they disembarked and then boarded another bound for Clermont via Montluçon. All went according to plan, though not without tension. Crossing the Demarcation Line required answers to many, many pointed questions. The German guards were relentless, looking for reasons to arrest and detain.

Rachel and Ilka proved they'd committed their cover story to memory. Not a single hitch in their recitation. Ilka even managed tears when she spoke of her dead family member. Paulette sensed she cried for another, possibly many others. *Too many untimely deaths*, she thought. *The wiping out of generations.*

When would the madness end?

Not today. However, today, at least two would survive. Paulette would make it so.

In Montluçon, she wound the blue scarf around her neck and guided her charges to a table at a small outdoor café near the train station. The handoff went smoothly. For the bulk of the trip back to Paris, she covered her face with her floppy cap and pretended to sleep.

Only once the train was pulling up to the Nevers platform did Paulette lift her head and look around the nearly empty compartment. She'd discovered two things about herself on this journey. She was a natural chameleon, efficiently donning countless personas—seamstress, party girl, model, student—and she was very good at lying to Nazis. The latter got her through another checkpoint. As she stuffed her identity card back in her bag, she sensed someone watching her.

Someone close—on the platform.

Steam billowed from the train, hissing loudly and swallowing all hope of visibility beyond the immediate vicinity. Paulette struggled to find an anchor in her disorientation, something besides the smoke and massive din of noise—the train whistle, the shouts, the growl of guard dogs. The air held the weight of heat and moisture from a previous rainstorm.

A movement in the smoke revealed a murky form coming directly toward her. The figure flickered and morphed into the shape of a man. Tall, broad-shouldered, solid and real. And very, very familiar. Paulette had a momentary slice of pleasure. Then came the confusion.

Rochon shouldn't be here. He should be back in Paris doing whatever black-marketeers did on their time off from running cargo and refugees across the border. A chill raced up her spine, knowing he would not have changed his plans for something minor.

"You," she said.

"Yes, me."

She'd posed hers as a question. His, an answer before she'd finished speaking, as if he'd known what she'd say. Slightly disturbing, how well he anticiated her, but it was the unspoken words that stopped Paulette's heart. "What's happened?"

"Our mutual friend has been injured on her recent journey, which has caused a significant delay in her return to Paris."

Nicolle. Nicolle had been hurt. Paulette felt like a fox cornered by hounds. "How significant?"

"Several days, possibly a week."

Too long. People would notice her absence and begin asking questions, as was still the case with Charlotte. "Will she… will she recover fully?"

"Yes, but…" He produced a weak smile. "We have decided she must leave for an extended holiday at once. Mademoiselle thought you would want to say goodbye. I'm here to escort you to her current location."

That was a lot of information in a very short amount of time. Paulette's skin prickled with some unknown sensation. Her face drained of heat. Pressing her hand to her stomach, she struggled to remain calm. *Nicolle will improve*, she told herself as she mixed slow pulls of air with hard swallows. *All will be well.* "Take me to her."

He offered no hesitation. Merely took her hand and drew her across the platform to his motorcar parked outside the train station. As she settled in the passenger seat, Paulette battled two contradictory emotions at once. She wanted her friend to return to Paris, but she also wanted Nicolle safe. The two could not coexist.

"How did it happen? Her injury?"

"We don't have all the details. A German soldier infiltrated the escape line and pretended to be a British airman. He kept the charade going all the way to the point where Nicolle relinquished him to the next *passeur*." Rochon stopped abruptly, and his eyes went hard. "We don't know the fate of the other girl. She's gone missing. What we do know is that the German stalked Nicolle into a dark alley, attempted to kill her. She was quicker and smarter."

"Of course, we're talking about Nicolle."

His lips twitched, then fell into a frown. "The Germans are systematically devastating our escape lines. We believe they're getting information from somewhere inside our operation. We have a mole. Until we can uncover his or her identity, Mademoiselle and I have suspended all rescue operations."

Heart thumping, Paulette shifted in her seat to better see Rochon's face. "What about Nicolle? How do you plan to get her out of the country if you're shutting down the escape line?"

"It's safer I don't tell you."

In other words, what she didn't know she couldn't reveal to the enemy. Sobering thought.

By the time they cleared the border and crossed into the Occupied Zone, black, ominous clouds had rolled in over the horizon. Thunder growled in the distance, and Paulette realized with absolute certainty that she would be a different woman by nightfall because Nicolle would no longer be in her life. She would be halfway to Spain while Paulette would be left to endure the rest of the war without her greatest friend and ally by her side.

Chapter Thirty

Nicolle

Nicolle snapped awake, startled and disoriented, a man's name on her lips. Not her husband's, but another's. She wanted to feel ashamed, embarrassed even, but the emotion simply wasn't there. Or, at least, not riding along the surface. Maybe deeper down, in that cool, separate place where Julien lived with her, always. A constant fixture, a part of her, the best part that had never endured German occupation or killed a man.

She didn't want to think about what she'd done. Falling asleep in the middle of the day always left her feeling as if the world had shifted on its axis and everything was slightly bent. The incident in the back alley, still so fresh in her mind, only further enhanced the teetering sensation. Maybe if she sat up…

Untangling her legs from the blanket on her lap proved a challenge. She prevailed, mostly, and glanced around the room. André was everywhere. In the harmonious order of his personal belongings, in the dark masculine wood of the furniture, in the warm scents of sandalwood and pepper that complemented his coal-black hair and startlingly blue-green eyes. Now André's image rattled around in her head.

Much more pleasant than blood and death and German soldiers with guns. She tried to stand and hissed at the stab of pain ripping across the left side of her abdomen. The bullet had done more than just graze her, as she'd originally thought. It had lodged deep within the flesh, in the meaty section between her rib cage and hip. No permanent damage, but a dangerous amount of blood loss. Adrenaline had gotten her across the miles of rough terrain. André's unbending will had kept her here. After he'd dug out the bullet and sewn up the wound, he'd insisted she stay until she was fully healed. As hours turned to days, he continued pampering her with his inherent kindness and stories of Julien from their childhood.

Hard not to care for a man like that. Perhaps she'd always cared, just a little, if for no other reason than the steadfast way he'd stood by her and Julien from the start.

Outside, a storm beat its angry fists against the house. Static electricity vibrated on the air. Nicolle sighed, accepting she would not be going home tonight. She tried to think of this as a bad thing, but somewhere in the past few days, she'd lost her desire to return to Paris.

At first, she'd blamed her reluctance on her injury. Now she wasn't certain that was the only reason. She was weary of telling lies, and hiding her identity, even from her own son. It gutted her to hear him call another woman *Maman*.

Restless inside her own skin, Nicolle tried to stand again. The pain stole her breath. She hated this physical weakness.

Again, she told herself. *Try again.* She found success on the third attempt. Her forehead was soaked with sweat, her side throbbed, but she was on her feet, bobbing and weaving but upright.

The sound of brisk footsteps clipping down the hallway grew

closer, louder. A moment later, the door swung open and André strode into the room, face scrunched into a frown. He vibrated with silent energy, like the air after a clap of thunder. "I heard you cry out."

"From exasperation." She gave up the fight and sat down. "I hate being confined."

He didn't look convinced. He looked worried.

A little flustered, she gave a tiny shrug, winced from the pain. "I'm not used to lounging around all day."

He came closer, his posture relaxed, his gaze intense. "You're not lounging, Nicolle. You're healing."

"I need to heal quicker." She sounded like a bereft child.

Chuckling softly, he leaned down and kissed the top of her head. "Patience, *chérie*."

The endearment surprised a lump in her throat. For a long moment after he'd straightened, Nicolle could do nothing other than stare up at him. His clothes never seemed to change. Same black trousers, same crisp white shirt, but they always looked freshly laundered, no matter the time of day or night. She liked that about him. Liked the way he took care of his belongings. Of her. "How long was I out this time?"

"Only a few hours."

Better than when she'd first arrived and had lost consciousness for an entire day.

"Are you hungry?"

"Not really." She struggled to stand again.

He left her to it—for three whole seconds. Then he swore softly under his breath. From there, she wasn't sure how it happened, he'd moved so quickly, but he'd scooped her up off the sofa and straight into his arms. He cradled her there, her cheek pressed to his chest.

Or maybe she was the one doing all the clinging.

Eventually, he released her. The doctor in him took over as he ran his gaze over her face, taking in her individual features one at a time, her eyes, her nose, her lips. He lowered his attention to her injury. Or rather the bandage that stuck out from beneath her shirt. He lifted the edge, nodded in satisfaction. "No new bloodstains."

"This is good?"

"Very good." He smiled, soft and gentle, and she saw something sweet in his expression. Something she'd seen in him before. Only now she was able to assign a name because the feeling was spreading through her.

Not affection, nothing so mild. Loyalty, sure, but also something true and permanent. Another time. Another place. Those were the thoughts in her head. Not him. Not now. And yet her hand was moving up to his cheek. She felt it again, the attraction she'd resisted for months. "André, I want…"

She couldn't say the traitorous words that would change everything.

"I know. I want it, too. But…" He took her hand and placed it on his heart. "Julien."

She closed her eyes, and took a deep breath, and thought of her husband. "But Julien."

"He will always be between us."

She nodded and dropped her hand. Surprising them both, she stood, lifted onto her toes, and pressed her lips to his. The kiss was tentative, more question than answer, a shuffling of past and present. He didn't react at first, just stood there, wooden and unmoving. Then she was wrapped in his arms again. There was no more thinking of the man they'd both lost, only sensation and feelings and the press of her lips.

Not a kiss, precisely, a promise. Nicolle didn't know who pulled away first, only that there were several feet between them and they were staring at each other rather intensely, breathing hard.

"I think…" He speared splayed fingers through his hair. "I'll leave you to rest."

He was nearly at the door when she said his name.

He paused, turned back around, eyebrows lifted.

"When this war is over, I...we..." How did she put into words the wish that they could move past this thorny tangle of emotions and become something more than friends?

Eyes locked with hers, André came back to stand before her again. He kissed her hard on the lips, then softer on her cheek, her nose, her chin, and said, simply, gently, "Yes. To all of it."

He was nearly to the door again when she whispered his name a second time. It was time to tell him the truth, all of it. She couldn't let him believe her heart could be wholly his. He deserved to know her secret. "I have a confession to make. Something that may change how you feel about me."

This time, when he came back to stand before her, he took her hands and kissed each palm. "Nothing you say will change how I feel."

She hoped that was true. Then again, if what she told him changed his feelings, then he wasn't the man she thought. And certainly not one she could love. "I gave birth to Julien's son nearly two years ago. He never knew. He..." She swallowed. "He died before I had a chance to tell him."

"The boy is somewhere safe?" His voice gave away nothing of his thoughts.

She nodded.

He remained feet away from her, still calm, still stoic. "How many people know of his existence?"

"Besides me, three others." Mademoiselle, Monique and Louis Lavigne. "No, make that four." She'd forgotten about Paulette, her clever, insightful friend who'd figured out Nicolle's secret on her own. "Counting you, that makes five."

His expression softened, then filled with a depth of understanding she hadn't expected from him, though she should have. André Dubois was a man of integrity, of kindness, a healer and lover of animals. "This is why you stay in France? To be near your son?"

She gave another nod, her heart tearing into pieces. The largest part belonged to her son, a smaller portion to the man she'd lost, a bit to Mademoiselle, another to Paulette, and now, this man had managed to scoop up what was left.

"Then I will find a way to get you both free."

The vow was pure André, and Nicolle had no doubt he meant every word. If she hadn't fallen for him already, she would have done so in this moment. "Escaping France with my son has been my greatest wish since I discovered I was carrying Julien's child."

"And now it is my greatest wish, too."

Oh, André. "But my son is already free." Her throat choked over the words. "He is being raised by good people who have come to love him as their own. They provide him with every comfort a child could ever need or want." Things she could never give him, even without a war waging on. "He lives without fear, without judgment, without pain. Is it fair of me to take him away from all that?"

"Children are resilient."

That had been her argument, once. Perhaps even her mantra. The selfish part of her wanted to keep believing Jules would make the transition to a new life without any bumps. "Starting over in a new country where the language, the people, even the culture are different from anything he has ever known, that's a lot to ask of a child."

He stroked his hand down her hair. "Others have done it and thrived."

That was true, but many of those children had lived with suffering prior to their escape. Her son knew nothing of sorrow or the loss of a loved one. He enjoyed a safe, pampered existence because Nicolle had surrendered her right to raise him herself.

She didn't regret her choice. "If I wish to continue giving my son the life he deserves, I have to leave him behind."

There, the words were out of her mouth. She braced for the grief. When it hit, her lungs emptied of air.

"You don't need to make that decision today."

The decision was already made. But she didn't want to argue with the man when he was trying so very hard to give her hope. "No," she whispered into his shirt. "Not today."

His arms came around her again, and she snuggled close, trying to hold on to the moment as long as she could. And then, without warning, her grief overwhelmed her, and she began crying. Hard, choking sobs that ripped from her mouth. André didn't try to talk her out of her sadness. He didn't tell her everything would be all right. He simply held her close, kissing her head, stroking her hair, whispering soft, kind words. He was so warm and solid, smelling of soap and fresh cotton, a scent she would forever know as his, a stark reminder that with loss came grief, but also hope for a better day. Different from the past. Not better, not worse, just different.

They stayed in that position for another few minutes. Then he gently pulled away, helped her sit, and covered her legs with the blanket. "Get some rest. I'll come check on you again in an hour."

The hour came and went, and the door remained firmly closed. Nicolle could hear voices. André's and two others. Both familiar, one that had become dear to her.

Shoving away the blanket, Nicolle scavenged the floor, looking for something to put on her feet. Giving up, she padded into the kitchen barefoot and said, *"Bonjour."*

André smiled. Rochon gave her a nod. Paulette, no smile or nod, nothing so mundane. She gasped, cried out Nicolle's name, then rushed to her, arms opened wide, eyes leaking tears.

"Oh, Nicolle, I've been so worried about you." Reaching for her shoulders, holding on gently, carefully Paulette gave her a thorough once-over. "You're so pale."

"Getting shot will do that to a woman."

A shadow swept across her face. Then her mouth quirked into a grin, and she was roping her arms gingerly around Nicolle. Her side protested, but only a little, nothing she couldn't muscle through, because she wanted this hug, from this woman. Her friend. Her confidant. Her sister. "Thank you, Paulette. Thank you for being the kind of friend I've always wanted, but never knew I needed."

"I think the same of you." Sniffing, she stepped back and took Nicolle's hand. "Come, sit, and tell me everything."

"Not much to tell."

"Let us be the judge." This from Rochon, seconded by Paulette, who helped her sit in a chair at the small kitchen table.

Her stomach growled, which of course André heard. That was how she found herself digging into the bowl of soup he'd set before her, describing what happened between bites. She left nothing out, no detail too small. They didn't interrupt her, not once. "And then I woke up, in André's home."

Paulette said, "Thank you, Monsieur Dubois," while Rochon asked, "What happened to the other *passeur*?"

Closing her eyes, Nicolle tried to draw the German's words into the circle of her memory. Her limbs felt leaden, her head full of muslin, but she forced herself to concentrate. What had he said, right before he rounded the corner? *I know you're here, Fräulein. Show yourself.* Yes, that. But something else. Something about the other girl. *I killed your friend. Now I will kill you.*

Feeling sick, Nicolle set down her spoon, her hand shaking. "He killed her."

Silence bled into the room, dark and mournful, broken only by the sound of the rain scratching against the windowpane.

Paulette squeezed her hand. "It's not your fault, Nicolle."

Not entirely true. She hadn't put the gun in the Nazi's hand, but she still bore some level of responsibility. Had she been more diligent, maybe she would have recognized him for an impostor. "I don't know how I missed the signs." She'd replayed the escape in her mind a hundred times over. "He spoke French with a British accent. He described his girl back home, gave me the name of the last picture show he'd seen before going to war. He even knew the current slang."

Rochon repeated Paulette's words. "Not your fault. The Germans are getting smarter, bolder, and you've killed one of them. It's highly unlikely they know who you are, but they may have a general description, height, weight, hair color. Mademoiselle is taking no chances, nor am I. We're getting you out of France as soon as you're able to travel. When will that be?" He asked the question of André.

"Two days."

"No sooner?"

"Not if you want her to survive the Pyrenees."

The conversation continued around her, turning to the logistics of her escape. Nicolle knew what would be expected of her. She stopped listening and embraced the darkness coiling inside her, the guilt and sadness. Two people were dead because of her, one by her own hand. She had to leave France, alone, and in two days, perhaps sooner if Rochon had his way.

The finality struck her like a fist. No more trips to Limoges. No more deliveries of stuffed toys. No more ferrying young soldiers to safety. No more fashion shows. No more sharing a cigarette and secrets with Paulette on the roof of the atelier. She was fighting back tears. Paulette covered her hand and squeezed. That's all it took. That small connection and Nicolle was crying again. She averted her gaze from the men.

A wasted effort. They were already rising from the table, Rochon asking for a map, André directing him to his private office.

Paulette waited until they left the room before leaning close and saying, "I'm going to miss you, dreadfully."

Nicolle looked at the young woman through her watery eyes, and saw the friend she'd become in a few short months also battling tears. Also losing the fight. "I'm going to miss you, too."

"It won't be the same at Maison de Ballard without you."

Nothing would be the same. The Nazis had destroyed what was good and right in the world. They'd inflicted mortal wounds on France, on her soil, her people. When recovery came, *if* recovery came, not all the wounds would heal. Not all the bitterness and resentment would evaporate with a peace agreement. No matter what side won.

There was one bright, shining light in all the darkness. Nicolle's beautiful little boy was safe and insulated from the harsh reality of this war. He would never know the sacrifice his parents made for him. Unless someone told him. "Promise me, Paulette, if I don't survive this—"

"You *will* survive."

Nicolle wasn't so sure. Her carefully constructed life was imploding. All the work. All the lies, they had been a temporary solution only, a stay of execution at best.

"Please, Paulette." She fisted her hand around her friend's wrist. "If something happens to me…*promise* me you'll find my son and tell him about his father. Give him this." She unhooked the locket around her neck. "Tell him what Julien sacrificed for his freedom. Tell him about his mother. Tell him how much I loved him and why I chose to leave him behind."

Paulette opened the locket, studied the picture inside. "Must you leave the boy behind?"

"It's too dangerous to take him with me. Rochon was right. I killed a German soldier. I'm also a Jew who dared to falsify my identity papers. I never wore the yellow star, and I escaped the roundups. If I'm caught and any of this comes out, I'll be executed on the spot. Jules cannot be a witness to that. Nor should he suffer because of me."

"What if you aren't caught?"

"I can't take that chance. It'll be safer if I travel alone."

Eyes downcast, Paulette snapped the locket closed. "All right.

I don't like it, but I promise, if something happens to you, I'll find your son."

"Thank you."

Rochon and André returned to the kitchen. They spread a map on the table between them and began coordinating her escape. Paulette watched and listened in silence. Nicolle added a few suggestions, but mostly she watched and listened as well. "Once you're in Spain, a British diplomat will get you to Gibraltar, where you'll find transport on a military flight to America. Your contact will meet you here." He pointed to a spot in Spain at the foot of the Pyrenees.

There was more. A lot more. Details she committed to memory. And then it was done, and the four of them were standing at the back door. Rochon handed Nicolle a bag with the usual contents. Identity card, free movement pass, cash. "Godspeed, Nicolle."

"Thank you, Philippe, for everything. Please give Mademoiselle my gratitude as well."

"It is us who should thank you. You saved many lives and brought much honor to our network. We're both forever grateful. May you find much happiness in your next life."

"I wish the same for you."

He offered her his hand. She shook it. And then, reluctantly, turned to Paulette. "Goodbye, my friend. I won't forget you."

"Nor I you."

They hugged. There were no more tears, they'd dried up. Nor were words about the future exchanged. No promises of finding one another after the war. And yet Nicolle knew they would meet again. "This is not the end."

"No," Paulette agreed. "Only a brief pause."

Two days later, Nicolle stood in the same spot, telling another person she loved goodbye. This man, with his capacity for knowing her, loving her, had found his way into her heart. Not as a replacement for the one she'd lost, but as something new yet equally special. He'd taught her how to defend herself, had nursed her back to health. *"Au revoir, mon amour."*

Their kiss was gentle and sweet. Nicolle had lost one man she loved, wishing that there had been one more moment together, one more kiss, one more tender touch of his hand to her cheek, her palm to his heart. One final time to tell him she loved him. She would not let that happen again. "I love you, André," she whispered into his lips.

Twice she'd found love. Twice with good men.

"I love you, too. Be safe out there." He opened the door and ushered her into the cool morning air. The fog hadn't yet lifted, cloaking them in a silent cocoon. "Until we meet again."

"May it not be long." Only once she was covered in fog did she give in to the urge to look back. She sensed him watching her from the back stoop. In the next moment, the sun broke through the clouds and mist, sending a ray of light over his tall form. Nicolle took it as a promise. A reminder that even in the darkest of times, light always found a way to shine.

Chapter Thirty-One

Sabine

In the early morning hours between midnight and dawn, Sabine stood at her office window, her hand pressed to the cool glass. She was still dressed in the previous day's clothing, a simple blue skirt and matching top, prepared for the worst, knowing the arrest would come soon—today, tomorrow, next week. Despite the precautions she'd put in place, the network had been compromised. It stood to reason she was the next target.

Time passed, minutes, an hour. Her body said longer, and the length of the shadows agreed. Still, she remained at the window, squinting into the abyss between the buildings across the street. There was nothing to see under the moonless sky as dark as her mood. No movement, no sign of life. Just a hard, empty absence of light.

She pushed away from the window and prowled through her office, around the desk, past the cabinet, the shelf of photographs. She touched her favorite one of Giselle. After years of living without her daughter, Sabine had thought she'd made peace with her death. But the years had not been kind, or healing, and her own failures were too glaring. She'd done the math. For every soul Sabine saved, she'd lost at least one other. Members of her network had been compromised, killed. Young *passeurs* and their families arrested.

And now, Nicolle was on the run, halfway to Spain if their plan held. Sabine had not been given the chance to tell the young woman goodbye. Better that way. Safer.

They were coming for Sabine. She could feel it in her bones. She'd been so careful, putting nothing in writing. There was no paper trail to discover. Yet a mole had infiltrated the network. Sabine thought she knew who, a woman bent on destroying her for some unknown offense she'd inflicted. The betrayal was another loss to add to all the others.

Swaying, she stumbled back to the window, grasped onto the sill, and scanned the dark for the monster heading her way. To her surprise, she wasn't ready to die.

Outside, the sky awakened with the first light of dawn. Sabine blinked at the infusion of light, wondering how she'd missed the changes in the sky that heralded a new day. There were still hours before her girls arrived to begin work. Perhaps she would rustle up some breakfast, wash up a bit, change her clothes.

The sound, when it came, was a low rumble, a vibration on the air, as distant as thunder, as real as death. She saw the military vehicles, two large, growling trucks, their gears grinding from beneath the metal cabs. Their canvas tarps covering their human cargo flapped in the wind.

The first truck pulled to a halt outside her atelier, the other right behind that, as if knowing she would be in the back of the building at this hour. The mole had shared her daily routine with the Nazis.

Soldiers, dressed in the gray uniforms of the Schutzstaffel, the Waffen-SS, spilled out the backs of the trucks. So many of them, one after another, hard-eyed, scowling. They moved as a single unit, an endless stream of demons bent on the destruction of all that was good and right. And they were heading for the atelier's entrance.

Were her girls still in bed? Sabine prayed for their safety, willing them to stay out of sight, knowing they'd done nothing wrong. She'd been careful to keep her two lives separate. Still, the Nazis came for her here, at the heart of her fashion house.

Her breath fogged the glass. How loud it sounded in the empty room.

Looking neither right nor left, the soldiers continued their march. Even through the glass, Sabine could hear their boots striking the pavement, hammers to nails on a coffin. Behind the trucks, a black Mercedes moved into view. A man near Philippe's age exited the vehicle. He was tall, muscular, and wore a Gestapo uniform. He swiveled his head and looked straight at her.

A rush of noise filled her head, the sound of a drumbeat. She shivered. Her knees wanted to give way. She couldn't watch anymore and pushed back, but then two more climbed out of the black Mercedes. A man and a woman, both known to Sabine. Hysteria clogged in her throat, stealing her air like an invisible noose wrapped around her neck, the knot in the front rather than the back.

The drumming in her head grew faster, louder. Ignoring the man she'd always known would turn on her, she stared at the woman, waiting for her eyes to catch hers. Sabine's entire body shook. Her assistant. Geneviève.

Betrayer.

How had she known of Sabine's Resistance work? Or was this a bluff? The drumbeat stopped abruptly. Silence. Pain. She squeezed her eyes shut, opened them again. Saw the soldiers progressing to the atelier's entrance, the Gestapo agent moving to the front of their ranks. Geneviève stayed across the street, at a distance, but not so far that Sabine couldn't see the smirk on her face, this woman whom she'd given every opportunity to rise to her own greatness. Instead she'd made her own deal with a devil. Marcel stood beside her, looking equally self-satisfied.

Checkmate.

A crash from the atelier had her spinning around. More crashes. The ripping of material. The SS soldiers were making their ham-fisted point. She braced for their arrival. Head high, shoulders back. She would go to her death with dignity.

In walked the Gestapo agent, flanked by two other men wearing the same black uniform, red swastika armband, disdainful expressions. The leader moved to stand before her. He didn't give his name. Didn't ask for hers. His blue-eyed gaze swept over her, so pale, so brilliant, yet absent of emotion. Almost benign. An evil trick of the light.

"Mademoiselle Sabine Ballard, you are under arrest for treason against the Reich."

It was a vague charge, encompassing any number of offenses, and something in her snapped. Defiance sounded in her voice. "That is the best you can do? No details of what I've done. No specifics?"

"Those will come at your sentencing."

There was no mention of a trial, or a chance to defend herself against the charges. Nazi justice would allow neither.

She held his cold gaze, again shocked at the lies she saw there, the silent promise that he would not hurt her. Just another way to torture her, a cruel joke. "Restrain her."

The man on her left dragged her hands behind her back, slapped manacles around her wrists, tugging needlessly hard. She bit her lip to keep from crying out.

"Do not struggle," the leader urged, more suggestion than threat. "That will only make the pain worse."

In the atelier, the soldiers continued tearing apart her workroom. They didn't seem to be looking for anything specific.

Their big hands smashed valuable equipment, tore expensive silks and satins into shreds. Their soulless eyes were ugly with hate.

And then Geneviève entered the building, Marcel keeping step beside her, a smirk on his face. Geneviève lifted her hand and slapped her. Hard. Sabine's cheek stung, but her eyes never left her assistant's. She'd learned firsthand that grief had stages. She went through all of them in the split second it took for her assistant to drop her hand. There was no sadness in her now, no need to bargain, no rage. She felt nothing but a cold numbness in her heart.

"You have made a grave mistake," she told Geneviève, "teaming up with Marcel. I'm sorry I won't be here to witness the moment you realize that."

Chapter Thirty-Two

Paulette

They arrived in Paris with the rosy fragments of dawn clinging to the low-hanging clouds. Philippe hadn't spoken much
on the silent drive home. Just as well, since Paulette hadn't been
in a talkative mood, either. She fiddled with the locket Nicolle
had given her to pass on to her son. Running her fingers over
the smooth gold brought back the sharp reminder of how little
she knew of Nicolle's husband. She wished she'd asked more
questions, small details that she could tell the boy. Perhaps the
picture would be enough.

Stowing the locket back in her pocket, she watched the buildings pass by, not really seeing them. Already she missed Nicolle.
It was an ache that she feared would never go away. What would
life be like at Maison de Ballard now that she had no friends?

Without taking his eyes off the road, Philippe said, "She's
going to be all right."

Paulette shivered. "I don't like that she has to travel most of the journey on her own."

"If anyone can do it, it's Nicolle."

She inhaled deeply. They'd rolled down the windows to bring in the cool of the night, but now, with dawn, the air smelled stale. Paulette knew something was wrong the moment Philippe took the final corner. Military vehicles stood empty outside Maison de Ballard. A black Mercedes was parked at the rear of the mini-convoy. Something sharp clutched in her chest. The smells, the lights, the sound of shattering glass. The shouts in guttural German.

A clatter. A crash. Masculine shrieks, the sound of madness and violence and rage. Paulette resisted the urge to scream herself. "What's happening, Philippe?"

He slammed the car to a stop. "The Gestapo is raiding Maison de Ballard."

Paulette's heart stopped in her chest. "Mademoiselle. We have to help her."

The eyes that turned to her were filled with such sorrow and helplessness, she thought, *This is what fresh grief looks like.* "It may be too late."

A ripple rose along her spine. The mole. It had to be the mole. "We have to try."

"Agreed."

They exited the car together in a fast, coordinated union of like minds. Another shout rang out. A gunshot. *Mon Dieu, no!* Paulette started running. Philippe was already three steps ahead of her, moving fast despite his limp. The street behind the fashion house remained empty but for the military vehicles. No one dared leave the safety of their buildings.

Still running, Paulette looked up to the dormer windows of the attic. Her remaining roommates, two young women, stared back at her, their eyes large and dark in their ashen faces. They would not help Mademoiselle. After all she'd done for them, they chose their own safety.

A movement from across the street had Paulette's feet slowing, then stopping altogether. Her breath caught. Her mind reeled. Two lone figures had ventured into the street. They faced the atelier, standing side by side, each carrying an expression of satisfaction. Paulette's stomach clenched. "Do you see them? The man and woman?"

Philippe made a growling sound low in his throat. "I see them."

She started toward the duo, but only made it a few steps before Philippe grabbed her arm. "They aren't our greatest concern right now."

No, they weren't, and yet she stared at Marcel and Geneviève a moment longer. They hadn't seen her yet, or Philippe. They were too busy quietly celebrating the destruction of Mademoiselle's legacy. They had something to do with this raid. The unmistakable glee in their expressions was proof of their evil intent. Absently, Geneviève rubbed at her palm, as if trying to make a sting go away.

Paulette thought matters couldn't get worse, but the door to the atelier burst open. Out came two men wearing Gestapo uniforms. They were followed by a taller, more menacing, black-clad monster. He gripped the arm of Mademoiselle, who walked beside him looking straight ahead, head high. She had an angry red mark on her cheek. From his hand or another?

Paulette glanced at Geneviève still rubbing her palm and thought she had the answer.

The sound of three sets of bootheels reverberated off the hard ground. A death march that had her swinging her gaze back to Mademoiselle, focusing in on the man hauling her toward the black Mercedes.

Shadows from the bill of his hat covered his face, but Paulette knew that build. She held her breath, praying she was wrong.

But no, that arrogant swagger belonged to only one man: Kriminalkommissar Wolfgang Mueller. The most ruthless of Gestapo agents. The man who'd arrested Paulette's mother now had Mademoiselle in his clutches. The older woman showed the ordeals and losses she'd endured, appearing beaten, nearly drained of life, with dark smudges in the hollows of her eyes.

The cold breath of terror filled Paulette. A dozen warnings opened in her mind. *Run, Mademoiselle. Fight back. Don't get in that car.* Once there, she would never be free.

Paulette bit her lip, then tried to rush to Mademoiselle, but Philippe still held her arm. "It's too late. Anything you say or do will only serve to make the situation worse."

This was her mother all over again. Paulette had to do something, say something. She could not remain passive. She tried to break free of Philippe's grip, but he held on, his hold firm but not especially biting.

Suddenly, images bombarded her. Philippe navigating Marcel's parties, charming men and women alike. Philippe talking to Mueller, their heads bent in conversation. Philippe never fully explaining how he knew the Gestapo agent. Philippe the bad guy.

Other images followed. Philippe patiently teaching Paulette how to read a map, to cross over rough terrain. Philippe coordinating Rachel and Ilka Berman's escape. Philippe taking Paulette to say goodbye to Nicolle. Philippe the good guy.

Which was real?

She wrenched her arm free and staggered toward the car. Too late. Mademoiselle was already sitting in the back seat of the black Mercedes. In her last glimpse, her mentor's face was stricken, pale, resolved. No different from her mother's final expression.

Rounding to the other side of the car, Mueller stopped and looked straight at Paulette. She had a sudden, immediate urge to slap him, kick him, but he was no longer looking at her.

Philippe had his entire attention. The men shared a short nod that, had she not been watching them closely, Paulette would have missed.

"Philippe, what are you—"

"I'll explain everything, but not here. We have an audience." He looked pointedly at a spot over her shoulder.

Marcel was the first to saunter over. "Well, well, look who it is. The two lovers, coming home from…" His eyes roved over them, taking in their clothing, their flushed faces. "Just where have you been?"

Philippe gave a short, brief, detail-rich answer that had Marcel slapping him on the back and Paulette blushing.

"You missed quite a show."

"We caught enough." Philippe's voice revealed nothing of his reaction to the *show*. "Your doing, I suppose?"

"Actually, it was mine." Geneviève joined their grim little group, looking wildly pleased with herself. Did she not realize who she was talking to? Philippe was Mademoiselle's son-in-law. Her family. And Paulette was the daughter of her closest friend. Yet Geneviève spoke as though they were just two random people who'd come across the raid. Then again, she was supposed to think that. As far as she knew, Paulette was a silly, flirty girl engaging in a torrid affair with a man who considered her more toy than woman.

Nevertheless, it took every ounce of willpower for Paulette not to slap the woman across the face, as she'd done to Mademoiselle. "How did you get the Gestapo to arrest Mademoiselle?"

"Oh, that." She studied her red fingernails from several angles. "I whispered in a few Nazi ears about her selling dresses to known Resistance workers. An American expat, a famous actress. Nothing substantiated, mind you, mostly lies and half-truths, a mention of a name that didn't exist. Enough to have her brought in for questioning. Honestly—" she glanced toward the atelier "—I didn't think they'd come for her quite this hard."

As if to punctuate her remark, a sewing machine came flying out the window, landing mere feet from where they stood. She frowned. "Well, that was unnecessary."

"What now?" Philippe asked in that calm, quiet voice that should have warned the woman she was on shaky ground with the closest person Mademoiselle had to family.

"I take over the fashion house until she returns, *if* she returns."

"Not much left to take over."

She shrugged. "Guy will help me rebuild, won't you, Guy?"

The gangster gave her a winking grin. "I'm sure we can come to some sort of an agreement."

A loud voice from inside the atelier shouted in German. "Halt!"

Immediately, the vandalism stopped and soon an impossible number of soldiers filed out of the building and climbed into the backs of the military trucks. Seconds after they roared away, the seamstresses began arriving for the day. They had an array of reactions to the destruction, none of them mild. All of them expressed considerable worry for Mademoiselle.

Assuming her new role, Geneviève took charge of the women, ushering them to the front of the building, where she promised all would be explained. Paulette hung back. But Philippe guided her away from Guy and said into her ear, "Go with them. Find out what she has to say. It could be important, what you hear."

She didn't want to go. Geneviève had turned on the one woman who'd given her a future, a career. She'd risen to great power in the fashion house, second only to Mademoiselle. She'd ruined a good woman's life out of spite and greed. "How do I bear being in the same room with her?"

"For Mademoiselle. You do it for her."

He was right. "For Mademoiselle," she whispered.

Paulette found a spot in the back of the room. The prevailing atmosphere among her coworkers was grim. Mademoiselle's girls were equally worried about their boss and their own future in the fashion house. Geneviève kept her speech short and simple, claiming the fashion designer had been taken in only for questioning. Nothing to worry about. "She will be released soon. In the meantime, we will honor Mademoiselle by salvaging what is left of her atelier and continue filling orders from the show as best we can."

The syrupy sincerity was over the top, and Paulette thought she might be sick.

As the day progressed, and the extent of the destruction became evident, Paulette fell into a pit of despair. Not long after her rallying speech, Geneviève disappeared into Mademoiselle's office under the guise of sorting through special orders. She left Marie Claire to organize the cleanup. The head seamstress assigned Paulette to salvaging ribbon. For hours she worked, wondering where Philippe had gone. Gestapo headquarters, she hoped, and prayed that his sway with Mueller was strong enough to save Mademoiselle.

He returned midafternoon. The door swung open, and there he was. Framed in the afternoon light. A hush fell over the room, all heads turned in his direction, and Paulette was reminded of the first time she'd laid eyes on the man. He'd been impressive back then, and still had the quintessential look of a Frenchman. Dark eyes, dark hair, the face of a poet, the lean build of an athlete. His gaze landed on Paulette. "A word, *s'il vous plaît*. Outside."

"Of course," she said, choking back her worry, her doubts. He had news and she wanted—needed—to hear what he had to say.

Marie Claire stopped them at the door. "Any news about Mademoiselle?"

"It's not good." He shut his eyes, scrubbed a hand over his face. "She's being detained overnight for questioning."

They all three knew what that meant. A long, unceasing interrogation that would be hard on any woman, doubly so on someone Mademoiselle's age.

"I'm borrowing Paulette for a few minutes. I'll have her back within the hour."

"Yes, yes. Of course." To Paulette, Marie Claire said, "You have earned your place on this team with hard work and talent. I'm grateful to Mademoiselle for bringing you here. With the events of today, and Nicolle still missing, it would be my honor to take over your training, should you wish it."

Her words left Paulette somewhat speechless. Eventually, she managed to say, "Thank you, madame. That means a lot coming from you. Yes, I would very much like to learn everything I can from you."

Marie Claire squeezed her arm. "The sooner you leave, the sooner you will return."

Philippe didn't speak again until they were outside and walking away from the building. They entered a park full of trees and flowering bushes, and the world should not look so beautiful. The scent of summer hung on the air. His limp was more pronounced this afternoon, a sign he'd pushed himself too hard. Her compassion ignited, but then she remembered all the questions she had. She would ask them now. "What is your connection to Wolfgang Mueller?"

"He is not the enemy you think him to be."

Paulette replayed the nod between the two men near this very spot behind the fashion house, a shared understanding of...what? Mueller made people disappear. That was his reputation. Disappear, where? *Your mother is with her people.* Paulette had assumed he'd meant a concentration camp with other Jews.

Why be so cryptic? Why give her hope? A cruel trick. Or a message?

"Is Mueller going to release Mademoiselle?"

"No." One small word, a single syllable, full of so much terrible meaning. The end of a life. The extinction of a woman's legacy. Gone.

"There's no hope of her returning to the atelier?"

"No, but I'm working on getting her out of France."

A daring rescue. Of course that would be where his mind went. "What can I do?"

"You can tell me what Geneviève revealed to the team."

"Nothing we can use to save Mademoiselle. She took charge, as you already knew. She made a few vague comments about pressing on in the face of adversity, working for Mademoiselle's honor, but she avoided anything concrete. It was an uninspiring call to arms."

"That's unfortunate. I was hoping she'd incriminate herself. Or at least give us…something."

Reality was sinking in, the knowledge that Mademoiselle was lost to her as surely as her mother. The ground swirled under Paulette's feet, and she thought her knees might give out. She looked frantically around, found a nearby bench, and sat down, hard. Philippe settled in next to her. She clung to one glimmer of hope. "What are the odds you will be able to break Mademoiselle out of custody?"

"I'd rather not do the math." His tone held more apology than confidence.

The silence grew between them, somber and heavy. Whatever his connection was to Mueller, it wasn't strong enough to secure Mademoiselle's release. Paulette felt his sorrow. It was there, whole and tangible, swirling in his silence, in the sad tilt of his head.

"What will you do now?" he asked. "Will you take Marie Claire's offer and stay on at the atelier?"

Paulette considered the question seriously. Her life had imploded a second time, so close to the first. Yet somewhere along the way, she'd found herself a purpose. Her desire to fight the enemy wasn't about atonement anymore. It was a higher calling. "I will continue on as before, at the atelier. Under Marie Claire."

He turned his head, slowly, eyes searching her face. "It would mean putting yourself in close proximity with Geneviève. She will bring clients to the fashion house who are as greedy and self-serving as her. Can you do that?"

In Philippe's question, Paulette found her answer. "I've been eavesdropping on Geneviève's crowd for months. Nothing has to change. Except instead of going to them at Marcel's parties, they will come to me. I will fit their dresses, tailor their suits, and continue doing what I've been doing all along. I will watch, listen, and pass on whatever I learn to you."

He shook his head. "Not me."

"Why not you?"

"Your plan would work better if you report to another woman. I have someone in mind, a close friend of Mademoiselle's. She is a famous French actress who runs in Marcel's crowd but is loyal to France." He gave her a soft smile. "In the very near future, she will become quite enamored with your impeccable craftsmanship and insist that only you fit her clothes."

With a fast, steady motion, Paulette sat back. "You've had this plan in place for a while."

"This is Mademoiselle's plan. In case something happened to her."

The older woman's strategic mind was astounding. Of course she would think of every possible outcome and have a plan in place for each. "And you?" she asked Philippe. "Is it business as usual?"

"I leave for England at the end of the week."

Paulette gaped at the man. "England? How?" Better yet, "Why?"

"You once asked me how I got my injury. I only gave you half the story." He took her hand, turned it over to stare at her palm, his eyes seeing another time, another place. "The escape line was my wife's idea. She had friends that needed to get out of France. We weren't trained yet. We didn't know what we were doing. But we were the good guys. What could possibly go wrong? A lot, as it turned out. We were ambushed in the mountains."

Hearing his bitterness, Paulette laid a cautious hand on his forearm. "You were the only survivor. That's what you told me."

"I vowed to continue Giselle's work. I began rescuing British airmen and putting them back into the sky, by any means possible. I also helped escaped POWs find their way home, with Mademoiselle's help. We were outrageously successful from the start, and I was tapped to train in England with MI9. The section of British Intelligence dedicated to escapes and rescues is under the guidance of a man I've known since we attended boarding school together in England."

So many revelations. Paulette could hardly keep them straight. Rochon's past. The British involvement.

"The Germans are infiltrating too many of our escape lines. We need to be smarter than them, more tactical."

"So this is goodbye."

"For now." He stood, reached out his hand, tugged her against him when she took it. "There's something between us, Paulette. I know you feel it, too."

She did feel a connection, had felt it from the start. She'd been afraid of her feelings, thinking she'd fallen for another Friedrich—different face, same man. But she'd been wrong on so many things, and yet she didn't regret leading with caution instead of emotion. Given a chance, she'd do it all over again the same way.

"It's not our time, Paulette."

No, it wasn't. Maybe their day would come. Maybe after the war. They had this moment, this day. A few hours of closeness. It was enough. She would relish every minute. And then, she would let him go.

Chapter Thirty-Three

Paulette

August 1944.
Paris, France.

German occupation continued for two more years. Food grew scarcer and Paulette became thinner, lonelier. Under Marie Claire's guidance, she resumed her education, becoming an expert seamstress in half the time it took her peers. She also listened, watched, and passed on vital information to the Resistance via the French actress Philippe sent as her contact.

While Marie Claire surely suspected Paulette's clandestine work, Geneviève never did. She was too busy grasping for notoriety within the fashion industry, an honor that forever eluded her. Her designs were ordinary, unexceptional, and, as one member of the press claimed, derivative. Nevertheless, the woman obstinately pushed her garments on the masses.

Months after the Normandy invasion, Paris remained firmly

under German control. Even with Allied troops closing in on the city, Hitler vowed that "Paris would not fall into enemy hands except lying in complete debris." Battles were waged on the streets. Posters calling French citizens to arms were pasted on the exteriors of every building. Next to those were flyers vowing punishment for Nazi sympathizers. When Paris was finally liberated in August, the Free French, or Fifis as they were called, unleashed their wrath on women they branded as *horizontal collaborators*.

With de Gaulle's rallying speech still ringing in French ears, they stormed homes and businesses and brutally hauled off their targets to the prison of Fresnes. Inside the concrete walls, they handed out their version of vigilante justice. They questioned the women without listening to their answers, beat them ruthlessly, chopped off their hair, then paraded them through the streets in their undergarments.

So far, Geneviève had escaped their notice. While Paulette wanted the woman punished for her crimes, she wished for it to be done through the proper channels. When she said as much to Marie Claire, the other woman sniffed rather uncharitably and said, "That foul woman is the reason Mademoiselle was arrested and made to disappear. I wish a similar ending for her, and may it come soon. Now—" *clap, clap, clap* "—finish those alterations. As long as we have paying clients, we will continue fulfilling their orders."

Paulette bent her head and went back to work. Her mind wandered to the future and all the possibilities that lay ahead. Her dream of opening her own fashion house would have to wait until she made peace with her sister. It was the last piece of her past that remained unresolved.

Not solely her fault. There'd been little communication from Gabrielle during the war. A few letters, a phone call or two, but no visits, and certainly no invitation to return home. That had come just last week. Gabrielle had been gracious on the telephone, if a bit cautious with her words. Paulette wasn't sure when she would take her sister up on her offer, but she would. Soon.

The persistent knocking on the atelier door had her looking over her shoulder, somewhat confused. Not many customers came to that entrance, nearly never.

Clicking her tongue in impatience, Marie Claire hurried to the door, her expression equally baffled. Two men in shirt-sleeves with sandals on their feet and berets on their heads stood on the threshold. Their clothing suggested they were members of the Free French. Their brutish behavior confirmed it as they shouldered their way into the workroom without waiting to be let in. It was not hard to guess their purpose. Geneviève's luck had run out.

The other seamstresses seemed to have come to the same conclusion. They, too, stopped working and, like Paulette, sat in shocked silence. The taller of the two brutes addressed Marie Claire with a fierce scowl and complete lack of civility. "Are you Mademoiselle Durand?"

Clearly offended, Marie Claire's chin snapped up. "I am not."

His flinty eyes narrowed. "You will take us to her now."

"With pleasure."

She'd barely taken the first step when Geneviève appeared in the atelier wearing her own design, a gaudy purple dress with black stripes that managed to make her look both matronly and youthful at the same time. "What is the meaning of this?" She spoke in the dismissive tone she reserved for people she considered beneath her. "Who dares interrupt my employees during the workday?"

Neither man answered her questions. "Geneviève Adrienne Durand," the taller one asked, "is that whom I am addressing?"

Her hands went to her hips in an open show of defiance. Only the slightest shake in her chin indicated she might—possibly—understand the danger she was in. "Who's asking?"

Again, he ignored her question. "My colleague and I are here to escort you to prison. You will come quietly or we will drag you there. The choice is, of course, up to you."

The words clearly caught her by surprise. "Prison? But I... I've done nothing wrong."

Her shock was real, as was her outrage. Even now, after what she'd done to Mademoiselle, and with so many of her fellow collaborators being carted away, Geneviève thought she could escape retaliation for her crimes against France.

For a split second, it appeared she would allow them to arrest her. But then she looked left, right, scanning the faces in the room. She would find no support from her employees. They sat perfectly still, silent as a tomb, hands in their laps, eyes cast down. Paulette included. She had not wished for this outcome—violence was not the answer—but she would not help the woman who'd shown so little respect to Mademoiselle.

Geneviève took a deep breath, pivoted on one foot, and then, with a yelp, ran. A foolish mistake. She made it three whole steps before the Fifis caught her, one by the arm, the other by the hair with a hard yank. Her scream turned Paulette's blood cold. She instinctively stood, not sure what she meant to do. She paused too long. Geneviève's fate was sealed.

As promised, the men dragged her out of the atelier. She did not go willingly. Her harrowing shrieks reverberated in Paulette's ears for hours after her arrest.

The following day, Marie Claire called the few remaining members of her team together and announced the fashion house was closing. "Effective immediately."

She gave the girls two days to clear out. Most only needed one, Paulette included. Last to leave, she stood in the attic dormitory room, leaning over her suitcase, studying its meager contents. Marie Claire came to stand beside her. "I brought you this." She handed Paulette a scarred thimble. "It belonged to Mademoiselle. She would want you to have it."

Touched, Paulette felt her eyes stinging. This woman who'd started as an adversary had become so very dear to her, a precious ally in a world turned upside down. "I'll treasure it always." As she tucked the gift in her pocket, the first trickle of tears slid down her cheeks. "What will you do now?"

A smile split her face, and she looked nearly like her old self. "I've been offered a position with a talented emerging designer in his own right. He is already gaining notoriety in the fashion community. His name is on everyone's lips. I like his vision very, very much."

She meant Christian Dior, of course, who was the talk of Paris. "He's lucky to have you."

"He is also willing to hire you."

A dream job for a seamstress. But Paulette didn't want to spend the rest of her life sewing other designers' garments. "Tempting," she admitted, "and greatly appreciated, but no. It's time I go home and settle matters with my family."

Marie Claire gave her a quick hug that was no less heartfelt for its brevity. "If you change your mind, you will let me know?"

"I will."

"Yes, well." Marie Claire swiped at her own eyes. "I'll leave you to finish your packing."

There wasn't much to pack. What she brought with her from Reims, plus two new dresses she'd made herself, her mother's shawl, and, of course, Giselle's gown. Her sketch pad went on top. She was closing the lid when Marie Claire entered the attic once again. "There's someone here to see you."

"Oh?" Paulette didn't have friends in Paris, not anyone who would seek her out at the fashion house.

A soft smile met her confusion. "He's waiting for you in the atelier."

He. Her heart lurched. Philippe. Who else? She was down the first flight of stairs in seconds. Her feet flew over wood and carpet as she conquered the next two. Her path had rarely crossed Philippe's, only twice after Mademoiselle's arrest. He'd left for England, as promised, and had been in and out of France sporadically ever since. In early 1944, he'd become a member of the British Pathfinder team charged with setting up drop zones and safe houses throughout France in preparation for the Normandy invasion. Paulette had only discovered that last bit after the storming of the beaches, from the actress who'd been her contact.

She rounded the final corner, her heart in her throat.

The atelier was dark and silent. Then she saw him. A warmth flickered within the depths of her heart. She heard the whisper of her name in his familiar deep voice. A moment later, she was across the room and in his arms. "I've missed you," she murmured into his chest, holding tightly to his waist. He'd lost weight, but hadn't they all?

The kiss that followed was long and sweet. Then they were sitting on the floor, Paulette's head resting against his shoulder. "Is it over for you?" she asked. "The war?"

"Not yet. I'm working with French authorities to bring Guy Marcel to justice. Eventually, once we've gathered all the evidence, he'll be tried for treason and punished accordingly."

"How long will that take?"

"Months."

They fell silent after that, each lost in their own thoughts. The hush grew between them, somber and heavy. So many things to say, yet no promises were uttered. They made no vows. They simply held on to the moment, to each other.

Slowly, almost reverently, Philippe turned Paulette in his arms, kissed her again, then settled her back against him. "I have to tell you about Mademoiselle." He shifted in the shadows, his discomfort evident in his rigid muscles. "I know what happened to her."

A long shiver ran through Paulette, a premonition of bad news. She could not bear to hear confirmation of Mademoiselle's death, but she must. The woman's story deserved to be heard, if only by Paulette. Before she could change her mind, she urged him to continue. "All right, I'm listening."

"She's in New York, alive and well." For a moment, she felt a flare of hope. It had barely sparked in her chest, a small sharp ping, when Philippe added, "We got her out of France."

We? "You mean other members of the network?"

"I mean me, and the man you know as Kriminalkommissar Wolfgang Mueller."

Mueller. He kept turning up. *Not the bad guy you think he is.* How could that be? Her stomach roiled. That awful conundrum of anger and guilt and sorrow she'd felt watching him take her mother away, then Mademoiselle, burned anew. "I don't understand."

"Mueller is actually a British secret agent working deep undercover in the Gestapo. His real name is Richard Doyle."

"But his reputation…"

"Was accurate, to a point. He made people disappear, but not to concentration camps. To safety."

Paulette's skin prickled, and her face went hot. Her eyes strained to see Philippe's face. She saw only sincerity in his eyes. Truth. "Mademoiselle is alive."

"And living in New York. Nicolle is with her."

Nicolle. Mademoiselle. Alive and together in America. As she sat up, a peculiar calmness fell across her soul. Almost instantly, she was less angry. Less filled with remorse. Her friend and mentor were safe. That had always been the dream, the reason for the escape routes, to rescue people who otherwise would have been sent to death.

Words began tumbling through her mind. Phrases uttered by Mueller. Her sister.

Things aren't always as they seem…

Your mother is with her people…

Philippe telling her the man was *not the enemy you think him to be*...

She had to ask, had to know the truth, all of it. "My mother? What happened to her?"

"She is alive and well and also in New York."

Alive and well. Hope flooded Paulette's heart. It came fast and hard and stung, stealing her breath. Her mind raced to the past, back to the initial days after her mother's arrest.

Gabrielle never quite meeting her eyes.

Gabrielle claiming Maman was "sent away," not sent to her death, or made to disappear.

Gabrielle telling Paulette she must prove she'd learned her lesson and changed her ways.

Her sister had known. All along, she'd known her mother was alive and well and living in New York. Wolfgang Mueller, Richard Doyle, whatever his name was, had brought Gabrielle into his confidence. Yet she'd withheld the truth from Paulette. Why?

As soon as the question materialized in her mind, a sickening feeling spread through her, and she was that vapid, flirty, self-centered girl again. The one who'd fallen into a romance with a very bad man. The one who'd betrayed her mother for all the right reasons in all the wrong ways. Sweat poured into her eyes, blurring her vision until all she could see was the harm she'd brought to the people she loved. *You are not that girl anymore.*

No, she was not. She hadn't been that girl for a long time.

"Paulette, *mon amour*." Philippe lifted her away from him again, staring into her eyes. "I'm sorry I didn't tell you any of this sooner."

There was such grief in his gaze, such remorse. How strange it all was. How unexpected to hear this news from him. How right it felt. The former Paulette would have blamed him for lying to her. A rush of understanding overtook her instead. "It was not your secret to tell."

"And yet I ask your forgiveness." Underneath the black-marketeer, and the lies upon lies upon lies, she'd always known Philippe was a good man.

Everything he'd done had been for the greater good. "There is nothing to forgive."

She understood that, better than most. Lives had been at stake, including Mueller's, the man who wasn't her enemy after all, but something quite different.

"I need you to say the words. I need to hear you say you forgive me."

She laid a hand on his forearm. "I forgive you, Philippe."

Embracing her, he kissed her nose, her chin, her lips with such tenderness. He was making a promise, something that could not happen now.

"Mueller, or rather, Richard Doyle and I have put together one final rescue, Paulette. Yours."

"Mine," she whispered, tears springing to her eyes. "Oh, Philippe. How can I thank you?"

"By living well. It is my greatest wish for you."

The tears flowed freely. This, she decided, was the new beginning she needed, provided by a man who had crept into her heart, who was sending her away from him, at least for now. Away from Paris and the memories of war. Away from Champagne and the past that would always haunt her, but not before she confronted Gabrielle. "I will need to go home first."

"I thought you might say that, which is why you leave for England in a week, to give you time to make the trip."

They talked all through the night, of nothing and everything, of hopes and dreams.

Too soon, the first light of dawn spread her gray melancholy into the room. Philippe kissed Paulette, handed her a muslin pouch with all the necessary documents for her trip, said, *"Au revoir, mon amour,"* and then he was gone.

Paulette made the trip to Reims the next morning. As expected, her conversation with Gabrielle did not go well. Her sister showed no remorse for her lies. She still saw Paulette through the lens of her worst act. But if Paulette had learned anything in her time in Paris, it was that she was not the sum total of her worst deed. She was more. So much more.

Three weeks after her final goodbye with Philippe, she arrived in New York on a ship carrying war brides to their American husbands. She'd been included among their ranks courtesy of the British government.

As the ship sailed into New York Harbor, Paulette joined the other women on deck. She kept her eyes locked on Lady Liberty, feeling the connection between her former country and her new homeland all the way to her bones. She wasn't forsaking France, but embracing America. A new life, in exchange for the old.

She joined the queue at the gangplank and began her journey into yet another beginning, another fresh start. This one, she prayed, would bring more joy than heartache. Calm over chaos. All she really wanted was a small, contented life free of war and death, lies and betrayal, an existence without anger forming a tight ball around her heart. She wished Philippe was here with her, but the war wasn't over for him.

A soft breeze kicked up against her skin, and Paulette found herself smiling as she stepped off the gangplank. The air felt alive, as if the city had a pulse. But where were they? She scanned the crowd, searching, and there, beside a vending cart selling cooking wares, they stood. All three of them. Her family. The family of her choosing.

Mother, mentor, friend.

The sight of them jarred Paulette into motion. She shouted their names, all but running in their direction. Nicolle saw her first. She, too, started to run. They slammed into each other, hard, nearly toppling over. Laughing, they found their balance and hugged, their words of greeting choked inside happy tears. Joining them a moment later, Mademoiselle placed a hand on

Paulette's head and said, softly, "Welcome to America, Paulette. Welcome home."

The two women stepped back. The third woman stepped forward, and Paulette was staring at her mother. Beautiful, elegant Hélène Leblanc with her sad, guilt-ridden eyes. She shifted uneasily from foot to foot, as if she didn't know how to proceed.

"Maman?"

"Paulette. I'm so sorry." The words spilled forth, spooling over one another. "I'm sorry for not telling you I was alive, for leaving you behind, for not being a better mother. I did so many things wrong. I…" She swiped at her eyes. "Can you ever forgive me?"

There'd been a time when Paulette had felt genuine resentment toward her mother, mostly in the days following Philippe's news of her fate and Gabrielle's own revelations. But she'd had a lot of time to think on the journey to America. She'd looked at the girl she'd been with the eyes of the woman she'd become and had found insight, understanding. Every offense her mother claimed had been motivated by love.

There was nothing to forgive, but she said the words anyway. "I forgive you, Maman."

"My dear, sweet girl."

She opened her arms, and Paulette walked into them. The past slipped away. Old hurts shattered into fragments at her feet. Shifting slightly, she reached out her arm and dragged the other two women into the embrace.

Now, Paulette thought. Now, with these women, her family, she could begin anew.

Epilogue

June 1950.
Leblanc-Cadieux Fashion House. New York City, New York.

Paulette navigated her way through the main artery of the fashion house she and Nicolle had built from a shared vision and five years of hard, backbreaking work. As was her habit, she kept her steps calm and unhurried. She stopped occasionally to view a garment in production, checking a seam, a hemline, the progress of a pleat. Sometimes she made corrections. Mostly she gave praise to her seamstresses and finishers.

They were a talented group, curated for their skill. Paulette and Nicolle had come a long way since the days they'd designed their first collection sitting at her mother's kitchen table in her tiny apartment. They'd started small, with a few handsewn gowns, and had almost instantly become the talk of New York. Now, five years later, thanks to Mademoiselle's creative guidance and Hélène's head for business, Leblanc-Cadieux was a complete fashion house, with divisions dedicated to haute couture, ready-to-wear, handbags, accessories, and hats.

A signature fragrance was Paulette's current project and the reason her stomach was currently twisted in knots. She tried not to show her nerves. It was the same every time Philippe came to New York. They'd created a strong friendship over the years. But there was always something keeping them from taking the next step. For Paulette, it had been her fledgling fashion house. For Philippe, the loose ends of the war followed by his father's death in 1945, which had put him in sole control of his family's company, though not without some pushback from his brother. The younger man had come around, eventually supporting Philippe and his decision to open stores in New York, Paris, and Milan. Soon, in a matter of minutes, he would arrive and present the crystal bottle she'd commissioned for her perfume.

She must look her best.

Heart racing, she entered her office, shut the door, and rummaged around in her top drawer for the spare cosmetics she kept for just such an occasion. With unsteady hands, she rouged her cheeks and kohled her eyes. After looking in the compact mirror, she decided only a few of the last five years showed on her face.

She was just snapping her compact closed when Nicolle bolted into the room, waving a letter in the air. "He's coming to New York. My son!" She wheezed, out of breath. "Jules is coming with his parents to meet me. It's all settled, the arrangements made. They'll arrive the first of July and leave on the fifteenth."

"Oh, Nicolle. This is wonderful news." Paulette popped out of her chair and rounded the desk. "He's going to love you as much as I do. You can give him the locket at last, and tell him about his father."

It was one of Paulette's greatest sorrows that she'd been unable to present the necklace to the boy herself. This was even better.

Nicolle swiped at her face, trying to brush aside the tears falling down her cheeks. "André did this for me. He made this happen."

"He's a good husband." He'd found Nicolle a year after the war ended, claiming he could treat pets anywhere, but not without Nicolle in his life.

They'd married six months later and had since produced two beautiful daughters. "I'm so happy for you, Nicolle. Really, really happy."

"I must tell Mademoiselle."

A faint rustle of movement was the last Paulette saw of Nicolle as she hurried back down the hallway. Left alone, she picked up the picture of her sister's three children. Two boys with the light sandy hair and blue eyes of their father, and a sweet baby girl with Gabrielle's dark hair. Paulette and Gabrielle had finally found a way past their differences, or rather, Paulette had let go of her bitterness toward her sister and had forgiven her for her lies.

It had come as a surprise that Richard Doyle and Gabrielle had fallen in love during his time in Reims, which explained why her sister had protected his secret. Not long after the war, they'd married.

A knock on her doorjamb had her spinning around to face the final piece of her past that had remained murky and unresolved. She recognized the curling in her stomach as longing, hope. "*Bonjour*, Philippe."

He gave her a slow, soul-splitting grin, the one that never failed to steal her breath. "Paulette, *mon amour*, you're looking well."

"As are you." The years had been kind to him, smoothing the roughened edges, returning him to the artist that had lurked beneath the Resistance soldier. "I trust your trip went well?"

"Very." He regarded her with kind, patient eyes, giving her

the feeling he understood her need to engage in polite small talk before launching into the murky depths of their past.

How she'd missed this man, even though it had only been three months since their last meeting.

She'd always felt cheated out of a life with him by her side, but she'd made her choices, and he'd made his. Neither had married since the war or had children of their own.

Now, here they were, with nothing between them but a bit of official business. "You brought the sketch?"

"I did one better." He retrieved an insulated box from within his bag and cracked open the lid. "I present to you Rochon Crystal's design for your latest venture."

With a dramatic flourish, he produced a small crystal perfume bottle with the Leblanc-Cadieux emblem on the glass and an elaborate stopper that stole her breath. The collection of three butterflies in various stages of flight, each more intricately designed than the last, was more than a top for a perfume bottle. It was art. "You…you designed this?"

"I did." The boyish grin came lightning-fast. "It's how I think of you. Delicate, airy, beautiful. A woman meant to fly and, Paulette, how you've soared since the war."

Words coaxed themselves to her throat, but they hung suspended midflight. She forced them to the surface. "I… It's…" Her hand shook. "It's beautiful."

"I'm glad you like it."

They stood smiling at each other. Then she was in his arms. He kissed her nose, her cheek, her lips, pulled back. "Paulette, *ma chérie*, we have danced around each other for years. I know you cannot leave America—"

"And you can't leave France," she reminded him.

A slow, beautiful grin came to his lips. "There you are wrong. It seems my youngest brother has a desire to try his hand at running the family business, and I have a desire to spend more time designing." He touched the wing of one of the butterflies. "I can do that anywhere. Paris, Milan…"

"New York?"

"That would be my first choice."

"Mine, too."

Again, he kissed her nose, her cheek, her lips. "What do you say, Paulette? Take a chance on me? On us?"

This was it. Their time had finally come. "I'm all in, Philippe. Whatever the future holds, I want to share it with you."

They shared the first of many more kisses.

Later that night, as they walked out onto the terrace of her apartment on Fifth Avenue, arm in arm, they took in the view of Central Park. It marked the first of a lifetime of evenings gazing out at the skyline in the distance, first as something more than friends, then as husband and wife.

★ ★ ★ ★ ★

Author's Note

The Last Fashion House in Paris has been in my head for years. I actually started plotting the story back in 2020, when I finished writing *The Widows of Champagne*. I always felt as though I'd shortchanged Paulette. She made a mistake and hurt the people she loved most, but I never gave her a chance to explain herself or, at the very least, make restitution for her bad decisions. In short, Paulette needed redemption.

I'd sent her to work with Mademoiselle Sabine at her fashion house, but what did that actually entail? What did Paulette do during her two years in Paris? So began my journey of discovery into the French fashion industry during German occupation. My greatest discovery was that, yes, there was an actual fashion industry during the war. Though it almost didn't happen. In July 1940, with Paris cut off from the rest of the world, Nazi officials raided the headquarters of the Chambre Syndicale de la Couture Parisienne (CSCP) and seized irreplaceable archives needed to conduct business. It was the first step in Hitler's plan to move the entire industry to Berlin.

Lucien Lelong, President of the CSCP, flew to Berlin and argued on behalf of his fellow designers. Prior to the German invasion, couture houses employed tens of thousands of skilled artisans, tailors, seamstresses, milliners, lacemakers, embroiderers, etc. Relocating these men and women to Germany was not feasible, nor could unskilled workers take their place without years of proper training. Due to Lelong's persuasive arguments, Hitler relented, and nearly sixty of the ninety-two couture houses remained open during the war.

While I'd laid the groundwork to put Paulette to work, I knew she could not operate in a bubble. I also knew she would have to do more than make pretty clothes if she was to find redemption. My research uncovered the intricate escape lines/networks that helped thousands of downed airmen, escaped POWs, and Jews leave France. Nicolle was born from that research, as was Philippe. Now Paulette had a mentor in Mademoiselle, a friend in Nicolle, and an adversary in the mysterious Philippe.

All my book needed was a villain. A Nazi would have made the most sense. Then I uncovered the story of Henri Lafont and Pierre Bonny. The two Frenchmen were gangsters, black-marketeers, and, basically, the worst criminals of their day. Although they worked closely with German military intelligence and the Gestapo, they were loyal only to themselves. They threw lavish society parties, rubbed elbows with German officials and French police alike, and helped the Nazis take down several Resistance cells in Paris. They enjoyed wild evenings at the best nightclubs and cabarets and were fans of extortion and brutality. They happily inflicted torture on Resistance workers in the basement of the house they'd commandeered from a wealthy Jewish woman in the sixteenth arrondissement. Guy Marcel would have enjoyed a close friendship with these two.

Much like Paulette, I could not have written this book in a bubble. I am grateful to my first reader, my confidant and close friend, Donnell Ann Bell. Thank you for always answering my calls, frantic texts, and jumbled emails.

I also want to thank my wonderful, loving, amazing husband, Mark. You have been with me through every iteration of every book (including the ones living in a trash heap somewhere in the Midwest). Thank you for listening to my rants, wiping away my tears, helping me punch through plot holes, and popping open the champagne bottle whenever I write "The End."

I am forever grateful to my readers. You are the reason I write. You make the long hours of sitting alone at my computer worth every minute. I love knowing that you will one day read my words. I only pray that I have brought you some level of entertainment, knowledge, and inspiration along the way.

Last, but never least, thank you to my editor, Melissa Endlich. I value your insight, your patience, and your loyal support through the years. Most of all, I treasure your friendship. When next we meet, dinner is on me! Cheers, my friend!